THE ADVENTURES

OF TOM SAWYER

To Matthew
I hope you're
going to read this
someday. It's history!
Love
Aunt Teeta

Aug. 23/03

To Jerry!
Allow me to introduce
you to the essence of
childhood!
Love, Paul
Christmas 2007

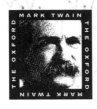

THE OXFORD MARK TWAIN

Shelley Fisher Fishkin, Editor

The Prince and the Pauper
  Introduction: Judith Martin
  Afterword: Everett Emerson

Life on the Mississippi
  Introduction: Willie Morris
  Afterword: Lawrence Howe

Adventures of Huckleberry Finn
  Introduction: Toni Morrison
  Afterword: Victor A. Doyno

A Connecticut Yankee in King Arthur's Court
  Introduction: Kurt Vonnegut, Jr.
  Afterword: Louis J. Budd

Merry Tales
  Introduction: Anne Bernays
  Afterword: Forrest G. Robinson

The American Claimant
  Introduction: Bobbie Ann Mason
  Afterword: Peter Messent

The £1,000,000 Bank-Note and Other New Stories
  Introduction: Malcolm Bradbury
  Afterword: James D. Wilson

Tom Sawyer Abroad
  Introduction: Nat Hentoff
  Afterword: M. Thomas Inge

The Tragedy of Pudd'nhead Wilson and the Comedy
Those Extraordinary Twins
  Introduction: Sherley Anne Williams
  Afterword: David Lionel Smith

The Adventures of Tom Sawyer

Mark Twain

FOREWORD

SHELLEY FISHER FISHKIN

INTRODUCTION

E.L. DOCTOROW

AFTERWORD

ALBERT E. STONE

New York   Oxford

OXFORD UNIVERSITY PRESS

1996

OXFORD UNIVERSITY PRESS

Oxford   New York

Athens, Auckland, Bangkok, Bogotá, Bombay

Buenos Aires, Calcutta, Cape Town, Dar es Salaam

Delhi, Florence, Hong Kong, Istanbul, Karachi

Kuala Lumpur, Madras, Madrid, Melbourne

Mexico City, Nairobi, Paris, Singapore

Taipei, Tokyo, Toronto

and associated companies in

Berlin, Ibadan

Published by

Oxford University Press, Inc.

198 Madison Avenue, New York,

New York 10016

Oxford is a registered trademark of

Oxford University Press

Library of Congress

Cataloging-in-Publication Data

Twain, Mark, 1835–1910.

The adventures of Tom Sawyer / by Mark Twain;

with an introduction by E.L. Doctorow; and an

afterword by Albert E. Stone.

p. cm. — (The Oxford Mark Twain)

Includes bibliographical references.

1. Sawyer, Tom (Fictitious character)—Fiction. 2.

Boys—Missouri—Fiction. I. Title. II. Series: Twain,

Mark, 1835–1910. Works. 1996.

PS1306.A1 1996

813'.4—dc20

96-17033

CIP

ISBN 0-19-510136-7 (trade ed.)

ISBN 0-19-511405-1 (lib. ed.)

ISBN 0-19-509088-8 (trade ed. set)

ISBN 0-19-511345-4 (lib. ed. set)

9 8 7 6 5 4 3 2 1

Printed in the United States of America

on acid-free paper

FRONTISPIECE

Samuel L. Clemens is seen here in his study at
Quarry Farm in Elmira, New York, in this
photograph taken by E. M. Van Aken in 1874, the
year Clemens started to write *The Adventures of Tom
Sawyer*. (The Mark Twain House, Hartford,
Connecticut)

CONTENTS

EDITOR'S NOTE

The Oxford Mark Twain consists of twenty-nine volumes of facsimiles of the first American editions of Mark Twain's works, with an editor's foreword, new introductions, afterwords, notes on the texts, and essays on the illustrations in volumes with artwork. The facsimiles have been reproduced from the originals unaltered, except that blank pages in the front and back of the books have been omitted, and any seriously damaged or missing pages have been replaced by pages from other first editions (as indicated in the notes on the texts).

In the foreword, introduction, afterword, and essays on the illustrations, the titles of Mark Twain's works have been capitalized according to modern conventions, as have the names of characters (except where otherwise indicated). In the case of discrepancies between the title of a short story, essay, or sketch as it appears in the original table of contents and as it appears on its own title page, the title page has been followed. The parenthetical numbers in the introduction, afterwords, and illustration essays are page references to the facsimiles.

FOREWORD

Shelley Fisher Fishkin

Samuel Clemens entered the world and left it with Halley's Comet, little dreaming that generations hence Halley's Comet would be less famous than Mark Twain. He has been called the American Cervantes, our Homer, our Tolstoy, our Shakespeare, our Rabelais. Ernest Hemingway maintained that "all modern American literature comes from one book by Mark Twain called *Huckleberry Finn*." President Franklin Delano Roosevelt got the phrase "New Deal" from *A Connecticut Yankee in King Arthur's Court. The Gilded Age* gave an entire era its name. "The future historian of America," wrote George Bernard Shaw to Samuel Clemens, "will find your works as indispensable to him as a French historian finds the political tracts of Voltaire."[1]

There is a Mark Twain Bank in St. Louis, a Mark Twain Diner in Jackson Heights, New York, a Mark Twain Smoke Shop in Lakeland, Florida. There are Mark Twain Elementary Schools in Albuquerque, Dayton, Seattle, and Sioux Falls. Mark Twain's image peers at us from advertisements for Bass Ale (his drink of choice was Scotch), for a gas company in Tennessee, a hotel in the nation's capital, a cemetery in California.

Ubiquitous though his name and image may be, Mark Twain is in no danger of becoming a petrified icon. On the contrary: Mark Twain lives. *Huckleberry Finn* is "the most taught novel, most taught long work, and most taught piece of American literature" in American schools from junior high to the graduate level.[2] Hundreds of Twain impersonators appear in theaters, trade shows, and shopping centers in every region of the country.[3] Scholars publish hundreds of articles as well as books about Twain every year, and he is the subject of daily exchanges on the Internet. A journalist somewhere in the world finds a reason to quote Twain just about every day. Television series such as *Bonanza*, *Star Trek: The Next Generation*, and *Cheers* broadcast episodes that feature Mark Twain as a character. Hollywood screenwriters regularly produce movies inspired by his works, and writers of mysteries and science fiction continue to weave him into their plots.[4]

A century after the American Revolution sent shock waves throughout Europe, it took Mark Twain to explain to Europeans and to his countrymen alike what that revolution had wrought. He probed the significance of this new land and its new citizens, and identified what it was in the Old World that America abolished and rejected. The founding fathers had thought through the political dimensions of making a new society; Mark Twain took on the challenge of interpreting the social and cultural life of the United States for those outside its borders as well as for those who were living the changes he discerned.

Americans may have constructed a new society in the eighteenth century, but they articulated what they had done in voices that were largely inter-changeable with those of Englishmen until well into the nineteenth century. Mark Twain became the voice of the new land, the leading translator of what and who the "American" was — and, to a large extent, is. Frances Trollope's *Domestic Manners of the Americans,* a best-seller in England, Hector St. John de Crèvecoeur's *Letters from an American Farmer,* and Tocqueville's *Democracy in America* all tried to explain America to Europeans. But Twain did more than that: he allowed European readers to *experience* this strange "new world." And he gave his countrymen the tools to do two things they had not quite had the confidence to do before. He helped them stand before the cultural icons of the Old World unembarrassed, unashamed of America's lack of palaces and shrines, proud of its brash practicality and bold inventiveness, unafraid to reject European models of "civilization" as tainted or corrupt. And he also helped them recognize their own insularity, boorishness, arrogance, or ignorance, and laugh at it — the first step toward transcending it and becoming more "civilized," in the best European sense of the word.

Twain often strikes us as more a creature of our time than of his. He appreciated the importance and the complexity of mass tourism and public relations, fields that would come into their own in the twentieth century but were only fledgling enterprises in the nineteenth. He explored the liberating potential of humor and the dynamics of friendship, parenting, and marriage. He narrowed the gap between "popular" and "high" culture, and he meditated on the enigmas of personal and national identity. Indeed, it would be difficult to find an issue on the horizon today that Twain did not touch on somewhere in his work. Heredity versus environment? Animal rights? The boundaries of gender? The place of black voices in the cultural heritage of the United States? Twain was there.

With startling prescience and characteristic grace and wit, he zeroed in on many of the key challenges — political, social, and technological — that would face his country and the world for the next hundred years: the challenge of race relations in a society founded on both chattel slavery and ideals of equality, and the intractable problem of racism in American life; the potential of new technologies to transform our lives in ways that can be both exhilarating and terrifying — as well as unpredictable; the problem of imperialism and the difficulties entailed in getting rid of it. But he never lost sight of the most basic challenge of all: each man or woman's struggle for integrity in the face of the seductions of power, status, and material things.

Mark Twain's unerring sense of the right word and not its second cousin taught people to pay attention when he spoke, in person or in print. He said things that were smart and things that were wise, and he said them incomparably well. He defined the rhythms of our prose and the contours of our moral map. He saw our best and our worst, our extravagant promise and our stunning failures, our comic foibles and our tragic flaws. Throughout the world he is viewed as the most distinctively American of American authors — and as one of the most universal. He is assigned in classrooms in Naples, Riyadh, Belfast, and Beijing, and has been a major influence on twentieth-century writers from Argentina to Nigeria to Japan. The Oxford Mark Twain celebrates the versatility and vitality of this remarkable writer.

The Oxford Mark Twain reproduces the first American editions of Mark Twain's books published during his lifetime.[5] By encountering Twain's works in their original format — typography, layout, order of contents, and illustrations — readers today can come a few steps closer to the literary artifacts that entranced and excited readers when the books first appeared. Twain approved of and to a greater or lesser degree supervised the publication of all of this material.[6] The Mark Twain House in Hartford, Connecticut, generously loaned us its originals.[7] When more than one copy of a first American edition was available, Robert H. Hirst, general editor of the Mark Twain Project, in cooperation with Marianne Curling, curator of the Mark Twain House (and Jeffrey Kaimowitz, head of Rare Books for the Watkinson Library of Trinity College, Hartford, where the Mark Twain House collection is kept), guided our decision about which one to use.[8] As a set, the volumes also contain more than eighty essays commissioned especially for The Oxford Mark Twain, in which distinguished contributors reassess Twain's achievement as a writer and his place in the cultural conversation that he did so much to shape.

Each volume of The Oxford Mark Twain is introduced by a leading American, Canadian, or British writer who responds to Twain — often in a very personal way — as a fellow writer. Novelists, journalists, humorists, columnists, fabulists, poets, playwrights — these writers tell us what Twain taught them and what in his work continues to speak to them. Reading Twain's books, both famous and obscure, they reflect on the genesis of his art and the characteristics of his style, the themes he illuminated, and the aesthetic strategies he pioneered. Individually and collectively their contributions testify to the place Mark Twain holds in the hearts of readers of all kinds and temperaments.

Scholars whose work has shaped our view of Twain in the academy today have written afterwords to each volume, with suggestions for further reading. Their essays give us a sense of what was going on in Twain's life when he wrote the book at hand, and of how that book fits into his career. They explore how each book reflects and refracts contemporary events, and they show Twain responding to literary and social currents of the day, variously accepting, amplifying, modifying, and challenging prevailing paradigms. Sometimes they argue that works previously dismissed as quirky or eccentric departures actually address themes at the heart of Twain's work from the start. And as they bring new perspectives to Twain's composition strategies in familiar texts, several scholars see experiments in form where others saw only formlessness, method where prior critics saw only madness. In addition to elucidating the work's historical and cultural context, the afterwords provide an overview of responses to each book from its first appearance to the present.

Most of Mark Twain's books involved more than Mark Twain's words: unique illustrations. The parodic visual send-ups of "high culture" that Twain himself drew for *A Tramp Abroad*, the sketch of financial manipulator Jay Gould as a greedy and sadistic "Slave Driver" in *A Connecticut Yankee in King Arthur's Court*, and the memorable drawings of Eve in *Eve's Diary* all helped Twain's books to be sold, read, discussed, and preserved. In their essays for each volume that contains artwork, Beverly R. David and Ray Sapirstein highlight the significance of the sketches, engravings, and photographs in the first American editions of Mark Twain's works, and tell us what is known about the public response to them.

The Oxford Mark Twain invites us to read some relatively neglected works by Twain in the company of some of the most engaging literary figures of our time. Roy Blount Jr., for example, riffs in a deliciously Twain-like manner on "An Item Which the Editor Himself Could Not Understand," which may well rank as one of the least-known pieces Twain ever published. Bobbie Ann Mason celebrates the "mad energy" of Twain's most obscure comic novel, *The American Claimant*, in which the humor "hurtles beyond tall tale into simon-pure absurdity."[9] Garry Wills finds that *Christian Science* "gets us very close to the heart of American culture." Lee Smith reads "Political Economy" as a sharp and funny essay on language. Walter Mosley sees "The Stolen White Elephant," a story "reduced to a series of ridiculous telegrams related by an untrustworthy narrator caught up in an adventure that is as impossible as it is ludicrous," as a stunningly compact and economical satire of a world we still recognize as our own. Anne Bernays returns to "The Private History of a Campaign That Failed" and finds "an antiwar manifesto that is also confession, dramatic monologue, a plea for understanding and absolution, and a romp that gradually turns into atrocity even as we watch." After revisiting Captain Stormfield's heaven, Frederik Pohl finds that there "is no imaginable place more pleasant to spend eternity." Indeed, Pohl writes, "one would almost be willing to die to enter it."

While less familiar works receive fresh attention in The Oxford Mark Twain, new light is cast on the best-known works as well. Judith Martin ("Miss Manners") points out that it is by reading a court etiquette book that Twain's pauper learns how to behave as a proper prince. As important as etiquette may be in the palace, Martin notes, it is even more important in the slums.

> That etiquette is a sorer point with the ruffians in the street than with the proud dignitaries of the prince's court may surprise some readers. As in our own streets, etiquette is always a more volatile subject among those who cannot count on being treated with respect than among those who have the power to command deference.

And taking a fresh look at *Adventures of Huckleberry Finn,* Toni Morrison writes,

> much of the novel's genius lies in its quiescence, the silences that pervade it and give it a porous quality that is by turns brooding and soothing. It lies in . . . the subdued images in which the repetition of a simple word, such as "lonesome," tolls like an evening bell; the moments when nothing is said, when scenes and incidents swell the heart unbearably precisely because unarticulated, and force an act of imagination almost against the will.

Engaging Mark Twain as one writer to another, several contributors to The Oxford Mark Twain offer new insights into the processes by which his books came to be. Russell Banks, for example, reads *A Tramp Abroad* as "an important revision of Twain's incomplete first draft of *Huckleberry Finn*, a second draft, if you will, which in turn made possible the third and final draft." Erica Jong suggests that *1601,* a freewheeling parody of Elizabethan manners and mores, written during the same summer Twain began *Huckleberry Finn*, served as "a warm-up for his creative process" and "primed the pump for other sorts of freedom of expression." And Justin Kaplan suggests that "one of the transcendent figures standing behind and shaping" *Joan of Arc* was Ulysses S. Grant, whose memoirs Twain had recently published, and who, like Joan, had risen unpredictably "from humble and obscure origins" to become a "military genius" endowed with "the gift of command, a natural eloquence, and an equally natural reserve."

As a number of contributors note, Twain was a man ahead of his times. *The Gilded Age* was the first "Washington novel," Ward Just tells us, because "Twain was the first to see the possibilities that had eluded so many others." Commenting on *The Tragedy of Pudd'nhead Wilson,* Sherley Anne Williams observes that "Twain's argument about the power of environment in shaping character runs directly counter to prevailing sentiment where the negro was concerned." Twain's fictional technology, wildly fanciful by the standards of his day, predicts developments we take for granted in ours. DNA cloning, fax machines, and photocopiers are all prefigured, Bobbie Ann Mason tells us, in *The American Claimant.* Cynthia Ozick points out that the "telelectrophonoscope" we meet in "From the 'London Times' of 1904" is suspiciously like what we know as "television." And Malcolm Bradbury suggests that in the "phrenophones" of "Mental Telegraphy" "the Internet was born."

Twain turns out to have been remarkably prescient about political affairs as well. Kurt Vonnegut sees in *A Connecticut Yankee* a chilling foreshadowing (or perhaps a projection from the Civil War) of "all the high-tech atrocities which followed, and which follow still." Cynthia Ozick suggests that "The Man That Corrupted Hadleyburg," along with some of the other pieces collected under that title — many of them written when Twain lived in a Vienna ruled by Karl Lueger, a demagogue Adolf Hitler would later idolize — shoot up moral flares that shed an eerie light on the insidious corruption, prejudice, and hatred that reached bitter fruition under the Third Reich. And Twain's portrait in this book of "the dissolving Austria-Hungary of the 1890s," in Ozick's view, presages not only the Sarajevo that would erupt in 1914 but also "the disintegrated components of the former Yugoslavia" and "the *fin-de-siècle* Sarajevo of our own moment."

Despite their admiration for Twain's ambitious reach and scope, contributors to The Oxford Mark Twain also recognize his limitations. Mordecai Richler, for example, thinks that "the early pages of *Innocents Abroad* suffer from being a tad broad, proffering more burlesque than inspired satire," perhaps because Twain was "trying too hard for knee-slappers." Charles Johnson notes that the Young Man in Twain's philosophical dialogue about free will and determinism (*What Is Man?*) "caves in far too soon," failing to challenge what through late-twentieth-century eyes looks like "pseudoscience" and suspect essentialism in the Old Man's arguments.

Some contributors revisit their first encounters with Twain's works, recalling what surprised or intrigued them. When David Bradley came across "Fenimore Cooper's Literary Offences" in his college library, he "did not at first realize that Twain was being his usual ironic self with all this business about the 'nineteen rules governing literary art in the domain of romantic fiction,' but by the time I figured out there was no such list outside Twain's own head, I had decided that the rules made *sense*. . . . It seemed to me they were a pretty good blueprint for writing — Negro writing included." Sherley Anne Williams remembers that part of what attracted her to *Pudd'nhead Wilson* when she first read it thirty years ago was "that Twain, writing at the end of the nineteenth century, could imagine negroes as characters, albeit white ones, who actually thought for and of themselves, whose actions were the product of their thinking rather than the spontaneous ephemera of physical instincts that stereotype assigned to blacks." Frederik Pohl recalls his first reading of *Huckleberry Finn* as "a watershed event" in his life, the first book he read as a child in which "bad people" ceased to exercise a monopoly on doing "bad things." In *Huckleberry Finn* "some seriously bad things — things like the possession and mistreatment of black slaves, like stealing and lying, even like killing other people in duels — were quite often done by people who not only thought of themselves as exemplarily moral but, by any other standards I knew how to apply, actually *were* admirable citizens." The world that

Tom and Huck lived in, Pohl writes, "was filled with complexities and con-tradictions," and resembled "the world I appeared to be living in myself."

Other contributors explore their more recent encounters with Twain, ex-plaining why they have revised their initial responses to his work. For Toni Morrison, parts of *Huckleberry Finn* that she "once took to be deliberate eva-sions, stumbles even, or a writer's impatience with his or her material," now strike her "as otherwise: as entrances, crevices, gaps, seductive invitations flashing the possibility of meaning. Unarticulated eddies that encourage div-ing into the novel's undertow — the real place where writer captures reader." One such "eddy" is the imprisonment of Jim on the Phelps farm. Instead of dismissing this portion of the book as authorial bungling, as she once did, Morrison now reads it as Twain's commentary on the 1880s, a period that "saw the collapse of civil rights for blacks," a time when "the nation, as well as Tom Sawyer, was deferring Jim's freedom in agonizing play." Morrison be-lieves that Americans in the 1880s were attempting "to bury the combustible issues Twain raised in his novel," and that those who try to kick Huck Finn out of school in the 1990s are doing the same: "The cyclical attempts to re-move the novel from classrooms extend Jim's captivity on into each genera-tion of readers."

Although imitation-Hemingway and imitation-Faulkner writing contests draw hundreds of entries annually, no one has ever tried to mount a faux-Twain competition. Why? Perhaps because Mark Twain's voice is too much a part of who we are and how we speak even today. Roy Blount Jr. suggests that it is impossible, "at least for an American writer, to parody Mark Twain. It would be like doing an impression of your father or mother: he or she is al-ready there in your voice."

Twain's style is examined and celebrated in The Oxford Mark Twain by fellow writers who themselves have struggled with the nuances of words, the structure of sentences, the subtleties of point of view, and the trickiness of opening lines. Bobbie Ann Mason observes, for example, that "Twain loved the sound of words and he knew how to string them by sound, like different shades of one color: 'The earl's barbaric eye,' 'the Usurping Earl,' 'a double-dyed humbug.'" Twain "relied on the punch of plain words" to show writers how to move beyond the "wordy romantic rubbish" so prevalent in nineteenth-century fiction, Mason says; he "was one of the first writers in America to deflower literary language." Lee Smith believes that "American writers have benefited as much from the way Mark Twain opened up the possibilities of first-person narration as we have from his use of vernacular language." (She feels that "the ghost of Mark Twain was hovering someplace in the background" when she decided to write her novel *Oral History* from the standpoint of multiple first-person narrators.) Frederick Busch maintains that "A Dog's Tale" "boasts one of the great opening sentences" of all time: "My father was a St. Bernard, my mother was a collie, but I am a Presbyterian." And Ursula Le Guin marvels at the ingenuity of the following sentence that she encounters in *Extracts from Adam's Diary*.

> . . . This made her sorry for the creatures which live in there, which she calls fish, for she continues to fasten names on to things that don't need them and don't come when they are called by them, which is a matter of no consequence to her, as she is such a numskull anyway; so she got a lot of them out and brought them in last night and put them in my bed to keep warm, but I have noticed them now and then all day, and I don't see that they are any happier there than they were before, only quieter.[10]

Le Guin responds,

> Now, that is a pure Mark-Twain-tour-de-force sentence, covering an immense amount of territory in an effortless, aimless ramble that seems to be heading nowhere in particular and ends up with breathtaking accuracy at the gold mine. Any sensible child would find that funny, perhaps not following all its divagations but delighted by the swing of it, by the word "numskull," by the idea of putting fish in the bed; and as that child grew older and reread it, its reward would only grow; and if that grown-up child had to write an essay on the piece and therefore earnestly studied and pored over this sentence, she would end up in unmitigated admiration of its vocabulary, syntax, pacing, sense, and rhythm, above all the beautiful

timing of the last two words; and she would, and she does, still find it funny.

The fish surface again in a passage that Gore Vidal calls to our attention, from *Following the Equator*: "'The Whites always mean well when they take human fish out of the ocean and try to make them dry and warm and happy and comfortable in a chicken coop,' which is how, through civilization, they did away with many of the original inhabitants. Lack of empathy is a principal theme in Twain's meditations on race and empire."

Indeed, empathy — and its lack — is a principal theme in virtually all of Twain's work, as contributors frequently note. Nat Hentoff quotes the following thoughts from Huck in *Tom Sawyer Abroad*:

> I see a bird setting on a dead limb of a high tree, singing with its head tilted back and its mouth open, and before I thought I fired, and his song stopped and he fell straight down from the limb, all limp like a rag, and I run and picked him up and he was dead, and his body was warm in my hand, and his head rolled about this way and that, like his neck was broke, and there was a little white skin over his eyes, and one little drop of blood on the side of his head; and laws! I could n't see nothing more for the tears; and I hain't never murdered no creature since that war n't doing me no harm, and I ain't going to.[11]

"The Humane Society," Hentoff writes, "has yet to say anything as powerful — and lasting."

Readers of The Oxford Mark Twain will have the pleasure of revisiting Twain's Mississippi landmarks alongside Willie Morris, whose own lower Mississippi Valley boyhood gives him a special sense of connection to Twain. Morris knows firsthand the mosquitoes described in *Life on the Mississippi* — so colossal that "two of them could whip a dog" and "four of them could hold a man down"; in Morris's own hometown they were so large during the flood season that "local wags said they wore wristwatches." Morris's Yazoo City and Twain's Hannibal shared a "rough-hewn democracy . . . complicated by all the visible textures of caste and class, . . . harmless boyhood fun and mischief right along with . . . rank hypocrisies, churchgoing sanctimonies, racial hatred, entrenched and unrepentant greed."

For the West of Mark Twain's *Roughing It*, readers will have George Plimpton as their guide. "What a group these newspapermen were!" Plimpton writes about Twain and his friends Dan De Quille and Joe Goodman in Virginia City, Nevada. "Their roisterous carryings-on bring to mind the kind of frat-house enthusiasm one associates with college humor magazines like the *Harvard Lampoon*." Malcolm Bradbury examines Twain as "a living example of what made the American so different from the European." And Hal Holbrook, who has interpreted Mark Twain on stage for some forty years, describes how Twain "played" during the civil rights movement, during the Vietnam War, during the Gulf War, and in Prague on the eve of the demise of Communism.

Why do we continue to read Mark Twain? What draws us to him? His wit? His compassion? His humor? His bravura? His humility? His understanding of who and what we are in those parts of our being that we rarely open to view? Our sense that he knows we can do better than we do? Our sense that he knows we can't? E. L. Doctorow tells us that children are attracted to *Tom Sawyer* because in this book "the young reader confirms his own hope that no matter how troubled his relations with his elders may be, beneath all their disapproval is their underlying love for him, constant and steadfast." Readers in general, Arthur Miller writes, value Twain's "insights into America's always uncertain moral life and its shifting but everlasting hypocrisies"; we appreciate the fact that he "is not using his alienation from the public illusions of his hour in order to reject the country implicitly as though he could live without it, but manifestly in order to correct it." Perhaps we keep reading Mark Twain because, in Miller's words, he "wrote much more like a father than a son. He doesn't seem to be sitting in class taunting the teacher but standing at the head of it challenging his students to acknowledge their own humanity, that is, their immemorial attraction to the untrue."

Mark Twain entered the public eye at a time when many of his countrymen considered "American culture" an oxymoron; he died four years before a world conflagration that would lead many to question whether the contradiction in terms was not "European civilization" instead. In between he worked in journalism, printing, steamboating, mining, lecturing, publishing, and editing, in virtually every region of the country. He tried his hand at humorous sketches, social satire, historical novels, children's books, poetry, drama, science fiction, mysteries, romance, philosophy, travelogue, memoir, polemic, and several genres no one had ever seen before or has ever seen since. He invented a self-pasting scrapbook, a history game, a vest strap, and a gizmo for keeping bed sheets tucked in; he invested in machines and processes designed to revolutionize typesetting and engraving, and in a food supplement called "Plasmon." Along the way he cheerfully impersonated himself and prior versions of himself for doting publics on five continents while playing out a charming rags-to-riches story followed by a devastating riches-to-rags story followed by yet another great American comeback. He had a long-running real-life engagement in a sumptuous comedy of manners, and then in a real-life tragedy not of his own design: during the last fourteen years of his life almost everyone he ever loved was taken from him by disease and death.

Mark Twain has indelibly shaped our views of who and what the United States is as a nation and of who and what we might become. He understood the nostalgia for a "simpler" past that increased as that past receded — and he saw through the nostalgia to a past that was just as complex as the present. He recognized better than we did ourselves our potential for greatness and our potential for disaster. His fictions brilliantly illuminated the world in which he lived, changing it — and us — in the process. He knew that our feet often danced to tunes that had somehow remained beyond our hearing; with perfect pitch he played them back to us.

My mother read *Tom Sawyer* to me as a bedtime story when I was eleven. I thought Huck and Tom could be a lot of fun, but I dismissed Becky Thatcher as a bore. When I was twelve I invested a nickel at a local garage sale in a book that contained short pieces by Mark Twain. That was where I met Twain's Eve. Now, *that's* more like it, I decided, pleased to meet a female character I could identify *with* instead of against. Eve had spunk. Even if she got a lot wrong, you had to give her credit for trying. "The Man That Corrupted

Hadleyburg" left me giddy with satisfaction: none of my adolescent reveries of getting even with my enemies were half as neat as the plot of the man who got back at that town. "How I Edited an Agricultural Paper" set me off in uncontrollable giggles.

People sometimes told me that I looked like Huck Finn. "It's the freckles," they'd explain — not explaining anything at all. I didn't read *Huckleberry Finn* until junior year in high school in my English class. It was the fall of 1965. I was living in a small town in Connecticut. I expected a sequel to *Tom Sawyer*. So when the teacher handed out the books and announced our assignment, my jaw dropped: "Write a paper on how Mark Twain used irony to attack racism in *Huckleberry Finn*."

The year before, the bodies of three young men who had gone to Mississippi to help blacks register to vote — James Chaney, Andrew Goodman, and Michael Schwerner — had been found in a shallow grave; a group of white segregationists (the county sheriff among them) had been arrested in connection with the murders. America's inner cities were simmering with pent-up rage that began to explode in the summer of 1965, when riots in Watts left thirty-four people dead. None of this made any sense to me. I was confused, angry, certain that there was something missing from the news stories I read each day: the why. Then I met Pap Finn. And the Phelpses.

Pap Finn, Huck tells us, "had been drunk over in town" and "was just all mud." He erupts into a drunken tirade about "a free nigger . . . from Ohio — a mulatter, most as white as a white man," with "the whitest shirt on you ever see, too, and the shiniest hat; and there ain't a man in town that's got as fine clothes as what he had."

> . . . they said he was a p'fessor in a college, and could talk all kinds of languages, and knowed everything. And that ain't the wust. They said he could *vote*, when he was at home. Well, that let me out. Thinks I, what is the country a-coming to? It was 'lection day, and I was just about to go and vote, myself, if I warn't too drunk to get there; but when they told me there was a State in this country where they'd let that nigger vote, I drawed out. I says I'll never vote agin. Them's the very words I said. . . . And to see the

cool way of that nigger — why, he wouldn't a give me the road if I hadn't shoved him out o' the way.[12]

Later on in the novel, when the runaway slave Jim gives up his freedom to nurse a wounded Tom Sawyer, a white doctor testifies to the stunning altruism of his actions. The Phelpses and their neighbors, all fine, upstanding, well-meaning, churchgoing folk,

> agreed that Jim had acted very well, and was deserving to have some notice took of it, and reward. So every one of them promised, right out and hearty, that they wouldn't curse him no more.
>
> Then they come out and locked him up. I hoped they was going to say he could have one or two of the chains took off, because they was rotten heavy, or could have meat and greens with his bread and water, but they didn't think of it.[13]

Why did the behavior of these people tell me more about why Watts burned than anything I had read in the daily paper? And why did a drunk Pap Finn railing against a black college professor from Ohio whose vote was as good as his own tell me more about white anxiety over black political power than anything I had seen on the evening news?

Mark Twain knew that there was nothing, absolutely *nothing*, a black man could do — including selflessly sacrificing his freedom, the only thing of value he had — that would make white society see beyond the color of his skin. And Mark Twain knew that depicting racists with chilling accuracy would expose the viciousness of their world view like nothing else could. It was an insight echoed some eighty years after Mark Twain penned Pap Finn's rantings about the black professor, when Malcolm X famously asked, "Do you know what white racists call black Ph.D.'s?" and answered, "'*Nigger!*'"[14]

Mark Twain taught me things I needed to know. He taught me to understand the raw racism that lay behind what I saw on the evening news. He taught me that the most well-meaning people can be hurtful and myopic. He taught me to recognize the supreme irony of a country founded in freedom that continued to deny freedom to so many of its citizens. Every time I hear of another effort to kick Huck Finn out of school somewhere, I recall everything that Mark Twain taught *this* high school junior, and I find myself jumping into the fray.[15] I remember the black high school student who called CNN during the phone-in portion of a 1985 debate between Dr. John Wallace, a black educator spearheading efforts to ban the book, and myself. She accused Dr. Wallace of insulting her and all black high school students by suggesting they weren't smart enough to understand Mark Twain's irony. And I recall the black cameraman on the *CBS Morning News* who came up to me after he finished shooting another debate between Dr. Wallace and myself. He said he had never read the book by Mark Twain that we had been arguing about — but now he really wanted to. One thing that puzzled him, though, was why a white woman was defending it and a black man was attacking it, because as far as he could see from what we'd been saying, the book made whites look pretty bad.

As I came to understand *Huckleberry Finn* and *Pudd'nhead Wilson* as commentaries on the era now known as the nadir of American race relations, those books pointed me toward the world recorded in nineteenth-century black newspapers and periodicals and in fiction by Mark Twain's black contemporaries. My investigation of the role black voices and traditions played in shaping Mark Twain's art helped make me aware of their role in shaping all of American culture.[16] My research underlined for me the importance of changing the stories we tell about who we are to reflect the realities of what we've been.[17]

Ever since our encounter in high school English, Mark Twain has shown me the potential of American literature and American history to illuminate each other. Rarely have I found a contradiction or complexity we grapple with as a nation that Mark Twain had not puzzled over as well. He insisted on taking America seriously. And he insisted on *not* taking America seriously: "I think that there is but a single specialty with us, only one thing that can be called by the wide name 'American,'" he once wrote. "That is the national devotion to ice-water."[18]

Mark Twain threw back at us our dreams and our denial of those dreams, our greed, our goodness, our ambition, and our laziness, all rattling around together in that vast echo chamber of our talk — that sharp, spunky American talk that Mark Twain figured out how to write down without robbing it of its energy and immediacy. Talk shaped by voices that the official arbiters of "culture" deemed of no importance — voices of children, voices of slaves, voices of servants, voices of ordinary people. Mark Twain listened. And he made us listen. To the stories he told us, and to the truths they conveyed. He still has a lot to say that we need to hear.

Mark Twain lives — in our libraries, classrooms, homes, theaters, movie houses, streets, and most of all in our speech. His optimism energizes us, his despair sobers us, and his willingness to keep wrestling with the hilarious and horrendous complexities of it all keeps us coming back for more. As the twenty-first century approaches, may he continue to goad us, chasten us, delight us, berate us, and cause us to erupt in unrestrained laughter in unexpected places.

NOTES

1. Ernest Hemingway, *Green Hills of Africa* (New York: Charles Scribner's Sons, 1935), 22. George Bernard Shaw to Samuel L. Clemens, July 3, 1907, quoted in Albert Bigelow Paine, *Mark Twain: A Biography* (New York: Harper and Brothers, 1912), 3:1398.

2. Allen Carey-Webb, "Racism and *Huckleberry Finn*: Censorship, Dialogue and Change," *English Journal* 82, no. 7 (November 1993):22.

3. See Louis J. Budd, "Impersonators," in J. R. LeMaster and James D. Wilson, eds., *The Mark Twain Encyclopedia* (New York: Garland Publishing Company, 1993), 389–91.

4. See Shelley Fisher Fishkin, "Ripples and Reverberations," part 3 of *Lighting Out for the Territory: Reflections on Mark Twain and American Culture* (New York: Oxford University Press, 1996).

5. There are two exceptions. Twain published chapters from his autobiography in the *North American Review* in 1906 and 1907, but this material was not published in book form in Twain's lifetime; our volume reproduces the material as it appeared in the *North American Review*. The other exception is our final volume, *Mark Twain's Speeches*, which appeared two months after Twain's death in 1910.

An unauthorized handful of copies of *1601* was privately printed by an Alexander Gunn of Cleveland at the instigation of Twain's friend John Hay in 1880. The first American edition authorized by Mark Twain, however, was printed at the United States Military Academy at West Point in 1882; that is the edition reproduced here.

It should further be noted that four volumes — *The Stolen White Elephant and Other Detective Stories, Following the Equator and Anti-imperialist Essays, The Diaries of Adam and Eve,* and *1601, and Is Shakespeare Dead?* — bind together material originally published separately. In each case the first American edition of the material is the version that has been reproduced, always in its entirety. Because Twain constantly recycled and repackaged previously published works in his collections of short pieces, a certain amount of duplication is unavoidable. We have selected volumes with an eye toward keeping this duplication to a minimum.

Even the twenty-nine-volume Oxford Mark Twain has had to leave much out. No edition of Twain can ever claim to be "complete," for the man was too prolix, and the file drawers of both ephemera and as yet unpublished texts are deep.

6. With the possible exception of *Mark Twain's Speeches*. Some scholars suspect Twain knew about this book and may have helped shape it, although no hard evidence to that effect has yet surfaced. Twain's involvement in the production process varied greatly from book to book. For a fuller sense of authorial intention, scholars will continue to rely on the superb definitive editions of Twain's works produced by the Mark Twain Project at the University of California at Berkeley as they become available. Dense with annotation documenting textual emendation and related issues, these editions add immeasurably to our understanding of Mark Twain and the genesis of his works.

7. Except for a few titles that were not in its collection. The American Antiquarian Society in Worcester, Massachusetts, provided the first edition of *King Leopold's Soliloquy*; the Elmer Holmes Bobst Library of New York University furnished the 1906–7 volumes of the *North American Review* in which *Chapters from My Autobiography* first appeared; the Harry Ransom Humanities Research Center at the University of Texas at Austin made their copy of the West Point edition of *1601* available; and the Mark Twain Project provided the first edition of *Extract from Captain Stormfield's Visit to Heaven*.

8. The specific copy photographed for Oxford's facsimile edition is indicated in a note on the text at the end of each volume.

9. All quotations from contemporary writers in this essay are taken from their introductions to the volumes of The Oxford Mark Twain, and the quotations from Mark Twain's works are taken from the texts reproduced in The Oxford Mark Twain.

10. *The Diaries of Adam and Eve*, The Oxford Mark Twain [hereafter OMT] (New York: Oxford University Press, 1996), p. 33.

11. *Tom Sawyer Abroad*, OMT, p. 74.

12. *Adventures of Huckleberry Finn*, OMT, p. 49–50.

13. Ibid., p. 358.

14. Malcolm X, *The Autobiography of Malcolm X*, with the assistance of Alex Haley (New York: Grove Press, 1965), p. 284.

15. I do not mean to minimize the challenge of teaching this difficult novel, a challenge for which all teachers may not feel themselves prepared. Elsewhere I have developed some concrete strategies for approaching the book in the classroom, including teaching it in the context of the history of American race relations and alongside books by black writers. See Shelley Fisher Fishkin, "Teaching *Huckleberry Finn*," in James S. Leonard, ed., *Making Mark Twain Work in the Classroom* (Durham: Duke University Press, forthcoming). See also Shelley Fisher Fishkin, *Was Huck Black? Mark Twain and African-American Voices* (New York: Oxford University Press, 1993), pp. 106–8, and a curriculum kit in preparation at the Mark Twain House in Hartford, containing teaching suggestions from myself, David Bradley, Jocelyn Chadwick-Joshua, James Miller, and David E. E. Sloane.

16. See Fishkin, *Was Huck Black?* See also Fishkin, "Interrogating 'Whiteness,' Complicating 'Blackness': Remapping American Culture," in Henry Wonham, ed., *Criticism and the Color Line: Desegregating American Literary Studies* (New Brunswick: Rutgers UP, 1996, pp. 251–90 and in shortened form in *American Quarterly* 47, no. 3 (September 1995):428–66.

17. I explore the roots of my interest in Mark Twain and race at greater length in an essay entitled "Changing the Story," in Jeffrey Rubin-Dorsky and Shelley Fisher Fishkin, eds., *People of the Book: Thirty Scholars Reflect on Their Jewish Identity* (Madison: U of Wisconsin Press, 1996), pp. 47–63.

18. "What Paul Bourget Thinks of Us," *How to Tell a Story and Other Essays*, OMT, p. 197.

INTRODUCTION

E.L. Doctorow

S am Clemens was thirty-seven when he began writing *The Adventures of Tom Sawyer*. He wrote most of it in the space of two summers, 1874 and 1875, devoting the year in between to the business schemes, lectures, writing projects, and domestic and financial matters with which they filled his exuberant life. He spent the summer of 1874 at Quarry Farm, in the countryside above Elmira, New York, with his young wife, Livy Langdon, and their two children, Susy, age two and Clara, a newborn. Each morning he went off to write in a self-contained study built specially for him, an octagonal room with big windows and panoramic views of the hills and valleys of upstate New York.

Clemens had made himself at home in many parts of the country, any one of which would have contained and nourished another writer for life. A Missourian by birth, he spoke with a slow Southern drawl. But it was out west that he had found fame as a journalist and humorist. His attachment to the state of New York came of his love and courtship of Livy, the daughter of a wealthy Elmira coal mine operator. And now, with his income as a popular American author and lecturer, he was building the grandiose mansion on Farmington Avenue in Hartford, Connecticut, that would establish him as a literary New Englander, a friend of the famous Beecher family — Harriet, the author of *Uncle Tom's Cabin*, and her brothers and sisters — a close colleague of William Dean Howells, the editor of the *Atlantic Monthly*, and a dinner companion of the elderly Brahmins Emerson and Oliver Wendell Holmes. He was the most peripatetic of authors, unparalleled in restlessness among

American writers until then. But the purposive direction of all his travels was up.

The upwardly mobile Clemens was quick to understand both the opportunities and the obligations of his success. Received into the well-to-do Langdon family, he'd muted his views of Christianity and joined their daily prayers. He'd been a bachelor and free-living Bohemian until his mid-thirties. As a young man he'd worked on the Mississippi and gone silver prospecting. He'd become a celebrated drinker and cigar smoker in San Francisco saloons. He was the major means of support of his elderly mother, a widowed sister, and a hapless improvident brother. He'd written himself out of genteel Southern poverty and Western frontier gaucherie, but his first fame was as a humorist, a lower-class literary identification that he was still struggling to surmount.

It is the thesis of the most insightful and astute of his biographers, Justin Kaplan, that Sam Clemens' discovery of his "usable past" constituted "the central drama of his mature literary life." *Tom Sawyer*, the first major act of the drama, would come not a moment too soon — the self-attenuation of a literary careerist was as dire in the America of 1874 as it is now. At his writing table in northern New York State, Clemens went back to his beginnings in Hannibal, Missouri, thirty or so years before, a time when "all the summer world was bright and fresh" and "the sun rose upon a tranquil world, and beamed down . . . like a benediction" (26, 42). It was of course the time when the internal conflicts, the stresses and strains, of an invented self complete with its ironic-nostalgic name could hardly have been imagined. In Hannibal, renamed St. Petersburgh in the book, a person needed no education, social position, money, or renown to feel the radiance of heaven. He didn't even need shoes.

Writing without plan from some hastily scribbled notes, Clemens invoked from his past the boy his genius would descry as the carrier of our national soul. He didn't know where Tom Sawyer's adventures would end, thinking at first that they would take him into adulthood. Improvising from one episode to the next, he ran out of inspiration by the end of summer and waited — confident of the empowering past — until it kicked back in a year later. In the months intervening, the book's dimensions managed to clarify themselves in his mind and he decided to leave Tom forever in his boyhood. He wrote to Howells when the book was finished, in July of 1875, "If I went on, now, & took him into manhood, he would just be like all the one-horse men in literature & the reader would conceive a hearty contempt for him." The decision was the right one. But it did not resolve the larger question in his mind of the book's true audience, and both Livy and Howells had to persuade him not to publish it as a work for adults.

The fact is that Clemens' vision of *Tom Sawyer* never quite came into focus. He seemed to want more from the book than it could give — a creative dissatisfaction that would only be resolved with the writing of *Huckleberry Finn*. "Although my book is intended mainly for the entertainment of boys and girls," he wrote in his preface, "I hope it will not be shunned by men and women on that account." The reader today, remembering his own responses to the book as a child, realizes its peculiar duality in adulthood. We can read with a child's eye or an adult's, and with a different focal resolution for each.

Ever since its publication in 1876, children have been able to read *Tom Sawyer* with a sense of recognition for the feelings of childhood truly rendered: how Tom finds solace for his unjust treatment at the hands of Aunt Polly by dreaming of running away; or how he loves Becky Thatcher, the sort of simpering little blond girl all boys love, and how he does the absolutely right thing in lying and taking her punishment in school to protect her; or how he and his friends pretend to be pirates or the Merry Men of Sherwood Forest, accurately interrupting their scenarios with arguments about who plays what part and what everyone must say and how they must fight and when they must die. In addition, child readers recognize as true and reasonable Tom's aversion to soap and water; they share his keen interest in the insect forms of life, and they relish the not always kind attention he pays to dogs and cats. They understand the value he and his friends place on such items as pulled teeth, marbles, tadpoles, pieces of colored glass. And because all children are given to myth and superstition, they take as seriously as he does the proper rituals and necessary incantations for ridding oneself of warts or reclaiming

XXXIV : E. L. DOCTOROW

lost possessions by using the divining powers of doodlebugs, as well as the efficacy of various spells, charms, and oaths drawn in blood, although it is sadly possible that children today, divested of their atavistic impulses by television cartoons and computer games, are no longer the natural repositories of such folklore.

There is perhaps less explicit recognition by young readers of the taxonomic world Tom Sawyer lives in, though it accredits and confirms their own: it is the world of two distinct and, for the most part, irreconcilable life forms, the Child and the Adult. As separate species children and adults have separate cultures which continually clash and cause trouble between them. All of Tom's adventures, from the simply mischievous to the seriously dangerous, arise in the disparity of the two cultures. And because power and authority reside in the Adult, he is necessarily a rebel acting in the name of freedom. Thus he is understood not as a bad boy but as a good boy who is amiably, creatively, and as a matter of political principle bad — unlike his half-brother Sid, who is that all too recognizable archetype of everyone's childhood, the actually bad boy who appears in the perverse eyesight of adults to be good. (The brothers stand in relation to each other as Tom Jones does to the wretched Blifil in Fielding's great work.)

The moral failures of the adult culture of St. Petersburgh are apparent to the child reader. They range from the imperceptions of the dithering Aunt Polly to the pure evil of Injun Joe. When, with chapter 9, the plot of the book is finally engaged, that is, when Tom and Huckleberry Finn witness the murder at night in the graveyard, the young reader finds everything from then on seriously satisfying, as how could it not be, in that it involves the fear of a murderer, the terror of being lost in a cave, the gratification of a court trial that rights an injustice, and the apotheosis of Tom Sawyer as hero of the whole town and possessor of a vast fortune.

Even more satisfying, though not to be consciously admitted as such, is the uniting of the child and adult communities in times of crisis. The whole town turns out along the river when it appears that Tom and Joe Harper have drowned. There is universal mourning. Similarly, when Tom and Becky are feared lost in the cave, the bereavement is understood as the entire community's. The government of the adults is washed away in their tearful expressions of love. And the young reader confirms his own hope that no matter how troubled his relations with his elders may be, beneath all their disapproval is their underlying love for him, constant and steadfast. This is the ultimate subtextual assurance Mark Twain provides his young reader, and it is no small thing for the child who understands, at whatever degree of consciousness, that his own transgressions are never as dire as they seem, and that there is a bond that unites old and young in one moral world in which truth can be realized and forgiveness is always possible.

But what the adult eye reads — ah, that is quite another matter. We open the book now and see Tom as a mysterious fellow, possibly, something of an anthropological construct, more a pastiche of boyhood qualities than a boy. He is a collection of traits we recognize as applicable to boyhood, or to American boyhood, all of them brought together and animated by the author's voice. In their encyclopedic accuracy they confer upon Tom an unnatural vividness rather than a human character.

Tom Sawyer is ageless. I don't mean that he is a boy for the ages, although he may be — I mean that he is a boy of no determinable age. When he falls in love he exhibits the behavior of a six-year-old. When he is cunning and manipulative he might be nine or ten. His athleticism places him nearer the age of twelve. And in self-dramatization and insensitivity to all feelings but his own he is unquestionably a teenager. The variety of his moods, including his deep funks when he feels unloved, his manic exhibitionism, his retributive fantasies, sweeps him up and down the scale of juvenile thought. The boy doing handstands to impress Becky Thatcher is not the same boy who swims across the river at night from Jackson's Island and, after eavesdropping on his grief-stricken aunt, elects not to relieve the poor woman's misery by telling her he is alive. Unlike Lewis Carroll's Alice, Tom does not have to drink anything to grow taller or shorter. (I note that the illustrations to the first edition can't seem to decide on Tom's proper height or bulk or the lineaments of his face.) He's a morally plastic trickster in part derived from the Trickster myths of the Afro-American and Native American traditions. He may also be the flighty, whimsical, sometimes kind, sometimes cruel minor sort of deity of classical myth, a god of mischief, with the capacity to manipulate the actions of normal human beings, evoke and deflect human emotions, and in general to arrange the course of history to bring honor to himself.

We do not minimize Mark Twain's achievement by noticing, as adults, some of the means by which it was accomplished. Tom Sawyer's thought has generative powers. What he fantasizes often comes to pass. In chapter 3 he receives a cuffing from his aunt when it is the detestable Sid who has broken the sugar bowl; in the sulking aftermath, he pictures himself "brought home from the river, dead, with his curls all wet and his sore heart at rest. How she [Aunt Polly] would throw herself upon him, and how her tears would fall like rain, and her lips pray God to give her back her boy and she would never, never abuse him any more! But he would lie there . . . and make no sign." As indeed he doesn't in chapter 15 when he hides under Aunt Polly's bed, still wet from his night swim, and listens as she weeps and mourns just as he once imagined, and remonstrates with herself in the belief that he has drowned. Tom's fantasies of buried pirate treasure metamorphose into the real buried treasure of Injun Joe. And after Tom and Huck thrill themselves imagining the devilish goings-on in graveyards at midnight in chapter 6, real deviltry arises in front of their eyes in chapter 9, when the grave robbers appear and fight among themselves until one of them is murdered in cold blood. Possibly we are ourselves witness to the author's exploratory method of composition, in which he first conceives of likely things for a boy's mind to imagine, and then decides some of them are too good not to be developed and played out as elements of a plot. In any event a godlike power of realization is conferred upon Tom, as if authorship itself is transferred, and we see a causal connection in what he seriously and intensely imagines and what comes to pass afterwards.

Lacking Tom's magical power, the other children in the book tend to be pallidly drawn, with the possible exception of Huck Finn, though he is clearly a preliminary one-dimensional Huck. Becky, we are disappointed to see, is too careless a sketch to be the ideal girl we half fell in love with ourselves as children, and Sid, though showing promise as a villainous Model Boy at the beginning, gradually fades into the background. Mary goes still once Tom's bath is administered, and finds no further reason to be included at all in the life of the village. It is as if the god of mischief sucks up all their vitality into himself — or as if Mark Twain put so much into this free-range American boyhood that he hadn't anything left for the others.

It is the same with the adult parents and authorities in St. Petersburgh, who lack any dimension except the forbearing kindness with which they foolishly greet every outrage perpetrated by the wretched children they have raised. They, too, are desultory parts of the composition, more impressive really as a village collective or chorus led by Aunt Polly. In some cases the author forgets the names he gives them and supplies them with others. Sometimes he so scants their reactions — as when Tom, the putative Bible-winning scholar, reveals his biblical illiteracy in Sunday school — that he pulls the curtain down over the scene before they can respond at all. And in the climactic return of Tom in time for his own funeral, they fall all over him unbelievably with kisses, and are allowed to ask no questions, let alone to work up an anger, before the chapter comes to its abrupt end.

And yet we indulge the flaws in the composition, perhaps in the author's own spirit of indulgence as he looks down on his lost rural world. In the post-industrial America of today, as in the industrial America of Clemens' own time, *Tom Sawyer* is a work of longing, a version of pastoral, with a built-in entreaty to our critical disbelief. What elicits our tolerance is the voice of the book, which first of all gives candid recognition to the true feelings of its people, and second of all grants them universal amnesty: it is Mark Twain's reigning voice of amused tolerance. Not only are we charmed by its perfect pitch for the American vernacular, but we derive from it a serious self-satisfaction. Its comic rhetoric, its hyperbole, its tongue-in-cheek ennoblement of the actions of a provincial country boy, ask to be read as implicit declaration of a young nation's cultural independence.

There is some indication that the author's own view of his work was less resolute. In his attempt to define what he had done, he claimed *Tom Sawyer* was a kind of hymn. It is "simply a hymn" to boyhood, Sam Clemens wrote to William Dean Howells as he struggled with the judgment that his book was more suitable for children than for adults. The claim has a defensive ring to it. Hymns ennoble or idealize life, express its pieties, and are made to be totally

proper and appropriate for all ears. In the painful evolution of his creative genius Clemens was finding it difficult to accept the value of what he had written. He was having to consider the possibility that the voice he had chosen for
the book was insufficient to the truth of his usable past. In its celebratory
comedy, *The Adventures of Tom Sawyer* might be too forgiving of the racist
backwater that had nurtured him. In that sense it purveyed a false sentimen-
tality. If he troubled to draw his boys on a chart, Tom would stand between
the Model Boy, Sid, on his right, and the unwashed, unschooled son of a
drunkard, Huck Finn, on his left. Tom was a centrist, like Clemens himself, a
play rebel who had been welcomed into the bosom of a ruling society he had
sallied against. He had been rewarded with every honor it could bestow. It
may even have occurred to Clemens that by some perverse act of literary
transmutation he had not anticipated, Tom had replaced Sid as the detestable
Model Boy.

How could his reviewing eye not wander then to the other one, the skinny,
ragged, unredeemable one, swearing to give up all the benefits of civilization
if only they would let him alone? What a glorious moment it must have been
when the squire of Quarry Farm, the master builder of Hartford's grandest
Eastern literary mansion, realized he was in creative contact with a true
outsider, the real unrepentant thing, a boy who would never conform, a boy
who couldn't read or write but who could turn the tables and speak for the
author — a boy who could speak for Sam Clemens from the free territory that
had once been his own.

THE ADVENTURES

OF TOM SAWYER

THE

ADVENTURES OF TOM SAWYER.

THE ADVENTURES

OF

TOM SAWYER

BY

MARK TWAIN.

———————

THE AMERICAN PUBLISHING COMPANY,

HARTFORD, CONN.: CHICAGO, ILL.: CINCINNATI, OHIO.

A. ROMAN & CO., SAN FRANCISCO, CAL.

1876.

To

MY WIFE

THIS BOOK

IS

AFFECTIONATELY DEDICATED.

PREFACE.

———————

Most of the adventures recorded in this book really occurred; one or two were experiences of my own, the rest those of boys who were schoolmates of mine. Huck Finn is drawn from life; Tom Sawyer also, but not from an individual—he is a combination of the characteristics of three boys whom I knew, and therefore belongs to the composite order of architecture.

The odd superstitions touched upon were all prevalent among children and slaves in the West at the period of this story—that is to say, thirty or forty years ago.

Although my book is intended mainly for the entertainment of boys and girls, I hope it will not be shunned by men and women on that account, for part of my plan has been to try to pleasantly remind adults of what they once were themselves, and of how they felt and thought and talked, and what queer enterprises they sometimes engaged in.

THE AUTHOR.

HARTFORD, 1876.

CONTENTS.

ILLUSTRATIONS.

THE ADVENTURES OF TOM SAWYER.

CHAPTER I.

TOM AT HOME.

"TOM!"

No answer.

"TOM!"

No answer.

"What's gone with that boy, I wonder? You TOM!"

No answer.

The old lady pulled her spectacles down and looked over them about the room; then she put them up and looked out under them. She seldom or never looked *through* them for so small a thing as a boy; they were her state pair, the pride of her heart, and were built for "style," not service— she could have seen through a pair of stove lids just as well. She looked perplexed for a moment, and then said, not fiercely, but still loud enough for the furniture to hear:

"Well, I lay if I get hold of you I'll—"

She did not finish, for by this time she was bending down and punching under the bed with the broom, and so she needed breath to punctuate the punches with.   She resurrected nothing but the cat.

"I never did see the beat of that boy!"

She went to the open door and stood in it and looked out among the tomato vines and "jimpson" weeds that constituted the garden.   No Tom.   So she

lifted up her voice at an angle calculated for distance, and shouted:

"Y-o-u-u *Tom!*"

There was a slight noise behind her and she turned just in time to seize a small boy by the slack of his roundabout and arrest his flight.

"There!   I might 'a' thought of that closet. What you been doing in there?"

"Nothing."

"Nothing!   Look at your hands.   And look at your mouth.   What *is* that truck?"

"*I* don't know, aunt."

"Well, *I* know.   It's jam—that's what it is. Forty times I've said if you didn't let that jam alone I'd skin you.   Hand me that switch."

The switch hovered in the air—the peril was desperate—

"My!   Look behind you, aunt!"

The old lady whirled round, and snatched her skirts out of danger.   The lad. fled, on the instant, scrambled up the high board-fence, and disappeared over it.

AUNT POLLY BEGUILED.

His aunt Polly stood surprised a moment, and then broke into a gentle laugh.

"Hang the boy, can't I never learn anything?   Ain't he played me tricks enough like that for me to be looking out for him by this time?   But old fools is the biggest fools there is. Can't learn an old dog new tricks, as the saying is. But my goodness, he never plays them alike, two days, and how is a body to know what's coming? He 'pears to know just how long he can torment me before I get my dander up, and he knows if he can make out to put me off for a minute or make me laugh, it's all down again and I can't hit him a lick. I ain't doing my duty by that boy, and that's the Lord's truth, goodness knows. Spare the rod and spile the child, as the Good Book says. I'm a laying up sin and suffering for us both, *I* know. He's full of the Old Scratch, but laws-a-me! he's my own dead sister's boy, poor thing, and I ain't got the heart to lash him, somehow. Every time I let him off, my conscience does hurt me so, and every time I hit him my old heart most breaks. Well-a-well, man that is born of woman is of few days and full of trouble, as the Scripture says, and I reckon it's so. He'll play hookey this evening, * and I'll just be obleeged to make him work, tomorrow, to punish him. It's mighty hard to make him work Saturdays, when all the boys is having holiday, but he hates work more than he hates anything else, and I've *got* to do some of my duty by him, or I'll be the ruination of the child."

Tom did play hookey, and he had a very good time. He got back home barely in season to help Jim, the small colored boy, saw next-day's wood and

A GOOD OPPORTUNITY.

split the kindlings before supper—at least he was there in time to tell his adventures to Jim while Jim did three-fourths of the work. Tom's younger brother (or rather, half-brother) Sid, was already through with his part of the work (picking up chips) for he was a quiet boy, and had no adventurous, troublesome ways.

While Tom was eating his supper, and stealing sugar as opportunity offered,

---

* South-western for "afternoon."

Aunt Polly asked him questions that were full of guile, and very deep—for she wanted to trap him into damaging revealments. Like many other simple-hearted souls, it was her pet vanity to believe she was endowed with a talent for dark and mysterious diplomacy, and she loved to contemplate her most transparent devices as marvels of low cunning. Said she:

"Tom, it was middling warm in school, warn't it?"

"Yes'm."

"Powerful warm, warn't it?"

"Yes'm."

"Didn't you want to go in a-swimming, Tom?"

A bit of a scare shot through Tom—a touch of uncomfortable suspicion. He searched Aunt Polly's face, but it told him nothing. So he said:

"No'm—well, not very much."

The old lady reached out her hand and felt Tom's shirt, and said:

"But you ain't too warm now, though." And it flattered her to reflect that she had discovered that the shirt was dry without anybody knowing that that was what she had in her mind. But in spite of her, Tom knew where the wind lay, now. So he forestalled what might be the next move:

"Some of us pumped on our heads—mine's damp yet. See?"

Aunt Polly was vexed to think she had overlooked that bit of circumstantial evidence, and missed a trick. Then she had a new inspiration:

"Tom, you didn't have to undo your shirt collar where I sewed it, to pump on your head, did you? Unbutton your jacket!"

The trouble vanished out of Tom's face. He opened his jacket. His shirt collar was securely sewed.

"Bother! Well, go 'long with you. I'd made sure you'd played hookey and been a-swimming. But I forgive ye, Tom. I reckon you're a kind of a singed cat, as the saying is—better'n you look. *This* time."

She was half sorry her sagacity had miscarried, and half glad that Tom had stumbled into obedient conduct for once.

But Sidney said:

"Well, **now,** if I didn't think you sewed his collar with white thread, but it's black."

"Why, I did sew it with white! Tom!"

But Tom did not wait for the rest. As he went out at the door he said:

"Siddy, I'll lick you for that."

In a safe place Tom examined two large needles which were thrust into the lappels of his jacket, and had thread bound about them—one needle carried white thread and the other black. He said:

"She'd never noticed if it hadn't been for Sid. Confound it! sometimes she sews it with white, and sometimes she sews it with black. I wish to geemini she'd stick to one or t'other—*I* can't keep the run of 'em. But I bet you I'll lam Sid for that. I'll learn him!"

He was not the Model Boy of the village. He knew the model boy very well though—and loathed him.

Within two minutes, or even less, he had forgotten all his troubles. Not because his troubles were one whit less heavy and bitter to him than a man's are to a man, but because a new and powerful interest bore them down and drove them out of his mind for the time—just as men's misfortunes are forgotten in the excitement of new enterprises. This new interest was a valued novelty in whistling, which he had just acquired from a negro, and he was suffering to practice it undisturbed. It consisted in a peculiar bird-like turn, a sort of liquid warble, produced by touching the tongue to the roof of the mouth at short intervals in the midst of the music—the reader probably remembers how to do it, if he has ever been a boy. Diligence and attention soon gave him the knack of it, and he strode down the street with his mouth full of harmony and his soul full of gratitude. He felt much as an astronomer feels who has discovered a new planet—no doubt, as far as strong, deep, unalloyed pleasure is concerned, the advantage was with the boy, not the astronomer.

The summer evenings were long. It was not dark, yet. Presently Tom checked his whistle. A stranger was before him—a boy a shade larger than himself. A new comer of any age or either sex was an impressive curiosity in the poor little shabby village of St. Petersburgh. This boy was well-dressed, too—well-dressed on a week-day. This was simply astounding. His cap was a dainty thing, his close-buttoned blue cloth roundabout was new and natty, and so were his pantaloons. He had shoes on—and it was only Friday. He even wore a necktie, a bright bit of ribbon. He had a citified air about him that ate into Tom's vitals. The more Tom stared at the splendid marvel, the higher he turned up his nose at his finery and the shabbier and shabbier his own outfit seemed to him to grow. Neither boy spoke. If one moved, the other moved—but only sidewise, in a circle; they kept face to face and eye to eye all the time. Finally Tom said:

" I can lick you! "

" I'd like to see you try it."

" Well, I can do it."

" No you can't, either."

" Yes I can."

" No you can't."

" I can."

" You can't."

" Can! "

" Can't! "

An uncomfortable pause. Then Tom said:

" What's your name? "

" ' Tisn't any of your business, maybe."

" Well I 'low I'll *make* it my business."

" Well why don't you ? "

" If you say much I will."

" Much—much—*much*. There now."

" Oh, you think you're mighty smart, *don't* you? I could lick you with one hand tied behind me, if I wanted to."

" Well why don't you *do* it ? You *say* you can do it."

" Well I *will*, if you fool with me."

" Oh yes—I've seen whole families in the same fix."

" Smarty ! You think you're *some*, now, *don't* you? Oh what a hat !"

" You can lump that hat if you don't like it. I dare you to knock it off—and anybody that'll take a dare will suck eggs."

" You're a liar! "

" You're another."

" You're a fighting liar and dasn't take it up."

"Aw—take a walk ! "

"Say—if you give me much more of your sass I'll take and bounce a rock off'n your head."

" Oh, of *course* you will."

" Well I *will*."

" Well why don't you *do* it then ? What do you keep *saying* you will for ? Why don't you *do* it ? It's because you're afraid."

WHO'S AFRAID ?

" I *ain't* afraid."

" You are."

" I ain't."

" You are."

Another pause, and more eyeing and sidling around each other. Presently they were shoulder to shoulder. Tom said :

" Get away from here ! "

" Go away yourself ! "

"I won't."

" *I* won't either."

So they stood, each with a foot placed at an angle as a brace, and both shoving with might and main, and glowering at each other with hate. But neither could get an advantage. After struggling till both were hot and flushed, each relaxed his strain with watchful caution, and Tom said :

" You're a coward and a pup. I'll tell my big brother on you, and he can thrash you with his little finger, and I'll make him do it, too."

" What do I care for your big brother ? I've got a brother that's bigger than he is—and what's more, he can throw him over that fence, too." [Both brothers were imaginary.]

" That's a lie."

" *Your* saying so don't make it so."

Tom drew a line in the dust with his big toe, and said :

" I dare you to step over that, and I'll lick you till you can't stand up.   Anybody that'll take a dare will steal sheep."

The new boy stepped over promptly, and said :

" Now you said you'd do it, now let's see you do it."

" Don't you crowd me now; you better look out."

" Well, you *said* you'd do it—why don't you do it ? "

" By jingo ! for two cents I *will* do it."

The new boy took two broad coppers out of his pocket and held them out with derision.   Tom struck them to the ground.   In an instant both boys were rolling and tumbling in the dirt, gripped together like cats; and for the space of a minute they tugged and tore at each other's hair and clothes, punched and scratched each other's noses, and covered themselves with dust and glory.   Presently the confusion took form and through the fog of battle Tom appeared, seated astride the new boy, and pounding him with his fists.

" Holler 'nuff ! " said he.

The boy only struggled to free himself.   He was crying,—mainly from rage.

"Holler 'nuff ! "—and the pounding went on.

At last the stranger got out a smothered " 'Nuff ! " and Tom let him up and said :

" Now that'll learn you.   Better look out who you're fooling with next time."

The new boy went off brushing the dust from his clothes, sobbing, snuffling, and occasionally looking back and shaking his head and threatening what he would do to Tom the " next time he caught him out."   To which Tom responded with jeers, and started off in high feather, and as soon as his back was turned the new boy snatched up a stone, threw it and hit him between the shoulders and then turned tail and ran like an antelope.   Tom chased the traitor home, and thus found out where he lived.   He then held a position at the gate for some time, daring the enemy to come outside, but the enemy only made faces at him through the window and declined.   At last the enemy's mother appeared, and called Tom a bad, vicious, vulgar child, and ordered him away.   So he went away; but he said he " 'lowed " to ' 'lay " for that boy.

He got home pretty late, that night, and when he climbed cautiously in at the window, he uncovered an ambuscade, in the person of his aunt; and when she saw the state his clothes were in her resolution to turn his Saturday holiday into captivity at hard labor became adamantine in its firmness.

CHAPTER II.

JIM.

SATURDAY morning was come, and all the summer world was bright and fresh, and brimming with life. There was a song in every heart; and if the heart was young the music issued at the lips. There was cheer in every face and a spring in every step. The locust trees were in bloom and the fragrance of the blossoms filled the air. Cardiff Hill, beyond the village and above it, was green with vegetation, and it lay just far enough away to seem a Delectable Land, dreamy, reposeful, and inviting.

Tom appeared on the sidewalk with a bucket of whitewash and a long-handled brush. He surveyed the fence, and all gladness left him and a deep melancholy settled down upon his spirit. Thirty yards of board fence nine feet high. Life to him seemed hollow, and existence but a burden. Sighing

26

he dipped his brush and passed it along the topmost plank; repeated the operation; did it again; compared the insignificant whitewashed streak with the far-reaching continent of unwhitewashed fence, and sat down on a tree-box discouraged. Jim came skipping out at the gate with a tin pail, and singing "Buffalo Gals." Bringing water from the town pump had always been hateful work in Tom's eyes, before, but now it did not strike him so. He remembered that there was company at the pump. White, mulatto, and negro boys and girls were always there waiting their turns, resting, trading playthings, quarreling, fighting, skylarking. And he remembered that although the pump was only a hundred and fifty yards off, Jim never got back with a bucket of water under an hour—and even then somebody generally had to go after him. Tom said:

"Say, Jim, I'll fetch the water if you'll whitewash some."

Jim shook his head and said:

"Can't, Mars Tom. Ole missis, she tole me I got to go an' git dis water an' not stop foolin' roun' wid anybody. She say she spec' Mars Tom gwine to ax me to whitewash, an' so she tole me go 'long an' 'tend to my own business—she 'lowed *she'd* 'tend to de whitewashin'."

"Oh, never you mind what she said, Jim. That's the way she always talks. Gimme the bucket—I won't be gone only a minute. *She* won't ever know."

"Oh, I dasn't Mars Tom. Ole missis she'd take an' tar de head off'n me. 'Deed she would."

"*She!* She never licks anybody—whacks 'em over the head with her thimble —and who cares for that, I'd like to know. She talks awful, but talk don't hurt —anyways it don't if she don't cry. Jim, I'll give you a marvel. I'll give you a white alley!"

Jim began to waver.

"White alley, Jim! And it's a bully taw."

"My! Dat's a mighty gay marvel, *I* tell you! But Mars Tom I's powerful 'fraid ole missis—"

"And besides, if you will I'll show you my sore toe."

Jim was only human—this attraction was too much for him. He put down his pail, took the white alley, and bent over the toe with absorbing interest while the

bandage was being unwound.   In another moment he was flying down the street
with his pail and a tingling rear, Tom was whitewashing with vigor, and Aunt Polly

TENDIN' TO BUSINESS.

was retiring from the field with a slipper in her hand and triumph in her eye.

But Tom's energy did not last.   He began to think of the fun he had planned
for this day, and his sorrows multiplied.   Soon the free boys would come tripping
along on all sorts of delicious expeditions, and they would make a world of fun of
him for having to work—the very thought of it burnt him like fire.   He got out
his worldly wealth and examined it—bits of toys, marbles, and trash; enough to
buy an exchange of *work*, maybe, but not half enough to buy so much as half an
hour of pure freedom.   So he returned his straightened means to his pocket, and
gave up the idea of trying to buy the boys.   At this dark and hopeless moment an
inspiration burst upon him !   Nothing less than a great, magnificent inspiration.

He took up his brush and went tranquilly to work.   Ben Rogers hove in sight
presently—the very boy, of all boys, whose ridicule he had been dreading.   Ben's

gait was the hop-skip-and-jump—proof enough that his heart was light and his anticipations high. He was eating an apple, and giving a long, melodious whoop, at intervals, followed by a deep-toned ding-dong-dong, ding-dong-dong, for he was personating a steamboat. As he drew near, he slackened speed, took the middle of the street, leaned far over to starboard and rounded to ponderously and with laborious pomp and circumstance—for he was personating the " Big Missouri," and considered himself to be drawing nine feet of water. He was boat, and captain, and engine-bells combined, so he had to imagine himself standing on his own hurricane-deck giving the orders and executing them:

"Stop her, sir! Ting-a-ling-ling!" The headway ran almost out and he drew up slowly toward the side-walk.

"Ship up to back! Ting-a-ling-ling!" His arms straightened and stiffened down his sides.

"Set her back on the stabboard! Ting-a-ling-ling! Chow! ch-chow-wow! Chow!" His right hand, meantime, describing stately circles,—for it was representing a forty-foot wheel.

" Let her go back on the labboard! Ting-a-ling-ling! Chow-ch-chow-chow!" The left hand began to describe circles.

"Stop the stabboard! Ting-a-ling-ling! Stop the labbord! Come ahead on the stabboard! Stop her! Let your outside turn over slow! Ting-a-ling-ling! Chow-ow-ow! Get out that head-line! *Lively* now! Come—out with your spring-line—what're you about there! Take a turn round that stump with the bight of it! Stand by that stage, now—let her go! Done with the engines, sir! Ting-a-ling-ling! *Sh't! s'h't! sh't!*" (trying the gauge-cocks.)

Tom went on whitewashing—paid no attention to the steamboat. Ben stared a moment and then said:

" Hi-*yi*! *You're* up a stump, ain't you!"

No answer. Tom surveyed his last touch with the eye of an artist; then he gave his brush another gentle sweep and surveyed the result, as before. Ben ranged up alongside of him. Tom's mouth watered for the apple, but he stuck to his work. Ben said:

" Hello, old chap, you got to work, hey?"

Tom wheeled suddenly and said:

"Why it's you Ben! I warn't noticing."

"Say—*I*'m going in a swimming, *I* am. Don't you wish you could? But of course you'd druther *work*—wouldn't you? Course you would!"

Tom contemplated the boy a bit, and said:

'AIN'T THAT WORK?

"What do you call work?"

"Why ain't *that* work?"

Tom resumed his whitewashing, and answered carelessly:

"Well, maybe it is, and maybe it aint. All I know, is, it suits Tom Sawyer."

"Oh come, now, you don't mean to let on that you *like* it?"

The brush continued to move.

"Like it? Well I don't see why I oughtn't to like it. Does a boy get a chance to whitewash a fence every day?"

That put the thing in a new light. Ben stopped nibbling his apple. Tom swept his brush daintily back and forth—stepped back to note the effect —added a touch here and there—criti- cised the effect again—Ben watching every move and getting more and more interested, more and more absorbed. Presently he said:

"Say, Tom, let *me* whitewash a little."

Tom considered, was about to consent; but he altered his mind:

"No—no—I reckon it wouldn't hardly do, Ben. You see, Aunt Polly's awful particular about this fence—right here on the street, you know—but if it was the back fence I wouldn't mind and *she* wouldn't. Yes, she's awful particular about this fence; it's got to be done very careful; I reckon there ain't one boy in a thousand, maybe two thousand, that can do it the way it's got to be done.

"No—is that so? Oh come, now—lemme just try. Only just a little—I'd let *you*, if you was me, Tom."

"Ben, I'd like to, honest injun; but Aunt Polly—well Jim wanted to do it, but she wouldn't let him; Sid wanted to do it, and she wouldn't let Sid. Now don't you see how I'm fixed? If you was to tackle this fence and anything was to happen to it—"

"Oh, shucks, I'll be just as careful. Now lemme try. Say—I'll give you the core of my apple."

"Well, here—. No, Ben, now don't. I'm afeard—"

"I'll give you *all* of it!"

Tom gave up the brush with reluctance in his face but alacrity in his heart. And while the late steamer "Big Missouri" worked and sweated in the sun, the retired artist sat on a barrel in the shade close by, dangled his legs, munched his apple, and planned the slaughter of more innocents. There was no lack of material; boys happened along every little while; they came to jeer, but remained to whitewash. By the time Ben was fagged out, Tom had traded the next chance to Billy Fisher for a kite, in good repair; and when *he* played out, Johnny Miller bought in for a dead rat and a string to swing it with—and so on, and so on, hour after hour. And when the middle of the afternoon came, from being a poor poverty-stricken boy in the morning, Tom was literally rolling in wealth. He had beside the things before mentioned, twelve marbles, part of a jews-harp, a piece of blue bottle-glass to look through, a spool cannon, a key that wouldn't unlock anything, a fragment of chalk, a glass stopper of a decanter, a tin soldier, a couple of tadpoles, six fire-crackers, a kitten with only one eye, a brass door-knob, a dog-collar—but no dog—the handle of a knife, four pieces of orange-peel, and a dilapidated old window-sash.

He had had a nice, good, idle time all the while—plenty of company—and **the** fence had three coats of whitewash on it! If he hadn't run out of whitewash, he would have bankrupted every boy in the village.

Tom said to himself that it was not such a hollow world, after all. He had discovered a great law of human action, without knowing it—namely, that in order to make a man or a boy covet a thing, it is only necessary to make the thing

difficult to attain. If he had been a great and wise philosopher, like the writer of this book, he would now have comprehended that Work consists of whatever a body is *obliged* to do, and that Play consists of whatever a body is not obliged to do. And this would help him to understand why constructing artificial flowers or performing on a tread-mill is work, while rolling ten-pins or climbing Mont Blanc is only amusement. There are wealthy gentlemen in England who drive four-horse passenger-coaches twenty or thirty miles on a daily line, in the summer, because the privilege costs them considerable money; but if they were offered wages for the service, that would turn it into work and then they would resign.

AMUSEMENT.

The boy mused a while over the substantial change which had taken place **in** his worldly circumstances, and then wended toward head-quarters to report.

CHAPTER III

TOM presented himself before Aunt Polly, who was sitting by an open window in a pleasant rearward apartment, which was bed-room, breakfast-room, dining-room, and library, combined. The balmy summer air, the restful quiet, the odor of the flowers, and the drowsing murmur of the bees had had their effect, and she was nodding over her knitting—for she had no company but the cat, and it was asleep in her lap. Her spectacles were propped up on her gray head for safety. She had thought that of course Tom had deserted long ago, and she wondered at seeing him place himself in her power again in this intrepid way. He said: "Mayn't I go and play now, aunt?"

"What, a'ready? How much have you done?"

BECKY THATCHER

3   33

"It's all done, aunt."

"Tom, don't lie to me—I can't bear it."

"I ain't, aunt; it *is* all done."

Aunt Polly placed small trust in such evidence. She went out to see for herself; and she would have been content to find twenty per cent of Tom's statement true. When she found the entire fence whitewashed, and not only whitewashed but elaborately coated and recoated, and even a streak added to the ground, her astonishment was almost unspeakable. She said:

"Well, I never! There's no getting round it, you *can* work when your'e a mind to, Tom." And then she diluted the compliment by adding, "But it's powerful seldom you're a mind to, I'm bound to say. Well, go 'long and play; but mind you get back sometime in a week, or I'll tan you."

She was so overcome by the splendor of his achievement that she took him

PAYING OFF.

into the closet and selected a choice apple and delivered it to him, along with an improving lecture upon the added value and flavor a treat took to itself when it came without sin through virtuous effort. And while she closed with a happy scriptural flourish, he "hooked" a doughnut.

Then he skipped out, and saw Sid just starting up the outside stairway that led to the back rooms on the second floor. Clods were handy and the air was full of them in a twinkling. They raged around Sid like a hail-storm; and before Aunt Polly could collect her surprised faculties and sally to the rescue, six or seven clods had taken personal effect, and Tom was over the fence and gone. There was a gate, but as a general thing he was too crowded for time to make use of it. His soul was at peace, now that he had settled with Sid for calling attention to his black thread and getting him into trouble.

Tom skirted the block, and came round into a muddy alley that led by the back of his aunt's cow-stable. He presently got safely beyond the reach of capture and punishment, and hasted toward the public square of the village, where two "military" companies of boys had met for conflict, according to previous appointment. Tom was General of one of these armies, Joe Harper (a bosom friend,) General of the other. These two great commanders did not condescend to fight in person—that being better suited to the still smaller fry —but sat together on an eminence and conducted the field operations by orders delivered through aides-de-camp. Tom's army won a great victory, after a long and hard-fought battle. Then the dead were counted, prisoners exchanged, the terms of the next disagreement agreed upon and the day for the necessary

AFTER THE BATTLE.

battle appointed; after which the armies fell into line and marched away, and Tom turned homeward alone.

As he was passing by the house where Jeff Thatcher lived, he saw a new girl in the garden—a lovely little blue-eyed creature with yellow hair plaited into two long tails, white summer frock and embroidered pantalettes. The fresh-crowned hero fell without firing a shot. A certain Amy Lawrence vanished out of his heart and left not even a memory of herself behind. He had thought he loved her to distraction, he had regarded his passion as adoration; and behold it was only a poor little evanescent partiality. He had been months winning her; she had confessed hardly a week ago; he had been the happiest and the proudest boy in the world only seven short days, and here in one instant of time she had gone out of his heart like a casual stranger whose visit is done.

" SHOWING OFF."

He worshiped this new angel with furtive eye, till he saw that she had discovered him; then he pretended he did not know she was present, and began to " show off " in all sorts of absurd boyish ways, in order to win her admiration. He kept up this grotesque foolishness for some time; but by and by, while he was in the midst of some dangerous gymnastic performances, he glanced aside and saw that the little girl was wending her way toward the house. Tom came up to the fence and leaned on it, grieving, and hoping she would tarry yet a while longer. She halted a moment on the steps and then moved toward the door. Tom heaved a great sigh as she put her foot on the threshold. But his face lit up, right away, for she tossed a pansy over the fence a moment before she disappeared.

The boy ran around and stopped within a foot or two of the flower, and then shaded his eyes with his hand and began to look down street as if he had discovered something of interest going on in that direction. Presently he picked up a straw and began trying to balance it on his nose, with his head tilted far back; and as he moved from side to side, in his efforts, he edged nearer and nearer toward the pansy; finally his bare foot rested upon it, his pliant toes closed upon it, and he hopped away with the treasure and disappeared round the corner. But only for a minute—only while he could button the flower inside his jacket, next his heart—or next his stomach, possibly, for he was not much posted in anatomy, and not hypercritical, anyway.

He returned, now, and hung about the fence till nightfall, "showing off," as before; but the girl never exhibited herself again, though Tom comforted himself a little with the hope that she had been near some window, meantime, and been aware of his attentions. Finally he rode home reluctantly, with his poor head full of visions.

All through supper his spirits were so high that his aunt wondered "what had got into the child." He took a good scolding about clodding Sid, and did not seem to mind it in the least. He tried to steal sugar under his aunt's very nose, and got his knuckles rapped for it. He said:

"Aunt, you don't whack Sid when he takes it."

"Well, Sid don't torment a body the way you do. You'd be always into that sugar if I warn't watching you."

Presently she stepped into the kitchen, and Sid, happy in his immunity, reached for the sugar-bowl—a sort of glorying over Tom which was well-nigh unbearable. But Sid's fingers slipped and the bowl dropped and broke. Tom was in ecstasies. In such ecstasies that he even controlled his tongue and was silent. He said to himself that he would not speak a word, even when his aunt came in, but would sit perfectly still till she asked who did the mischief; and then he would tell, and there would be nothing so good in the world as to see that pet model "catch it." He was so brim-full of exultation that he could hardly hold himself when the old lady came back and stood above the wreck discharging lightnings of wrath from over her spectacles. He said to himself, "Now it's coming!" And the next instant he was sprawling on the floor! The potent palm was uplifted to strike again when Tom cried out:

"Hold on, now, what 'er you belting *me* for?—Sid broke it!"

Aunt Polly paused, perplexed, and Tom looked for healing pity. But when she got her tongue again, she only said:

"Umf! Well, you didn't get a lick amiss, I reckon. You been into some other audacious mischief when I wasn't around, like enough."

NOT AMISS.

Then her conscience reproached her, and she yearned to say something kind and loving; but she judged that this would be construed into a confession that she had been in the wrong, and discipline forbade that. So she kept silence, and went about her affairs with a troubled heart. Tom sulked in a corner and exalted his woes. He knew that in her heart his aunt was on her knees to him, and he was morosely gratified by the consciousness of it. He would hang out no signals, he would take notice of none. He knew that a yearning glance fell upon him, now and then, through a film of tears, but he refused recognition of it. He pictured himself lying sick unto death and his aunt bending over him beseeching one little forgiving word, but he would turn his face to the wall, and die with that word unsaid. Ah, how would she feel then? And he pictured himself brought home from the river, dead, with his curls all wet, and his sore heart at rest. How she would throw herself upon him, and how her tears would fall like rain, and her lips pray God to give her back her boy and she would never, never abuse him any more! But he would lie there cold and white and make no sign—a poor little sufferer, whose griefs were at an end. He so worked upon his feelings with the pathos of these dreams, that he had to keep swallowing, he was so like to choke; and his eyes swam in a blur of water, which overflowed when he winked, and ran down and trickled from the end of his nose. And such a luxury to him was this petting of his sorrows, that he could not bear to have any worldly cheeriness or any grating delight intrude upon

MARY.

it; it was too sacred for such contact; and so, presently, when his cousin Mary danced in, all alive with the joy of seeing home again after an age-long visit of one week to the country, he got up and moved in clouds and darkness out at one door as she brought song and sunshine in at the other.

He wandered far from the accustomed haunts of boys, and sought desolate places that were in harmony with his spirit. A log raft in the river invited him, and he seated himself on its outer edge and contemplated the dreary vastness of the stream, wishing, the while, that he could only be drowned, all at once and unconsciously, without undergoing the uncomfortable routine devised by nature. Then he thought of his flower. He got it out, rumpled and wilted, and it mightily increased his dismal felicity. He wondered if *she* would pity him if she knew? Would she cry, and wish that she had a right to put her arms around his neck and comfort him? Or would she turn coldly away like all the hollow world? This picture brought such an agony of pleasureable suffering that he worked it over and over again in his mind and set it up in new and varied lights, till he wore it threadbare. He departed in the darkness.

At last he rose up sighing and

About half past nine or ten o'clock he came along the deserted street to where the Adored Unknown lived; he paused a moment; no sound fell upon his listening ear; a candle was casting a dull glow upon the curtain of a second-story window. Was the sacred presence there? He climbed the fence, threaded his stealthy way through the plants, till he stood under that window; he looked up at it long, and with emotion; then he laid him down on the ground under it, disposing himself upon his back, with his hands clasped upon his breast and holding his poor wilted flower. And thus he would die—out in the cold world, with no shelter over his homeless head, no friendly hand to wipe the death-damps from his brow, no loving face to bend pityingly over him when the great agony came. And thus *she* would see him when she looked out upon the glad morning, and oh! would she drop one little tear upon his poor, lifeless form, would she heave one little sigh to see a bright young life so rudely blighted, so untimely cut down?

The window went up, a maid-servant's discordant voice profaned the holy calm, and a deluge of water drenched the prone martyr's remains!

The strangling hero sprang up with a relieving snort. There was a whiz as of a missile in the air, mingled with the murmur of a curse, a sound as of shivering glass followed, and a small, vague form went over the fence and shot away in the gloom.

Not long after, as Tom, all undressed for bed, was surveying his drenched garments by the light of a tallow dip, Sid woke up; but if he had any dim idea of making any " references to allusions," he thought better of it and held his peace, for there was danger in Tom's eye.

Tom turned in without the added vexation of prayers, and Sid made mental note of the omission.

CHAPTER IV.

THE sun rose upon a tranquil world, and beamed down upon the peaceful village like a benediction. Breakfast over, Aunt Polly had family worship; it began with a prayer built from the ground up of solid courses of Scriptural quotations, welded together with a thin mortar of originality; and from the summit of this she delivered a grim chapter of the Mosaic Law, as from Sinai.

Then Tom girded up his loins, so to speak, and went to work to "get his verses." Sid had learned his lesson days before. Tom bent all his energies to the memorizing of five verses, and he chose part of the Sermon on the Mount, because he could find no verses that were shorter. At the end of half an hour Tom had a vague general idea of his lesson, but no more, for his

42

mind was traversing the whole field of human thought, and his hands were busy with distracting recreations. Mary took his book to hear him recite, and he tried to find his way through the fog:

"Blessed are the—a—a—"

"Poor"—

"Yes—poor; blessed are the poor—a—a—"

"In spirit—"

"In spirit; blessed are the poor in spirit, for they—they—"

"*Theirs*—"

"For *theirs*. Blessed are the poor in spirit, for *theirs* is the kingdom of heaven. Blessed are they that mourn, for they—they—"

"Sh—"

"For they—a—"

"S, H, A—"

"For they S, H—Oh I don't know what it is!"

"*Shall!*"

"Oh, *shall!* for they shall—for they shall—a—a—shall mourn—a—a—blessed are they that shall—they that—a—they that shall mourn, for they shall—a—shall *what*? Why don't you tell me Mary?—what do you want to be so mean for?"

"Oh, Tom, you poor thick-headed thing, I'm not teasing you. I wouldn't do that. You must go and learn it again. Don't you be discouraged, Tom, you'll manage it—and if you do, I'll give you something ever so nice. There, now, that's a good boy."

"All right! What is it, Mary, tell me what it is."

"Never you mind, Tom. You know if I say it's nice, it *is* nice."

"You bet you that's so, Mary. All right, I'll tackle it again."

And he did "tackle it again"—and under the double pressure of curiosity and prospective gain, he did it with such spirit that he accomplished a shining success. Mary gave him a bran-new "Barlow" knife worth twelve and a half cents; and the convulsion of delight that swept his system shook him to his foundations. True, the knife would not cut anything, but it was a "sure-enough" Barlow, and there was inconceivable grandeur in that—though where the western boys ever got the idea that such a weapon could possibly be counterfeited to its injury, is an imposing mystery and will always remain so, perhaps. Tom contrived to scarify the cupboard with it, and was arranging to begin on the bureau, when he was called off to dress for Sunday-School.

USING THE "BARLOW."

Mary gave him a tin basin of water and a piece of soap, and he went outside the door and set the basin on a little bench there; then he dipped the soap in the water and laid it down; turned up his sleeves; poured out the water on the ground, gently, and then entered the kitchen and began to wipe his face diligently on the towel behind the door. But Mary removed the towel and said:

"Now ain't you ashamed, Tom. You mustn't be so bad. Water won't hurt you."

Tom was a trifle disconcerted. The basin was refilled, and this time he stood over it a little while, gathering resolution; took in a big breath and began. When he entered the kitchen presently, with both eyes shut and groping for the towel with his hands, an honorable testimony of suds and water was dripping from his face. But when he emerged from the towel, he was not yet satisfactory, for the clean territory stopped short at his chin and his jaws, like a mask; below and beyond this line there was a dark expanse of unirrigated soil that spread downward in front and backward around his neck. Mary took him in hand, and when she was done with him he was a man and a brother, without distinction of color, and his saturated hair was neatly brushed, and its short curls wrought into a dainty and symmetrical general effect. [He privately smoothed out the curls, with labor and difficulty, and plastered his hair close down to his head; for he held curls to be effeminate, and his own filled his life with bitterness.] Then Mary got out a suit of his clothing that had been used only on Sundays during two years —they were simply called his "other clothes"—and so by that we know the size of his wardrobe. The girl "put him to rights" after he had dressed himself; she buttoned his neat roundabout up to his chin, turned his vast shirt collar down over his shoulders, brushed him off and crowned him with his speckled straw hat. He now looked exceedingly improved and uncomfortable. He was fully as uncomfortable as he looked; for there was a restraint about whole clothes and cleanliness that galled him. He hoped that Mary would forget his shoes, but the hope was blighted; she coated them thoroughly with tallow, as was the custom, and brought them out. He lost his temper and said he was always being made to do everything he didn't want to do. But Mary said, persuasively:

"Please, Tom—that's a good boy."

So he got into the shoes snarling. Mary was soon ready, and the three children set out for Sunday-school—a place that Tom hated with his whole heart; but Sid and Mary were fond of it.

THE CHURCH.

Sabbath-school hours were from nine to half past ten; and then church service. Two of of the children always remained for the sermon voluntarily, and the other always remained too—for stronger reasons. The church's high-backed, uncushioned pews would seat about three hundred persons; the edifice was but a small, plain affair, with a sort of pine board tree-box on top of it for a steeple. At the door Tom dropped back a step and accosted a Sunday-dressed comrade:

"Say, Billy, got a yaller ticket?"

"Yes."

"What'll you take for her?"

"What'll you give?"

"Piece of lickrish and a fish-hook."

"Less see 'em."

Tom exhibited. They were satisfactory, and the property changed hands. Then Tom traded a couple of white alleys for three red tickets, and some small trifle or other for a couple of blue ones. He waylaid other boys as they came, and went on buying tickets of various colors ten or fifteen minutes longer. He entered the church, now, with a swarm of clean and noisy boys and girls, proceeded to his seat and started a quarrel with the first boy that came handy. The teacher, a grave, elderly man, interfered; then turned his back a moment and Tom pulled a boy's hair in the next bench, and was absorbed in his book when the boy turned around; stuck a pin in another boy, presently, in order to hear him say "Ouch!" and got a new reprimand from his teacher. Tom's whole class were of a pattern—restless, noisy, and troublesome. When they came to recite their lessons, not one of them knew his verses perfectly, but had to be prompted all along. However, they worried through, and each got his reward—in small blue tickets, each with a passage of Scripture on it; each blue ticket was pay for two verses of the recitation. Ten blue tickets equalled a red one, and could be exchanged for it; ten red tickets equalled a yellow one: for ten yellow tickets the Superintendant gave a very plainly bound Bible, (worth forty cents in those easy times,) to the pupil. How many of my readers would have the industry and application to memorize two thousand verses, even for a Doré Bible? And yet Mary had acquired two Bibles in this way—it was the patient work of two years—and a boy of German parentage had won four or five. He once recited three thousand verses without stopping; but the strain upon his mental faculties was too great, and he was little better than an idiot from that day forth—a grievous misfortune for the school, for on great occasions, before company, the Superintendent (as Tom expressed it) had always made this boy come out and "spread himself." Only the older pupils managed to keep their tickets and stick to their tedious work long enough to get a Bible, and so the delivery of one of these prizes was a rare and noteworthy circumstance; the successful pupil was so great and conspicuous for that day that on the spot every scholar's heart was fired with a fresh ambition that often lasted a couple of weeks. It is possible that Tom's mental stomach had never really hungered for one of those prizes, but unquestionably his entire being had for many a day longed for the glory and the eclat that came with it.

In due course the Superintendent stood up in front of the pulpit, with a closed hymn book in his hand and his forefinger inserted between its leaves, and commanded attention. When a Sunday-school Superintendent makes his customary little speech, a hymn-book in the hand is as necessary as is the inevitable sheet of

NECESSITIES.

music in the hand of a singer who stands forward on the platform and sings a solo at a concert—though why, is a mystery: for neither the hymn-book nor the sheet of music is ever referred to by the sufferer. This Superintendent was a slim creature of thirty-five, with a sandy goatee and short sandy hair; he wore a stiff standing-collar whose upper edge almost reached his ears and whose sharp points curved forward abreast the corners of his mouth—a fence that compelled a straight lookout ahead, and a turning of the whole body when a side view was required; his chin was propped on a spreading cravat which was as broad and as long as a bank note, and had fringed ends; his boot toes were turned sharply up, in the fashion of the day, like sleigh-runners—an effect patiently and laboriously produced by the young men by sitting with their toes pressed against a wall for hours together. Mr. Walters was very earnest of mein, and very sincere and honest at heart; and he held sacred things and places in such reverence, and so separated them from worldly matters, that unconsciously to himself his Sunday-school voice had acquired a peculiar intonation which was wholly absent on week-days. He began after this fashion:

"Now children, I want you all to sit up just as straight and pretty as you can and give me all your attention for a minute or two. There—that is it. That is the way good little boys and girls should do. I see one little girl who is looking out of the window—I am afraid she thinks I am out there somewhere—perhaps up in one of the trees making a speech to the little birds. [Applausive titter.] I want to tell you how good it makes me feel to see so many bright, clean little faces assembled in a place like this, learning to do right and be good." And so forth and so on. It is not necessary to set down the rest of the oration. It was of a pattern which does not vary, and so it is familiar to us all.

The latter third of the speech was marred by the resumption of fights and other recreations among certain of the bad boys, and by fidgetings and whisperings that extended far and wide, washing even to the bases of isolated and incorruptible rocks like Sid and Mary. But now every sound ceased suddenly, with the subsidence of Mr. Walters' voice, and the conclusion of the speech was received with a burst of silent gratitude.

A good part of the whispering had been occasioned by an event which was more or less rare—the entrance of visitors; lawyer Thatcher, accompanied by a very feeble and aged man; a fine, portly, middle-aged gentleman with iron-gray hair; and a dignified lady who was doubtless the latter's wife. The lady was leading a child. Tom had been restless and full of chafings and repinings; conscience-smitten, too—he could not meet Amy Lawrence's eye, he could not brook her loving gaze. But when he saw this small new-comer his soul was all ablaze with bliss in a moment. The next moment he was "showing off" with all his might—cuffing boys, pulling hair, making faces—in a word, using every art that seemed likely to fascinate a girl and win her applause. His exaltation had but one alloy—the memory of his humiliation in this angel's garden—and that record in sand was fast washing out, under the waves of happiness that were sweeping over it now.

The visitors were given the highest seat of honor, and as soon as Mr. Walters' speech was finished, he introduced them to the school. The middle-aged man turned out to be a prodigious personage—no less a one than the county judge—altogether the most august creation these children had ever looked upon— and they wondered what kind of material he was made of—and they half wanted to hear him roar, and were half afraid he might, too. He was from Constantinople, twelve miles away—so he had traveled, and seen the world—these very eyes had looked upon the county court house—which was said to have a tin roof. The awe which these reflections inspired was attested by the impressive silence and the ranks of staring eyes. This was the great Judge Thatcher, brother of their own lawyer. Jeff Thatcher immediately went forward, to be familiar with the great man and be envied by the school. It would have been music to his soul to hear the whisperings:

"Look at him, Jim! He's a going up there. Say—look! he's a going to shake hands with him—he *is* shaking hands with him! By jings, don't you wish you was Jeff?"

Mr. Walters fell to "showing off," with all sorts of official bustlings and activities giving orders, delivering judgments, discharging directions here, there, everywhere that he could find a target. The librarian "showed off"—running hither and thither with his arms full of books and making a deal of the splutter and fuss that insect authority delights in. The young lady teachers "showed off"—bending sweetly over pupils that were lately being boxed, lifting pretty warning fingers at bad little boys and patting good ones lovingly. The young gentlemen teachers "showed off" with small scoldings and other little displays of authority and fine attention to discipline—and most of the teachers, of both sexes, found business up at the library, by the pulpit; and it was business that frequently had to be done over again two or three times, (with much seeming vexation.) The little girls "showed off" in various ways, and the little boys "showed off" with such diligence that the air was thick with paper wads and the murmur of scufflings. And above it all the great man sat and beamed a majestic judicial smile upon all the house, and warmed himself in the sun of his own grandeur—for he was "showing off," too. 4

There was only one thing wanting, to make Mr. Walters' ecstacy complete. and that was a chance to deliver a Bible-prize and exhibit a prodigy. Several pupils had a few yellow tickets, but none had enough—he had been around among the star pupils inquiring. .He would have given worlds, now, to have that German lad back again with a sound mind.

And now at this moment, when hope was dead, **Tom** Sawyer came forward with nine yellow tickets, nine red tickets, and ten blue ones, and demanded a Bible. This was a thunderbolt out of a clear sky. Walters was not expecting an application from this source for the next ten years. But there was no getting around it—here were the certified checks, and they were good for their face. Tom was therefore elevated to a place with the Judge and the other elect, and the great news was announced from head-quarters. It was the most stunning surprise of the decade, and so profound was the sensation that it lifted the new hero up to the judicial one's altitude, and the school had two marvels to gaze upon in place of one. The boys were all eaten up with envy—but those that suffered the bitterest pangs were those who perceived too late that they themselves had contributed to this hated splendor by trading tickets to Tom for the wealth he had amassed in selling whitewashing privileges. These despised themselves, as being the dupes of a wily fraud, a guileful snake in the grass.

The prize was delivered to Tom with as much effusion as the Superintendent could pump up under the circumstances; but it lacked somewhat of the true gush, for the poor fellow's instinct taught him that there was a mystery here that could not well bear the light, perhaps; it was simply preposterous that *this* boy had warehoused two thousand sheaves of Scriptural wisdom on his premises—a dozen would strain his capacity, without a doubt.

Amy Lawrence was proud and glad, and she tried to make Tom see it in her face—but he wouldn't look. She wondered; then she was just a grain troubled; next a dim suspicion came and went—came again; she watched; a furtive glance told her worlds—and then her heart broke, and she was jealous, and angry, and the tears came and she hated everybody. Tom most of all, (she thought.)

Tom was introduced to the Judge; but his tongue was tied, his breath would hardly come, his heart quaked—partly because of the awful greatness of the man, but mainly because he was *her* parent. He would have liked to fall down and worship him, if it were in the dark. The Judge put his hand on Tom's head and called him a fine little man, and asked him what his name was. The boy stammered, gasped, and got it out :

"Tom."

"Oh, no, not Tom—it is — "

"Thomas."

"Ah, that's it. I thought there was more to it, maybe. That's very well. But you've another one I daresay, and you'll tell it to me, won't you ? "

"Tell the gentleman your other name, Thomas," said Walters, "and say *sir.*—You mustn't forget your manners."

"Thomas Sawyer—sir."

"That's it ! That's a good boy. Fine boy. Fine, manly little fellow. Two thousand verses is a great many—very, very great many. And you never can be

TOM AS A SUNDAY-SCHOOL HERO.

sorry for the trouble you took to learn them ; for knowledge is worth more than anything there is in the world ; it's what makes great men and good men ; you'll be a great man and a good man yourself, some day, Thomas, and then you'll look back and say, It's all owing to the precious Sunday-school privileges of my boyhood—it's all owing to my dear teachers that taught me to learn—it's all owing to the good Superintendent, who encouraged me, and watched over me, and gave me a beautiful Bible—a splendid elegant Bible, to keep and have it all for my own, always—it's all owing to right bringing up ! That is what you will say, Thomas—and you wouldn't take any money for those two thousand verses—no indeed you wouldn't. And now you wouldn't mind telling me and this lady some of the things you've learned—no, I know you wouldn't—for we are proud of little boys that learn. Now no doubt you know the names of all the twelve disciples. Won't you tell us the names of the first two that were appointed ? "

Tom was tugging at a button hole and looking sheepish. He blushed, now, and his eyes fell. Mr. Walters' heart sank within him. He said to himself, it is not possible that the boy can answer the simplest question—why *did* the Judge ask him? Yet he felt obliged to speak up and say ;

"Answer the gentleman, Thomas—don't be afraid."

Tom still hung fire.

"Now I know you'll tell *me*" said the lady. "The names of the first two disciples were—"

"DAVID AND GOLIAH!"

Let us draw the curtain of charity over the rest of the scene.

Chapter V.

ABOUT half-past ten the cracked bell of the small church began to ring, and presently the people began to gather for the morning sermon. The Sunday school children distributed themselves about the house and occupied pews with their parents, so as to be under supervision. Aunt Polly came, and Tom and Sid and Mary sat with her—Tom being placed next the aisle, in order that he might be as far away from the open window and the seductive outside summer scenes as possible. The crowd filed up the aisles: the aged and needy postmaster, who had seen better days; the mayor and his wife—for they had a mayor there, among other unnecessaries; the justice of the peace; the widow

53

Douglass, fair, smart and forty, a generous, good-hearted soul and well-to-do, her hill mansion the only palace in the town, and the most hospitable and much the most lavish in the matter of festivities that St. Petersburg could boast; the bent and venerable Major and Mrs. Ward; lawyer Riverson, the new notable from a distance; next the belle of the village, followed by a troop of lawn-clad and ribbon-decked young heart-breakers; then all the young clerks in town in a body—for they had stood in the vestibule sucking their cane-heads, a circling

THE MODEL BOY.

wall of oiled and simpering admirers, till the last girl had run their gauntlet; and last of all came the Model Boy, Willie Mufferson, taking as heedful care of his mother as if she were cut glass. He always brought his mother to church, and was the pride of all the matrons. The boys all hated him, he was so good. And besides, he had been "thrown up to them" so much. His white handkerchief was hanging out of his pocket behind, as usual on Sundays—accidentally. Tom had no handkerchief, and he looked upon boys who had, as snobs.

The congregation being fully assembled, now, the bell rang once more, to warn laggards and stragglers, and then a solemn hush fell upon the church which was only broken by the tittering and whispering of the choir in the gallery. The choir always tittered and whispered all through service. There was once a church choir that was not ill-bred, but I have forgotten where it was, now. It was a great many years ago, and I can scarcely remember anything about it, but I think it was in some foreign country.

The minister gave out the hymn, and read it through with a relish, in a peculiar style which was much admired in that part of the country. His voice began on a medium key and climbed steadily up till it reached a certain point, where it bore with strong emphasis upon the topmost word and then plunged down as if from a spring-board:

Shall I be car-ri-ed toe the skies, on flow'ry *beds*

of ease,

Whilst others fight to win the prize, and sail thro' *blood-*

-y seas?

He was regarded as a wonderful reader. At church "sociables" he **was**

THE CHURCH CHOIR.

always called upon to read poetry; and when he was through, the ladies would lift up their hands and let them fall helplessly in their laps, and "wall" their eyes, and shake their heads, as much as to say, "Words cannot express it; it is too beautiful, *too* beautiful for this mortal earth."

After the hymn had been sung, the Rev. Mr. Sprague turned himself into a bulletin board, and read off "notices" of meetings and societies and things till it seemed that the list would stretch out to the crack of doom—a queer custom which is still kept up in America, even in cities, away here in this age of abundant newspapers. Often, the less there is to justify a traditional custom, the harder it is to get rid of it.

And now the minister prayed. A good, generous prayer, it was, and went into details: it pleaded for the church, and the little children of the church; for the other churches of the village; for the village itself; for the county; for the State; for the State officers; for the United States; for the churches of the United States; for Congress; for the President; for the officers of the Government; for poor sailors, tossed by stormy seas; for the oppressed millions groaning under the heel of European monarchies and Oriental despotisms; for such as have the light and the good tidings, and yet have not eyes to see nor ears to hear withal; for the heathen in the far islands of the sea; and closed with a supplication that the words he was about to speak might find grace and favor, and be as seed sown in fertile ground, yielding in time a grateful harvest of good. Amen.

There was a rustling of dresses, and the standing congregation sat down. The boy whose history this book relates did not enjoy the prayer, he only endured it—if he even did that much. He was restive all through it; he kept tally of the details of the prayer, unconsciously—for he was not listening, but he knew the ground of old, and the clergyman's regular route over it—and when a little trifle of new matter was interlarded, his ear detected it and his whole nature resented it; he considered additions unfair, and scoundrelly. In the midst of the prayer a fly had lit on the back of the pew in front of him and tortured his spirit by calmly rubbing its hands together, embracing its head with its arms, and polishing it so vigorously that it seemed to almost part company with the body, and the slender thread of a neck was exposed to view; scraping its wings with its hind legs and smoothing them to its body as if they had been coat tails; going through its whole toilet as tranquilly as if it knew it was perfectly safe. As indeed it was; for as sorely as Tom's hands itched to grab for it they did not dare—he believed his soul would be instantly destroyed if he did such a thing while the prayer was going on. But with the closing sentence his hand began to curve and steal forward; and the instant the "Amen" was out the fly was a prisoner of war. His aunt detected the act and made him let it go.

The minister gave out his text and droned along monotonously through an argument that was so prosy that many a head by and by began to nod—and yet it was an argument that dealt in limitless fire and brimstone and thinned the predestined elect down to a company so small as to be hardly worth the saving. Tom counted the pages of the sermon ; after church he always knew how many pages there had been, but he seldom knew anything else about the discourse. However, this time he was really interested for a little while. The minister made a grand and moving picture of the assembling together of the world's hosts at the millennium when the lion and the lamb should lie down together and a little child should lead them. But the pathos, the lesson, the moral of the great spectacle were lost upon the boy; he only thought of the conspicuousness of the principal character before the on-looking nations; his face

lit with the thought, and he said to himself that he wished he could be that child, if it was a tame lion.

Now he lapsed into suffering again, as the dry argument was resumed. Presently he bethought him of a treasure he had and got it out. It was a large black beetle with formidable jaws — a "pinch-bug," he called it. It was in a percussion-cap box. The first thing the beetle did was to take him by the finger. A natural fillip followed, the beetle went floundering into the aisle and lit on its back, and the hurt finger went into the boy's mouth. The beetle lay there working its helpless legs, unable to turn over. Tom eyed it, and longed for it; but it was safe out of his reach. Other people uninterested in the sermon, found relief in

A SIDE SHOW.

the beetle, and they eyed it too. Presently a vagrant poodle dog came idling along, sad at heart, lazy with the summer softness and the quiet, weary of captivity, sighing for change. He spied the beetle; the drooping tail lifted and wagged. He surveyed the prize; walked around it; smelt at it from a safe distance; walked around it again; grew bolder, and took a closer smell; then lifted his lip and made a gingerly snatch at it, just missing it; made another, and another; began to enjoy the diversion; subsided to his stomach with the beetle between his paws, and continued his experiments; grew weary at last, and then indifferent and absent-minded. His head nodded, and little by little his chin descended and touched the enemy, who seized it. There was a sharp yelp, a flirt of the poodle's head, and the beetle fell a couple of yards away, and lit on its back once more. The neighboring spectators shook with a gentle inward joy, several faces went behind fans and handkerchiefs, and Tom was entirely happy. The dog looked foolish, and probably felt so; but there was resentment in his heart, too, and a craving for revenge. So he went to the beetle and began a wary attack on it again; jumping at it from every point of a circle, lighting with his fore paws within an inch of the creature, making even closer snatches at it with his teeth, and jerking his head till

RESULT OF PLAYING IN CHURCH.

his ears flapped again. But he grew tired once more, after a while; tried to amuse himself with a fly but found no relief; followed an ant around, with his nose close to the floor, and quickly wearied of that; yawned, sighed, forgot the beetle entirely, and sat down on it! Then there was a wild yelp of agony and the poodle went sailing up the aisle; the yelps continued, and so did the dog; he crossed the house in front of the altar; he flew down the other aisle; he crossed before the doors; he clamored up the home-stretch; his anguish grew with his progress, till presently he was but a woolly comet moving in its orbit with the gleam and the speed of light. At last the frantic sufferer sheered from its course, and sprang into its master's lap; he flung it out of the window, and the voice of distress quickly thinned away and died in the distance.

By this time the whole church was red-faced and suffocating with suppressed laughter, and the sermon had come to a dead stand-still. The discourse was resumed presently, but it went lame and halting, all possibility of impressiveness being at an end; for even the gravest sentiments were constantly being received with a smothered burst of unholy mirth, under cover of some remote pew-back, as if the poor parson had said a rarely facetious thing. It was a genuine relief to the whole congregation when the ordeal was over and the benediction pronounced.

Tom Sawyer went home quite cheerful, thinking to himself that there was some satisfaction about divine service when there was a bit of variety in it. He had but one marring thought; he was willing that the dog should play with his pinch-bug, but he did not think it was upright in him to carry it off.

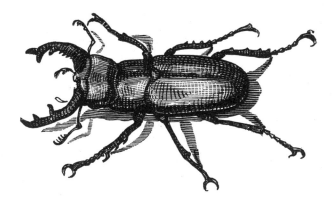

CHAPTER VI.

MONDAY morning found Tom Sawyer miserable. Monday morning always found him so—because it began another week's slow suffering in school. He generally began that day with wishing he had had no intervening holiday, it made the going into captivity and fetters again so much more odious.

Tom lay thinking. Presently it occurred to him that he wished he was sick; then he could stay home from school. Here was a vague possibility. He canvassed his system. No ailment was found, and he investigated again. This time he thought he could detect colicky symptoms, and he began to encourage them with considerable hope. But they soon grew feeble, and presently died wholly away. He reflected further.

60

Suddenly he discovered something. One of his upper front teeth was loose. This was lucky ; he was about to begin to groan, as a "starter," as he called it, when it occurred to him that if he came into court with that argument, his aunt would pull it out, and that would hurt. So he thought he would hold the tooth in reserve for the present, and seek further. Nothing offered for some little time, and then he remembered hearing the doctor tell about a certain thing that laid up a patient for two or three weeks and threatened to make him lose a finger. So the boy eagerly drew his sore toe from under the sheet and held it up for inspection. But now he did not know the necessary symptoms. However, it seemed well worth while to chance it, so he fell to groaning with considerable spirit.

But Sid slept on unconscious.

Tom groaned louder, and fancied that he began to feel pain in the toe.

No result from Sid.

Tom was panting with his exertions by this time. He took a rest and then swelled himself up and fetched a succession of admirable groans.

Sid snored on.

Tom was aggravated. He said, "Sid, Sid!" and shook him. This course worked well, and Tom began to groan again. Sid yawned, stretched, then brought himself up on his elbow with a snort, and began to stare at Tom. Tom went on groaning. Sid said :

"Tom ! Say, Tom!" [No response.] "Here Tom! *Tom!* What is the matter, Tom ? " And he shook him and looked in his face anxiously.

Tom moaned out :

"O don't, Sid. Don't joggle me."

"Why what's the matter Tom? I must call auntie."

"No—never mind. It'll be over by and by, maybe. Don't call anybody."

"But I must! *Don't* groan so, Tom, it's awful. How long you been this way ? "

"Hours. Ouch! O don't stir so, Sid, you'll kill me."

"Tom, why didn't you wake me sooner? O, Tom, *don't!* It makes my flesh crawl to hear you. Tom, what *is* the matter?"

"I forgive you everything, Sid. [Groan.] Everything you've ever done to me. When I'm gone—"

"O, Tom, you ain't dying are you? Don't, Tom—O, don't. Maybe—"

"I forgive everybody, Sid. [Groan.] Tell 'em so, Sid. And Sid, you give my window-sash and my cat with one eye to that new girl that's come to town, and tell her—"

But Sid had snatched his clothes and gone. Tom was suffering in reality, now, so handsomely was his imagination working, and so his groans had gathered quite a genuine tone.

Sid flew down stairs and said:

"O, Aunt Polly, come! Tom's dying!"

"Dying!"

"Yes'm. Don't wait—come quick!"

"Rubbage! I don't believe it!"

But she fled up stairs, nevertheless, with Sid and Mary at her heels. And her face grew white, too, and her lip trembled. When she reached the bedside she gasped out:

"You Tom! Tom, what's the matter with you?"

"O, auntie, I'm—"

"What's the matter with you—what *is* the matter with you, child?"

"O auntie, my sore toe's mortified!"

The old lady sank down into a chair and laughed a little, then cried a little, then did both together. This restored her and she said:

"Tom, what a turn you did give me. Now you shut up that nonsense and climb out of this."

The groans ceased and the pain vanished from the toe. The boy felt a little foolish, and he said:

"Aunt Polly it *seemed* mortified, and it hurt so I never minded my tooth at all."

"Your tooth, indeed! What's the matter with your tooth?"

"One of them's loose, and it aches perfectly awful."

"There, there, now, don't begin that groaning again. Open your mouth. Well —your tooth *is* loose, but you're not going to die about that. Mary get me a silk thread, and a chunk of fire out of the kitchen."

Tom said:

"O, please auntie, don't pull it out. It don't hurt any more. I wish I may never stir if it does. Please don't, auntie. *I* don't want to stay home from school."

"Oh, you don't, don't you? So all this row was because you thought you'd get to stay home from school and go a fishing? Tom, Tom, I love you so, and you seem to try every way you can to break my old heart with your outrageousness." By this time the dental instruments were ready. The old lady made one end of the silk thread fast to Tom's tooth with a loop and tied the other to the bed-post. Then she seized the chunk of fire and suddenly thrust it almost into the boy's face. The tooth hung dangling by the bedpost, now.

DENTISTRY.

But all trials bring their compensations. As Tom wended to school after breakfast, he was the envy of every boy he met because the gap in his upper row of teeth enabled him to expectorate in a new and admirable way. He gathered quite a following of lads interested in the exhibition; and one that had cut his finger and had been a centre of fascination and homage up to this time, now found himself suddenly without an adherent, and shorn of his glory. His heart was heavy, and he said with a disdain which he did not feel, that it wasn't anything to spit like Tom Sawyer; but another boy said "Sour grapes!" and he wandered away a dismantled hero.

Shortly Tom came upon the juvenile pariah of the village, Huckleberry Finn, son of the town drunkard. Huckleberry was cordially hated and dreaded by all the mothers of the town, because he was idle, and lawless, and vulgar and bad—and because all their children admired him so, and delighted in his forbidden society, and wished they dared to be like him. Tom was like the rest of the respectable boys, in that he envied Huckleberry his gaudy outcast condition, and was under strict orders not to play with him. So he played with him every time he got a chance. Huckleberry was always dressed in the cast-off clothes of full-grown men, and they were in perennial bloom and fluttering with rags. His hat was a vast ruin with a wide crescent lopped out of its brim; his coat, when he wore one, hung nearly to his heels and had the rearward buttons far down the back; but one suspender supported his trousers; the seat of the trousers bagged low and contained nothing; the fringed legs dragged in the dirt when not rolled up.

Huckleberry came and went, at his own free will. He slept on door-steps in fine weather and in empty hogsheads in wet; he did not have to go to school or to church, or call any being master or obey anybody; he could go fishing or swimming when and where he chose, and stay as long as it suited him; nobody forbade him to fight; he could sit up as late as he pleased;

HUCKLEBERRY FINN.

he was always the first boy that went barefoot in the spring and the last to resume leather in the fall; he never had to wash, nor put on clean clothes; he could swear wonderfully. In a word, everything that goes to make life precious, that boy had. So thought every harassed, hampered, respectable boy in St. Petersburgh.

Tom hailed the romantic outcast:

"Hello, Huckleberry!"

"Hello yourself, and see how you like it."

"What's that you got?"

"Dead cat."

"Lemme see him Huck. My, he's pretty stiff. Where'd you get him?"

"Bought him off'n a boy."

"What did you give?"

"I give a blue ticket and a bladder that I got at the slaughter house."

"Where'd you get the blue ticket?"

"Bought it off'n Ben Rogers two weeks ago for a hoop-stick."

"Say—what is dead cats good for, Huck?"

"Good for? Cure warts with."

"No! Is that so? I know something that's better."

"I bet you don't. What is it?"

"Why, spunk-water."

"Spunk-water! I wouldn't give a dern for spunk-water."

"You wouldn't wouldn't you? D'you ever try it?"

"No, I hain't. But Bob Tanner did."

"Who told you so!"

"Why he told Jeff Thatcher, and Jeff told Johnny Baker, and Johnny told Jim Hollis, and Jim told Ben Rogers, and Ben told a nigger, and the nigger told me. There now!"

"Well, what of it? They'll all lie. Leastways all but the nigger. I don't know *him*. But I never see a nigger that *wouldn't* lie. Shucks! Now you tell me how Bob Tanner done it, Huck."

"Why he took and dipped his hand in a rotten stump where the rain water was."

"In the day time?"

"Certainly."

"With his face to the stump?"

"Yes. Least I reckon so."

"Did he *say* anything?"

"I don't reckon he did. I don't know."

"Aha! Talk about trying to cure warts with spunk-water such a blame fool way as that! Why that ain't a going to do any good. You got to go all by yourself, to the middle of the woods, where you know there's a spunk-water stump, and just as it's midnight you back up against the stump and jam your hand in and say:

> "Barley-corn, Barley-corn, injun-meal shorts,
> Spunk-water, spunk-water, swaller these warts."

and then walk away quick, eleven steps, with your eyes shut, and then turn around three times and walk home without speaking to anybody. Because if you speak the charm's busted."

5

"Well that sounds like a good way; but that ain't the way Bob Tanner done."

"No, sir, you can bet he didn't, becuz he's the wartiest boy in this town; and he wouldn't have a wart on him if he'd knowed how to work spunk-water. I've took off thousands of warts off of my hands that way Huck. I play with frogs so much that I've always got considerable many warts. Sometimes I take 'em off with a bean."

"Yes, bean's good. I've done that."

"Have you? What's your way?"

"You take and split the bean, and cut the wart so as to get some blood, and then you put the blood on one piece of the bean and take and dig a hole and bury it 'bout midnight at the cross-roads in the dark of the moon, and then you burn up the rest of the bean. You see that piece that's got the blood on it will keep drawing and drawing, trying to fetch the other piece to it, and so that helps the blood to draw the wart, and pretty soon off she comes."

"Yes that's it Huck—that's it; though when you're burying it if you say 'Down bean; off wart; come no more to bother me!' it's better. That's the way Jo Harper does, and he's been nearly to Coonville and most everywheres. But say—how do you cure 'em with dead cats?"

"Why you take your cat and go and get in the graveyard 'long about midnight when somebody that was wicked has been buried; and when it's midnight a devil will come, or maybe two or three, but you can't see 'em, you can only hear something like the wind, or maybe hear 'em talk; and when they're taking that feller away, you heave your cat after 'em and say 'Devil follow corpse, cat follow devil, warts follow cat, *I*'m done with ye!' That'll fetch *any* wart."

"Sounds right. D'you ever try it, Huck?"

"No, but old mother Hopkins told me."

"Well I reckon it's so, then. Becuz they say she's a witch."

"Say! Why Tom I *know* she is. She witched pap. Pap says so his own self. He come along one day, and he see she was a witching him, so he took up a rock, and if she hadn't dodged, he'd a got her. Well that very night he rolled off'n a shed wher' he was a layin drunk, and broke his arm."

"Why that's awful. How did he know she was a witching him."

"Lord, pap can tell, easy. Pap says when they keep looking at you right stiddy, they're a witching you. Specially if they mumble. Becuz when they mumble they're saying the Lord's Prayer back-ards."

"Say, Hucky, when you going to try the cat?"

"To-night. I reckon they'll come after old Hoss Williams to-night."

"But they buried him Saturday. Didn't they get him Saturday night?"

"Why how you talk! How could their charms work till midnight?—and *then* it's Sunday. Devils don't slosh around much of a Sunday, I don't reckon."

"I never thought of that. That's so. Lemme go with you?"

"Of course—if you ain't afeard."

"Afeard! 'Tain't likely. Will you meow?"

"Yes—and you meow back, if you get a chance. Last time, you kep' me a meowing around till old Hays went to throwing rocks at me and says 'Dern that cat!' and so I hove a brick through his window—but don't you tell."

MOTHER HOPKINS.

"I won't. I couldn't meow that night, becuz auntie was watching me, but I'll meow this time. Say—what's that?"

"Nothing but a tick."

"Where'd you get him?"

"Out in the woods."

"What'll you take for him?"

"I don't know. I don't want to sell him."

"All right. It's a mighty small tick, anyway."

"O, anybody can run a tick down that don't belong to them. I'm satisfied with it. It's a good enough tick for me."

"Shó, there's ticks a plenty.   I could have a thousand of 'em if I wanted to."

"Well why don't you?   Becuz you know mighty well you can't.   This is a pretty early tick, I reckon.   It's the first one I've seen this year."

"Say Huck—I'll give you my tooth for him."

"Less see it."

Tom got out a bit of paper and carefully unrolled it.   Huckleberry viewed it wistfully.   The temptation was very strong.   At last he said:

"Is it genuwyne?"

Tom lifted his lip aud showed the vacancy.

"Well, all right," said Huckleberry, "it's a trade."

Tom enclosed the tick in the percussion-cap box that had lately been the pinch-bug's prison, and the boys separated, each feeling wealthier than before.

When Tom reached the little isolated frame School-house, he strode in briskly, with the manner of one who had come with all honest speed.   He hung his hat on a peg and flung himself into his seat with business-like alacrity.   The master, throned on high in his great splint-bottom arm-chair, was dozing, lulled by the drowsy hum of study.   The interruption roused him.

"Thomas Sawyer!"

Tom knew that when his name was pronounced in full, it meant trouble.

"Sir!"

"Come up here.   Now sir, why are you late again, as usual?"

Tom was about to take refuge in a lie, when he saw two long tails of yellow hair hanging down a back that he recognized by the electric sympathy of love; and by that form was *the only vacant place* on the girl's side of the school-house.   He instantly said:

"I STOPPED TO TALK WITH HUCKLEBERRY FINN!"

The master's pulse stood still, and he stared helplessly.   The buzz of study ceased.   The pupils wondered if this fool-hardy boy had lost his mind.   The master said:

"You—you did what?"

"Stopped to talk with Huckleberry Finn."

There was no mistaking the words.

"Thomas Sawyer, this is the most astounding confession I have ever listened to. No mere ferule will answer for this offence. Take off your jacket."

The master's arm performed until it was tired and the stock of switches notably diminished. Then the order followed:

"Now sir, go and sit with the *girls!* And let this be a warning to you."

The titter that rippled around the room appeared to abash the boy, but in reality that result was caused rather more by his worshipful awe of his unknown idol and the dread pleasure that lay in his high good fortune. He sat down upon the end of the pine bench and the girl hitched herself away from him with a toss of her head. Nudges and winks and whispers traversed the room, but Tom sat still, with his arms upon the long, low desk before him, and seemed to study his book.

By and by attention ceased from him, and the accustomed school murmur rose upon the dull air once more. Presently

RESULT OF TOM'S TRUTHFULNESS.

the boy began to steal furtive glances at the girl. She observed it, "made a mouth" at him and gave him the back of her head for the space of a minute. When she cautiously faced around again, a peach lay before her. She thrust it away. Tom gently put it back. She thrust it away, again, but with less animosity. Tom patiently returned it to its place. Then she let it remain. Tom scrawled on his slate, "Please take it—I got more." The girl glanced at the words, but made no sign. Now the boy began to draw something on the slate, hiding his work with his left hand. For a time the girl refused to notice; but her human curiosity presently began to manifest itself by hardly perceptible signs. The boy worked on, apparently unconcious. The girl made a sort of non-committal attempt to see, but the boy did not betray that he was aware of it. At last she gave in and hesitatingly whispered:

"Let me see it."

Tom partly uncovered a dismal caricature of a house with two gable ends to it and a cork-screw of smoke issuing from the chimney. Then the girl's interest began to fasten itself upon the work and she forgot everything else. When it was finished, she gazed a moment, then whispered:

"It's nice—make a man."

The artist erected a man in the front yard, that resembled a derrick. He could have stepped over the house; but the girl was not hypercritical; she was satisfied with the monster, and whispered:

"It's a beautiful man—now make me coming along."

Tom drew an hour-glass with a full moon and straw limbs to it and armed the spreading fingers with a portentous fan. The girl said:

TOM AS AN ARTIST.

"It's ever so nice—I wish I could draw."

"It's easy," whispered Tom, "I'll learn you."

"O, will you? When?"

"At noon. Do you go home to dinner?"

"I'll stay if you will."

"Good,—that's a whack. What's your name?"

"Becky Thatcher. What's yours? Oh, I know. It's Thomas Sawyer."

"That's the name they lick me by. I'm Tom when I'm good. You call me Tom, will you?"

"Yes."

Now Tom began to scrawl something on the slate, hiding the words from the girl. But she was not backward this time. She begged to see. Tom said:

"Oh it ain't anything."

"Yes it is."

"No it ain't. You don't want to see."

"Yes I do, indeed I do. Please let me."

"You'll tell."

"No I won't—deed and deed and double deed I won't."

"You won't tell anybody at all? Ever, as long as you live?"

"No I won't ever tell *any*body. Now let me."

"Oh, *you* don't want to see!"

"Now that you treat me so, I *will* see." And she put her small hand upon his and a little scuffle ensued, Tom pretending to resist in earnest but letting his hand slip by degrees till these words were revealed: "*I love you.*"

INTERRUPTED COURTSHIP.

"O, you bad thing!" And she hit his hand a smart rap but reddened and looked pleased, nevertheless.

Just at this juncture the boy felt a slow, fateful grip closing on his ear, and a steady lifting impulse. In that vise he was borne across the house and deposited in his own seat, under a peppering fire of giggles from the whole school. Then the master stood over him during a few awful moments, and finally moved away to his throne without saying a word. But although Tom's ear tingled, his heart was jubilant.

As the school quieted down Tom made an honest effort to study, but the turmoil within him was too great. In turn he took his place in the reading class and made a botch of it; then in the geography class and turned lakes into mountains, mountains into rivers, and rivers into continents, till chaos was come again; then in the spelling class, and got "turned down," by a succession of mere baby words till he brought up at the foot and yielded up the pewter medal which he had worn with ostentation for months.

CHAPTER VII.

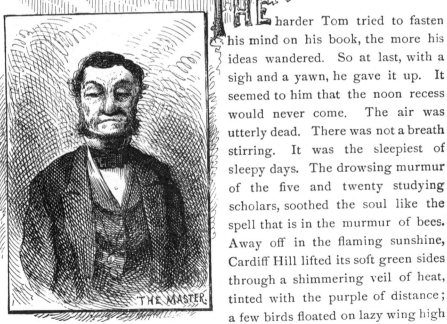

THE MASTER.

THE harder Tom tried to fasten his mind on his book, the more his ideas wandered. So at last, with a sigh and a yawn, he gave it up. It seemed to him that the noon recess would never come. The air was utterly dead. There was not a breath stirring. It was the sleepiest of sleepy days. The drowsing murmur of the five and twenty studying scholars, soothed the soul like the spell that is in the murmur of bees. Away off in the flaming sunshine, Cardiff Hill lifted its soft green sides through a shimmering veil of heat, tinted with the purple of distance; a few birds floated on lazy wing high in the air; no other living thing was visible but some cows, and they were asleep. Tom's heart ached to be free, or else to have something of interest to do to pass the dreary time. His hand wandered into his pocket and his face lit up with a glow of gratitude that was prayer, though he did not know it. Then furtively the percussion-cap box came out. He released the tick and put him on the long flat desk. The creature probably glowed with a gratitude that amounted to prayer, too, at this moment, but it was premature: for when he started thankfully to travel off, Tom turned him aside with a pin and made him take a new direction.

Tom's bosom friend sat next him, suffering just as Tom had been, and now he was deeply and gratefully interested in this entertainment in an instant. This bosom friend was Joe Harper. The two boys were sworn friends all the week, and embattled enemies on Saturdays. Joe took a pin out of his lappel and began to assist in exercising the prisoner. The sport grew in interest momently. Soon Tom said that they were interfering with each other, and neither getting the fullest benefit of the tick. So he put Joe's slate on the desk and drew a line down the middle of it from top to bottom.

"Now," said he, "as long as he is on your side you can stir him up and I'll let him alone; but if you let him get away and get on my side, you're to leave him alone as long as I can keep him from crossing over."

"All right, go ahead; start him up."

The tick escaped from Tom, presently, and crossed the equator. Joe harassed him a while, and then he got away and crossed back again. This change of base occurred often. While one boy was worrying the tick with absorbing interest, the other would look on with interest as strong, the two heads bowed together over the slate, and the two souls dead to all things else. At last luck seemed to settle and abide with Joe. The tick tried this, that, and the other course, and got as excited and as anxious as the boys themselves, but time and again just as he would have victory in his very grasp, so to speak, and Tom's fingers would be twitching to begin, Joe's pin would deftly head him off, and keep possession. At last Tom could stand it no longer. The temptation was too strong. So he reached out and lent a hand with his pin. Joe was angry in a moment. Said he:

"Tom, you let him alone."

"I only just want to stir him up a little, Joe."

"No, sir, it ain't fair; you just let him alone."

"Blame it, I ain't going to stir him much."

"Let him alone, I tell you!"

"I won't!"

"You shall—he's on my side of the line."

"Look here, Joe Harper, whose is that tick?"

"*I* don't care whose tick he is—he's on my side of the line, and you shan't touch him."

"Well I'll just bet I will, though. He's my tick and. I'll do what I blame please with him, or die!"

A tremendous whack came down on Tom's shoulders, and its duplicate on Joe's; and for the space of two minutes the dust continued to fly from the two jackets and the whole school to enjoy it. The boys had been too absorbed to notice the hush that had stolen upon the school a while before when the master came tip-toeing down the room and stood over them. He had contemplated a good part of the performance before he contributed his bit of variety to it.

When school broke up at noon, Tom flew to Becky Thatcher, and whispered in her ear:

"Put on your bonnet and let on you're going home; and when you get to the corner, give the rest of 'em the slip, and turn down through the lane and come back. I'll go the other way and come it over 'em the same way."

So the one went off with one group of scholars, and the other with another. In a little while the two met at the bottom of the lane, and when they reached the school they had it all to themselves. Then they sat together, with a slate before them, and Tom gave Becky the pencil and held her hand in his, guiding it, and so created another surprising house. When the interest in art began to wane, the two fell to talking. Tom was swimming in bliss. He said:

"Do you love rats?"

"No! I hate them!"

"Well, I do too—*live* ones. But I mean dead ones, to swing round your head with a string."

" No, I don't care for rats much, anyway. What *I* like is chewing-gum."

" O, I should say so ! I wish I had some now."

" Do you ? I've got some. I'll let you chew it awhile, but you must give it back to me."

That was agreeable, so they chewed it turn about, and dangled their legs against the bench in excess of contentment.

" Was you ever at a circus ? " said Tom.

" Yes, and my pa's going to take me again some time, if I'm good."

" I been to the circus three or four times—lots of times. Church ain't shucks to a circus. There's things going on at a circus all the time. I'm going to be a clown in a circus when I grow up."

" O, are you ! That will be nice. They're so lovely, all spotted up."

" Yes, that's so. And they get slathers of money—most a dollar a day, Ben Rogers says. Say, Becky, was you ever engaged ? "

" What's that ? "

" Why, engaged to be married."

" No."

" Would you like to ? "

" I reckon so. I don't know. What is it like ? "

" Like ? " Why it ain't like anything. You only just tell a boy you won't ever have any body but him, ever ever *ever*, and then you kiss and that's all. Anybody can do it."

" Kiss ? What do you kiss for ? "

" Why that, you know, is to—well, they always do that."

" Everybody ? "

" Why yes, everybody that's in love with each other. Do you remember what I wrote on the slate ? "

" Ye—yes."

" What was it ? "

" I shant tell you."

" Shall I tell *you* ? "

" Ye—yes—but some other time."

" No, now."

" No, not now—to-morrow."

" O, no, *now.* Please Becky—I'll whisper it, I'll whisper it ever so easy."

Becky hesitating, Tom took silence for consent, and passed his arm about her waist and whispered the tale ever so softly, with his mouth close to her ear. And then he added :

" Now you whisper it to me—just the same."

She resisted, for a while, and then said :

" You turn your face away so you can't see, and then I will. But you mustn't ever tell anybody—*will* you, Tom ? Now you won't, *will* you ? "

" No, indeed indeed I won't. Now Becky."

He turned his face away. She bent timidly around till her breath stirred his curls and whispered, " I—love—you ! "

Then she sprang away and ran around and around the desks and benches, with Tom after her, and took refuge in a corner at last, with her little white apron to her face. Tom clasped her about her neck and pleaded :

" Now Becky, it's all done—all over but the kiss. Don't you be afraid of that —it aint anything at all. Please, Becky."—And he tugged at her apron and the hands.

By and by she gave up, and let her hands drop ; her face, all glowing with the struggle, came up and submitted. Tom kissed the red lips and said :

" Now it's all done, Becky. And always after this, you know, you ain't ever to love anybody but me, and you ain't ever to marry anybody but me, never never and forever. Will you ? "

" No, I'll never love anybody but you, Tom, and I'll never marry anybody but you—and you ain't to ever marry anybody but me, either."

" Certainly. Of course. That's *part* of it. And always coming to school or when we're going home, you're to walk with me, when there ain't anybody looking—and you choose me and I choose you at parties, because that's the way you do when you're engaged."

" It's so nice. I never heard of it before."

" Oh its ever so gay ! Why me and Amy Lawrence "—

The big eyes told Tom his blunder and he stopped, confused.

"O, Tom! Then I ain't the first you've ever been engaged to!"

The child began to cry. Tom said:

"O don't cry, Becky, I don't care for her any more."

"Yes you do, Tom,—you know you do."

Tom tried to put his arm about her neck, but she pushed him away and turned her face to the wall, and went on crying. Tom tried again, with soothing words in his mouth, and was repulsed again. Then his pride was up, and he strode away and went outside. He stood about, restless and uneasy, for a while, glancing at the door, every now and then, hoping she would repent and come to find him. But she did not. Then he began to feel badly and fear that he was in the wrong. It was a hard struggle with him to make new advances, now, but he nerved himself to it and entered. She was still standing back there in the corner, sobbing, with her face to the wall. Tom's heart smote him. He went to her and stood a moment, not knowing exactly how to proceed. Then he said hesitatingly:

"Becky, I—I don't care for anybody but you."

No reply—but sobs.

"Becky,"— pleadingly. "Becky, won't you say something?"

More sobs.

Tom got out his chiefest jewel, a brass knob from the top of an andiron, and passed it around'her so that she could see it, and said:

VAIN PLEADING.

"Please, Becky, won't you take it?"

She struck it to the floor. Then Tom marched out of the house and over the hills and far away, to return to school no more that day. Presently Becky began to suspect. She ran to the door; he was not in sight; she flew around to the play-yard; he was not there. Then she called:

"Tom! Come back Tom!"

She listened intently, but there was no answer. She had no companions but silence and loneliness. So she sat down to cry again and upbraid herself; and by this time the scholars began to gather again, and she had to hide her griefs and still her broken heart and take up the cross of a long, dreary, aching afternoon, with none among the strangers about her to exchange sorrows with.

CHAPTER VIII.

TOM dodged hither and thither through lanes until he was well out of the track of returning scholars, and then fell into a moody jog. He crossed a small "branch" two or three times, because of a prevailing juvenile superstition that to cross water baffled pursuit. Half an hour later he was disappearing behind the Douglas mansion on the summit of Cardiff Hill, and the school-house was hardly distinguishable away off in the valley behind him. He entered a dense wood, picked his pathless way to the centre of it, and sat down on a mossy spot under a spreading oak. There was not even a zephyr stirring; the dead noonday heat had even stilled the songs of the birds; nature lay in a trance that was broken by no sound but the occasional far-off hammering of a woodpecker, and this seemed to render the pervading silence and sense of loneliness the more profound. The boy's soul was steeped in melancholy; his feelings were in happy accord with his surroundings. He sat long with his elbows on his knees and his chin in his hands, meditating. It seemed to him that life was but a trouble, at best, and he more than half envied Jimmy Hodges, so lately released; it must be very peaceful, he thought, to lie and slumber and dream forever and ever, with the wind whispering through the trees and caressing the grass and the flowers over the grave, and nothing to bother and grieve about, ever any more. If he only had a clean Sunday-school record he could be willing to go, and be done with it all. Now as to this girl. What had he done? Nothing. He had meant the best in the world, and been treated like a dog—like a very dog. She would be sorry some day—maybe when it was too late. Ah, if he could only die *temporarily!*

But the elastic heart of youth cannot be compressed into one constrained shape long at a time. Tom presently began to drift insensibly back into the concerns of this life again. What if he turned his back, now, and disappeared mysteriously? What if he went away—ever so far away, into unknown countries beyond the seas —and never come back any more! How would she feel then! The idea of being a clown recurred to him now, only to fill him with disgust. For frivolity and jokes and spotted tights were an offense, when they intruded themselves upon a spirit that was exalted into the vague august realm of the romantic. No, he would be a soldier, and return after long years, all war-worn and illustrious. No—better still, he would join the Indians, and hunt buffaloes and go on the warpath in the mountain ranges and the trackless great plains of the Far West, and away in the future come back a great chief, bristling with feathers, hideous with paint, and prance into Sunday-school, some drowsy summer morning, with a blood-curdling war-whoop, and sear the eye-balls of all his companions with unappeasable envy. But no, there was something gaudier even than this. He would be a pirate! That was it! *Now* his future lay plain before him, and glowing with unimaginable splendor. How his name would fill the world, and make people shudder! How gloriously he would go plowing the dancing seas, in his long, low, black-hulled racer, the "Spirit of the Storm," with his grisly flag

flying at the fore! And at the zenith of his
fame, how he would suddenly appear at the
old village and stalk into church, brown and
weather-beaten, in his black velvet doublet
and trunks, his great jack-boots, his crimson
sash, his belt bristling with horse-pistols, his
crime-rusted cutlass at his side, his slouch
hat with waving plumes, his black flag un-
furled, with the skull and cross-bones on it,
and hear with swelling ecstasy the whisperings, "It's Tom Sawyer the Pirate! — the
Black Avenger of the Spanish Main!"

Yes, it was settled; his career was determined. He would run away from home and
enter upon it. He would start the very next
morning. Therefore he must now begin to
get ready. He would collect his resources
together. He went to a rotten log near at
hand and began to dig under one end of it
with his Barlow knife. He soon struck
wood that sounded hollow. He put his
hand there and uttered this incantation
impressively:

"What hasn't come here, *come !* What's
here, *stay* here!"

Then he scraped away the dirt, and exposed a pine shingle. He took it up and
disclosed a shapely little treasure-house
whose bottom and sides were of shingles.
In it lay a marble. Tom's astonishment
was boundless! He scratched his head
with a perplexed air, and said:

6

TOM MEDITATES.

"Well, that beats anything?"

Then he tossed the marble away pettishly, and stood cogitating. The truth was, that a superstition of his had failed, here, which he and all his comrades had always looked upon as infallible. If you buried a marble with certain necessary incantations, and left it alone a fortnight, and then opened the place with the incantation he had just used, you would find that all the marbles you had ever lost had gathered themselves together there, meantime, no matter how widely they had been separated. But now, this thing had actually and unquestionably failed. Tom's whole structure of faith was shaken to its foundations. He had many a time heard of this thing succeeding, but never of its failing before. It did not occur to him that he had tried it several times before, himself, but could never find the hiding places afterwards. He puzzled over the matter some time, and finally decided that some witch had interfered and broken the charm. He thought he would satisfy himself on that point; so he searched around till he found a small sandy spot with a little funnel-shaped depression in it. He laid himself down and put his mouth close to this depression and called:

"Doodle-bug, doodle-bug, tell me what I want to know! Doodle-bug, doodle-bug tell me what I want to know!"

The sand began to work, and presently a small black bug appeared for a second and then darted under again in a fright.

"He dasn't tell! So it *was* a witch that done it. I just knowed it."

He well knew the futility of trying to contend against witches, so he gave up discouraged. But it occurred to him that he might as well have the marble he had just thrown away, and therefore he went and made a patient search for it. But he could not find it. Now he went back to his treasure-house and carefully placed himself just as he had been standing when he tossed the marble away; then he took another marble from his pocket and tossed it in the same way, saying:

"Brother go find your brother!"

He watched where it stopped, and went there and looked. But it must have fallen short or gone too far; so he tried twice more. The last repetition was successful. The two marbles lay within a foot of each other.

Just here the blast of a toy tin trumpet came faintly down the green aisles of the forest. Tom flung off his jacket and trousers, turned a suspender into a belt, raked away some brush behind the rotten log, disclosing a rude bow and arrow, a lath sword and a tin trumpet, and in a moment had seized these things and bounded away. bare legged, with fluttering shirt. He presently halted under a great elm, blew an answering blast, and then began to tip-toe and look warily out, this way and that. He said cautiously—to an imaginary company:

"Hold, my merry men! Keep hid till I blow."

Now appeared Joe Harper, as airily clad and elaborately armed as Tom. Tom called:

"Hold! Who comes here into Sherwood Forest without my pass?"

ROBIN HOOD AND HIS FOE.

"Guy of Guisborne wants no man's pass. Who art thou that—that—"

"Dares to hold such language," said Tom, prompting—for they talked "by the book," from memory.

"Who art thou that dares to hold such language?"

"I, indeed! I am Robin Hood, as thy caitiff carcase soon shall know."

"Then art thou indeed that famous outlaw? Right gladly will I dispute with thee the passes of the merry wood. Have at thee!"

They took their lath swords, dumped their other traps on the ground, struck a fencing attitude, foot to foot, and began a grave, careful combat, "two up and two down." Presently Tom said:

"Now if you've got the hang, go it lively!"

So they "went it lively," panting and perspiring with the work. By and by Tom shouted:

"Fall! fall! Why don't you fall?"

"I shan't! Why don't you fall yourself? You're getting the worst of it."

"Why that ain't anything. *I* can't fall; that ain't the way it is in the book. The book says 'Then with one back-handed stroke he slew poor Guy of Guis-borne.' You're to turn around and let me hit you in the back."

There was no getting around the authorities, so Joe turned, received the whack and fell.

"Now," said Joe, getting up, "You got to let me kill *you*. That's fair."

"Why I can't do that, it ain't in the book."

"Well it's blamed mean,—that's all."

"Well, say, Joe, you can be Friar Tuck or Much the miller's son and lam me

DEATH OF ROBIN HOOD.

with a quarter-staff; or I'll be the Sheriff of Nottingham and you be Robin Hood a little while and kill me."

This was satisfactory, and so these adventures were carried out. Then Tom became Robin Hood again, and was allowed by the treacherous nun to bleed his strength away through his neglected wound. And at last Joe, representing a whole tribe of weeping outlaws, dragged him sadly forth, gave his bow into his feeble hands, and Tom said, "Where this arrow falls, there bury poor Robin Hood under the greenwood tree." Then he shot the arrow and fell back and would have died but he lit on a nettle and sprang up too gaily for a corpse.

The boys dressed themselves, hid their accoutrements, and went off grieving that there were no outlaws any more, and wondering what modern civilization could claim to have done to compensate for their loss. They said they would rather be outlaws a year in Sherwood Forest than President of the United States forever.

CHAPTER IX.

AT half past nine, that night, Tom and Sid were sent to bed, as usual. They said their prayers, and Sid was soon asleep. Tom lay awake and waited, in restless impatience. When it seemed to him that it must be nearly daylight, he heard the clock strike ten! This was despair. He would have tossed and fidgeted, as his nerves demanded, but he was afraid he might wake Sid. So he lay still, and stared up into the dark. Everything was dismally still. By and by, out of the stillness, little, scarcely preceptible noises began to emphasize themselves. The ticking of the clock began to bring itself into notice. Old beams began to crack mysteriously. The stairs creaked faintly. Evidently spirits were abroad. A measured, muffled snore issued from Aunt Polly's chamber. And now the tiresome chirping of a cricket that no human ingenuity could locate, began. Next the ghastly ticking of a death-watch in the wall at the bed's head made Tom shudder—it meant that somebody's days were numbered. Then the howl of a far-off dog rose on the night air, and was answered by a fainter howl from a remoter distance. Tom was in an agony. At last he was satisfied that time had ceased and eternity begun; he began to doze, in spite of himself; the clock chimed eleven but he did not hear it. And then there came mingling with his half-formed dreams,

TOM'S MODE OF EGRESS.

a most melancholy caterwauling. The raising of a neighboring window disturbed him. A cry of "Scat! you devil!" and the crash of an empty bottle against the back of his aunt's woodshed brought him wide awake, and a single minute later he was dressed and out of the window and creeping along the roof of the "ell" on all fours. He "meow'd" with caution once or twice, as he went; then jumped to the roof of the woodshed and thence to the ground. Huckleberry Finn was there, with his dead cat. The boys moved off and disappeared in the gloom. At the end of half an hour they were wading through the tall grass of the graveyard.

It was a graveyard of the old-fashioned western kind. It was on a hill, about a mile and a half from the village. It had a crazy board fence around it, which leaned inward in places, and outward the rest of the time, but stood upright nowhere. Grass and weeds grew rank over the whole cemetery. All the old graves were sunken in, there was not a tombstone on the place; round-topped, worm-eaten boards staggered over the graves, leaning for support and finding none. "Sacred to the memory of" So-and-So had been painted on them once, but it could no longer have been read, on the most of them, now, even if there had been light.

A faint wind moaned through the trees, and Tom feared it might be the spirits of the dead, complaining at being disturbed. The boys talked little, and only under their breath, for the time and the place and the pervading solemnity and silence oppressed their spirits. They found the sharp new heap they were seeking, and ensconsced themselves within the protection of three great elms that grew in a bunch within a few feet of the grave.

Then they waited in silence for what seemed a long time. The hooting of a distant owl was all the sound that troubled the dead stillness. Tom's reflections grew oppressive. He must force some talk. So he said in a whisper:

"Hucky, do you believe the dead people like it for us to be here?"

Huckleberry whispered:

"I wisht I knowed. It's awful solemn like, *ain't* it?"

"I bet it is."

There was a considerable pause, while the boys canvassed this matter inwardly. Then Tom whispered:

"Say, Hucky—do you reckon Hoss Williams hears us talking?"

"O' course he does. Least his sperrit does."

Tom, after a pause:

"I wish I'd said *Mister* Williams. But I never meant any harm. Everybody calls him Hoss."

"A body can't be too partic'lar how they talk 'bout these-yer dead people, Tom."

This was a damper, and conversation died again. Presently Tom seized his comrade's arm and said:

"Sh!"

"What is it, Tom?" And the two clung together with beating hearts.

"Sh! There 'tis again! Didn't you hear it?"

"I—"

"There! Now you hear it."

"Lord, Tom they're coming! They're coming, sure. What'll we do?"

"I dono.   Think they'll see us?"

"O, Tom, they can see in the dark, same as cats.   I wisht I hadn't come."

"O, don't be afeard. *I* don't believe they'll bother us.   We ain't doing any harm.   If we keep perfectly still, maybe they won't notice us at all."

"I'll try to, Tom, but Lord I'm all of a shiver."

"Listen!"

The boys bent their heads together and scarcely breathed.   A muffled sound of voices floated up from the far end of the graveyard.

TOM'S EFFORT AT PRAYER.

"Look! See there!" whispered Tom. "What is it?"

"It's devil-fire.   O, Tom, this is awful."

Some vague figures approached through the gloom, swinging an old-fashioned tin lantern that freckled the ground with innumerable little spangles of light.   Presently Huckleberry whispered with a shudder:

"It's the devils sure enough.   Three of 'em!   Lordy, Tom, we're goners!   Can you pray?"

"I'll try, but don't you be afeard.   They ain't going to hurt us.   Now I lay me down to sleep, I—"

"Sh!"

"What is it, Huck?"

"They're *humans!*   One of 'em is, anyway.   One of 'em's old Muff Potter's voice."

"No—tain't so, is it?"

"I bet I know it.   Don't you stir nor budge.   *He* ain't sharp enough to notice us.   Drunk, same as usual, likely—blamed old rip!"

"All right, I'll keep still.   Now they're stuck.   Can't find it.   Here they come again.   Now they're hot.   Cold again.   Hot again.   Red hot!   They're p'inted right, this time.   Say Huck, I know another o' them voices; it's Injun Joe."

"That's so—that murderin' half-breed! I'd druther they was devils a dern sight. What kin they be up to?"

The whispers died wholly out, now, for the three men had reached the grave and stood within a few feet of the boys' hiding-place."

"Here it is," said the third voice; and the owner of it held the lantern up and revealed the face of young Dr. Robinson.

Potter and Injun Joe were carrying a handbarrow with a rope and a couple of shovels on it. They cast down their load and began to open the grave. The doctor put the lantern at the head of the grave and came and sat down with his back against one of the elm trees. He was so close the boys could have touched him.

"Hurry, men!" he said in a low voice; "the moon might come out at any moment."

They growled a response and went on digging. For some time there was no noise but the grating sound of the spades discharging their freight of mould and gravel. It was very monotonous. Finally a spade struck upon the coffin with a dull woody accent, and within another minute or two the men had hoisted it out on the ground. They pried off the lid with their shovels, got out the body and dumped it rudely on the ground. The moon drifted from behind the clouds and exposed the pallid face. The barrow was got ready and the corpse placed on it, covered with a blanket, and bound to its place with the rope. Potter took out a large spring-knife and cut off the dangling end of the rope and then said:

"Now the cussed thing's ready, Sawbones, and you'll just out with another five, or here she stays."

"That's the talk!" said Injun Joe.

"Look here, what does this mean?" said the doctor. "You required your pay in advance, and I've paid you."

"Yes, and you done more than that," said Injun Joe, approaching the doctor, who was now standing. "Five years ago you drove me away from your father's kitchen one night, when I come to ask for something to eat, and you said I warn't there for any good; and when I swore I'd get even with you if it

took a hundred years, your father had me jailed for a vagrant. Did you think
I'd forget? The Injun blood ain't in me for nothing. And now I've *got* you,
and you got to *settle*, you know!"

He was threatening the doctor, with his fist in his face, by this time. The
doctor struck out suddenly and stretched the ruffian on the ground. Potter
dropped his knife, and exclaimed:

"Here, now, don't you hit my pard!" and the next moment he had grappled
with the doctor and the two were struggling with might and main, trampling
the grass and tearing the ground with their heels. Injun Joe sprang to his
feet, his eyes flaming with passion, snatched up Potter's knife, and went creeping, catlike and stooping, round and round about the combatants, seeking an
opportunity. All at once the doctor flung himself free, seized the heavy head
board of Williams' grave and felled Potter to the earth with it—and in the
same instant the half-breed saw his chance and drove the knife to the hilt in
the young man's breast. He reeled and fell partly upon Potter, flooding him
with his blood, and in the same moment the clouds blotted out the dreadful
spectacle and the two frightened boys went speeding away in the dark.

Presently, when the moon emerged again, Injun Joe was standing over the
two forms, contemplating them. The doctor murmured inarticulately, gave a
long gasp or two and was still. The half-breed muttered:

"*That* score is settled—damn you."

Then he robbed the body. After which he put the fatal knife in Potter's
open right hand, and sat down on the dismantled coffin. Three—four—five
minutes passed, and then Potter began to stir and moan. His hand closed
upon the knife; he raised it, glanced at it, and let it fall, with a shudder. Then
he sat up, pushing the body from him, and gazed at it, and then around him,
confusedly. His eyes met Joe's.

"Lord, how is this, Joe?" he said.

"It's a dirty business," said Joe, without moving. "What did you do it for?"

"I! I never done it!"

"Look here! That kind of talk won't wash."

Potter trembled and grew white.

"I thought I'd got sober. I'd no business to drink to-night. But it's in my head yet—worse'n when we started here. I'm all in a muddle; can't recollect anything of it hardly. Tell me, Joe—*honest*, now, old feller—did I do it? Joe, I never meant to—'pon my soul and honor I never meant to, Joe. Tell me how it was Joe. O, it's awful—and him so young and promising."

"Why you two was scuffling, and he fetched you one with the head-board and you fell flat; and then up you come, all reeling and staggering, like, and snatched the knife and jammed it into him, just as he fetched you another awful clip—and here you've laid, as dead as a wedge till now."

"O, I didn't know what I was a doing. I wish I may die this minute if I

MUFF POTTER OUTWITTED.

did. It was all on account of the whisky; and the excitement, I reckon. I never used a weepon in my life before, Joe. I've fought, but never with weepons. They'll all say that. Joe, don't tell! Say you won't tell, Joe—that's a good feller. I always liked you Joe, and stood up for you, too. Don't you remember? You *won't* tell, *will* you Joe?" And the poor creature dropped on his knees before the stolid murderer, and clasped his appealing hands.

"No, you've always been fair and square with me, Muff Potter, and I won't go back on you.—There, now, that's as fair as a man can say."

"O, Joe, you're an angel. I'll bless you for this the longest day I live." And Potter began to cry.

"Come, now, that's enough of that. This ain't any time for blubbering. You be off yonder way and I'll go this. Move, now, and don't leave any tracks behind you."

Potter started on a trot that quickly increased to a run. The half-breed stood looking after him. He muttered:

"If he's as much stunned with the lick and fuddled with the rum as he had the look of being, he won't think of the knife till he's gone so far he'll be afraid to come back after it to such a place by himself—chicken-heart!"

Two or three minutes later the murdered man, the blanketed corpse, the lidless coffin and the open grave were under no inspection but the moon's. The stillness was complete again, too.

CHAPTER X.

The two boys flew on and on, toward the village, speechless with horror. They glanced backward over their shoulders from time to time, apprehensively, as if they feared they might be followed. Every stump that started up in their path seemed a man and an enemy, and made them catch their breath; and as they sped by some outlying cottages that lay near the village, the barking of the aroused watch-dogs seemed to give wings to their feet.

"If we can only get to the old tannery, before we break down!" whispered Tom, in short catches between breaths, "I can't stand it much longer."

Huckleberry's hard pantings were his only reply, and the boys fixed their eyes on the goal of their hopes and bent to their work to win it. They gained steadily on it, and at last, breast to breast they burst through the open door and fell grateful and exhausted in the sheltering shadows beyond. By and by their pulses slowed down, and Tom whispered:

"Huckleberry, what do you reckon 'll come of this?"

"If Dr. Robinson dies, I reckon hanging 'll come of it."

"Do you though?"

"Why I *know* it, Tom."

Tom thought a while, then he said:

"Who'll tell? We?"

"What are you talking about? S'pose something happened and Injun Joe *didn't* hang? Why he'd kill us some time or other, just as dead sure as we're a laying here."

"That's just what I was thinking to myself, Huck."

"If anybody tells, let Muff Potter do it, if he's fool enough. He's generally drunk enough."

Tom said nothing—went on thinking. Presently he whispered:

"Huck, Muff Potter don't *know* it. How can he tell?"

"What's the reason he don't know it?"

"Because he'd just got that whack when Injun Joe done it. D' you reckon he could see anything? D' you reckon he knowed anything?"

"By hokey, that's so Tom!"

"And besides, look-a-here—maybe that whack done for *him*!"

"No, 'taint likely Tom. He had liquor in him; I could see that; and besides, he always has. Well when pap's full, you might take and belt him over the head with a church and you couldn't phase him. He says so, his own self. So it's the same with Muff Potter, of course. But if a man was dead sober, I reckon maybe that whack might fetch him; I dono."

After another reflective silence, Tom said:

"Hucky, you sure you can keep mum?"

"Tom, we *got* to keep mum. *You* know that. That Injun devil would'nt make any more of drownding us than a couple of cats, if we was to squeak 'bout this and they didn't hang him. Now look-a-here, Tom, less take and swear to one another—that's what we got to do—swear to keep mum."

"I'm agreed. It's the best thing. Would you just hold hands and swear that we—"

"O, no, that wouldn't do for this. That's good enough for little rubbishy common things—specially with gals, cuz *they* go back on you anyway, and blab if they get in a huff—but there orter be writing 'bout a big thing like this. And blood."

Tom's whole being applauded this idea. It was deep, and dark, and awful; the hour, the circumstances, the surroundings, were in keeping with it. He picked up a clean pine shingle that lay in the moonlight, took a little fragment of "red keel" out of his pocket, got the moon on his work, and painfully scrawled these lines, emphasizing each slow down-stroke by clamping his tongue between his teeth, and letting up the pressure on the up-strokes:

> "Huck Finn and
> Tom Sawyer swears
> they will keep mum
> about this and they
> wish they may drop
> down dead in their
> tracks if they ever
> tell and Rot."

Huckleberry was filled with admiration of Tom's facility in writing, and the sublimity of his language. He at once took a pin from his lappel and was going to prick his flesh, but Tom said:

"Hold on! Don't do that. A pin's brass. It might have verdigrease on it."

"What's verdigrease?"

"It's p'ison. That's what it is. You just swaller some of it once—you'll see."

So Tom unwound the thread from one of his needles, and each boy pricked the ball of his thumb and squeezed out a drop of blood. In time, after many squeezes, Tom managed to sign his initials, using the ball of his little finger for a pen. Then he showed Huckleberry how to make an H and an F, and the oath was complete. They buried the shingle close to the wall, with some dismal ceremonies and incantations, and the fetters that bound their tongues were considered to be locked and the key thrown away.

A figure crept stealthily through a break in the other end of the ruined building, now, but they did not notice it.

"Tom," whispered Huckleberry, "does this keep us from *ever* telling—*always?*"

"Of course it does. It don't make any difference *what* happens, we got to keep mum. We'd drop down dead—don't *you* know that?"

"Yes, I reckon that's so."

They continued to whisper for some little time. Presently a dog set up a long, lugubrious howl just outside—within ten feet of them. The boys clasped each other suddenly, in an agony of fright.

"Which of us does he mean?" gasped Huckleberry.

"I dono—peep through the crack. Quick!"

"No, *you*, Tom!"

"I can't—I can't *do* it, Huck!"

"Please, Tom. There 'tis again!"

"O, lordy, I'm thankful!" whispered Tom. "I know his voice. It's Bull Harbison." *

---

* If Mr. Harbison had owned a slave named Bull, Tom would have spoken of him as " Harbison's Bull," but a son or a dog of that name was " Bull Harbison."

"O, that's good—I tell you, Tom, I was most scared to death; I'd a bet any-thing it was a *stray* dog."

The dog howled again. The boys' hearts sank once more.

"O, my! that ain't no Bull Harbison!" whispered Huckleberry. "*Do*, Tom!"

Tom, quaking with fear, yielded, and put his eye to the crack. His whisper was hardly audible when he said:

"O, Huck, IT'S A STRAY DOG!"

"Quick, Tom, quick! Who does he mean?"

"Huck, he must mean us both—we're right together."

"O, Tom, I reckon we're goners. I reckon there ain't no mistake 'bout where *I'll* go to. I been so wicked."

"Dad fetch it! This comes of playing hookey and doing everything a feller's told *not* to do. I might a been good, like Sid, if I'd a tried—but no, I wouldn't, of course. But if ever I get off this time, I lay I'll just *waller* in Sunday-schools!" And Tom began to snuffle a little.

"*You* bad!" and Huckleberry began to snuffle too. "Consound it, Tom Sawyer, you're just old pie, 'longside o'what *I* am. O, *lordy*, lordy, lordy, I wisht I only had half your chance."

Tom choked off and whispered:

"Look, Hucky, look! He's got his *back* to us!"

Hucky looked, with joy in his heart.

"Well he has, by jingoes! Did he before?"

"Yes, he did. But I, like a fool, never thought. O, this is bully, you know. *Now* who can he mean?"

The howling stopped. Tom pricked up his ears.

"Sh! What's that?" he whispered.

"Sounds like—like hogs grunting. No—it's somebody snoring, Tom."

"That *is* it? Where 'bouts is it, Huck?"

"I bleeve it's down at 'tother end. Sounds so, anyway. Pap used to sleep there, sometimes, 'long with the hogs, but laws bless you, he just lifts things when *he* snores. Besides, I reckon he ain't ever coming back to this town any more."

The spirit of adventure rose in the boys' souls once more.

7

" Hucky, do you das't to go if I lead ? "

" I don't like to, much.   Tom, s'pose it's Injun Joe ! "

Tom quailed.   But presently the temptation rose up strong again and the boys agreed to try, with the understanding that they would take to their heels if the snoring stopped.   So they went tip-toeing stealthily down, the one behind the other.   When they had got to within five steps of the snorer, Tom stepped on a stick, and it broke with a sharp snap.   The man moaned, writhed a little, and his

DISTURBING MUFF'S SLEEP.

face came into the moonlight.   It was Muff Potter.   The boys' hearts had stood still, and their hopes too, when the man moved, but their fears passed away now. They tip-toed out, through the broken weather-boarding, and stopped at a little distance to exchange a parting word.   That long, lugubrious howl rose on the night air again !   They turned and saw the strange dog standing within a few feet of where Potter was lying, and *facing* Potter, with his nose pointing heavenward.

" O, geeminy it's *him*! " exclaimed both boys, in a breath.

" Say, Tom — they say a stray dog come howling around Johnny Miller's house, 'bout midnight, as much as two weeks ago; and a whippoorwill come in and lit on the bannisters and sung, the very same evening; and there ain't anybody dead there yet."

" Well I know that. And suppose there ain't. Didn't Gracie Miller fall in the kitchen fire and burn herself terrible the very next Saturday ? "

" Yes, but she ain't *dead*. And what's more, she's getting better, too."

" All right, you wait and see. She's a goner, just as dead sure as Muff Potter's a goner. That's what the niggers say, and they know all about these kind of things, Huck."

Then they separated, cogitating. When Tom crept in at his bedroom window, the night was almost spent. He undressed with excessive caution, and fell asleep congratulating himself that nobody knew of his escapade. He was not aware that the gently-snoring Sid was awake, and had been so for an hour.

When Tom awoke, Sid was dressed and gone. There was a late look in the light, a late sense in the atmosphere. He was startled. Why had he not been called—persecuted till he was up, as usual ? The thought filled him with bodings. Within five minutes he was dressed and down stairs, feeling sore and drowsy. The family were still at table, but they had finished breakfast. There was no voice of rebuke; but there were averted eyes; there was a silence and an air of solemnity that struck a chill to the culprit's heart. He sat down and tried to seem gay, but it was up-hill work ; it roused no smile, no response, and he lapsed into silence and let his heart sink down to the depths.

After breakfast his aunt took him aside, and Tom almost brightened in the hope that he was going to be flogged; but it was not so. His aunt wept over him and asked him how he could go and break her old heart so; and finally told him to go on, and ruin himself and bring her grey hairs with sorrow to the grave, for it was no use for her to try any more. This was worse than a thousand whippings, and Tom's heart was sorer now than his body. He cried, he pleaded for forgiveness, promised reform over and over again and then received his dismissal, feeling that he had won but an imperfect forgiveness and established but a feeble confidence.

He left the presence too miserable to even feel revengeful toward Sid; and so the latter's prompt retreat through the back gate was unnecessary. He moped to school gloomy and sad, and took his flogging, along with Joe Harper, for playing hooky the day before, with the air of one whose heart was busy with heavier woes and wholly dead to trifles. Then he betook himself to his seat, rested his elbows on his desk and his jaws in his hands and stared at the wall with the stony stare of suffering that has reached the limit and can no further go. His elbow was pressing against some hard substance. After a long time he slowly and sadly changed his position, and took up this object with a sigh. It was in a paper. He unrolled it. A long, lingering, colossal sigh followed, and his heart broke. It was his brass andiron knob!

This final feather broke the camel's back.

MUFF POTTER.

CLOSE upon the hour of noon the whole village was suddenly electrified with the ghastly news. No need of the as yet undreamed-of telegraph; the tale flew from man to man, from group to group, from house to house, with little less than telegraphic speed. Of course the schoolmaster gave holiday for that afternoon; the town would have thought strangely of him if he had not.

A gory knife had been found close to the murdered man, and it had been recognized by somebody as belonging to Muff Potter—so the story ran. And it was said that a belated citizen had come upon Potter washing himself in the "branch" about one or two o'clock in the morning, and that Potter had at once sneaked off—suspicious circumstances, especially the washing, which was not a habit with Potter. It was also said that the town had been ransacked for this "murderer,"

A SUSPICIOUS INCIDENT.

(the public are not slow in the matter of sifting evidence and arriving at a verdict), but that he could not be found. Horsemen had departed down all the roads in every direction, and the Sheriff "was confident" that he would be captured before night.

All the town was drifting toward the graveyard. Tom's heart-break vanished and he joined the procession, not because he would not a thousand times rather go anywhere else, but because an awful, unaccountable fascination drew him on. Arrived at the dreadful place, he wormed his small body through the crowd and saw the dismal spectacle. It seemed to him an age since he was there before. Somebody pinched his arm. He turned, and his eyes met Huckleberry's. Then both looked elsewhere at once, and wondered if anybody had noticed anything in their mutual glance. But everybody was talking, and intent upon the grisly spectacle before them.

"Poor fellow!" "Poor young fellow!" "This ought to be a lesson to grave-robbers!" "Muff Potter'll hang for this if they catch him!" This was the drift of remark; and the minister said, "It was a judgment; His hand is here."

Now Tom shivered from head to heel; for his eye fell upon the stolid face of Injun Joe. At this moment the crowd began to sway and struggle, and voices shouted, "It's him! it's him! he's coming himself!"

"Who? Who?" from twenty voices.

"Muff Potter!"

"Hallo, he's stopped!—Look out, he's turning! Don't let him get away!"

People in the branches of the trees over Tom's head, said he wasn't trying to get away—he only looked doubtful and perplexed.

"Infernal impudence!" said a bystander; "wanted to come and take a quiet look at his work, I reckon—didn't expect any company."

The crowd fell apart, now, and the Sheriff came through, ostentatiously leading Potter by the arm. The poor fellow's face was haggard, and his eyes

INJUN JOE'S TWO VICTIMS.

showed the fear that was upon him. When he stood before the murdered man, he shook as with a palsy, and he put his face in his hands and burst into tears.

"I didn't do it, friends," he sobbed; "'pon my word and honor I never done it."

"Who's accused you?" shouted a voice.

This shot seemed to carry home. Potter lifted his face and looked around him with a pathetic hopelessness in his eyes. He saw Injun Joe, and exclaimed:

"O, Injun Joe, you promised me you'd never—"

"Is that your knife?" and it was thrust before him by the Sheriff.

Potter would have fallen if they had not caught him and eased him to the ground. Then he said:

"Something told me 't if I didn't come back and get—" He shuddered; then waved his nerveless hand with a vanquished gesture and said, "Tell 'em, Joe, tell 'em—it ain't any use any more."

Then Huckleberry and Tom stood dumb and staring, and heard the stony-hearted liar reel off his serene statement, they expecting every moment that the clear sky would deliver God's lightnings upon his head, and wondering to see how long the stroke was delayed. And when he had finished and still stood alive and whole, their wavering impulse to break their oath and save the poor betrayed prisoner's life faded and vanished away, for plainly this miscreant had sold himself to Satan and it would be fatal to meddle with the property of such a power as that.

"Why didn't you leave? What did you want to come here for?" somebody said.

"I couldn't help it—I couldn't help it," Potter moaned. "I wanted to run away, but I couldn't seem to come anywhere but here." And he fell to sobbing again.

Injun Joe repeated his statement, just as calmly, a few minutes afterward on the inquest, under oath; and the boys, seeing that the lightnings were still withheld, were confirmed in their belief that Joe had sold himself to the devil. He was now become, to them, the most balefully interesting object they had ever looked upon, and they could not take their fascinated eyes from his face.

They inwardly resolved to watch him, nights, when opportunity should offer, in the hope of getting a glimpse of his dread master.

Injun Joe helped to raise the body of the murdered man and put it in a wagon for removal; and it was whispered through the shuddering crowd that the wound bled a little! The boys thought that this happy circumstance would turn suspicion in the right direction; but they were disappointed, for more than one villager remarked:

" It was within three feet of Muff Potter when it done it."

Tom's fearful secret and gnawing conscience disturbed his sleep for as much as a week after this; and at breakfast one morning Sid said:

" Tom, you pitch around and talk in your sleep so much that you keep me awake about half the time."

Tom blanched and dropped his eyes.

" It's a bad sign," said Aunt Polly, gravely. " What you got on your mind, Tom?"

" Nothing. Nothing 't I know of." But the boy's hand shook so that he spilled his coffee.

" And you do talk such stuff," Sid said. " Last night you said 'it's blood, it's blood, that's what it is!' You said that over and over. And you said, 'Don't torment me so—I'll tell!' Tell *what?* What is it you'll tell?"

Everything was swimming before Tom. There is no telling what might have happened, now, but luckily the concern passed out of Aunt Polly's face and she came to Tom's relief without knowing it. She said:

" Sho! It's that dreadful murder. I dream about it most every night myself. Sometimes I dream it's me that done it."

Mary said she had been affected much the same way. Sid seemed satisfied. Tom got out of the presence as quick as he plausibly could, and after that he complained of toothache for a week, and tied up his jaws every night. He never knew that Sid lay nightly watching, and frequently slipped the bandage free and then leaned on his elbow listening a good while at a time, and afterward slipped the bandage back to its place again. Tom's distress of mind wore off gradually and the toothache grew irksome and was discarded. If Sid really managed to make anything out of Tom's disjointed mutterings, he kept it to himself.

It seemed to Tom that his schoolmates never would get done holding inquests on dead cats, and thus keeping his trouble present to his mind. Sid noticed that Tom never was coroner at one of these inquiries, though it had been his habit to take the lead in all new enterprises; he noticed, too, that Tom never acted as a witness,—and that was strange; and Sid did not overlook the fact that Tom even showed a marked aversion to these inquests, and always avoided them when he could. Sid marveled, but said nothing. However, even inquests went out of vogue at last, and ceased to torture Tom's conscience.

Every day or two, during this time of sorrow, Tom watched his opportunity and went to the little grated jail-window and smuggled such small comforts through to the "murderer" as he could get hold of. The jail was a trifling little brick den that stood in a marsh at the edge of the village, and no guards were afforded for it; indeed it was seldom occupied. These offerings greatly helped to ease Tom's conscience.

The villagers had a strong desire to tar-and-feather Injun Joe and ride him on a rail, for body-snatching, but so formidable was his character that nobody could be found who was willing to take the lead in the matter, so it was dropped. He had been careful to begin both of his inquest-statements with the fight, without confessing the grave-robbery that preceded it; therefore it was deemed wisest not to try the case in the courts at present.

CHAPTER XII.

PETER.

ONE of the reasons why Tom's mind had drifted away from its secret troubles was, that it had found a new and weighty matter to interest itself about. Becky Thatcher had stopped coming to school. Tom had struggled with his pride a few days, and tried to "whistle her down the wind," but failed. He began to find himself hanging around her father's house, nights, and feeling very miserable. She was ill. What if she should die! There was distraction in the thought. He no longer took an interest in war, nor even in piracy. The charm of life was gone; there was nothing but dreariness left. He put his hoop away, and his bat; there was no joy in them any more. His aunt was concerned. She began to try all manner of remedies on him. She was one of those people who are infatuated with patent medicines and all new-fangled methods of producing health or mending it. She was an inveterate experimenter in these things. When something fresh in this line came out she was in a fever, right away, to try it; not on herself, for she was never ailing, but on anybody else that came handy. She was a subscriber for all the "Health" periodicals and phreneological frauds; and the solemn ignorance they were inflated with was breath to her nostrils. All the "rot" they contained about

AUNT POLLY SEEKS INFORMATION.

ventilation, and how to go to bed, and how to get up, and what to eat, and what to drink, and how much exercise to take, and what frame of mind to keep one's self in, and what sort of clothing to wear, was all gospel to her, and she never observed that her health-journals of the current month customarily upset everything they had recommended the month before. She was as simple-hearted and honest as the day was long, and so she was an easy victim. She gathered together her quack periodicals and her quack medicines, and thus armed with death, went about on her pale horse, metaphorically speaking, with "hell following after." But she never suspected that she was not an angel of healing and the balm of Gilead in disguise, to the suffering neighbors.

The water treatment was new, now, and Tom's low condition was a windfall to her. She had him out at daylight every morning, stood him up in the woodshed and drowned him with a deluge of cold water; then she scrubbed him down with a towel like a file, and so brought him to; then she rolled him up in a wet sheet and put him away under blankets till she sweated his soul clean and "the yellow stains of it came through his pores"—as Tom said.

Yet notwithstanding all this, the boy grew more and more melancholy and pale and dejected. She added hot baths, sitz baths, shower baths and plunges. The boy remained as dismal as a hearse. She began to assist the water with a slim oatmeal diet and blister plasters. She calculated his capacity as she would a jug's, and filled him up every day with quack cure-alls.

Tom had become indifferent to persecution by this time. This phase filled the old lady's heart with consternation. . This indifference must be broken up at any cost. Now she heard of Pain-killer for the first time. She ordered a lot at once. She tasted it and was filled with gratitude. It was simply fire in a liquid form. She dropped the water treatment and everything else, and pinned her faith to Pain-killer. She gave Tom a tea-spoonful and watched with the deepest anxiety for the result. Her troubles were instantly at rest, her soul at peace again ; for the " indifference " was broken up. The boy could not have shown a wilder, heartier interest, if she had built a fire under him.

Tom felt that it was time to wake up ; this sort of life might be romantic enough, in his blighted condition, but it was getting to have too little sentiment and too much distracting variety about it. So he thought over various plans for relief, and finally hit upon that of professing to be fond of Pain-killer. He asked for it so often that he became a nuisance, and his aunt ended by telling him to help himself and quit bothering her. If it had been Sid, she would have had no misgivings to alloy her delight ; but since it was Tom, she watched the bottle clandestinely. She found that the medicine did really diminish, but it did not occur to her that the boy was mending the health of a crack in the sitting-room floor with it.

One day Tom was in the act of dosing the crack when his aunt's yellow cat came along, purring, eyeing the teaspoon avariciously, and begging for a taste. Tom said:

" Don't ask for it unless you want it, Peter."

But Peter signified that he did want it.

" You better make sure."

Peter was sure.

" Now you've asked for it, and I'll give it to you, because there ain't anything mean about *me* ; but if you find you don't like it, you musn't blame anybody but your own self."

Peter was agreeable. So Tom pried his mouth open and poured down the

Pain-killer. Peter sprang a couple of yards in the air, and then delivered a war-whoop and set off round and round the room, banging against furniture, upsetting flower pots and making general havoc. Next he rose on his hind feet and pranced around, in a frenzy of enjoyment, with his head over his shoulder and his voice proclaiming his unappeasable happiness. Then he went tearing around the house again spreading chaos and destruction in his path. Aunt Polly entered in time to see him throw a few double summersets, deliver a final mighty hurrah,

A GENERAL GOOD TIME.

and sail through the open window, carrying the rest of the flower-pots with him. The old lady stood petrified with astonishment, peering over her glasses; Tom lay on the floor expiring with laughter.

"Tom, what on earth ails that cat?"

"*I* don't know, aunt," gasped the boy.

"Why I never see anything like it. What *did* make him act so?"

"Deed I don't know Aunt Polly; cats always act so when they're having a good time."

" They do, do they ? " There was something in the tone that made Tom apprehensive.

" Yes'm. That is, I believe they do."

" You *do* ? "

" Yes'm."

The old lady was bending down, Tom watching, with interest emphasized by anxiety. Too late he divined her " drift." The handle of the tell-tale tea-spoon was visible under the bed-valance. Aunt Polly took it, held it up. Tom winced, and dropped his eyes. Aunt Polly raised him by the usual handle—his ear—and cracked his head soundly with her thimble.

" Now, sir, what did you want to treat that poor dumb beast so, for ? "

" I done it out of pity for him—because he hadn't any aunt."

" Hadn't any aunt !—you numscull. What has that got to do with it ? "

" Heaps. Because if he'd a had one she'd a burnt him out herself ! She'd a roasted his bowels out of him 'thout any more feeling than if he was a human ! "

Aunt Polly felt a sudden pang of remorse. This was putting the thing in a new light ; what was cruelty to a cat *might* be cruelty to a boy, too. She began to soften ; she felt sorry. Her eyes watered a little, and she put her hand on Tom's head and said gently :

" I was meaning for the best, Tom. And Tom, it *did* do you good."

Tom looked up in her face with just a preceptible twinkle peeping through his gravity :

" I know you was meaning for the best, aunty, and so was I with Peter. It done *him* good, too. I never see him get around so since — "

" O, go 'long with you, Tom, before you aggravate me again. And you try and see if you can't be a good boy, for once, and you needn't take any more medicine."

Tom reached school ahead of time. It was noticed that this strange thing had been occurring every day latterly. And now, as usual of late, he hung about the gate of the school-yard instead of playing with his comrades. He was sick, he said, and he looked it. He tried to seem to be looking everywhere but whither he really was looking—down the road. Presently Jeff Thatcher hove in sight, and Tom's face lighted ; he gazed a moment, and then turned sorrowfully away. When

Jeff arrived, Tom accosted him, and "led up" warily to opportunities for remark about Becky, but the giddy lad never could see the bait. Tom watched and watched, hoping whenever a frisking frock came in sight, and hating the owner of it as soon as he saw she was not the right one. At last frocks ceased to appear, and he dropped hopelessly into the dumps; he entered the empty school house and sat down to suffer. Then one more frock passed in at the gate, and Tom's heart gave a great bound. The next instant he was out, and "going on" like an Indian; yelling, laughing, chasing boys, jumping over the fence at risk of life and limb, throwing hand-springs, standing on his head—doing all the heroic things he could conceive of, and keeping a furtive eye out, all the while, to see if Becky Thatcher was noticing. But she seemed to be unconscious of it all; she never looked. Could it be posssble that she was not aware that he was there? He carried his exploits to her immediate vicinity; came war-whooping around, snatched a boy's cap, hurled it to the roof of the school-house, broke through a group of boys, tumbling them in every direction, and fell sprawling, himself, under Becky's nose, almost upsetting her—and she turned, with her nose in the air, and he heard her say. "Mf! some people think they're mighty smart—always showing off!"

Tom's cheeks burned. He gathered himself up and sneaked off, crushed and crestfallen.

CHAPTER XIII.

JOE HARPER.

TOM'S mind was made up now. He was gloomy and desperate. He was a forsaken, friendless boy, he said; nobody loved him; when they found out what they had driven him to, perhaps they would be sorry; he had tried to do right and get along, but they would not let him; since nothing would do them but to be rid of him, let it be so; and let them blame *him* for the consequences— why shouldn't they? What right had the friendless to complain? Yes, they had forced him to it at last: he would lead a life of crime. There was no choice.

By this time he was far down Meadow Lane, and the bell for school to "take up" tinkled faintly upon his ear. He sobbed, now, to think he should never, never hear that old familiar

sound any more—it was very hard, but it was forced on him; since he was
driven out into the cold world, he must submit—but he forgave them. Then
the sobs came thick and fast.

Just at this point he met his soul's sworn comrade, Joe Harper—hard-eyed,
and with evidently a great and dismal purpose in his heart. Plainly here were
"two souls with but a single thought." Tom, wiping his eyes with his sleeve,
began to blubber out something about a resolution to escape from hard usage
and lack of sympathy at home by roaming abroad into the great world never
to return; and ended by hoping that Joe would not forget him.

But it transpired that this was a request which Joe had just been going to
make of Tom, and had come to hunt him up for that purpose. His mother had
whipped him for drinking some cream which he had never tasted and knew
nothing about; it was plain that she was tired of him and wished him to go;
if she felt that way, there was nothing for him to do but succumb; he hoped
she would be happy, and never regret having driven her poor boy out into the
unfeeling world to suffer and die.

As the two boys walked sorrowing along, they made a new compact to stand
by each other and be brothers and never separate till death relieved them of
their troubles. Then they began to lay their plans. Joe was for being a hermit,
and living on crusts in a remote cave, and dying, some time, of cold, and want,
and grief; but after listening to Tom, he conceded that there were some conspicuous advantages about a life of crime, and so he consented to be a pirate.

Three miles below St. Petersburg, at a point where the Mississippi river was
a trifle over a mile wide, there was a long, narrow, wooded island, with a shallow bar at the head of it, and this offered well as a rendezvous. It was not
inhabited; it lay far over toward the further shore, abreast a dense and almost
wholly unpeopled forest. So Jackson's Island was chosen. Who were to be
the subjects of their piracies, was a matter that did not occur to them. Then
they hunted up Huckleberry Finn, and he joined them promptly, for all careers
were one to him; he was indifferent. They presently separated to meet at a
lonely spot on the river bank two miles above the village at the favorite hour
—which was midnight. There was a small log raft there which they meant to

capture. Each would bring hooks and lines, and such provision as he could steal in the most dark and mysterious way—as became outlaws. And before the afternoon was done, they had all managed to enjoy the sweet glory of spreading the fact that pretty soon the town would " hear something." All who got this vague hint were cautioned to " be mum and wait."

About midnight Tom arrived with a boiled ham and a few trifles, and stopped in a dense undergrowth on a small bluff overlooking the meeting-place. It was starlight, and very still. The mighty river lay like an ocean at rest. Tom listened a moment, but no sound disturbed the quiet. Then he gave a low, distinct whistle. It was answered from under the bluff. Tom whistled twice more; these signals were answered in the same way. Then a guarded voice said :

" Who goes there ? "

" Tom Sawyer, the Black Avenger of the Spanish Main. Name your names."

" Huck Finn the Red-Handed, and Joe Harper the Terror of the Seas." Tom had furnished these titles, from his favorite literature.

" Tis well. Give the countersign."

Two hoarse whispers delivered the same awful word simultaneously to the brooding night :

" BLOOD ! "

Then Tom tumbled his ham over the bluff and let himself down after it, tearing both skin and clothes to some extent in the effort. There was an easy, comfortable path along the shore under the bluff, but it lacked the advantages of difficulty and danger so valued by a pirate.

The Terror of the Seas had brought a side of bacon, and had about worn himself out with getting it there. Finn the Red-Handed had stolen a skillet and a quantity of half-cured leaf tobacco, and had also brought a few corn-cobs to make pipes with. But none of the pirates smoked or " chewed" but himself. The Black Avenger of the Spanish Main said it would never do to start without some fire. That was a wise thought; matches were hardly known there in that day. They saw a fire smouldering upon a great raft a hundred yards above, and they went stealthily thither and helped themselves to a chunk.

They made an imposing adventure of it, saying "Hist!" every now and then, and suddenly halting with finger on lip; moving with hands on imaginary dagger-hilts; and giving orders in dismal whispers that if "the foe" stirred, to "let him have it to the hilt," because "dead men tell no tales." They knew well enough that the raftsmen were all down at the village laying in stores or having a spree, but still that was no excuse for their conducting this thing in an unpiratical way.

They shoved off, presently, Tom in command, Huck at the after oar and Joe at the forward. Tom stood amidships, gloomy-browed, and with folded arms, and gave his orders in a low, stern whisper:

"Luff, and bring her to the wind!"

"Aye-aye, sir!"

"Steady, stead-y-y-y!"

"Steady it is, sir!"

"Let her go off a point!"

"Point it is, sir!"

As the boys steadily and monotonously drove the raft toward mid-stream it was no doubt understood that these orders were given only for "style," and were not intended to mean anything in particular.

"What sail's she carrying?"

"Courses, tops'ls and flying-jib, sir."

"Send the r'yals up! Lay out aloft, there, half a dozen of ye,—foretopmast-stuns'l! Lively, now!"

"Aye-aye, sir!"

"Shake out that maintogalans'l! Sheets and braces! *Now*, my hearties!"

"Aye-aye, sir!"

"Hellum-a-lee—hard a port! Stand by to meet her when she comes! Port, port! *Now*, men! With a will! Stead-y-y-y!"

"Steady it is, sir!"

The raft drew beyond the middle of the river; the boys pointed her head right, and then lay on their oars. The river was not high, so there was not more than a two or three-mile current. Hardly a word was said during the next three-quarters of an hour. Now the raft was passing before the distant

town.   Two or three glimmering lights showed where it lay, peacefully sleeping, beyond the vague vast sweep of star-gemmed water, unconscious of the
tremendous event that was happening.   The Black Avenger stood still with
folded arms, " looking his last " upon the scene of his former joys and his later

ON BOARD THEIR FIRST PRIZE.

sufferings, and wishing " she " could see him now, abroad on the wild sea,
facing peril and death with dauntless heart, going to his doom with a grim
smile on his lips.   It was but a small strain on his imagination to remove Jackson's Island beyond eye-shot of the village, and so he " looked his last " with
a broken and satisfied heart.   The other pirates were looking their last, too ;
and they all looked so long that they came near letting the current drift them
out of the range of the island.   But they discovered the danger in time, and
made shift to avert it.   About two o'clock in the morning the raft grounded on
the bar two hundred yards above the head of the island, and they waded
back and forth until they had landed their freight.   Part of the little raft's

belongings consisted of an old sail, and this they spread over a nook in the bushes for a tent to shelter their provisions; but they themselves would sleep in the open air in good weather, as became outlaws.

They built a fire against the side of a great log twenty or thirty steps within the sombre depths of the forest, and then cooked some bacon in the frying-pan

for supper, and used up half of the corn "pone" stock they had brought. It seemed glorious sport to be feasting in that wild free way in the virgin forest of an unexplored and uninhabited island, far from the haunts of men, and they said they never would return to civilization. The climbing fire lit up their faces and threw its ruddy glare upon the pillared tree trunks of their forest temple, and upon the varnished foliage and festooning vines.

When the last crisp slice of bacon was gone, and the last allowance of corn pone devoured, the boys stretched themselves out on the grass, filled with contentment. They could have found a

THE PIRATES ASHORE.

cooler place, but they would not deny themselves such a romantic feature as the roasting camp-fire.

"*Ain't* it gay?" said Joe.

"It's *nuts!*" said Tom. "What would the boys say if they could see us?"

"Say? Well they'd just die to be here—hey Hucky!"

"I reckon so," said Huckleberry; "anyways *I'm* suited. I dont want nothing better'n this. I don't ever get enough to eat, gen'ally—and here they can't come and pick at a feller and bullyrag him so."

"It's just the life for me," said Tom. "You don't have to get up, mornings, and you don't have to go to school, and wash, and all that blame foolishness. You see a pirate don't have to do *anything*, Joe, when he's ashore, but a hermit *he* has to be praying considerable, and then he don't have any fun, anyway, all by himself that way."

" O yes, that's so," said Joe, " but I hadn't thought much about it, you know. I'd a good deal rather be a pirate, now that I've tried it."

" You see," said Tom, "people don't go much on hermits, now-a-days, like they used to in old times, but a pirate's always respected.   And a hermit's got to sleep on the hardest place he can find, and put sack-cloth and ashes on his head, and stand out in the rain, and— "

" What does he put sack-cloth and ashes on his head for ? " inquired Huck.

" *I* dono.   But they've *got* to do it.   Hermits always do.   You'd have to **do** that if you was a hermit."

" Dern'd if I would," said Huck.

" Well what would you do ? "

" I dono.   But I wouldn't do that."

" Why Huck, you'd *have* to.   How'd you get around it ? "

" Why I just wouldn't stand it.   I'd run away."

" Run away !   Well you *would* be a nice old slouch of a hermit.   You'd be a disgrace."

The Red-Handed made no response, being better employed.   He had finished gouging out a cob, and now he fitted a weed stem to it, loaded it with tobacco, and was pressing a coal to the charge and blowing a cloud of fragrant smoke —he was in the full bloom of luxurious contentment.   The other pirates envied him this majestic vice, and secretly resolved to acquire it shortly.   Presently Huck said :

" What does pirates have to do ? "

Tom said :

" Oh they have just a bully time—take ships, and burn them, and get the money and bury it in awful places in their island where there's ghosts and things to watch it, and kill everybody in the ships—make 'em walk a plank."

" And they carry the women to the island," said Joe; " they don't kill the women."

" No," assented Tom, " they don't kill the women—they're too noble.   And the women's always beautiful, too."

"And don't they wear the bulliest clothes! Oh, no! All gold and silver and di'monds," said Joe, with enthusiasm.

"Who?" said Huck.

"Why the pirates."

Huck scanned his own clothing forlornly.

"I reckon I ain't dressed fitten for a pirate," said he, with a regretful pathos in his voice; "but I ain't got none but these."

But the other boys told him the fine clothes would come fast enough, after they should have begun their adventures. They made him understand that his poor rags would do to begin with, though it was customary for wealthy pirates to start with a proper wardrobe.

Gradually their talk died out and drowsiness began to steal upon the eyelids of the little waifs. The pipe dropped from the fingers of the Red-Handed, and he slept the sleep of the conscience-free and the weary. The Terror of the Seas and the Black Avenger of the Spanish Main had more difficulty in getting to sleep. They said their prayers inwardly, and lying down, since there was nobody there with authority to make them kneel and recite aloud; in truth they had a mind not to say them at all, but they were afraid to proceed to such lengths as that, lest they might call down a sudden and special thunderbolt from Heaven. Then at once they reached and hovered upon the imminent verge of sleep—but an intruder came, now, that would not "down." It was conscience. They began to feel a vague fear that they had been doing wrong to run away; and next they thought of the stolen meat, and then the real torture came. They tried to argue it away by reminding conscience that they had purloined sweetmeats and apples scores of times; but conscience was not to be appeased by such thin plausibilities; it seemed to them, in the end, that there was no getting around the stubborn fact that taking sweetmeats was only "hooking," while taking bacon and hams and such valuables was plain simple *stealing*—and there was a command against that in the Bible. So they inwardly resolved that so long as they remained in the business, their piracies should not again be sullied with the crime of stealing. Then conscience granted a truce, and these curiously inconsistent pirates fell peacefully to sleep.

CHAPTER XIV.

WHEN Tom awoke in the morning, he wondered where he was. He sat up and rubbed his eyes and looked around. Then he comprehended. It was the cool gray dawn, and there was a delicious sense of repose and peace in the deep pervading calm and silence of the woods. Not a leaf stirred; not a sound obtruded upon great Nature's meditation. Beaded dew-drops stood upon the leaves and grasses. A white layer of ashes covered the fire, and a thin blue breath of smoke rose straight into the air. Joe and Huck still slept.

Now, far away in the woods a bird called; another answered; presently the hammering of a woodpecker was heard. Gradually the cool dim gray of the morning whitened, and as gradually sounds multiplied and life manifested itself. The marvel of Nature shaking off sleep and going to work unfolded itself to the musing boy. A little green worm came crawling over a dewy leaf, lifting two-thirds of his body into the air from time to time and "sniffing around," then proceeding again—for he was measuring, Tom said; and when the worm approached him, of its own accord, he sat as still as a stone, with his hopes rising and falling, by turns, as the creature still came toward him or seemed inclined to go elsewhere; and when at last it considered a painful moment with its curved body in the air and then came decisively down upon Tom's leg and began a journey over him, his whole heart was glad—for that meant that he was going to have a new suit of clothes—without the shadow of a doubt a gaudy piratical uniform. Now a procession of ants appeared, from nowhere in particular, and went about their labors; one struggled manfully by with a dead spider five times as big as itself in its arms, and lugged it straight up a tree-trunk. A brown spotted lady-bug climbed the dizzy height of a grass blade, and Tom bent down close to it and said, " Lady-bug, lady-bug, fly away home, your house is on fire, your children's alone," and she took wing and went off to see about it— which did not surprise the boy, for he knew of old that this insect was credulous about conflagrations and he had practiced upon its simplicity more than once. A tumble-bug came next, heaving sturdily at its ball, and Tom touched the creature, to see it shut its legs against its body and pretend to be dead. The birds were fairly rioting by this time. A cat-bird, the northern mocker, lit in a tree over Tom's head, and trilled out her imitations of her neighbors in a rapture of enjoy- ment; then a shrill jay swept down, a flash of blue flame, and stopped on a twig almost within the boy's reach, cocked his head to one side and eyed the strangers with a consuming curiosity ; a gray squirrel and a big fellow of the " fox " kind came skurrying along, sitting up at intervals to inspect and chatter at the boys, for the wild things had probably never seen a human being before and scarcely knew whether to be afraid or not. All Nature was wide awake and stirring, now ; long lances of sunlight pierced down through the dense foliage far and near, and a few butterflies came fluttering upon the scene.

Tom stirred up the other pirates and they all clattered away with a shout, and in a minute or two were stripped and chasing after and tumbling over each other in the shallow limpid water of the white sand-bar. They felt no longing for the little village sleeping in the distance beyond the majestic waste of water. A vagrant current or a slight rise in the river had carried off their raft, but this only

gratified them, since its going was something like burning the bridge between them and civilization.

They came back to camp wonderfully refreshed, glad-hearted, and ravenous; and they soon had the camp-fire blazing up again. Huck found a spring of clear cold water close by, and the boys made cups of broad oak or hickory leaves, and felt that water, sweetened with such a wild-wood charm as that, would be a good enough substitute for coffee. While Joe was slicing bacon for breakfast, Tom and Huck asked him to hold on a minute; they stepped to a promising nook in the river bank and threw in their lines; almost immediately they had reward. Joe had not had time to

THE PIRATES' BATH.

get impatient before they were back again with some handsome bass, a couple of sun-perch and a small catfish—provisions enough for quite a family. They fried the fish with the bacon and were astonished; for no fish had ever seemed so delicious before. They did not know that the quicker a fresh water fish is on the fire after he is caught the better he is; and they reflected little upon what a sauce open air sleeping, open air exercise, bathing, and a large ingredient of hunger makes, too.

They lay around in the shade, after breakfast, while Huck had a smoke, and then went off through the woods on an exploring expedition. They tramped gaily along, over decaying logs, through tangled underbrush, among solemn monarchs of the forest, hung from their crowns to the ground with a drooping regalia of grape-vines. Now and then they came upon snug nooks carpeted with grass and jeweled with flowers.

They found plenty of things to be delighted with but nothing to be astonished at. They discovered that the island was about three miles long and a quarter of

THE PLEASANT STROLL.

a mile wide, and that the shore it lay closest to was only separated from it by a narrow channel hardly two hundred yards wide. They took a swim about every hour, so it was close upon the middle of the afternoon when they got back to camp. They were too hungry to stop to fish, but they fared sumptuously upon cold ham, and then threw themselves down in the shade to talk. But the talk soon began to drag, and then died. The stillness, the solemnity that brooded in the woods, and the sense of loneliness, began to tell upon the spirits of the boys. They fell to thinking. A sort of undefined longing crept upon them. This took dim shape, presently—it was budding home-sickness. Even Finn the Red-Handed was dreaming of his door-steps and empty hogsheads. But they were all ashamed of their weakness, and none was brave enough to speak his thought.

For some time, now, the boys had been dully conscious of a peculiar sound in the distance, just as one sometimes is of the ticking of a clock which he takes no distinct note of. But now this mysterious sound became more pronounced, and forced a recognition. The boys started, glanced at each other, and then each assumed a listening attitude. There was a long silence, profound and unbroken ; then a deep, sullen boom came floating down out of the distance.

"What is it!" exclaimed Joe, under his breath.

"I wonder," said Tom in a whisper.

"'Tain't thunder," said Huckleberry, in an awed tone, "becuz thunder — "

"Hark!" said Tom. "Listen—don't talk."

They waited a time that seemed an age, and then the same muffled boom troubled the solemn hush.

"Let's go and see."

They sprang to their feet and hurried to the shore toward the town. They

THE SEARCH FOR THE DROWNED.

parted the bushes on the bank and peered out over the water. The little steam ferry boat was about a mile below the village, drifting with the current. Her broad deck seemed crowded with people. There were a great many skiffs rowing about or floating with the stream in the neighborhood of the ferry boat, but the boys could not determine what the men in them were doing. Presently a great jet of white smoke burst from the ferry boat's side, and as it expanded and rose in a lazy cloud, that same dull throb of sound was borne to the listeners again.

"I know now!" exclaimed Tom; "somebody's drownded!"

"That's it!" said Huck; "they done that last summer, when Bill Turner got drownded; they shoot a cannon over the water, and that makes him come up to the top.   Yes, and they take loaves of bread and put quicksilver in 'em and set 'em afloat, and wherever there's anybody that's drownded, they'll float right there and stop."

"Yes, I've heard about that," said Joe. "I wonder what makes the bread do that."

"Oh it ain't the bread, so much," said Tom; "I reckon it's mostly what they *say* over it before they start it out."

"But they don't say anything over it," said Huck. "I've seen 'em and they don't."

"Well that's funny," said Tom. "But maybe they say it to themselves. Of *course* they do. Anybody might know that."

The other boys agreed that there was reason in what Tom said, because an ignorant lump of bread, uninstructed by an incantation, could not be expected to act very intelligently when sent upon an errand of such gravity.

"By jings I wish I was over there, now," said Joe.

"I do too," said Huck. "I'd give heaps to know who it is."

The boys still listened and watched. Presently a revealing thought flashed through Tom's mind, and he exclaimed :

"Boys, I know who's drownded—it's us!"

They felt like heroes in an instant. Here was a gorgeous triumph; they were missed; they were mourned; hearts were breaking on their account; tears were being shed; accusing memories of unkindnesses to these poor lost lads were rising up, and unavailing regrets and remorse were being indulged; and best of all, the departed were the talk of the whole town, and the envy of all the boys, as far as this dazzling notoriety was concerned. This was fine. It was worth while to be a pirate, after all.

As twilight drew on, the ferry boat went back to her accustomed business and the skiffs disappeared. The pirates returned to camp. They were jubilant with vanity over their new grandeur and the illustrious trouble they were making. They caught fish, cooked supper and ate it, and then fell to guessing at what the village was thinking and saying about them; and the pictures they drew of the public distress on their account were gratifying to look upon—from their point of view. But when the shadows of night closed them in, they gradually ceased to talk, and sat gazing into the fire, with their minds evidently wandering elsewhere. The excitement was gone, now, and Tom and Joe could not keep back thoughts of certain persons at home who were not enjoying this fine frolic as much as they were. Misgivings came; they grew troubled and unhappy; a sigh or two escaped, unawares. By and by Joe timidly ventured upon a round-about "feeler" as to how the others might look upon a return to civilization—not right now, but—

Tom withered him with derision! Huck, being uncommitted, as yet, joined in with Tom, and the waverer quickly "ex-plained," and was glad to get out of the scrape with as little taint of chicken-hearted home-sickness clinging to his garments as he could. Mutiny was effectually laid to rest for the moment.

As the night deepened, Huck began to nod, and presently to snore. Joe followed next. Tom lay upon his elbow motionless, for some time, watching the two intently. At last he got up cautiously, on his knees, and went searching among the grass and the flickering reflections flung by the camp-fire. He picked up and inspected several large semi-cylinders of the thin white bark of a sycamore, and finally chose two which seemed to suit

TOM'S MYSTERIOUS WRITING.

him. Then he knelt by the fire and painfully wrote something upon each of these with his "red keel;" one he rolled up and put in his jacket pocket, and the other he put in Joe's hat and removed it to a little distance from the owner. And he also put into the hat certain school-boy treasures of almost inestimable value— among them a lump of chalk, an India rubber ball, three fish-hooks, and one of that kind of marbles known as a "sure 'nough crystal." Then he tip-toed his way cautiously among the trees till he felt that he was out of hearing, and straightway broke into a keen run in the direction of the sand-bar.

CHAPTER XV.

A FEW minutes later Tom was in the shoal water of the bar, wading toward the Illinois shore. Before the depth reached his middle he was half way over; the current would permit no more wading, now, so he struck out confidently to swim the remaining hundred yards. He swam quartering up stream, but still was swept downward rather faster than he had expected. However, he reached the shore finally, and drifted along till he found a low place and drew himself out. He put his hand on his jacket pocket, found his piece of bark safe, and then struck through the woods, following the shore, with streaming garments. Shortly before ten o'clock he came out into an open place opposite the village, and saw the ferry boat lying in the shadow of the trees and the high bank. Everything was quiet under the blinking stars. He crept down the bank, watching with all his eyes, slipped into the water, swam three or four strokes and climbed into the skiff that did "yawl" duty at the boat's stern. He laid himself down under the thwarts and waited, panting.

Presently the cracked bell tapped and a voice gave the order to "cast off." A minute or two later the skiff's head was standing high up, against the boat's swell, and the voyage was begun. Tom felt happy in his success, for he knew it was the boat's last trip for the night. At the end of a long twelve or fifteen minutes the wheels stopped, and Tom slipped overboard and swam ashore in the dusk, landing fifty yards down stream, out of danger of possible stragglers.

He flew along unfrequented alleys, and shortly found himself at his aunt's back fence. He climbed over, approached the "ell" and looked in at the sitting-room window, for a light was burning there. There sat Aunt Polly, Sid, Mary, and Joe Harper's mother, grouped together, talking. They were by the bed, and the bed was between them and the door. Tom went to the door and began to softly lift the latch; then he pressed gently and the door yielded a crack; he continued pushing cautiously, and quaking every time it creaked, till he judged he might squeeze through on his knees; and so he put his head through and began, warily.

"What makes the candle blow so?" said Aunt Polly. Tom hurried up. "Why that door's open, I believe. Why of course it is. No end of strange things now. Go 'long and shut it, Sid."

Tom disappeared under the bed just in time. He lay and "breathed" himself for a time, and then crept to where he could almost touch his aunt's foot.

"But as I was saying," said Aunt Polly, "he warn't *bad*, so to say—only mischeevous. Only just giddy, and harum-scarum, you know. He warn't any more responsible than a colt. *He* never meant any harm, and he was the best-hearted boy that ever was"—and she began to cry.

"It was just so with my Joe—always full of his devilment, and up to **every** kind of mischief, but he was just as unselfish and kind as he could be—

9

and laws bless me, to think I went and whipped him for taking that cream, never once recollecting that I throwed it out myself because it was sour, and I never to see him again in this world, never, never, never, poor abused boy!" And Mrs Harper sobbed as if her heart would break.

"I hope Tom's better off where he is," said Sid, "but if he'd been better in some ways—"

"*Sid!*" Tom felt the glare of the old lady's eye, though he could not see it. "Not a word against my Tom, now that he's gone! God'll take care of *him*— never you trouble *your*self, sir! Oh, Mrs. Harper, I don't know how to give

WHAT TOM SAW.

him up! I don't know how to give him up! He was such a comfort to me, although he tormented my old heart out of me, 'most."

"The Lord giveth and the Lord hath taken away,—Blessed be the name of the Lord! But it's *so* hard—Oh, it's so hard! Only last Saturday my Joe busted a fire-cracker right under my nose and I knocked him sprawling.   Little did I know then, how soon—O, if it was to do over again I'd hug him and bless him for it."

"Yes, yes, yes, I know just how you feel, Mrs. Harper, I know just exactly how you feel.   No longer ago than yesterday noon, my Tom took and filled the cat full of Pain-Killer, and I did think the cretur would tear the house down.   And God forgive me, I cracked Tom's head with my thimble, poor boy, poor dead boy.   But he's out of all his troubles now.   And the last words I ever heard him say was to reproach—"

But this memory was too much for the old lady, and she broke entirely down. Tom was snuffling, now, himself—and more in pity of himself than anybody else.   He could hear Mary crying, and putting in a kindly word for him from time to time.   He began to have a nobler opinion of himself than ever before.   Still he wás sufficiently touched by his aunt's grief to long to rush out from under the bed and overwhelm her with joy—and the theatrical gorgeousness of the thing appealed strongly to his nature, too, but he resisted and lay still.

He went on listening, and gathered by odds and ends that it was conjectured at first that the boys had got drowned while taking a swim; then the small raft had been missed; next, certain boys said the missing lads had promised that the village should "hear something" soon; the wise-heads had "put this and that together" and decided that the lads had gone off on that raft and would turn up at the next town below, presently; but toward noon the raft had been found, lodged against the Missouri shore some five or six miles below the village,—and then hope perished; they must be drowned, else hunger would have driven them home by nightfall if not sooner.   It was believed that the search for the bodies had been a fruitless effort merely because the drowning must have occurred in mid-channel, since the boys, being good swimmers, would otherwise have escaped to shore.   This was Wednesday night.   If the bodies continued missing until Sunday, all hope would be given over, and the funerals would be preached on that morning.   Tom shuddered.

Mrs. Harper gave a sobbing good-night and turned to go.   Then with a mutual impulse the two bereaved women flung themselves into each other's arms and had a good, consoling cry, and then parted. Aunt Polly was tender far beyond her wont, in her good-night to Sid and Mary. Sid snuffled a bit and Mary went off crying with all her heart.

Aunt Polly knelt down and prayed for Tom so touchingly, so appealingly, and with such measureless love in her words and her old trembling voice, that he was weltering in tears again, long before she was through.

He had to keep still long after she went to bed, for she kept making broken-hearted ejaculations from time to time, tossing unrestfully, and turning over. But at last she was still, only moaning a little in her sleep. Now the boy stole out, rose gradually by the bedside, shaded the candle-light with his hand, and stood regarding her. His heart was full of pity for her. He took out his sycamore scroll and placed it by the candle. But something occurred to him, and he lingered considering. His face lighted with a happy solution of his thought; he put the bark hastily in his pocket. Then he bent over and kissed the faded lips, and straightway made his stealthy exit, latching the door behind him.

He threaded his way back to the ferry landing, found nobody at large there, and walked boldly on board the boat, for he knew she was tenantless except that there was a watchman, who always turned in and slept like a graven image. He untied the skiff at the stern, slipped into it, and was soon rowing cautiously up stream. When he had pulled a mile above the village, he started quartering across and bent himself stoutly to his work. He hit the landing on the other side neatly, for this was a familiar bit of work to him. He was moved to capture the skiff, arguing that it might be considered a ship and therefore legitimate prey for a pirate, but he knew a thorough search would be made for it and that might end in revelations. So he stepped ashore and entered the wood.

He sat down and took a long rest, torturing himself meantime to keep awake, and then started wearily down the home-stretch. The night was far spent. It was broad daylight before he found himself fairly abreast the island bar. He rested again until the sun was well up and gilding the great river with its splendor, and then he plunged into the stream. A little later he paused, dripping, upon the threshold of the camp, and heard Joe say:

"No, Tom's true-blue, Huck, and he'll come back. He won't desert. He knows that would be a disgrace to a pirate, and Tom's too proud for that sort of thing. He's up to something or other. Now I wonder what?"

"Well, the things is ours, anyway, ain't they?"

"Pretty near, but not yet, Huck. The writing says they are if he ain't back here to breakfast."

"Which he is!" exclaimed Tom, with fine dramatic effect, stepping grandly into camp.

A sumptuous breakfast of bacon and fish was shortly provided, and as the boys set to work upon it, Tom recounted (and adorned) his adventures. They were a vain and boastful company of heroes when the tale was done. Then Tom hid himself away in a shady nook to sleep till noon, and the other pirates got ready to fish and explore.

CHAPTER XVI.

AFTER dinner all the gang turned out to hunt for turtle eggs on the bar. They went about poking sticks into the sand, and when they found a soft place they went down on their knees and dug with their hands. Sometimes they would take fifty or sixty eggs out of one hole. They were perfectly round white things a trifle smaller than an English walnut. They had a famous fried-egg feast that night, and another on Friday morning.

After breakfast they went whooping and prancing out on the bar, and chased each other round and round, shedding clothes as they went, until they were naked, and then continued the frolic far away up the shoal water of the bar, against the stiff current, which latter tripped their legs from under them from time to time and greatly increased the fun. And now and then they stooped in a group and splashed water in each other's faces with their palms, gradually approaching each other, with averted faces to avoid the strangling sprays and finally gripping and struggling till the best man ducked his neighbor, and then they all went under in a tangle of white legs and arms and came up blowing, sputtering, laughing and gasping for breath at one and the same time.

When they were well·exhausted, they would run out and sprawl on the dry, hot sand, and lie there and cover themselves up with it, and by and by break for the water again and go through the original performance once more. Finally it occurred to them that their naked skin represented flesh-colored "tights" very fairly; so they drew a ring in the sand and had a circus—with three clowns in it, for none would yield this proudest post to his neighbor.

THE PIRATES' EGG MARKET.

Next they got their marbles and played "knucks" and "ring-taw" and "keeps" till that amusement grew stale. Then Joe and Huck had another swim, but Tom would not venture, because he found that in kicking off his trousers he had kicked his string of rattlesnake rattles off his ankle, and he wondered how he had escaped cramp so long without the protection of this mysterious charm. He did not venture again until he had found it, and by that time the other boys were tired and ready to rest. They gradually wandered apart, dropped into the "dumps," and fell to gazing longingly across the wide river to where the village lay drowsing in the sun. Tom found himself writing "BECKY" in the sand with his big toe; he scratched it out, and was angry with himself for his weakness. But he wrote it again, nevertheless; he could not help it. He erased it once more and then took himself out of temptation by driving the other boys together and joining them.

But Joe's spirits had gone down almost beyond resurrection.   He was so homesick that he could hardly endure the misery of it.   The tears lay very near the
surface.   Huck was melancholy, too.   Tom was down-hearted, but tried hard not
to show it.   He had a secret which he was not ready to tell, yet, but if this muti-
nous depression was not broken up soon, he would have to bring it out.   He said,
with a great show of cheerfulness :

"I bet there's been pirates on this island before, boys.   We'll explore it again.
They've hid treasures here somewhere.   How'd you feel to light on a rotten chest
full of gold and silver—hey ? "

But it roused only a faint enthusiasm, which faded out, with no reply.   Tom
tried one or two other seductions; but they failed, too.   It was discouraging
work.   Joe sat poking up the sand with a stick and looking very gloomy.   Finally
he said :

"O, boys, let's give it up.   I want to go home.   It's so lonesome."

"Oh, no, Joe, you'll feel better by and by," said Tom.   "Just think of the fishing that's here."

"I don't care for fishing.   I want to go home."

"But Joe, there ain't such another swimming place anywhere."

"Swimming's no good.   I don't seem to care for it, somehow, when there ain't
anybody to say I shan't go in.   I mean to go home."

"O, shucks!   Baby!   You want to see your mother, I reckon."

"Yes, I *do* want to see my mother—and you would too, if you had one.   I ain't
any more baby than you are."   And Joe snuffled a little.

"Well, we'll let the cry-baby go home to his mother, *won't* we Huck?   Poor
thing—does it want to see its mother?   And so it shall.   *You* like it here, *don't*
you Huck?   We'll stay, won't we ? "

Huck said " Y-e-s "—without any heart in it.

"I'll never speak to you again as long as I live," said Joe, rising.   "There
now ! "   And he moved moodily away and began to dress himself.

"Who cares ! " said Tom.   "Nobody wants you to.   Go 'long home and get
laughed at.   O, you're a nice pirate.   Huck and me ain't cry-babies.   We'll stay,

won't we Huck? Let him go if he wants to. I reckon we can get along without him, per'aps."

But Tom was uneasy, nevertheless, and was alarmed to see Joe go sullenly on with his dressing. And then it was discomforting to see Huck eyeing Joe's preparations so wistfully, and keeping up such an ominous silence. Presently, without a parting word, Joe began to wade off toward the Illinois shore. Tom's heart began to sink. He glanced at Huck. Huck could not bear the look, and dropped his eyes. Then he said:

"I want to go, too, Tom. It was getting so lonesome anyway, and now it'll be worse. Let's us go too, Tom."

"I won't! You can all go, if you want to. I mean to stay."

"Tom, I better go."

"Well go 'long—who's hendering you."

Huck began to pick up his scattered clothes. He said:

"Tom, I wisht you'd come too. Now you think it over. We'll wait for you when we get to shore."

"Well you'll wait a blame long time, that's all."

Huck started sorrowfully away, and Tom stood looking after him, with a strong desire tugging at his heart to yield his pride and go along too. He hoped the boys would stop, but they still waded slowly on. It suddenly dawned on Tom that it was become very lonely and still. He made one final struggle with his pride, and then darted after his comrades, yelling:

"Wait! Wait! I want to tell you something!"

They presently stopped and turned around. When he got to where they were, he began unfolding his secret, and they listened moodily till at last they saw the "point" he was driving at, and then they set up a war-whoop of applause and said it was "splendid!" and said if he had told them at first, they wouldn't have started away. He made a plausible excuse; but his real reason had been the fear that not even the secret would keep them with him any very great length of time, and so he had meant to hold it in reserve as a last seduction.

The lads came gaily back and went at their sports again with a will, chattering all the time about Tom's stupendous plan and admiring the genius of it. After a dainty egg and fish dinner, Tom said he wanted to learn to smoke, now. Joe caught at the idea and said he would like to try, too. So Huck made pipes and filled them. These novices had never smoked anything before but cigars made of grape-vine and they "bit" the tongue and were not considered manly, anyway.

Now they stretched themselves out on their elbows and began to puff, charily, and with slender confidence. The smoke had an unpleasant taste, and they gagged a little, but Tom said :

"Why it's just as easy! If I'd a knowed *this* was all, I'd a learnt long ago."

"So would I," said Joe. "It's just nothing."

"Why many a time I've looked at people smoking, and thought well I wish I could do that; but I never thought I could," said Tom.

"That's just the way with me, hain't it Huck? You've heard me talk just that way—haven't you Huck? I'll leave it to Huck if I haven't."

"Yes—heaps of times," said Huck.

"Well I have too," said Tom; "O, hundreds of times. Once down by the slaughter-house. Don't you remember, Huck? Bob Tanner was there, and Johnny Miller, and Jeff Thatcher, when I said it. Don't you remember Huck, 'bout me saying that?"

"Yes, that's so," said Huck. "That was the day after I lost a white alley. No, 'twas the day before."

"There—I told you so," said Tom. "Huck recollects it."

"I bleeve I could smoke this pipe all day," said Joe. "*I* don't feel sick.'

"Neither do I," said Tom. "*I* could smoke it all day. But I bet you Jeff Thatcher couldn't."

"Jeff Thatcher! Why he'd keel over just with two draws. Just let him try it once. *He'd* see!"

"I bet he would. And Johnny Miller—I wish I could see Johnny Miller tackle it once."

"O, dont *I!*" said Joe, "Why I bet you Johnny Miller couldn't any more do this than nothing. Just one little snifter would fetch *him*."

"'Deed it would, Joe. Say—I wish the boys could see us now."

"So do I."

"Say—boys, don't say anything about it, and some time when they're around, I'll come up to you and say 'Joe, got a pipe? I want a smoke.' And you'll say, kind of careless like, as if it warn't anything, you'll say, 'Yes, I got my *old* pipe, and another one, but my tobacker ain't very good.' And I'll say, 'Oh, that's all right, if it's *strong* enough.' And then you'll out with the pipes, and we'll light up just as ca'm, and then just see 'em look!"

"By jings that'll be gay, Tom! I wish it was *now*!"

"So do I! And when we tell 'em we learned when we was off pirating, won't they wish they'd been along?"

"O, I reckon not! I'll just *bet* they will!"

So the talk ran on. But presently it began to flag a trifle, and grow disjointed. The silences widened; the expectoration marvelously increased. Every pore inside the boys' cheeks became a spouting fountain; they could scarcely bail out the cellars under their tongues fast enough to prevent an inundation; little overflowings down their throats occurred in spite of all they could do, and sudden retchings followed every time. Both boys were looking very pale and miserable, now. Joe's pipe dropped from his nerveless fingers. Tom's followed. Both fountains were going furiously and both pumps bailing with might and main. Joe said feebly:

TOM LOOKING FOR JOE'S KNIFE.

"I've lost my knife. I reckon I better go and find it."

Tom said, with quivering lips and halting utterance:

"I'll help you. You go over that way and I'll hunt around by the spring. No, you needn't come, Huck—we can find it."

So Huck sat down again, and waited an hour. Then he found it lonesome, and went to find his comrades. They were wide apart in the woods, both very pale, both fast asleep. But something informed him that if they had had any trouble they had got rid of it.

They were not talkative at supper that night. They had a humble look, and when Huck prepared his pipe after the meal and was going to prepare theirs, they said no, they were not feeling very well—something they ate at dinner had disagreed with them.

About midnight Joe awoke, and called the boys. There was a brooding oppressiveness in the air that seemed to bode something. The boys huddled themselves together and sought the friendly companionship of the fire, though the dull dead heat of the breathless atmosphere was stifling. They sat still, intent and waiting. The solemn hush continued. Beyond the light of the fire everything was swallowed up in the blackness of darkness. Presently there came a quivering glow that vaguely revealed the foliage for a moment and then vanished. By and by another came, a little stronger. Then another. Then a faint moan came sighing through the branches of the forest and the boys felt a fleeting breath upon their cheeks, and shuddered with the fancy that the Spirit of the Night had gone by. There was a pause. Now a wierd flash turned night into day and showed every little grass-blade, separate and distinct, that grew about their feet. And it showed three white, startled faces, too. A deep peal of thunder went rolling and tumbling down the heavens and lost itself in sullen rumblings in the distance. A sweep of chilly air passed by, rustling all the leaves and snowing the flaky ashes broadcast about the fire. Another fierce glare lit up the forest and an instant crash followed that seemed to rend the tree-tops right over the boys' heads. They clung together in terror, in the thick gloom that followed. A few big rain-drops fell pattering upon the leaves.

"Quick! boys, go for the tent!" exclaimed Tom.

They sprang away, stumbling over roots and among vines in the dark, no two plunging in the same direction. A furious blast roared through the trees, making everything sing as it went. One blinding flash after another came, and peal on peal of deafening thunder. And now a drenching rain poured down and the rising hurricane drove it in sheets along the ground. The boys cried out to each

other, but the roaring wind and the
booming thunder-blasts drowned their
voices utterly. However one by one
they straggled in at last and took shelter
under the tent, cold, scared, and streaming with water; but to have company in
misery seemed something to be grateful
for. They could not talk, the old sail
flapped so furiously, even if the other
noises would have allowed them. The
tempest rose higher and higher, and
presently the sail tore loose from its
fastenings and went winging away on
the blast. The boys seized each others'
hands and fled, with many tumblings and
bruises, to the shelter of a great oak that
stood upon the river bank. Now the
battle was at its highest. Under the
ceaseless conflagration of lightning that
flamed in the skies, everything below
stood out in clean-cut and shadowless
distinctness: the bending trees, the bil-
lowy river, white with foam, the driving
spray of spume-flakes, the dim outlines
of the high bluffs on the other side,
glimpsed through the drifting cloud-rack
and the slanting veil of rain. Every little
while some giant tree yielded the fight
and fell crashing through the younger
growth; and the unflagging thunder-peals
came now in ear-splitting explosive
bursts, keen and sharp, and unspeakably

appalling. The storm culminated in one matchless effort that seemed likely to tear the island to pieces, burn it up, drown it to the tree tops, blow it away, and deafen every creature in it, all at one and the same moment. It was a wild night for homeless young heads to be out in.

But at last the battle was done, and the forces retired with weaker and weaker threatenings and grumblings, and peace resumed her sway. The boys went back to camp, a good deal awed; but they found there was still something to be thankful for, because the great sycamore, the shelter of their beds, was a ruin, now, blasted by the lightnings, and they were not under it when the catastrophe happened.

Everything in camp was drenched, the camp-fire as well; for they were but heedless lads, like their generation, and had made no provision against rain. Here was matter for dismay, for they were soaked through and chilled. They were eloquent in their distress; but they presently discovered that the fire had eaten so far up under the great log it had been built against, (where it curved upward and separated itself from the ground,) that a hand-breadth or so of it had escaped wetting; so they patiently wrought until, with shreds and bark gathered from the under sides of sheltered logs, they coaxed the fire to burn again. Then they piled on great dead boughs till they had a roaring furnace and were glad-hearted once more. They dried their boiled ham and had a feast, and after that they sat by the fire and expanded and glorified their midnight adventure until morning, for there was not a dry spot to sleep on, anywhere around.

As the sun began to steal in upon the boys, drowsiness came over them and they went out on the sand-bar and lay down to sleep. They got scorched out by and by, and drearily set about getting breakfast. After the meal they felt rusty, and stiff-jointed, and a little homesick once more. Tom saw the signs, and fell to cheering up the pirates as well as he could. But they cared nothing for marbles, or circus, or swimming, or anything. He reminded them of the imposing secret, and raised a ray of cheer. While it lasted, he got them interested in a new device. This was to knock off being pirates, for a while, and be Indians for a change. They were attracted by this idea; so it was not long before they were stripped, and striped from head to heel with black mud, like so many zebras,—all of them chiefs, of course—and then they went tearing through the woods to attack an English settlement.

By and by they separated into three hostile tribes, and darted upon each other from ambush with dreadful war-whoops, and killed and scalped each other by thousands. It was a gory day. Consequently it was an extremely satisfactory one.

They assembled in camp toward supper time, hungry and happy; but now a difficulty arose—hostile Indians could not break the bread of hospitality together without first making peace, and this was a simple impossibility without smoking a pipe of peace. There was no other process that ever they had heard of. Two of the savages almost wished they had remained pirates. However, there was no other way; so with such show of cheerfulness as they could muster they called for the pipe and took their whiff as it passed, in due form.

And behold they were glad they had gone into savagery, for they had gained something; they found that they could now smoke a little without having to go and

TERRIBLE SLAUGHTER.

hunt for a lost knife; they did not get sick enough to be seriously uncomfortable. They were not likely to fool away this high promise for lack of effort. No, they practiced cautiously, after supper, with right fair success, and so they spent a jubilant evening. They were prouder and happier in their new acquirement than they would have been in the scalping and skinning of the Six Nations. We will leave them to smoke and chatter and brag, since we have no further use for them at present.

CHAPTER XVII.

BUT there was no hilarity in the little town that same tranquil Saturday afternoon. The Harpers, and Aunt Polly's family, were being put into mourning, with great grief and many tears. An unusual quiet possessed the village, although it was ordinarily quiet enough, in all conscience. The villagers conducted their concerns with an absent air, and talked little; but they sighed often. The Saturday holiday seemed a burden to the children. They had no heart in their sports, and gradually gave them up.

In the afternoon Becky Thatcher found herself moping about the deserted school-house yard, and feeling very melancholy. But she found nothing there to comfort her. She soliloquised:

"Oh, if I only had his brass andiron-knob again! But I haven't got anything now to remember him by." And she choked back a little sob.

Presently she stopped, and said to herself:

"It was right here. O, if it was to do over again, I wouldn't say that—I wouldn't say it for the whole world. But he's gone now; I'll never never never see him any more."

This thought broke her down and she wandered away, with the tears rolling down her cheeks. Then quite a group of boys and girls,—playmates of Tom's and Joe's—came by, and stood looking over the paling fence and talking in reverent tones of how Tom did so-and-so, the last time they saw him, and how Joe said this and that small trifle (pregnant with awful prophecy, as they could easily see now!)—and each speaker pointed out the exact spot where the lost lads stood at the time, and then added something like "and I was a standing just so—just as I am now, and as if you was him—I was as close as that—and he smiled, just this way—and then something seemed to go all over me, like,—awful, you know—and I never thought what it meant, of course, but I can see now!"

Then there was a dispute about who saw the dead boys last in life, and many claimed that dismal distinction, and offered evidences, more or less tampered with by the witness; and when it was ultimately decided who *did* see the departed last, and exchanged the last words with them, the lucky parties took upon themselves a sort of sacred importance, and were gaped at and envied by all the rest. One poor chap, who had no other grandeur to offer, said with tolerably manifest pride in the remembrance:

"Well, Tom Sawyer he licked me once."

But that bid for glory was a failure. Most of the boys could say that, and so that cheapened the distinction too much. The group loitered away, still recalling memories of the lost heroes, in awed voices.

When the Sunday-school hour was finished, the next morning, the bell began to toll, instead of ringing in the usual way. It was a very still Sabbath, and the mournful sound seemed in keeping' with the musing hush that lay upon nature. The villagers began to gather, loitering a moment in the vestibule to converse in whispers about the sad event. But there was no whispering in the house; only the funereal rustling of dresses as the women gathered to their seats, disturbed the silence there. None could remember when the little church

10

had been so full before.   There was finally a waiting pause, an expectant dumb-
ness, and then Aunt Polly entered, followed by Sid and Mary, and they by the
Harper family, all in deep black, and the whole congregation, the old minister
as well, rose reverently and stood, until the mourners were seated in the front
pew.   There was another communing silence, broken at intervals by muffled
sobs, and then the minister spread his hands abroad and prayed.   A moving
hymn was sung, and the text followed : " I am the Resurrection and the Life."

As the service proceeded, the clergyman drew such pictures of the graces,
the winning ways and the rare promise of the lost lads, that every soul there,
thinking he recognized these pictures, felt a pang in remembering that he had
persistently blinded himself to them, always before, and had as persistently
seen only faults and flaws in the poor boys.   The minister related many a
touching incident in the lives of the departed, too, which illustrated their sweet,
generous natures, and the people could easily see, now, how noble and beautiful those episodes were, and remembered with grief that at the time they
occurred they had seemed rank rascalities, well deserving of the cowhide.   The
congregation became more and more moved, as the pathetic tale went on, till
at last the whole company broke down and joined the weeping mourners in a
chorus of anguished sobs, the preacher himself giving way to his feelings, and
crying in the pulpit.

There was a rustle in the gallery, which nobody noticed ; a moment later the
church door creaked ; the minister raised his streaming eyes above his handkerchief, and stood transfixed !   First one and then another pair of eyes followed the minister's, and then almost with one impulse the congregation rose
and stared while the three dead boys came marching up the aisle, Tom in the lead,
Joe next, and Huck, a ruin of drooping rags, sneaking sheepishly in the rear !
They had been hid in the unused gallery listening to their own funeral sermon !

Aunt Polly, Mary and the Harpers threw themselves upon their restored
ones, smothered them with kisses and poured out thanksgivings, while poor
Huck stood abashed and uncomfortable, not knowing exactly what to do or
where to hide from so many unwelcoming eyes.   He wavered, and started to
slink away, but Tom seized him and said :

" Aunt Polly, it ain't fair.   Somebody's got to be glad to see Huck."

"And so they shall. *I*'m glad to see him, poor motherless thing!" And the loving attentions Aunt Polly lavished upon him were the one thing capable of making him more uncomfortable than he was before.

Suddenly the minister shouted at the top of his voice: "Praise God from whom all blessings flow—SING!—and put your hearts in it!"

And they did. Old Hundred swelled up with a triumphant burst, and while

TOM'S PROUDEST MOMENT.

it shook the rafters Tom Sawyer the Pirate looked around upon the envying juveniles about him and confessed in his heart that this was the proudest moment of his life.

As the "sold" congregation trooped out they said they would almost be willing to be made ridiculous again to hear Old Hundred sung like that once more.

Tom got more cuffs and kisses that day—according to Aunt Polly's varying moods—than he had earned before in a year; and he hardly knew which expressed the most gratefulness to God and affection for himself.

CHAPTER XVIII.

AMY LAWRENCE.

THAT was Tom's great secret — the scheme to return home with his brother pirates and attend their own funerals. They had paddled over to the Missouri shore on a log, at dusk on Saturday, landing five or six miles below the village; they had slept in the woods at the edge of the town till nearly daylight, and had then crept through back lanes and alleys and finished their sleep in the gallery of the church among a chaos of invalided benches.

At breakfast, Monday morning, Aunt Polly and Mary were very loving to Tom, and very attentive to his wants. There was an unusual amount of talk. In the course of it Aunt Polly said:

"Well, I don't say it wasn't a fine joke, Tom, to keep everybody suffering 'most a week so you boys had a good time, but it is a pity you could be so hard-hearted as to let *me* suffer so. If you could come over on a log to go to your funeral, you could have come over and give me a hint some way that you warn't *dead*, but only run off."

"Yes, you could have done that, Tom," said Mary; "and I believe you would if you had thought of it."

"Would you Tom?" said Aunt Polly, her face lighting wistfully. "Say, now, would you, if you'd thought of it?"

"I—well I don't know. 'Twould a spoiled everything."

"Tom, I hoped you loved me that much," said Aunt Polly, with a grieved tone that discomforted the boy. "It would been something if you'd cared enough to *think* of it, even if you didn't *do* it."

"Now auntie, that ain't any harm," pleaded Mary; "it's only Tom's giddy way —he is always in such a rush that he never thinks of anything."

"More's the pity. Sid would have thought. And Sid would have come and *done* it, too. Tom, you'll look back, some day, when it's too late, and wish you'd cared a little more for me when it would have cost you so little."

"Now auntie, you know I do care for you," said Tom.

"I'd know it better if you acted more like it."

"I wish now I'd thought," said Tom, with a repentant tone; "but I dreamed about you, anyway. That's something, ain't it?"

"It ain't much—a cat does that much—but it's better than nothing. What did you dream?"

"Why Wednesday night I dreamt that you was sitting over there by the bed, and Sid was sitting by the wood-box, and Mary next to him."

"Well, so we did. So we always do. I'm glad your dreams could take even that much trouble about us."

"And I dreamt that Joe Harper's mother was here."

"Why, she *was* here! Did you dream any more?"

"O, lots. But it's so dim, now."

"Well, *try* to recollect—can't you?"

"Some how it seems to me that the wind—the wind blowed the—the—"

"Try harder, Tom! The wind did blow something. Come!"

Tom pressed his fingers on his forehead an anxious minute, and then said :

"I've got it now! I've got it now! It blowed the candle!"

"Mercy on us! Go on, Tom—go on!"

TOM TRIES TO REMEMBER.

"And it seems to me that you said, 'Why I believe that that door—'"

"Go *on*, Tom!"

"Just let me study a moment—just a moment. Oh, yes—you said you believed the door was open."

"As I'm a sitting here, I did! Didn't I, Mary! Go on!"

"And then—and then—well I won't be certain, but it seems like as if you made Sid go and—and—"

"Well? Well? What did I make him do, Tom? What did I make him do?"

"You made him—you—O, you made him shut it."

"Well for the land's sake! I never heard the beat of that in all my days! Don't tell *me* there ain't anything in dreams, any more. Sereny Harper shall know of this before I'm an hour older. I'd like to see her get around *this* with her rubbage 'bout superstition. Go on, Tom!"

"Oh, it's all getting just as bright as day, now. Next you said I warn't *bad,* only mischeevous and harum-scarum, and not any more responsible than—than— I think it was a colt, or something."

" And so it was! Well, goodness gracious! Go on, Tom!"

" And then you began to cry."

" So I did. So I did. Not the first time, neither. And then—"

" Then Mrs. Harper she began to cry, and said Joe was just the same and she wished she hadn't whipped him for taking cream when she'd throwed it out her own self—"

" Tom! The sperrit was upon you! You was a prophecying—that's what you was doing! Land alive, go on, Tom!"

" Then Sid he said—he said—"

" I don't think I said anything," said Sid.

" Yes you did, Sid," said Mary.

" Shut your heads and let Tom go on! What did he say, Tom?"

" He said—I *think* he said he hoped I was better off where I was gone to, but if I'd been better sometimes—"

" *There*, d'you hear that! It was his very words!"

" And you shut him up sharp."

" I lay I did! There must a been an angel there. There *was* an angel there, somewheres!"

" And Mrs. Harper told about Joe scaring her with a fire-cracker, and you told about Peter and the Pain-killer—"

" Just as true as I live!"

" And then there was a whole lot of talk 'bout dragging the river for us, and 'bout having the funeral Sunday, and then you and old Miss Harper hugged and cried, and she went."

" It happened just so! It happened just so, as sure as I'm a sitting in these very tracks. Tom you couldn't told it more like, if you'd a seen it! And *then* what? Go on, Tom?"

" Then I thought you prayed for me—and I could see you and hear every word you said. And you went to bed, and I was so sorry, that I took and wrote on a piece of sycamore bark, ' *We ain't dead—we are only off being pirates,*' and put it on the table by the candle ; and then you looked so good, laying there asleep, that I thought I went and leaned over and kissed you on the lips."

"Did you, Tom, *did* you! I just forgive you everything for that!" And she siezed the boy in a crushing embrace that made him feel like the guiltiest of villains.

"It was very kind, even though it was only a—dream," Sid soliloquised just audibly.

"Shut up Sid! A body does just the same in a dream as he'd do if he was awake. Here's a big Milum apple I've been saving for you Tom, if you was ever found again—now go 'long to school. I'm thankful· to the good God and Father of us all I've got you back, that's long-suffering and merciful to them that believe on Him and keep His word, though goodness knows I'm unworthy of it, but if only the worthy ones got His blessings and had His hand to help them over the rough places, there's few enough would smile here or ever enter into His rest when the long night comes. Go 'long Sid, Mary, Tom—take yourselves off—you've hendered me long enough."

THE HERO.

The children left for school, and the old lady to call on Mrs. Harper and vanquish her realism with Tom's marvelous dream. Sid had better judgment than to utter the thought that was in his mind as he left the house. It was this: "Pretty thin—as long a dream as that, without any mistakes in it!"

What a hero Tom was become, now! He did not go skipping and prancing, but moved with a dignified swagger as became a pirate who felt that the public eye was on him. And indeed it was; he tried not to seem to see the looks or hear the remarks as he passed along, but they were food and drink to him. Smaller boys than himself flocked at his heels, as proud to be seen with him, and tolerated by him, as if he had been the drummer at the head of a procession or the elephant leading a menagerie into town. Boys of his own

.size pretended not to know he had been away at all; but they were consuming with envy, nevertheless. They would have given anything to have that swarthy sun-tanned skin of his, and his glittering notoriety; and Tom would not have parted with either for a circus.

At school the children made so much of him and of Joe, .and delivered such eloquent admiration from their eyes, that the two heroes were not long in becoming insufferably "stuck-up." They began to tell their adventures to hungry listeners —but they only began; it was not a thing likely to have an end, with imaginations like theirs to furnish material. And finally, when they got out their pipes and went serenely puffing around, the very summit of glory was reached.

Tom decided that he could be independent of Becky Thatcher now. Glory was sufficient. He would live for glory. Now that he was distinguished, maybe .she would be wanting to "make up." Well, let her—she should see that he could be as indifferent as some other people. Presently she arrived. Tom pretended not to see her. He moved away and joined a group of boys and girls and began to talk. Soon he observed that she was tripping gayly back and forth with flushed face and dancing eyes, pretending to be busy chasing school-mates, and screaming with laughter when she made a capture; but he noticed that she always made her captures in his vicinity, and that she seemed to cast a conscious eye in his direction at such times, too. It gratified all the vicious vanity that was in him; and so, instead of winning him it only "set him up" the more and made him the more diligent to avoid betraying that he knew she was about. Presently she gave over skylarking, and moved irresolutely about, sighing once or twice and glancing furtively and wistfully toward Tom. Then she observed that now Tom was talking more particularly to Amy Lawrence than to any one else. She felt a sharp pang and grew disturbed and uneasy at once. She tried to go away, but her feet were treacherous, and carried her to the group instead. She said to a girl .almost at Tom's elbow—with sham vivacity:

"Why Mary Austin! you bad girl, why didn't you come to Sunday-school?"

"I did come—didn't you see me?"

"Why no! Did you? Where did you sit?"

"I was in Miss Peter's class, where I always go. I saw *you*."

"Did you ? Why it's funny I didn't see you. I wanted to tell you about the pic-nic."

"O, that's jolly. Who's going to give it ? "

"My ma's going to let me have one."

"O, goody ; I hope she'll let *me* come."

"Well she will. The pic-nic's for me. She'll let anybody come that I want, and I want you."

"That's ever so nice. When is it going to be ? "

"By and by. Maybe about vacation."

A FLIRTATION.

"O, won't it be fun ! You going to have all the girls and boys ? "

"Yes, every one that's friends to me— or wants to be ; " and she glanced ever so furtively at Tom, but he talked right along to Amy Lawrence about the terrible storm on the island, and how the lightning tore the great sycamore tree "all to flinders" while he was "standing within three feet of it."

"O, may I come ? " said Gracie Miller.

"Yes."

"And me ? " said Sally Rogers.

"Yes."

"And me, too ? " said Susy Harper. "And Joe ? "

"Yes."

And so on, with clapping of joyful hands till all the group had begged for invitations but Tom and Amy. Then Tom turned coolly away, still talking, and took Amy with him. Becky's lips trembled and the tears came to her eyes ; she hid these signs with a forced gayety and went on chattering, but the life had gone out of the pic-nic, now, and out of everything else ; she got away as soon as she could and hid herself and had what her sex call "a good cry." Then she sat moody, with wounded pride till the bell rang. She roused up, now, with a vindictive cast in her eye, and gave her plaited tails a shake and said she knew what *she'd* do.

At recess Tom continued his flirtation with Amy with jubilant self-satisfaction. And he kept drifting about to find Becky and lacerate her with the performance.

At last he spied her, but there was a sudden falling of his mercury. She was sitting cosily on a little bench behind the school-house looking at a picture book with Alfred Temple—and so absorbed were they, and their heads so close together over the book that they did not seem to be conscious of anything in the world besides. Jealousy ran red hot through Tom's veins. He began to hate himself for throwing away the chance Becky had offered for a reconciliation. He called himself a fool, and all the hard names he could think of. He wanted to cry with vexation. Amy chatted happily along, as they walked, for her heart was singing, but Tom's tongue had lost its function. He did not hear what Amy

BECKY RETALIATES.

was saying, and whenever she paused expectantly he could only stammer an awkward assent, which was as often misplaced as otherwise. He kept drifting to the rear of the school-house, again and again, to sear his eye-balls with the hateful spectacle there. He could not help it. And it maddened him to see, as he thought he saw, that Becky Thatcher never once suspected that he was even in the land of the living. But she did see, nevertheless; and she knew she was winning her fight, too, and was glad to see him suffer as she had suffered.

Amy's happy prattle became intolerable. Tom hinted at things he had to attend to; things that must be done; and time was fleeting. But in vain—the girl chirped on. Tom thought, "O hang her, ain't I ever going to get rid of her?" At last he *must* be attending to those things—and she said artlessly that she would be "around" when school let out. And he hastened away, hating her for it.

"Any other boy!" Tom thought, grating his teeth. "Any boy in the whole town but that Saint Louis smarty that thinks he dresses so fine and is aristocracy! O, all right, I licked you the first day you ever saw this town, mister, and I'll lick you again! You just wait till I catch you out! I'll just take and—"

And he went through the motions of thrashing an imaginary boy—pummeling the air, and kicking and gouging. "Oh, you do, do you? You holler 'nough, do you? Now, then, let that learn you!" And so the imaginary flogging was finished to his satisfaction.

Tom fled home at noon. His conscience could not endure any more of Amy's

A SUDDEN FROST.

grateful happiness, and his jealousy could bear no more of the other distress. Becky resumed her picture-inspections with Alfred, but as the minutes dragged along and no Tom came to suffer, her triumph began to cloud and she lost interest; gravity and absent-mindedness followed, and then melancholy; two or three times she pricked up her ear at a footstep, but it was a false hope; no Tom came. At last she grew entirely miserable and wished she hadn't carried it so far. When poor Alfred, seeing that he was losing her, he did not know how, and kept exclaiming: "O here's a jolly one! look at this!" she lost patience at last, and said, "Oh, don't bother me! I don't care for them!" and burst into tears, and got up and walked away.

Alfred dropped alongside and was going to try to comfort her, but she said: "Go away and leave me alone, can't you! I hate you!"

So the boy halted, wondering what he could have done—for she had said she would look at pictures all through the nooning—and she walked on, crying. Then Alfred went musing into the deserted school-house. He was humiliated and angry. He easily guessed his way to the truth—the girl had simply made a convenience of him to vent her spite upon Tom Sawyer. He was far from hating

Tom the less when this thought occurred to him. He wished there was some way to get that boy into trouble without much risk to himself. Tom's spelling book fell under his eye. Here was his opportunity. He gratefully opened to the lesson for the afternoon and poured ink upon the page.

COUNTER-IRRITATION.

Becky, glancing in at a window behind him at the moment, saw the act, and moved on, without discovering herself. She started homeward, now, intending to find Tom and tell him; Tom would be thankful and their troubles would be healed. Before she was half way home, however, she had changed her mind. The thought of Tom's treatment of her when she was talking about her pic-nic came scorching back and filled her with shame. She resolved to let him get whipped on the damaged spelling-book's account, and to hate him forever, into the bargain.

CHAPTER XIX.

AUNT POLLY.

TOM arrived at home in a dreary mood, and the first thing his aunt said to him showed him that he had brought his sorrows to an unpromising market:

"Tom, I've a notion to skin you alive!"

"Auntie, what have I done?"

"Well, you've done enough. Here I go over to Sereny Harper, like an old softy, expecting I'm going to make her believe all that rubbage about that dream, when lo and behold you she'd found out from Joe that you was over here and heard all the talk we had that night. Tom I don't know what is to become of a boy that will act like that. It makes me feel so bad to think you could let me go to Sereny Harper and make such a fool of myself and never say a word."

This was a new aspect of the thing. His smartness of the morning had seemed to Tom a good joke before, and very ingenious. It merely looked mean and shabby now. He hung his head and could not think of anything to say for a moment. Then he said:

"Auntie, I wish I hadn't done it—but I didn't think."

"O, child you never think. You never think of anything but your own selfishness. You could think to come all the way over here from Jackson's island in the night to laugh at our troubles, and you could think to fool me with a lie about a dream; but you couldn't ever think to pity us and save us from sorrow."

"Auntie, I know now it was mean, but I didn't mean to be mean. I didn't, honest. And besides I didn't come over here to laugh at you that night."

"What did you come for, then?"

"It was to tell you not to be uneasy about us, because we hadn't got drowned."

"Tom, Tom, I would be the thankfullest soul in this world if I could believe you ever had as good a thought as that, but you know you never did—and *I* know it, Tom."

"Indeed and 'deed I did, auntie—I wish I may never stir if I didn't."

"O, Tom, don't lic—don't do it. It only makes things a hundred times worse."

"It ain't a lie, auntie, it's the truth. I wanted to keep you from grieving—that was all that made me come."

"I'd give the whole world to believe that—it would cover up a power of sins Tom. I'd 'most be glad you'd run off and acted so bad. But it aint reasonable; because, why didn't you tell me, child?"

"Why, you see, auntie, when you got to talking about the funeral, I just got all full of the idea of our coming and hiding in the church, and I couldn't somehow bear to spoil it. So I just put the bark back in my pocket and kept mum."

"What bark?"

"The bark I had wrote on to tell you we'd gone pirating. I wish, now, you'd waked up when I kissed you—I do, honest."

The hard lines in his aunt's face relaxed and a sudden tenderness dawned in her eyes.

"*Did* you kiss me, Tom?"

" Why yes I did."

" Are you sure you did, Tom?"

" Why yes I did, auntie—certain sure."

" What did you kiss me for, Tom?"

"Because I loved you so, and you laid there moaning and I was so sorry."

The words sounded like truth. The old lady could not hide a tremor in her voice when she said:

" Kiss me again, Tom!—and be off with you to school, now, and don't bother me any more."

TOM JUSTIFIED.

The moment he was gone, she ran to a closet and got out the ruin of a jacket which Tom had gone pirating in. Then she stopped, with it in her hand, and said to herself:

" No, I don't dare. Poor boy, I reckon he's lied about it—but it's a blessed, blessed lie, there's such comfort come from it. I hope the Lord—I *know* the Lord will forgive him, because it was such goodheartedness in him to tell it. But I don't want to find out it's a lie. I won't look."

She put the jacket away, and stood by musing a minute. Twice she put out her hand to take the garment again, and twice she refrained. Once more she ventured, and this time she fortified herself with the thought: "It's a good lie—it's a good lie—I won't let it grieve me." So she sought the jacket pocket. A moment later she was reading Tom's piece of bark through flowing tears and saying: " I could forgive the boy, now, if he'd committed a million sins!"

Chapter XX.

THE DISCOVERY.

There was something about Aunt Polly's manner, when she kissed Tom, that swept away his low spirits and made him light-hearted and happy again. He started to school and had the luck of coming upon Becky Thatcher at the head of Meadow Lane. His mood always determined his manner. Without a moment's hesitation he ran to her and said:

"I acted mighty mean to-day, Becky, and I'm so sorry. I won't ever, ever do that way again, as long as ever I live— please make up, won't you?"

The girl stopped and looked him scornfully in the face:

"I'll thank you to keep yourself *to* yourself, Mr. Thomas Sawyer. I'll **never** speak to you again."

She tossed her head and passed on. Tom was so stunned that he had not even presence of mind enough to say "Who cares, Miss Smarty?" until the right time to say it had gone by. So he said nothing. But he was in a fine rage, nevertheless. He moped into the school-yard wishing she were a boy, and imagining how he would trounce her if she were. He presently encountered her and delivered a stinging remark as he passed. She hurled one in return, and the angry breach was complete. It seemed to Becky, in her hot resentment, that she could hardly wait for school to "take in," she was so impatient to see Tom flogged for the injured spelling-book. If she had had any lingering notion of exposing Alfred Temple, Tom's offensive fling had driven it entirely away.

Poor girl, she did not know how fast she was nearing trouble herself. The master, Mr. Dobbins, had reached middle age with an unsatisfied ambition. The darling of his desires was, to be a doctor, but poverty had decreed that he should be nothing higher than a village schoolmaster. Every day he took a mysterious book out of his desk and absorbed himself in it at times when no classes were reciting. He kept that book under lock and key. There was not an urchin in school but was perishing to have a glimpse of it, but the chance never came. Every boy and girl had a theory about the nature of that book; but no two theories were alike, and there was no way of getting at the facts in the case. Now, as Becky was passing by the desk, which stood near the door, she noticed that the key was in the lock! It was a precious moment. She glanced around; found herself alone, and the next instant she had the book in her hands. The title-page —Professor somebody's "Anatomy"—carried no information to her mind; so she began to turn the leaves. She came at once upon a handsomely engraved and colored frontispiece—a human figure, stark naked. · At that moment a shadow fell on the page and Tom Sawyer stepped in at the door, and caught a glimpse of the picture. Becky snatched at the book to close it, and had the hard luck to tear the pictured page half down the middle. She thrust the volume into the desk, turned the key, and burst out crying with shame and vexation.

"Tom Sawyer, you are just as mean as you can be, to sneak up on a person and look at what they're looking at."

"How could *I* know you was looking at anything?"

"You ought to be ashamed of yourself Tom Sawyer; you know you're going to tell on me, and O, what shall I do, what shall I do! I'll be whipped, and I never was whipped in school."

Then she stamped her little foot and said:

"*Be* so mean if you want to! *I* know something that's going to happen. You just wait and you'll see! Hateful, hateful, hateful!"—and she flung out of the house with a new explosion of crying.

Tom stood still, rather flustered by this onslaught. Presently he said to himself:

"What a curious kind of a fool a girl is. Never been licked in school! Shucks. What's a licking! That's just like a girl —they're so thin-skinned and chicken hearted. Well, of course *I* ain't going to tell old Dobbins on this little fool, because there's other ways of getting even on her,

CAUGHT IN THE ACT.

that ain't so mean; but what of it? Old Dobbins will ask who it was tore his book. Nobody'll answer. Then he'll do just the way he always does—ask first one and then t'other, and when he comes to the right girl he'll know it, without any telling. Girl's faces always tell on them. They ain't got any back-bone. She'll get licked. Well, it's a kind of a tight place for Becky Thatcher, because there ain't any way out of it." Tom conned the thing a moment longer and then added: "All right, though; she'd like to see me in just such a fix—let her sweat it out!"

Tom joined the mob of skylarking scholars outside. In a few moments the master arrived and school "took in." Tom did not feel a strong interest in his studies. Every time he stole a glance at the girls' side of the room Becky's face troubled him. Considering all things, he did not want to pity her, and yet it was all he could do to help it. He could get up no exultation that was really worthy the name. Presently the spelling-book discovery was made, and Tom's mind was entirely full of his own matters for a while after that. Becky roused up from her lethargy of distress and showed good interest in the proceedings. She did not expect that Tom could get out of his trouble by denying that he spilt the ink on the book himself; and she was right. The denial only seemed to make the thing worse for Tom. Becky supposed she would be glad of that, and she tried to believe she was glad of it, but she found she was not certain. When the worst came to the worst, she had an impulse to get up and tell on Alfred Temple, but she made an effort and forced herself to keep still—because, said she to herself, "he'll tell about me tearing the picture sure. I wouldn't say a word, not to save his life!"

Tom took his whipping and went back to his seat not at all broken-hearted, for he thought it was possible that he had unknowingly upset the ink on the spelling-book himself, in some skylarking bout—he had denied it for form's sake and because it was custom, and had stuck to the denial from principle.

A whole hour drifted by, the master sat nodding in his throne, the air was drowsy with the hum of study. By and by, Mr. Dobbins straightened himself up, yawned, then unlocked his desk, and reached for his book, but seemed undecided whether to take it out or leave it. Most of the pupils glanced up languidly, but there were two among them that watched his movements with intent eyes. Mr. Dobbins fingered his book absently for a while, then took it out and settled himself in his chair to read! Tom shot a glance at Becky. He had seen a hunted and helpless rabbit look as she did, with a gun leveled at its head. Instantly he forgot his quarrel with her. Quick—something must be done! done in a flash, too! But the very imminence of the emergency paralyzed his invention. Good! —he had an inspiration! He would run and snatch the book, spring through the door and fly. But his resolution shook for one little instant, and the chance was lost—the master opened the volume. If Tom only had the wasted opportunity back again! Too late. There was no help for Becky now, he said. The next moment the master faced the school. Every eye sunk under his gaze. There was that in it which smote even the innocent with fear. There was silence while one might count ten, the master was gathering his wrath. Then he spoke:

"Who tore this book?"

There was not a sound. One could have heard a pin drop. The stillness continued; the master searched face after face for signs of guilt.

"Benjamin Rogers, did you tear this book?"

A denial. Another pause.

"Joseph Harper, did you?"

Another denial. Tom's uneasiness grew more and more intense under the slow

torture of these proceedings. The master scanned the ranks of boys—considered a while, then turned to the girls:

"Amy Lawrence?"

A shake of the head.

"Gracie Miller?"

The same sign.

"Susan Harper, did you do this?"

Another negative. The next girl was Becky Thatcher. Tom was trembling from head to foot with excitement and a sense of the hopelessness of the situation.

"Rebecca Thatcher," [Tom glanced at her face—it was white with terror,]—"did you tear—no, look me in the face"—[her hands rose in appeal]—"did you tear this book?"

TOM ASTONISHES THE SCHOOL.

A thought shot like lightning through Tom's brain. He sprang to his feet and shouted—"*I* done it!"

The school stared in perplexity at this incredible folly. Tom stood a moment, to gather his dismembered faculties; and when he stepped forward to go to his punishment the surprise, the gratitude, the adoration that shone upon him out of poor Becky's eyes seemed pay enough for a hundred floggings. Inspired by the splendor of his own act, he took without an outcry the most merciless flaying that even Mr. Dobbins had ever administered; and also received with indifference the added cruelty of a command to remain two hours after school should be dismissed —for he knew who would wait for him outside till his captivity was done, and not count the tedious time as loss, either.

Tom went to bed that night planning vengeance against Alfred Temple ; for with shame and repentance Becky had told him all, not forgetting her own treachery ; but even the longing for vengeance had to give way, soon, to pleasanter musings, and he fell asleep at last, with Becky's latest words lingering dreamily in his ear—

"Tom, how *could* you be so noble !"

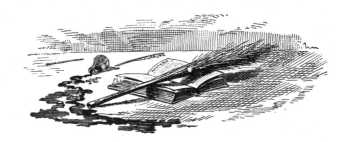

CHAPTER XXI.

VACATION was approaching. The schoolmaster, always severe, grew severer and more exacting than ever, for he wanted the school to make a good showing on "Examination" day. His rod and his ferule were seldom idle now—at least among the smaller pupils. Only the biggest boys, and young ladies of eighteen and twenty escaped lashing. Mr. Dobbins's lashings were very vigorous ones, too; for although he carried, under his wig, a perfectly bald and shiny head, he had only reached middle age and there was no sign of feebleness in his muscle. As the great day approached, all the tyranny that was in him came to the surface; he seemed to take a vindictive pleasure in punishing the least shortcomings. The consequence was, that the

TOM DECLAIMS.

167

smaller boys spent their days in terror and suffering and their nights in plotting revenge. They threw away no opportunity to do the master a mischief. But he kept ahead all the time. The retribution that followed every vengeful success was so sweeping and majestic that the boys always retired from the field badly worsted. At last they conspired together and hit upon a plan that promised a dazzling victory. They swore-in the sign-painter's boy, told him the scheme, and asked his help. He had his own reasons for being delighted, for the master boarded in his father's family and had given the boy ample

EXAMINATION EVENING.

cause to hate him. The master's wife would go on a visit to the country in a few days, and there would be nothing to interfere with the plan; the master always prepared himself for great occasions by getting pretty well fuddled, and the sign-painter's boy said that when the dominie had reached the proper condition on Examination Evening he would " manage the thing " while he napped in his chair; then he would have him awakened at the right time and hurried away to school.

In the fullness of time the interesting occasion arrived. At eight in the evening the schoolhouse was brilliantly lighted, and adorned with wreaths and festoons of foliage and flowers. The master sat throned in his great chair upon a raised platform, with his blackboard behind him. He was looking tolerably mellow. Three rows of benches on each side and six rows in front of him were occupied by the dignitaries of the town and by the parents of the pupils. To his left, back of the rows of citizens, was a spacious temporary platform upon which were seated the scholars who were to take part in the exercises of the evening; rows of small boys, washed and dressed to an intolerable state of discomfort; rows of gawky big boys; snow-banks of girls and young ladies clad in lawn and muslin and conspiciously conscious of their bare arms, their grandmothers' ancient trinkets, their bits of pink and blue ribbon and the flowers in their hair. All the rest of the house was filled with non-participating scholars.

The exercises began. A very little boy stood up and sheepishly recited, "You'd scarce expect one of my age to speak in public on the stage, etc "—accompanying himself with the painfully exact and spasmodic gestures which a machine might have used—supposing the machine to be a trifle out of order. But he got through safely, though cruelly scared, and got a fine round of applause when he made his manufactured bow and retired.

A little shame-faced girl lisped "Mary had a little lamb, etc.," performed a compassion-inspiring curtsy, got her meed of applause, and sat down flushed and happy.

Tom Sawyer stepped forward with conceited confidence and soared into the unquenchable and indestructible "Give me liberty or give me death" speech, with fine fury and frantic gesticulation, and broke down in the middle of it. A ghastly stage-fright siezed him, his legs quaked under him and he was like to choke. True, he had the manifest sympathy of the house—but he had the house's silence, too, which was even worse than its sympathy. The master frowned, and this completed the disaster. Tom struggled a while and then retired, utterly defeated. There was a weak attempt at applause, but it died early.

"The Boy stood on the Burning Deck" followed; also "The Assyrian Came Down," and other declamatory gems. Then there were reading exercises, and a spelling fight. The meager Latin class recited with honor. The prime

ON EXHIBITION.

feature of the evening was in order, now—original "compositions" by the young ladies. Each in her turn stepped forward to the edge of the platform, cleared her throat, held up her manuscript (tied with dainty ribbon), and proceeded to read, with labored attention to "expression" and punctuation. The themes were the same that had been illuminated upon similar occasions by their mothers before them, their grandmothers, and doubtless all their ancestors in the female line clear back to the Crusades. "Friendship" was one; "Memories of Other Days;" "Religion in History;" "Dream Land;" "The Advantages of Culture;" "Forms of Political Government Compared and

Contrasted; " " Melancholy; " " Filial Love; " " Heart Longings," etc., etc.

A prevalent feature in these compositions was a nursed and petted melancholy; another was a wasteful and opulent gush of "fine language;" another was a tendency to lug in by the ears particularly prized words and phrases until they were worn entirely out; and a peculiarity that conspicuously marked and marred them was the inveterate and intolerable sermon that wagged its crippled tail at the end of each and every one of them. No matter what the subject might be, a brain-racking effort was made to squirm it into some aspect or other that the moral and religious mind could contemplate with edification. The glaring insincerity of these sermons was not sufficient to compass the banishment of the fashion from the schools, and it is not sufficient to-day; it never will be sufficient while the world stands, perhaps. There is no school in all our land where the young ladies do not feel obliged to close their compositions with a sermom; and you will find that the sermon of the most frivolous and least religious girl in the school is always the longest and the most relentlessly pious. But enough of this. Homely truth is unpalatable.

Let us return to the "Examination." The first composition that was read was one entitled "Is this, then, Life?" Perhaps the reader can endure an extract from it:

"In the common walks of life, with what delightful emotions does the youthful mind look forward to some anticipated scene of festivity! Imagination is busy sketching rose-tinted pictures of joy. In fancy, the voluptuous votary of fashion sees herself amid the festive throng, 'the observed of all observers.' Her graceful form, arrayed in snowy robes, is whirling through the mazes of the joyous dance; her eye is brightest, her step is lightest in the gay assembly.

"In such delicious fancies time quickly glides by, and the welcome hour arrives for her entrance into the elysian world, of which she has had such bright dreams. How fairy-like does every thing appear to her enchanted vision! each new scene is more charming than the last. But after a while she finds that beneath this goodly exterior, all is vanity: the flattery which once charmed her soul, now grates harshly upon her ear; the ball-room has lost its charms; and with wasted health and imbittered heart, she turns away with the conviction that earthly pleasures cannot satisfy the longings of the soul!"

And so forth and so on. There was a buzz of gratification from time to time during the reading, accompanied by whispered ejaculations of "How sweet!" "How eloquent!" "So true!" etc., and after the thing had closed with a peculiarly afflicting sermon the applause was enthusiastic.

Then arose a slim, melancholy girl, whose face had the "interesting" pale-
ness that comes of pills and indigestion, and read a "poem." Two stanzas of
it will do:

A MISSOURI MAIDEN'S FAREWELL TO ALABAMA.

ALABAMA, good-bye! I love thee well!
  But yet for awhile do I leave thee now!
Sad, yes, sad thoughts of thee my heart doth swell,
  And burning recollections throng my brow!
For I have wandered through thy flowery woods;
  Have roamed and read near Tallapoosa's stream;
Have listened to Tallassee's warring floods,
  And wooed on Coosa's side Aurora's beam.

Yet shame I not to bear an o'er-full heart,
  Nor blush to turn behind my tearful eyes;
'Tis from no stranger land I now must part,
  'Tis to no strangers left I yield these sighs.
Welcome and home were mine within this State,
  Whose vales I leave—whose spires fade fast from me:
And cold must be mine eyes, and heart, and tête,
  When, dear Alabama! they turn cold on thee!

There were very few there who knew what " *tête* " meant, but the poem was
very satisfactory, nevertheless.

Next appeared a dark complexioned, black eyed, black haired young lady,
who paused an impressive moment, assumed a tragic expression and began to
read in a measured, solemn tone.

A VISION.

Dark and tempestuous was night. Around the throne on high not a single star quivered; but
the deep intonations of the heavy thunder constantly vibrated upon the ear; whilst the terrific
lightning revelled in angry mood through the cloudy chambers of heaven, seeming to scorn the
power exerted over its terror by the illustrious Franklin! Even the boisterous winds unanimously
came forth from their mystic homes, and blustered about as if to enhance by their aid the wildness
of the scene.

At such a time, so dark, so dreary, for human sympathy my very spirit sighed; but instead
thereof,

    " My dearest friend, my counsellor, my comforter and guide—
    My joy in grief, my second bliss in joy," came to my side.

She moved like one of those bright beings pictured in the sunny walks of fancy's Eden by the romantic and young, a queen of beauty unadorned save by her own transcendent loveliness. So soft was her step, it failed to make even a sound, and but for the magical thrill imparted by her genial touch, as other unobtrusive beauties, she would have glided away unperceived—unsought. A strange sadness rested upon her features, like icy tears upon the robe of December, as she pointed to the contending elements without, and bade me contemplate the two beings presented.

This nightmare occupied some ten pages of manuscript and wound up with a sermon so destructive of all hope to non-Presbyterians that it took the first

"*A Poem.*" "*A Vision.*"

PRIZE AUTHORS.

prize. This composition was considered to be the very finest effort of the evening. The mayor of the village, in delivering the prize to the author of it, made a warm speech in which he said that it was by far the most "eloquent" thing he had ever listened to, and that Daniel Webster himself might well be proud of it.

It may be remarked, in passing, that the number of compositions in which the word " beauteous " was over-fondled, and human experience referred to as " life's page," was up to the usual average.

Now the master, mellow almost to the verge of geniality, put his chair aside, turned his back to the audience, and began to draw a map of America on the blackboard, to exercise the geography class upon. But he made a sad business of it with his unsteady hand, and a smothered titter rippled over the house. He knew what the matter was and set himself to right it. He sponged out lines and re-made them; but he only distorted them more than ever, and the tittering was more pronounced. He threw his entire attention upon his work, now, as if determined not to be put down by the mirth. He felt that all eyes were fastened upon him; he imagined he was succeeding, and yet the tittering continued; it even manifestly increased. And well it might. There was a garret above, pierced with a scuttle over his head; and down through this scuttle came a cat, suspended around the haunches by a string; she had a rag tied about her head and jaws to keep her from mewing; as she slowly descended she curved upward and clawed at the string, she swung downward and clawed at the intangible air. The tittering rose higher and higher—the cat was within six inches of the absorbed teacher's head—down, down, a little lower, and

she grabbed his wig with her desperate claws, clung to it and was snatched up into the garret in an instant with her trophy still in her possession! And how the light did blaze abroad from the master's bald pate—for the sign-painter's boy had *gilded* it!

That broke up the meeting. The boys were avenged. Vacation had come.

NOTE.—The pretended "compositions" quoted in this chapter are taken without alteration from a volume entitled "Prose and Poetry, by a Western Lady"—but they are exactly and precisely after the school-girl pattern and hence are much happier than any mere imitations could be.

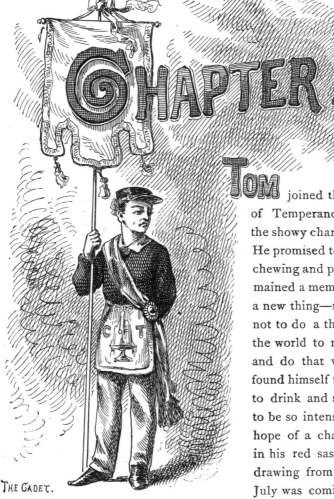

CHAPTER XXII.

TOM joined the new order of Cadets of Temperance, being attracted by the showy character of their "regalia." He promised to abstain from smoking, chewing and profanity as long as he remained a member. Now he found out a new thing—namely, that to promise not to do a thing is the surest way in the world to make a body want to go and do that very thing. Tom soon found himself tormented with a desire to drink and swear; the desire grew to be so intense that nothing but the hope of a chance to display himself in his red sash kept him from withdrawing from the order. Fourth of July was coming; but he soon gave that up—gave it up before he had worn his shackles over forty-eight hours—and fixed his hopes upon old Judge Frazer, justice of the peace, who was apparently

THE CADET.

on his death-bed and would have a big public funeral, since he was so high an official. During three days Tom was deeply concerned about the Judge's condition and hungry for news of it. Sometimes his hopes ran high—so high that he would venture to get out his regalia and practice before the looking-glass. But the Judge had a most discouraging way of fluctuating. At last he was pronounced upon the mend—and then convalescent. Tom was disgusted; and felt a sense of injury, too. He handed in his resignation at once—and that night the Judge

HAPPY FOR TWO DAYS.

suffered a relapse and died. Tom resolved that he would never trust a man like that again.

The funeral was a fine thing. The Cadets paraded in a style calculated to kill the late member with envy. Tom was a free boy again, however—there was something in that. He could drink and swear, now—but found to his surprise

12

that he did not want to. The simple fact that he could, took the desire away, and the charm of it.

Tom presently wondered to find that his coveted vacation was beginning to hang a little heavily on his hands.

He attempted a diary—but nothing happened during three days, and so he abandoned it.

The first of all the negro minstrel shows came to town, and made a sensation. Tom and Joe Harper got up a band of performers and were happy for two days.

Even the Glorious Fourth was in some sense a failure, for it rained hard, there was no procession in consequence, and the greatest man in the world (as Tom supposed) Mr. Benton, an actual United States Senator, proved an overwhelming disappointment—for he was not twenty-five feet high, nor even anywhere in the neighborhood of it.

ENJOYING THE VACATION.

A circus came. The boys played circus for three days afterward in tents made of rag carpeting—admission, three pins for boys, two for girls—and then circusing was abandoned.

A phrenologist and a mesmerizer came —and went again and left the village duller and drearier than ever.

There were some boys-and-girls' parties, but they were so few and so delightful that they only made the aching voids between ache the harder.

Becky Thatcher was gone to her Constantinople home to stay with her parents during vacation—so there was no bright side to life anywhere.

The dreadful secret of the murder was a chronic misery. It was a very cancer for permanency and pain.

Then came the measles.

During two long weeks Tom lay a prisoner, dead to the world and its happenings. He was very ill, he was interested in nothing. When he got upon his feet at last and moved feebly down town, a melancholy change had come over everything and every creature. There had been a " revival," and everybody had " got religion," not only the adults, but even the boys and girls. Tom went about, hoping against hope for the sight of one blessed sinful face, but disappointment crossed him everywhere. He found Joe Harper studying a Testament, and turned sadly away from the depressing spectacle. He sought Ben Rogers, and found him visiting the poor with a basket of tracts. He hunted up Jim Hollis, who called his attention to the precious blessing of his late measles as a warning. Every boy he encountered added another ton to his depression ; and when, in desperation, he flew for refuge at last to the bosom of Huckleberry Finn and was received with a scriptural quotation, his heart broke and he crept home and to bed realizing that he alone of all the town was lost, forever and forever.

And that night there came on a terrific storm, with driving rain, awful claps of thunder and blinding sheets of lightning. He covered his head with the bedclothes and waited in a horror of suspense for his doom; for he had not the shadow of a doubt that all this hubbub was about him. He believed he had taxed the forbearance of the powers above to the extremity of endurance and that this was the result. It might have seemed to him a waste of pomp and ammunition to kill a bug with a battery of artillery, but there seemed nothing incongruous about the getting up such an expensive thunder storm as this to knock the turf from under an insect like himself.

By and by the tempest spent itself and died without accomplishing its object. The boy's first impulse was to be grateful, and reform. His second was to wait —for there might not be any more storms.

The next day the doctors were back ; Tom had relapsed. The three weeks he spent on his back this time seemed an entire age. When he got abroad at last he was hardly grateful that he had been spared, remembering how lonely was his estate, how companionless and forlorn he was. He drifted listlessly down the street and found Jim Hollis acting as judge in a juvenile court that was trying a cat for murder, in the presence of her victim, a bird.   He found Joe Harper and Huck Finn up an alley eating a stolen melon.   Poor lads! they—like Tom—had suffered a relapse.

CHAPTER XXIII.

THE JUDGE.

AT last the sleepy atmosphere was stirred—and vigorously: the murder trial came on in the court. It became the absorbing topic of village talk immediately. Tom could not get away from it. Every reference to the murder sent a shudder to his heart, for his troubled conscience and fears almost persuaded him that these remarks were put forth in his hearing as "feelers;" he did not see how he could be suspected of knowing anything about the murder, but still he could not be comfortable in the midst of this gossip. It kept him in a cold shiver all the time. He took Huck to a lonely place to have a talk with him. It would be some relief to unseal his tongue for a little while; to divide his burden of distress with another sufferer. Moreover, he wanted to assure himself that Huck had remained discreet.

"Huck, have you ever told anybody about—that?"

"'Bout what?"

"You know what."

"Oh—'course I haven't."

"Never a word?"

"Never a solitary word, so help me. What makes you ask?"

"Well, I was afeard."

"Why Tom Sawyer, we wouldn't be alive two days if that got found out. *You* know that."

Tom felt more comfortable. After a pause:

"Huck, they couldn't anybody get you to tell, could they?"

"Get me to tell? Why if I wanted that half-breed devil to drownd me they could get me to tell. They ain't no different way."

"Well, that's all right, then. I reckon we're safe as long as we keep mum. But let's swear again, anyway. It's more surer."

"I'm agreed."

So they swore again with dread solemnities.

"What is the talk around, Huck? I've heard a power of it."

"Talk? Well, it's just Muff Potter, Muff Potter, Muff Potter all the time. It keeps me in a sweat, constant, so's I want to hide som'ers."

"That's just the same way they go on round me. I reckon he's a goner. Don't you feel sorry for him, sometimes?"

"Most always—most always. He ain't no account; but then he hain't ever done anything to hurt anybody. Just fishes a little, to get money to get drunk on—and loafs around considerable; but lord we all do that—leastways most of us,—preachers and such like. But he's kind of good—he give me half a fish, once, when there warn't enough for two; and lots of times he's kind of stood by me when I was out of luck."

"Well, he's mended kites for me, Huck, and knitted hooks on to my line. I wish we could get him out of there."

"My! we couldn't get him out Tom. And besides, 'twouldn't do any good; they'd ketch him again."

" Yes—so they would. But I hate to hear 'em abuse him so like the dickens when he never done—that."

" I do too, Tom. Lord, I hear 'em say he's the bloodiest looking villain in this country, and they wonder he wasn't ever hung before."

" Yes, they talk like that, all the time. I've heard 'em say that if he was to get free they'd lynch him."

" And they'd do it, too."

The boys had a long talk, but it brought them little comfort. As the twilight drew on, they found themselves hanging about the neighborhood of the little isolated jail, perhaps with an undefined hope that something would happen that might clear away their difficulties. But nothing happened; there seemed to be no angels or fairies interested in this luckless captive.

The boys did as they had often done before—went to the cell grating and gave Potter some tobacco and matches. He was on the ground floor and there were no guards.

His gratitude for their gifts had always smote their consciences before—it cut deeper than ever, this time. They felt cowardly and treacherous to the last degree when Potter said:

" You've been mighty good to me, boys—better'n anybody else in this town. And I don't forget it, I don't. Often I says to myself, says I, ' I used to mend all the boys' kites and things, and show 'em where the good fishin' places was, and befriend 'em what I could, and now they've all forgot old Muff when he's in trouble; but Tom don't, and Huck don't—*they* don't forget him,' says I, ' and I don't forget them.' Well, boys, I done an awful thing—drunk and crazy at the time—that's the only way I account for it—and now I got to swing for it, and it's right. Right, and *best*, too I reckon—hope so, anyway. Well, we won't talk about that. I don't want to make *you* feel bad; you've befriended me. But what I want to say, is, don't *you* ever get drunk—then you won't ever get here. Stand a little furder west—so—that's it; it's a prime comfort to see faces that's friendly when a body's in such a muck of trouble, and there don't none come here but yourn. Good friendly faces—good friendly faces. Git up on one another's backs and let me touch 'em. That's it. Shake hands—

yourn'll come through the bars, but mine's too big. Little hands, and weak — but they've helped Muff Potter a power, and they'd help him more if they could."

Tom went home miserable, and his dreams that night were full of horrors. The next day and the day after, he hung about the court room, drawn by an almost irresistible impulse to go in, but forcing himself to stay out. Huck was having the same experience. They studiously avoided each other. Each wandered away, from time to time, but the same dismal fascination always brought them back presently. Tom kept his ears open when idlers sauntered out of the court room, but invariably heard distressing news— the toils were closing more and more relentlessly around poor Potter. At the end of the second day the village talk was to the effect that Injun Joe's evidence stood firm and unshaken, and that there was not the slightest question as to what the jury's verdict would be.

Tom was out late, that night, and came to bed through the window. He was in a tremendous state of excitement. It was hours before he got to sleep. All the village flocked to the Court house the next morning, for this was to be the great day. Both sexes were about equally represented in the packed audience. After a long wait the jury filed in and took their places; shortly afterward, Potter, pale and haggard, timid and hopeless, was brought in, with chains upon him, and seated where all the curious eyes could stare at him; no less conspicuous was Injun Joe, stolid as ever. There was another pause, and then the judge arrived and the sheriff proclaimed the opening of the court. The usual whisperings among the lawyers and gathering together of papers followed. These details and accompanying delays worked up an atmosphere of preparation that was as impressive as it was fascinating.

Now a witness was called who testified that he found Muff Potter washing in the brook, at an early hour of the morning that the murder was discovered, and that he immediately sneaked away. After some further questioning, counsel for the prosecution said—

"Take the witness."

The prisoner raised his eyes for a moment, but dropped them again when his own counsel said—

"I have no questions to ask him."

The next witness proved the finding of the knife near the corpse. Counsel for the prosecution said:

"Take the witness."

"I have no questions to ask him," Potter's lawyer replied.

A third witness swore he had often seen the knife in Potter's possession.

"Take the witness."

Counsel for Potter declined to question him. The faces of the audience began to betray annoyance. Did this attorney mean to throw away his client's life without an effort?

Several witnesses deposed concerning Potter's guilty behavior when brought to the scene of the murder. They were allowed to leave the stand without being cross-questioned.

Every detail of the damaging circumstances that occurred in the graveyard upon that morning which all present remembered so well, was brought out by credible witnesses, but none of them were cross-examined by Potter's lawyer. The perplexity and dissatisfaction of the house expressed itself in murmurs and provoked a reproof from the bench. Counsel for the prosecution now said :

" By the oaths of citizens whose simple word is above suspicion, we have fastened this awful crime beyond all possibility of question, upon the unhappy prisoner at the bar. We rest our case here."

A groan escaped from poor Potter, and he put his face in his hands and rocked his body softly to and fro, while a painful silence reigned in the court-room. Many men were moved, and many women's compassion testified itself in tears. Counsel for the defence rose and said:

" Your honor, in our remarks at the opening of this trial, we foreshadowed

TOM SWEARS.

our purpose to prove that our client did this fearful deed while under the influence of a blind and irresponsible delirium produced by drink. We have changed our mind. We shall not offer that plea." [Then to the clerk]: " Call Thomas Sawyer ! "

A puzzled amazement awoke in every face in the house, not even excepting Potter's. Every eye fastened itself with wondering interest upon Tom as he rose and took his place upon the stand. The boy looked wild enough, for he was badly scared. The oath was administered.

" Thomas Sawyer, where were you on the seventeenth of June, about the hour of midnight ? "

Tom glanced at Injun Joe's iron face and his tongue failed him. The audience listened breathless, but the words refused to come. After a few moments, however, the boy got a little of his strength back, and managed to put enough of it into his voice to make part of the house hear:

" In the graveyard ! "

"A little bit louder, please. Don't be afraid. You were—"

"In the graveyard."

A contemptuous smile flitted across Injun Joe's face.

"Were you anywhere near Horse Williams's grave?"

"Yes, sir."

"Speak up—just a trifle louder. How near were you?"

"Near as I am to you."

"Were you hidden, or not?"

"I was hid."

"Where?"

"Behind the elms that's on the edge of the grave."

Injun Joe gave a barely perceptible start.

"Any one with you?"

"Yes, sir. I went there with—"

"Wait—wait a moment. Never mind mentioning your companion's name. We will produce him at the proper time. Did you carry anything there with you."

Tom hesitated and looked confused.

"Speak out my boy—don't be diffident. The truth is always respectable. What did you take there?"

"Only a—a—dead cat."

There was a ripple of mirth, which the court checked.

"We will produce the skeleton of that cat. Now my boy, tell us everything that occurred—tell it in your own way—don't skip anything, and don't be afraid."

Tom began—hesitatingly at first, but as he warmed to his subject his words flowed more and more easily; in a little while every sound ceased but his own voice; every eye fixed itself upon him; with parted lips and bated breath the audience hung upon his words, taking no note of time, rapt in the ghastly fascinations of the tale. The strain upon pent emotion reached its climax when the boy said—

"—and as the doctor fetched the board around and Muff Potter fell, Injun Joe jumped with the knife and—"

Crash! Quick as lightning the half-breed sprang for a window, tore his way through all opposers, and was gone!

CHAPTER XXIV.

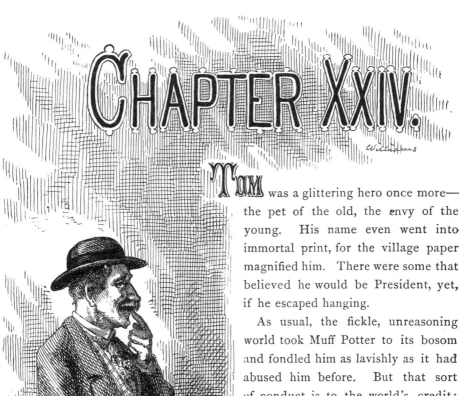

THE DETECTIVE.

TOM was a glittering hero once more—the pet of the old, the envy of the young. His name even went into immortal print, for the village paper magnified him. There were some that believed he would be President, yet, if he escaped hanging.

As usual, the fickle, unreasoning world took Muff Potter to its bosom and fondled him as lavishly as it had abused him before. But that sort of conduct is to the world's credit; therefore it is not well to find fault with it.

Tom's days were days of splendor and exultation to him, but his nights were seasons of horror. Injun Joe infested all his dreams, and always with doom in his eye. Hardly any temptation could persuade the boy to stir abroad after nightfall. Poor Huck was in the same state of wretchedness and terror, for Tom had told the whole story to the lawyer the night before the great day of the trial, and Huck was sore afraid that

TOM DREAMS.

his share in the business might leak out, yet, notwithstanding Injun Joe's flight had saved him the suffering of testifying in court. The poor fellow had got the attorney to promise secrecy, but what of that? Since Tom's harrassed conscience had managed to drive him to the lawyer's house by night and wring a dread tale from lips that had been sealed with the dismalest and most formidable of oaths, Huck's confidence in the human race was well nigh obliterated.

Daily Muff Potter's gratitude made Tom glad he had spoken; but nightly he wished he had sealed up his tongue.

Half the time Tom was afraid Injun Joe would never be captured; the other half he was afraid he would be. He felt sure he never could draw a safe breath again until that man was dead and he had seen the corpse.

Rewards had been offered, the country had been scoured, but no Injun Joe was found. One of those omniscient and awe-inspiring marvels, a detective, came up from St Louis, moused around, shook his head, looked wise, and made that sort of astounding success which members of that craft usually achieve. That is to say he "found a clew." But you can't hang a "clew" for murder and so after that detective had got through and gone home, Tom felt just as insecure as he was before.

The slow days drifted on, and each left behind it a slightly lightened weight of apprehension.

CHAPTER XXV

TREASURE

THERE comes a time in every rightly constructed boy's life when he has a raging desire to go somewhere and dig for hidden treasure. This desire suddenly came upon Tom one day. He sallied out to find Joe Harper, but failed of success. Next he sought Ben Rogers; he had gone fishing. Presently he stumbled upon Huck Finn the Red-Handed. Huck would answer. Tom took him to a private place and opened the matter to him confidentially. Huck was willing. Huck was always willing to take a hand in any enterprise that offered entertainment and required no capital, for he had a troublesome superabundance of that sort of time which is *not* money. "Where'll we dig?" said Huck.

"O, most anywhere."

"Why, is it hid all around?"

"No indeed it ain't. It's hid in mighty particular places, Huck—sometimes on islands, sometimes in rotten chests under the end of a limb of an old dead tree, just

THE PRIVATE CONFERENCE.

where the shadow falls at midnight; but mostly under the floor in ha'nted houses."

"Who hides it?"

"Why robbers, of course — who'd you reckon? Sunday-school sup'rintendents?"

"I don't know. If 'twas mine I wouldn't hide it; I'd spend it and have a good time."

"So would I. But robbers don't do that way. They always hide it and leave it there."

"Don't they come after it any more?"

"No, they think they will, but they generally forget the marks, or else they die. Anyway it lays there a long time and gets rusty; and by and by somebody finds an old yellow paper that tells how to find the marks—a paper that's got to be ciphered over about a week because it's mostly signs and hy'roglyphics."

"Hyro—which?"

"Hy'rogliphics—pictures and things, you know, that don't seem to mean anything."

"Have you got one of them papers, Tom?"

"No."

"Well then, how you going to find the marks?"

"I don't want any marks. They always bury it under a ha'nted house or on an island, or under a dead tree that's got one limb sticking out. Well, we've tried Jackson's Island a little, and we can try it again some time; and there's the old ha'nted house up the Still-House branch, and there's lots of dead-limb trees— dead loads of 'em."

"Is it under all of them?"

"How you talk! No!"

"Then how you going to know which one to go for?"

"Go for all of 'em!"

"Why Tom, it'll take all summer."

"Well, what of that? Suppose you find a brass pot with a hundred dollars in it, all rusty and gay, or a rotten chest full of di'monds. How's that?"

Huck's eyes glowed.

"That's bully. Plenty bully enough for me. Just you gimme the hundred dollars and I don't want no di'monds."

"All right. But I bet you *I* ain't going to throw off on di'monds. Some of 'em's worth twenty dollars apiece—there ain't any, hardly, but's worth six bits or a dollar."

"No! Is that so?"

"Cert'nly—anybody'll tell you so. Hain't you ever seen one, Huck?"

"Not as I remember."

"O, kings have slathers of them."

"Well, I don't know no kings, Tom."

"I reckon you don't. But if you was to go to Europe you'd see a raft of 'em hopping around."

"Do they hop?"

"Hop? —your granny! No!"

"Well what did you say they did, for?"

"Shucks, I only meant you'd *see* 'em—not hopping, of course—what do they want to hop for?—but I mean you'd just see 'em—scattered around, you know, in a kind of a general way. Like that old hump-backed Richard."

"Richard? What's his other name?"

"He didn't have any other name. Kings don't have any but a given name."

"No?"

"But they don't."

"Well, if they like it, Tom, all right; but I don't want to be a king and have

13

only just a given name, like a nigger. But say—where you going to dig first?"

"Well, I don't know. S'pose we tackle that old dead-limb tree on the hill t'other side of Still-House branch?"

"I'm agreed."

So they got a crippled pick and a shovel, and set out on their three-mile tramp. They arrived hot and panting, and threw themselves down in the shade of a neighboring elm to rest and have a smoke.

"I like this," said Tom.

"So do I."

"Say, Huck, if we find a treasure here, what you going to do with your share?"

"Well I'll have pie and a glass of soda every day, and I'll go to every circus that comes along. I bet I'll have a gay time."

"Well ain't you going to save any of it?"

A KING, POOR FELLOW!   "Save it? What for?"

"Why so as to have something to live on, by and by."

"O, that ain't any use. Pap would come back to thish-yer town some day and get his claws on it if I didn't hurry up, and I tell you he'd clean it out pretty quick. What you going to do with yourn, Tom?"

"I'm going to buy a new drum, and a sure-'nough sword, and a red neck-tie and a bull pup, and get married."

"Married!"

"That's it."

"Tom, you—why you ain't in your right mind."

"Wait—you'll see."

"Well that's the foolishest thing you could do. Look at pap and my mother. Fight! Why they used to fight all the time. I remember, mighty well."

"That ain't anything. The girl I'm going to marry won't fight."

"Tom, I reckon they're all alike. They'll all comb a body. Now you better think 'bout this a while. I tell you you better. What's the name of the gal?"

"It ain't a gal at all—it's a girl."

"It's all the same, I reckon; some says gal, some says girl—both's right, like enough. Anyway, what's her name, Tom?"

"I'll tell you some time—not now."

"All right—that'll do. Only if you get married I'll be more lonesomer than ever."

"No you won't. You'll come and live with me. Now stir out of this and we'll go to digging."

They worked and sweated for half an hour. No result. They toiled another half hour. Still no result. Huck said:

"Do they always bury it as deep as this?"

"Sometimes—not always. Not generally. I reckon we haven't got the right place."

So they chose a new spot and began again. The labor dragged a little, but still they made progress. They pegged away in silence for some time. Finally Huck leaned on his shovel, swabbed the beaded drops from his brow with his sleeve, and said:

BUSINESS.

"Where you going to dig next, after we get this one?"

"I reckon maybe we'll tackle the old tree that's over yonder on Cardiff Hill back of the widow's."

"I reckon that'll be a good one. But won't the widow take it away from us Tom? It's on her land."

"*She* take it away! Maybe she'd like to try it once. Whoever finds one of these hid treasures, it belongs to him. It don't make any difference whose land it's on."

That was satisfactory. The work went on. By and by Huck said:—

"Blame it, we must be in the wrong place again. What do you think?"

"It *is* mighty curious Huck. I don't understand it. Sometimes witches interfere. I reckon maybe that's what's the trouble now."

"Shucks, witches ain't got no power in the daytime."

"Well, that's so. I didn't think of that. Oh, *I* know what the matter is! What a blamed lot of fools we are! You got to find out where the shadow of the limb falls at midnight, and that's where you dig!"

"Then consound it, we've fooled away all this work for nothing. Now hang it all, we got to come back in the night. It's an awful long way. Can you get out?"

"I bet I will. We've got to do it to night, too, because if some body sees these holes they'll know in a minute what's here and they'll go for it."

"Well, I'll come around and maow to night."

"All right. Let's hide the tools in the bushes."

The boys were there that night, about the appointed time. They sat in the shadow waiting. It was a lonely place, and an hour made solemn by old traditions. Spirits whispered in the rustling leaves, ghosts lurked in the murky nooks, the deep baying of a hound floated up out of the distance, an owl answered with his sepulchral note. The boys were subdued by these solemnities, and talked little. By and by they judged that twelve had come ; they marked where the shadow fell, and began to dig. Their hopes commenced to rise. Their interest grew stronger, and their industry kept pace with it. The hole deepened and still deepened, but every time their hearts jumped to hear the pick strike upon something, they only suffered a new disappointment. It was only a stone or a chunk. At last Tom said :—

"It ain't any use, Huck, we're wrong again."

"Well but we *can't* be wrong. We spotted the shadder to a dot."

"I know it, but then there's another thing."

"What's that?"

"Why we only guessed at the time. Like enough it was too late or too early."

Huck dropped his shovel.

"That's it," said he. "That's the very trouble. We got to give this one up. We can't ever tell the right time, and besides this kind of thing's too awful, here this time of night with witches and ghosts a fluttering around so. I feel as if something's behind me all the time; and I'm afeard to turn around, becuz maybe there's others in front a-waiting for a chance. I been creeping all over, ever since I got here."

"Well, I've been pretty much so, too, Huck. They most always put in a dead man when they bury a treasure under a tree, to look out for it."

"Lordy!"

"Yes, they do. I've always heard that."

"Tom I don't like to fool around much where there's dead people. A body's bound to get into trouble with 'em, sure."

"I don't like to stir 'em up, either. S'pose this one here was to stick his skull out and say something!"

"Don't, Tom! It's awful."

"Well it just is. Huck, I don't feel comfortable a bit."

"Say, Tom, let's give this place up, and try somewheres else."

"All right, I reckon we better."

"What'll it be?"

Tom considered a while; and then said—

"The ha'nted house. That's it!"

"Blame it, I don't like ha'nted houses Tom. Why they're a dern sight worse'n dead people. Dead people might talk, maybe, but they don't come sliding around in a shroud, when you ain't noticing, and peep over your shoulder all of a sudden and grit their teeth, the way a ghost does. I couldn't stand such a thing as that, Tom—nobody could."

"Yes, but Huck, ghosts don't travel around only at night. They won't hender us from digging there in the day time."

"Well that's so. But you know mighty well people don't go about that ha'nted house in the day nor the night."

"Well, that's mostly because they don't like to go where a man's been murdered, anyway—but nothing's ever been seen around that house except in the night—just some blue lights slipping by the windows—no regular ghosts."

"Well where you see one of them blue lights flickering around, Tom, you can bet there's a ghost mighty close behind it. It stands to reason. Becuz *you* know that they don't anybody but ghosts use 'em."

"Yes, that's so. But anyway they don't come around in the daytime, so what's the use of our being afeared?"

"Well, all right. We'll tackle the ha'nted house if you say so—but I reckon it's taking chances."

They had started down the hill by this time. There in the middle of the moonlit valley below them stood the "ha'nted" house, utterly isolated, its fences gone

THE HA'NTED HOUSE.

long ago, rank weeds smothering the very doorsteps, the chimney crumbled to ruin, the window-sashes vacant, a corner of the roof caved in. The boys gazed a while, half expecting to see a blue light flit past a window; then talking in a low tone, as befitted the time and the circumstances, they struck far off to the right, to give the haunted house a wide berth, and took their way homeward through the woods that adorned the rearward side of Cardiff Hill.

CHAPTER XXVI.

INJUN JOE.

ABOUT noon the next day the boys arrived at the dead tree; they had come for their tools. Tom was impatient to go to the haunted house; Huck was measurably so, also—but suddenly said—

"Lookyhere, Tom, do you know what day it is?"

Tom mentally ran over the days of the week, and then quickly lifted his eyes with a startled look in them—

"My! I never once thought of it, Huck!"

"Well I didn't neither, but all at once it popped onto me that it was Friday."

"Blame it, a body can't be too careful, Huck. We might a got into an awful scrape, tackling such a thing on a Friday."

199

"*Might!* Better say we *would!* There's some lucky days, maybe, but Friday ain't."

"Any fool knows that. I don't reckon *you* was the first that found it out, Huck."

"Well, I never said I was, did I? And Friday ain't all, neither. I had a rotten bad dream last night—dreampt about rats."

"No! Sure sign of trouble. Did they fight?"

"No."

"Well that's good, Huck. When they don't fight it's only a sign that there's trouble around, you know. All we got to do is to look mighty sharp and keep out of it. We'll drop this thing for to-day, and play. Do you know Robin Hood, Huck?"

THE GREATEST AND BEST.

"No. Who's Robin Hood?"

"Why he was one of the greatest men that was ever in England—and the best. He was a robber."

"Cracky, I wisht I was. Who did he rob?"

"Only sheriffs and bishops and rich people and kings, and such like. But he never bothered the poor. He loved 'em. He always divided up with 'em perfectly square."

"Well, he must 'a' been a brick."

"I bet you he was, Huck. Oh, he was the noblest man that ever was. They ain't any such men now, I can tell you. He could lick any man in England, with one hand tied behind him; and he could take his yew bow and plug a ten cent piece every time, a mile and a half."

"What's a *yew* bow?"

"*I* don't know. It's some kind of a bow, of course. And if he hit that dime only on the edge he would set down and cry—and curse. But we'll play Robin Hood—it's noble fun. I'll learn you."

"I'm agreed."

So they played Robin Hood all the afternoon, now and then casting a yearning eye down upon the haunted house and passing a remark about the morrow's prospects and possibilities there. As the sun began to sink into the west they took their way homeward athwart the long shadows of the trees and soon were buried from sight in the forests of Cardiff Hill.

On Saturday, shortly after noon, the boys were at the dead tree again. They had a smoke and a chat in the shade, and then dug a little in their last hole, not with great hope, but merely because Tom said there were so many cases where people had given up a treasure after getting down within six inches of it, and then somebody else had come along and turned it up with a single thrust of a shovel. The thing failed this time, however, so the boys shouldered their tools and went away feeling that they had not trifled with fortune but had fulfilled all the requirements that belong to the business of treasure-hunting.

When they reached the haunted house there was something so wierd and grisly about the dead silence that reigned there under the baking sun, and something so depressing about the loneliness and desolation of the place, that they were afraid, for a moment, to venture in. Then they crept to the door and took a trembling peep. They saw a weed-grown, floorless room, unplastered, an ancient fireplace, vacant windows, a ruinous staircase; and here, there, and everywhere, hung ragged and abandoned cobwebs. They presently entered, softly, with quickened pulses, talking in whispers, ears alert to catch the slightest sound, and muscles tense and ready for instant retreat.

In a little while familiarity modified their fears and they gave the place a critical and interested examination, rather admiring their own boldness, and wondering at it, too. Next they wanted to look up stairs. This was something like cutting off retreat, but they got to daring each other, and of course there could be but one result—they threw their tools into a corner and made the ascent. Up there were the same signs of decay. In one corner they found a closet that promised mystery, but the promise was a fraud—there was nothing in it. Their courage was up now and well in hand. They were about to go down and begin work when—

"Sh!" said Tom.

"What is it?" whispered Huck, blanching with fright.

"Sh! . . . . . There! . . . . . Hear it?"

"Yes! . . . . . O, my! Let's run!"

"Keep still! Don't you budge! They're coming right toward the door."

The boys stretched themselves upon the floor with their eyes to knot holes in the planking, and lay waiting, in a misery of fear.

"They've stopped . . . . . . No—coming . . . . . . Here they are. Don't whisper another word, Huck. My goodness, I wish I was out of this!"

Two men entered. Each boy said to himself: "There's the old deaf and dumb Spaniard that's been about town once or twice lately—never saw t'other man before."

"T'other" was a ragged, unkempt creature, with nothing very pleasant in his face. The Spaniard was wrapped in a *serape;* he had bushy white whiskers; long white hair flowed from under his sombrero, and he wore green goggles. When they came in, "t'other" was talking in a low voice; they sat down on the ground, facing the door, with their backs to the wall, and the speaker continued his remarks. His manner became less guarded and his words more distinct as he proceeded:

"No," said he, "I've thought it all over, and I don't like it. It's dangerous."

"Dangerous!" grunted the "deaf and dumb" Spaniard,—to the vast surprise of the boys. "Milksop!"

This voice made the boys gasp and quake. It was Injun Joe's! There was silence for some time. Then Joe said:

"What's any more dangerous than that job up yonder—but nothing's come of it."

"That's different. Away up the river so, and not another house about. 'Twon't ever be known that we tried, anyway, long as we didn't succeed."

"Well, what's more dangerous than coming here in the day time!—anybody would suspicion us that saw us."

"*I* know that. But there warn't any other place as handy after that fool of a job. I want to quit this shanty. I wanted to yesterday, only it warn't any use trying to stir out of here, with those infernal boys playing over there **on** the hill right in full view."

"Those infernal boys," quaked again under the inspiration of this remark, and thought how lucky it was that they had remembered it was Friday and concluded to wait a day. They wished in their hearts they had waited a year.

The two men got out some food and made a luncheon. After a long and thoughtful silence, Injun Joe said:

"Look here, lad—you go back up the river where you belong. Wait there till you hear from me. I'll take the chances on dropping into this town just once more, for a look. We'll do that 'dangerous' job after I've spied around a little and think things look well for it. Then for Texas! We'll leg it together!"

This was satisfactory. Both men presently fell to yawning, and Injun Joe said:

"I'm dead for sleep! It's your turn to watch."

He curled down in the weeds and soon began to snore. His comrade stirred him once or twice and he became quiet. Presently the watcher began to nod; his head drooped lower and lower, both men began to snore now.

The boys drew a long, grateful breath. Tom whispered—

"Now's our chance—come!"

Huck said:

"I can't—I'd die if they was to wake."

Tom urged—Huck held back. At last Tom rose slowly and softly, and started alone. But the first step he made wrung such a hideous creak from the crazy floor that he sank down almost dead with fright. He never made a second attempt. The boys lay there counting the dragging moments till it seemed to them that time must be done and eternity growing gray; and then they were grateful to note that at last the sun was setting.

Now one snore ceased. Injun Joe sat up, stared around—smiled grimly upon his comrade, whose head was drooping upon his knees—stirred him up with his foot and said—

"Here! *You're* a watchman, ain't you! All right, though — nothing's happened."

"My! have I been asleep?"

" Oh, partly, partly.   Nearly time for us to be moving, pard.   What'll we do with what little swag we've got left? "

" I don't know—leave it here as we've always done, I reckon.   No use to take it away till we start south.   Six hundred and fifty in silver's something to carry."

" Well—all right—it won't matter to come here once more."

" No—but I'd say come in the night as we used to do—it's better."

" Yes; but look here; it may be a good while before I get the right chance at that job; accidents might happen; 'tain't in such a very good place; we'll just regularly bury it—and bury it deep."

" Good idea," said the comrade, who walked across the room, knelt down, raised one of the rearward hearthstones and took out a bag that jingled pleasantly.   He subtracted from it twenty or thirty dollars for himself and as much for Injun Joe and passed the bag to the latter, who was on his knees in the corner, now, digging with his bowie knife.

The boys forgot all their fears, all their miseries in an instant.   With gloating eyes they watched every movement.   Luck!—the splendor of it was beyond all imagination!   Six hundred dollars was money enough to make half a dozen boys rich!   Here was treasure-hunting under the happiest auspices—there would not be any bothersome uncertainty as to where to dig.   They nudged each other every moment—eloquent nudges and easily understood, for they simply meant—" O, but ain't you glad *now* we're here!"

Joe's knife struck upon something.

" Hello!" said he.

" What is it?" said his comrade.

" Half-rotten plank—no it's a box, I believe.   Here—bear a hand and we'll see what it's here for.   Never mind, I've broke a hole."

He reached his hand in and drew it out—

" Man, it's money!"

The two men examined the handful of coins.   They were gold.   The boys above were as excited as themselves, and as delighted.

Joe's comrade said—

"We'll make quick work of this. There's an old rusty pick over amongst the weeds in the corner the other side of the fire-place—I saw it a minute ago."

He ran and brought the boys' pick and shovel. Injun Joe took the pick, looked it over critically, shook his head, muttered something to himself, and then began to use it. The box was soon unearthed. It was not very large;

HIDDEN TREASURES UNEARTHED.

it was iron bound and had been very strong before the slow years had injured it. The men contemplated the treasure a while in blissful silence.

"Pard, there's thousands of dollars here," said Injun Joe.

"'Twas always said that Murrel's gang used around here one summer," the stranger observed.

"I know it," said Injun Joe; "and this looks like it, I should say."

"*Now* you won't need to do that job."

The half-breed frowned. Said he—

"You don't know me. Least you don't know all about that thing. 'Tain't robbery altogether—it's *revenge!*" and a wicked light flamed in his eyes. "I'll need your help in it. When it's finished—then Texas. Go home to your Nance and your kids, and stand by till you hear from me."

"Well—if you say so, what'll we do with this—bury it again?"

"Yes. [Ravishing delight overhead.] *No!* by the great Sachem, no! [Profound distress overhead.] I'd nearly forgot. That pick had fresh earth on it! [The boys were sick with terror in a moment.] What business has a pick and a shovel here? What business with fresh earth on them? Who brought them here—and where are they gone? Have you heard anybody?—seen anybody? What! bury it again and leave them to come and see the ground disturbed? Not exactly—not exactly. We'll take it to my den."

"Why of course! Might have thought of that before. You mean Number One?"

"No—Number Two—under the cross. The other place is bad—too common."

"All right. It's nearly dark enough to start."

Injun Joe got up and went about from window to window cautiously peeping out. Presently he said:

"Who could have brought those tools here? Do you reckon they can be up stairs?"

The boys' breath forsook them. Injun Joe put his hand on his knife, halted a moment, undecided, and then turned toward the stairway. The boys thought of the closet, but their strength was gone. The steps came creaking up the stairs—the intolerable distress of the situation woke the stricken resolution of the lads—they were about to spring for the closet, when there was a crash of rotten timbers and Injun Joe landed on the ground amid the *débris* of the ruined stairway. He gathered himself up cursing, and his comrade said:

"Now what's the use of all that? If it's anybody, and they're up there, let them *stay* there—who cares? If they want to jump down, now, and get into trouble, who objects? It will be dark in fifteen minutes—and then let them follow us if they want to. I'm willing. In my opinion, whoever hove those things in here caught a sight of us and took us for ghosts or devils or something. I'll bet they're running yet."

Joe grumbled a while; then he agreed with his friend that what daylight was left ought to be economized in getting things ready for leaving. Shortly afterward they slipped out of the house in the deepening twilight, and moved toward the river with their precious box.

Tom and Huck rose up, weak but vastly relieved, and stared after them through the chinks between the logs of the house. Follow? Not they. They were content to reach ground again without broken necks, and take the townward track over the hill. They did not talk much. They were too much absorbed in hating themselves— hating the ill luck that made them take the spade and the pick there. But for that, Injun Joe never would have suspected. He would have hidden the

THE BOYS' SALVATION.

silver with the gold to wait there till his "revenge" was satisfied, and then he would have had the misfortune to find that money turn up missing. Bitter, bitter luck that the tools were ever brought there!

They resolved to keep a lookout for that Spaniard when he should come to town spying out for chances to do his revengeful job, and follow him to "Number Two," wherever that might be. Then a ghastly thought occurred to Tom:

"Revenge?" What if he means *us*, Huck!"

"O, don't!" said Huck, nearly fainting.

They talked it all over, and as they entered town they agreed to believe that he might possibly mean somebody else—at least that he might at least mean nobody but Tom, since only Tom had testified.

Very, very small comfort it was to Tom to be alone in danger! Company would be a palpable improvement, he thought.

CHAPTER XXVII.

THE adventure of the day mightily tormented Tom's dreams that night. Four times he had his hands on that rich treasure and four times it wasted to nothingness in his fingers as sleep forsook him and wakefulness brought back the hard reality of his misfortune. As he lay in the early morning recalling the incidents of his great adventure, he noticed that they seemed curiously subdued and far away — somewhat as if they had happened in another world, or in a time long gone by. Then it occurred to him that the great adventure itself must be a dream! There was one very strong argument in favor of this idea — namely, that the quantity of coin he had seen was too vast to be real. He had never seen as much as fifty dollars in one mass before, and he was like all boys of his age and station in life, in that he imagined that all references to "hundreds" and "thousands" were mere fanciful forms of speech, and that no such sums really existed in the world. He never had supposed for a moment that so large a sum as a hundred dollars was to be found in actual money in any one's possession. If his notions of hidden treasure had been analyzed, they would have been found to consist of a handful of real dimes and a bushel of vague, splendid, ungraspable dollars.

But the incidents of his adventure grew sensibly sharper and clearer under the

THE NEXT DAY'S CONFERENCE.

attrition of thinking them over, and so he presently found himself leaning to the impression that the thing might not have been a dream, after all. This uncertainty must be swept away. He would snatch a hurried breakfast and go and find Huck.

Huck was sitting on the gunwale of a flatboat, listlessly dangling his feet in the water and looking very melancholy. Tom concluded to let Huck lead up to the subject. If he did not do it, then the adventure would be proved to have been only a dream.

"Hello, Huck!"

"Hello, yourself."

Silence, for a minute.

"Tom, if we'd a left the blame tools at the dead tree, we'd 'a' got the money. O, ain't it awful!"

"'Tain't a dream, then, 'tain't a dream! Somehow I most wish it was. Dog'd if I don't, Huck."

"What ain't a dream?"

"Oh, that thing yesterday. I been half thinking it was."

"Dream! If them stairs hadn't broke down you'd 'a' seen how much dream it was! I've had dreams enough all night—with that patch-eyed Spanish devil going for me all through 'em—rot him!"

14

"No, not rot him. *Find* him! Track the money!"

"Tom, we'll never find him. A feller don't have only once chance for such a pile—and that one's lost. I'd feel mighty shaky if I was to see him, anyway."

"Well, so'd I; but I'd like to see him, anyway—and track him out—to his Number Two."

"Number Two—yes, that's it. I ben thinking 'bout that. But I can't make nothing out of it. What do you reckon it is?"

"I dono. It's too deep. Say, Huck—maybe it's the number of a house!"

"Goody! . . . . . . No, Tom, that ain't it. If it is, it ain't in this one-horse town. They ain't no numbers here."

"Well, that's so. Lemme think a minute. Here—it's the number of a room— in a tavern, you know!"

"O, that's the trick! They ain't only two taverns. We can find out quick."

"You stay here, Huck, till I come."

Tom was off at once. He did not care to have Huck's company in public places. He was gone half an hour. He found that in the best tavern, No. 2 had long been occupied by a young lawyer, and was still so occupied. In the less ostentatious house No. 2 was a mystery. The tavern-keeper's young son said it was kept locked all the time, and he never saw anybody go into it or come out of it except at night; he did not know any particular reason for this state of things; had had some little curiosity, but it was rather feeble; had made the most of the mystery by entertaining himself with the idea that that room was "ha'nted;" had noticed that there was a light in there the night before.

"That's what I've found out, Huck. I reckon that's the very No. 2 we're after."

"I reckon it is, Tom. Now what you going to do?"

"Lemme think."

Tom thought a long time. Then he said:

"I'll tell you. The back door of that No. 2 is the door that comes out into that little close alley between the tavern and the old rattle-trap of a brick store. Now you get hold of all the door-keys you can find, and I'll nip all of Auntie's and the first dark night we'll go there and try 'em. And mind you keep a lookout for Injun Joe, because he said he was going to drop into town and spy around once more for a chance to get his revenge. If you see him, you just follow him; and if he don't go to that No. 2, that ain't the place."

"Lordy I don't want to foller him by myself!"

"Why it'll be night, sure. He mightn't ever see you—and if he did, maybe he'd never think anything."

"Well, if it's pretty dark I reckon I'll track him. I dono—I dono. I'll try."

"You bet *I*'ll follow him, if it's dark, Huck. Why he might 'a' found out he couldn't get his revenge, and be going right after that money."

"It's so, Tom, it's so. I'll foller him; I will, by jingoes!"

"Now you're *talking!* Don't you ever weaken, Huck, and I won't."

CHAPTER XXVIII.

UNCLE JAKE

That night Tom and Huck were ready for their adventure. They hung about the neighborhood of the tavern until after nine, one watching the alley at a distance and the other the tavern door. Nobody entered the alley or left it; nobody resembling the Spaniard entered or left the tavern door. The night promised to be a fair one; so Tom went home with the understanding that if a considerable degree of darkness came on, Huck was to come and "maow," whereupon he would slip out and try the keys. But the night remained clear, and Huck closed his watch and retired to bed in an empty sugar hogshead about twelve.

Tuesday the boys had the same ill luck. Also Wednesday. But Thursday night promised better. Tom slipped out in good season with his aunt's old tin lantern, and a large towel to blindfold it with. He hid the lantern in Huck's sugar hogshead and the watch began. An hour before midnight the tavern closed up and its lights (the only ones thereabouts) were put out. No Spaniard had been seen. Nobody had entered or left the alley. Everything was auspicious. The blackness of darkness reigned, the perfect stillness was interrupted only by occasional mutterings of distant thunder.

HUCK AT HOME.

Tom got his lantern, lit it in the hogshead, wrapped it closely in the towel, and the two adventurers crept in the gloom toward the tavern. Huck stood sentry and Tom felt his way into the alley. Then there was a season of waiting anxiety that weighed upon Huck's spirits like a mountain. He began to wish he could see a flash from the lantern — it would frighten him, but it would at least tell him that Tom was alive yet. It seemed hours since Tom had disappeared. Surely he must have fainted; maybe he was dead; maybe his heart had burst under terror and excitement. In his uneasiness Huck found himself drawing closer and closer to the alley; fearing all sorts of dreadful things, and momentarily expecting some catastrophe to happen that would take away his breath. There was not much to take away, for he seemed only able to inhale it by thimblefuls, and his heart would soon wear itself out, the way it was beating. Suddenly there was a flash of light and Tom came tearing by him:

"Run!" said he; "run, for your life!"

He needn't have repeated it; once was enough; Huck was making thirty or forty miles an hour before the repetition was uttered. The boys never stopped till they reached the shed of a deserted slaughter-house at the lower end of the

village.   Just as they got within its shelter the storm burst and the rain poured
down.   As soon as Tom got his breath he said :

"Huck, it was awful!   I tried two of the keys, just as soft as I could; but they
seemed to make such a power of racket that I couldn't hardly get my breath I
was so scared.   They wouldn't turn in the lock, either.   Well, without noticing

THE HAUNTED ROOM.

what I was doing, I took hold of the knob, and open comes the door!   It warn't
locked!   I hopped in, and shook off the towel, and, *great Cæsar's ghost!*"

"What!—what 'd you see, Tom!"

"Huck, I most stepped onto Injun Joe's hand!"

"No!"

"Yes!   He was laying there, sound asleep on the floor, with his old patch on
his eye and his arms spread out."

"Lordy, what did you do?   Did he wake up?"

"No, never budged. Drunk, I reckon. I just grabbed that towel and started!"

" I'd never 'a' thought of the towel, I bet!"

"Well, *I* would. My aunt would make me mighty sick if I lost it."

"Say, Tom, did you see that box?"·

"Huck I didn't wait to look around. I didn't see the box, I didn't see the cross. I didn't see anything but a bottle and a tin cup on the floor by Injun Joe; yes, and I saw two barrels and lots more bottles in the room. Don't you see, now, what's the matter with that ha'nted room?"

"How?"

"Why it's ha'nted with whisky! Maybe *all* the Temperance Taverns have got a ha'nted room, hey Huck?"

"Well I reckon maybe that's so. Who'd 'a' thought such a thing? But say, Tom, now's a mighty good time to get that box, if Injun Joe's drunk."

"It is, that! You try it!"

Huck shuddered.

"Well, no—I reckon not."

"And *I* reckon not, Huck. Only one bottle alongside of Injun Joe ain't enough. If there'd been three, he'd be drunk enough and I'd do it."

There was a long pause for reflection, and then Tom said:

"Lookyhere, Huck, less not try that thing any more till we know Injun Joe's not in there. It's too scary. Now if we watch every night, we'll be dead sure to see him go out, some time or other, and then we'll snatch that box quicker'n lightning."

"Well, I'm agreed. I'll watch the whole night long, and I'll do it every night, too, if you'll do the other part of the job."

"All right, I will. All you got to do is to trot up Hooper street a block and maow—and if I'm asleep, you throw some gravel at the window and that'll fetch me."

"Agreed, and good as wheat!"

"Now Huck, the storm's over, and I'll go home. It'll begin to be daylight in a couple of hours. You go back and watch that long, will you?"

"I said I would, Tom, and I will. I'll ha'nt that tavern every night for a year! I'll sleep all day and I'll stand watch all night."

" That's all right.   Now where you going to sleep? "

" In Ben Rogers's hayloft.   He let's me, and so does his pap's nigger man, Uncle Jake.   I tote water for Uncle Jake whenever he wants me to, and any time I ask him he gives me a little something to eat if he can spare it.   That's a mighty good nigger, Tom.   He likes me, becuz I don't ever act as if I was above him.   Sometimes I've set right down and eat *with* him.   But you needn't tell that. A body's got to do things when he's awful hungry he wouldn't want to do as a steady thing."

" Well, if I don't want you in the day time, I'll let you sleep.   I won't come bothering around.   Any time you see something's up, in the night, just skip right around and maow."

CHAPTER XXIX.

The first thing Tom heard on Friday morning was a glad piece of news—Judge Thatcher's family had come back to town the night before. Both Injun Joe and the treasure sunk into secondary importance for a moment, and Becky took the chief place in the boy's interest. He saw her and they had an exhausting good time playing "hi-spy" and "gully-keeper" with a crowd of their schoolmates. The day was completed and crowned in a peculiarly satisfactory way: Becky teased her mother to appoint the next day for the long-promised and long-delayed picnic, and she consented. The child's delight was boundless; and Tom's not more moderate. The invitations were sent out before sunset, and straightway the young folks of the

McDOUGAL'S CAVE.

village were thrown into a fever of preparation and pleasurable anticipation. Tom's excitement enabled him to keep awake until a pretty late hour, and he had good hopes of hearing Huck's "maow," and of having his treasure to astonish Becky and the pic-nickers with, next day; but he was disappointed. No signal came that night.

Morning came, eventually, and by ten or eleven o'clock a giddy and rollicking company were gathered at Judge Thatcher's, and everything was ready for a start. It was not the custom for elderly people to mar pic-nics with their presence. The children were considered safe enough under the wings of a few young ladies of eighteen and a few young gentlemen of twenty-three or thereabouts. The old steam ferry-boat was chartered for the occasion; presently the gay throng filed up the main street laden with provision baskets. Sid was sick and had to miss the fun; Mary remained at home to entertain him. The last thing Mrs. Thatcher said to Becky, was—

"You'll not get back till late. Perhaps you'd better stay all night with some of the girls that live near the ferry landing, child."

"Then I'll stay with Susy Harper, mamma."

"Very well. And mind and behave yourself and don't be any trouble."

Presently, as they tripped along, Tom said to Becky:

"Say—I'll tell you what we'll do. 'Stead of going to Joe Harper's we'll climb right up the hill and stop at the Widow Douglas's. She'll have ice cream! She has it most every day—dead loads of it. And she'll be awful glad to have us."

"O, that will be fun!"

Then Becky reflected a moment and said:

"But what will mamma say?"

"How'll she ever know?"

The girl turned the idea over in her mind, and said reluctantly:

"I reckon it's wrong—but—"

"But shucks! Your mother won't know, and so what's the harm? All she wants is that you'll be safe; and I bet you she'd 'a' said go there if she'd 'a' thought of it. I know she would!"

The widow Douglas's splendid hospitality was a tempting bait. It and Tom's persuasions presently carried the day. So it was decided to say nothing to anybody about the night's programme. Presently it occurred to Tom that maybe Huck might come this very night and give the signal. The thought took a deal of the spirit out of his anticipations. Still he could not bear to give up the fun at Widow Douglas's. And why should he give it up, he reasoned—the signal did not come the night before, so why should it be any more likely to come to-night? The sure fun of the evening outweighed the uncertain treasure; and boy like, he determined to yield to the stronger inclination and not allow himself to think of the box of money another time that day.

Three miles below town the ferry-boat stopped at the mouth of a woody hollow and tied up. The crowd swarmed ashore and soon the forest distances and craggy heights echoed far and near with shoutings and laughter. All the different ways of getting hot and tired were gone through with, and by and by the rovers straggled back to camp fortified with responsible appetites, and then the destruction of the good things began. After the feast there was a refreshing season of rest and chat in the shade of spreading oaks. By and by somebody shouted—

"Who's ready for the cave?"

Everybody was. Bundles of candles were procured, and straightway there was a general scamper up the hill. The mouth of the cave was up the hillside—an opening shaped like a letter A. It's massive oaken door stood unbarred. Within was a small chamber, chilly as an ice-house, and walled by Nature with solid limestone that was dewy with a cold sweat. It was romantic and mysterious to stand here in the deep gloom and look out upon the green valley shining in the sun. But the impressiveness of the situation quickly wore off, and the romping began again. The moment a candle was lighted there was a general rush upon the owner of it; a struggle and a gallant defense followed, but the candle was soon knocked down or blown out, and then there was a glad clamor of laughter and a new chase. But all things have an end. By and by the procession went filing down the steep descent of the main avenue, the flickering rank of lights dimly revealing the lofty walls of rock almost to their point of junction sixty feet overhead. This main avenue was not more than eight or ten feet wide. Every few steps other lofty and still narrower crevices branched from it on either hand

—for McDougal's cave was but a vast labyrinth of crooked isles that ran into each other and out again and led nowhere. It was said that one might wander days and nights together through its intricate tangle of rifts and chasms, and never find the end of the cave; and that he might go down, and down, and still down, into the earth, and it was just the same—labyrinth underneath labyrinth, and no end to any of them. No man "knew" the cave. That was an impossible thing. Most of the young men knew a portion of it, and it was not customary to venture much beyond this known portion. Tom Sawyer knew as much of the cave as any one.

The procession moved along the main avenue some three-quarters of a mile, and then groups and couples began to slip aside into branch avenues, fly along the dismal corridors, and take each other by surprise at points where the corridors joined again. Parties were able to elude each other for the space of half an hour without going beyond the "known" ground.

By and by, one group after another came straggling back to the mouth of the cave, panting, hilarious, smeared from head to foot with tallow drippings, daubed with clay, and entirely delighted with the success of the day. Then they were astonished to find that they had been taking no note of time and that night was about at hand. The clanging bell had been calling for half an hour. However, this sort of close to the day's adventures was romantic and therefore satisfactory. When the ferry-boat with her wild freight pushed into the stream, nobody cared sixpence for the wasted time but the captain of the craft.

Huck was already upon his watch when the ferry-boat's lights went glinting past the wharf. He heard no noise on board, for the young people were as subdued and still as people usually are who are nearly tired to death. He wondered what boat it was, and why she did not stop at the wharf—and then he dropped her out of his mind and put his attention upon his business. The night was growing cloudy and dark. Ten o'clock came, and the noise of vehicles ceased, scattered lights began to wink out, all straggling foot passengers disappeared, the village betook itself to its slumbers and left the small watcher alone with the silence and the ghosts.

Eleven o'clock came, and the tavern lights were put out; darkness every-where, now. Huck waited what seemed a weary long time, but nothing happened. His faith was weakening. Was there any use? Was there really any use? Why not give it up and turn in?

A noise fell upon his ear. He was all attention in an instant. The alley door closed softly. He sprang to the corner of the brick store. The next moment two men brushed by him, and one seemed to have something under his arm. It must be that box! So they were going to re-move the treasure. Why call Tom now? It would be absurd—the men would get away with the box and never be found

HUCK ON DUTY.

again. No, he would stick to their wake and follow them; he would trust to the darkness for security from discovery. So communing with himself, Huck stepped out and glided along behind the men, cat-like, with bare feet, allowing them to keep just far enough ahead not to be invisible.

They moved up the river street three blocks, then turned to the left up a cross street. They went straight ahead, then, until they came to the path that led up Cardiff Hill; this they took. They passed by the old Welchman's house, half way up the hill without hesitating, and still climbed upward. Good, thought Huck, they will bury it in the old quarry. But they never stopped at the quarry. They passed on, up the summit. They plunged into the narrow path between the tall sumach bushes, and were at once hidden in the gloom. Huck closed up and shortened his distance, now, for they would never be able to see him. He trotted along a while; then slackened his pace, fearing he was gaining too fast; moved on a piece, then stopped altogether; listened; no sound; none, save that he seemed to hear the beating of his own heart. The hooting of an owl came from over the hill—ominous sound! But no footsteps. Heavens, was everything lost! He was about to spring with winged feet, when a man cleared his throat not four feet from him! Huck's heart shot into his throat, but he swallowed it again; and then he stood there shaking as if a dozen agues had taken charge of him at once, and so weak that he thought he must surely fall to the ground. He knew where he was. He knew he was within five steps of the stile leading into Widow Douglas's grounds. Very well, he thought, let them bury it there; it won't be hard to find.

Now there was a voice—a very low voice—Injun Joe's:

" Damn her, maybe she's got company—there's lights, late as it is."

" I can't see any."

This was that stranger's voice—the stranger of the haunted house. A deadly chill went to Huck's heart—this, then, was the "revenge" job! His thought was, to fly. Then he remembered that the Widow Douglas had been kind to him more than once, and maybe these men were going to murder her. He wished he dared venture to warn her; but he knew he didn't dare—they might come and catch him. He thought all this and more in the moment that elapsed between the stranger's remark and Injun Joe's next—which was—

" Because the bush is in your way. Now—this way—now you see, don't you?"

"Yes. Well there *is* company there, I reckon. Better give it up."

"Give it up, and I just leaving this country forever! Give it up and maybe never have another chance. I tell you again, as I've told you before, I don't care for her swag—you may have it. But her husband was rough on me—many times he was rough on me—and mainly he was the justice of the peace that jugged me for a vagrant. And that ain't all. It ain't a millionth part of it! He had me *horsewhipped!*—horsewhipped in front of the jail, like a nigger!—with all the town looking on! HORSEWHIPPED!—do you understand? He took advantage of me and died. But I'll take it out of *her*."

"Oh, don't kill her! Don't do that!"

"Kill? Who said anything about killing? I would kill *him* if he was here; but not her. When you want to get revenge on a woman you don't kill her— bosh! you go for her looks. You slit her nostrils—you notch her ears like a sow!"

"By God, that's—"

"Keep your opinion to yourself! It will be safest for you. I'll tie her to the bed. If she bleeds to death, is that my fault? I'll not cry, if she does. My friend, you'll help in this thing—for *my* sake—that's why you're here—I mightn't be able alone. If you flinch, I'll kill you. Do you understand that? And if I have to kill you, I'll kill her—and then I reckon nobody'll ever know much about who done this business."

"Well, if it's got to be done, let's get at it. The quicker the better—I'm all in a shiver."

"Do it *now?* And company there? Look here—I'll get suspicious of you, first thing you know. No—we'll wait till the lights are out—there's no hurry."

Huck felt that a silence was going to ensue—a thing still more awful than any amount of murderous talk; so he held his breath and stepped gingerly back; planted his foot carefully and firmly, after balancing, one-legged, in a precarious way and almost toppling over, first on one side and then on the other. He took another step back, with the same elaboration and the same risks; then another and another, and—a twig snapped under his foot! His breath stopped and he listened. There was no sound—the stillness was perfect. His gratitude was measureless. Now he turned in his tracks, between the walls of sumach bushes. —turned himself as carefully as if he were a ship—and then stepped quickly but cautiously along. When he emerged at the quarry he felt secure, and so he picked up his nimble heels and flew. Down, down he sped, till he reached the Welch-

A ROUSING ACT.

man's. He banged at the door, and presently the heads of the old man and his two stalwart sons were thrust from windows.

"What's the row there? Who's banging? What do you want?"

"Let me in—quick! I'll tell everything."

"Why who are you?"

"Huckleberry Finn—quick, let me in!"

"Huckleberry Finn, indeed! It ain't a name to open many doors, I judge! But let him in, lads, and let's see what's the trouble."

"Please don't ever tell *I* told you," were Huck's first words when he got in

"Please don't—I'd be killed, sure—but the Widow's been good friends to me sometimes, and I want to tell—I *will* tell if you'll promise you won't ever say it was me."

"By George he *has* got something to tell, or he wouldn't act so!" exclaimed the old man; "out with it and nobody here'll ever tell, lad."

Three minutes later the old man and his sons, well armed, were up the hill, and just entering the sumach path on tip-toe, their weapons in their hands. Huck accompanied them no further. He hid behind a great bowlder and fell to listening. There was a lagging, anxious silence, and then all of a sudden there was an explosion of firearms and a cry.

Huck waited for no particulars. He sprang away and sped down the hill as fast as his legs could carry him.

CHAPTER XXX.

As the earliest suspicion of dawn appeared on Sunday morning, Huck came groping up the hill and rapped gently at the old Welchman's door. The inmates were asleep but it was a sleep that was set on a hair-trigger, on account of the exciting episode of the night. A call came from a window—

"Who's there!"

Huck's scared voice answered in a low tone:

"Please let me in! It's only Huck Finn!"

"It's a name that can open this door night or day, lad!—and welcome!"

These were strange words to the vagabond boy's ears, and the pleasantest he had ever heard. He could not recollect that the closing word had ever been applied in his case before. The door

THE WELSHMAN.

226

was quickly unlocked, and he entered. Huck was given a seat and the old man and his brace of tall sons speedily dressed themselves.

" Now my boy I hope you're good and hungry, because breakfast will be ready as soon as the sun's up, and we'll have a piping hot one, too—make yourself easy about that! I and the boys hoped you'd turn up and stop here last night."

" I was awful scared," said Huck, " and I run. I took out when the pistols went off, and I didn't stop for three mile. I've come now becuz I wanted to know about it, you know; and I come before daylight becuz I didn't want to run acrost them devils, even if they was dead."

" Well, poor chap, you do look as if you'd **had a hard night of it**—but there's a bed here for you when you've had your breakfast. No, they ain't dead, lad—we are sorry enough for that. You see we knew right where to put our hands on them, by your description; so we crept along on tip-toe till we got within fifteen feet of them—dark as a cellar that sumach path was—and just then I found I was going to sneeze. It was the meanest kind of luck! I tried to keep it back, but no use—'twas bound to come, and it did come! I was in the lead with my pistol raised, and when the sneeze started those scoundrels a-rustling to get out of the path, I sung out, ' Fire, boys!' and blazed away at the place where the rustling was. So did the boys. But they were off in a

RESULT OF A SNEEZE.

jiffy, those villains, and we after them, down through the woods. I judge we never touched them. They fired a shot apiece as they started, but their bullets whizzed by and didn't do us any harm. As soon as we lost the sound of their feet we quit chasing, and went down and stirred up the constables. They got a posse together, and went off to guard the river bank, and as soon as it is light the sheriff and a gang are going to beat up the woods. My boys will be with them presently. I wish we had some sort of description of those rascals— 'twould help a good deal. But you could'nt see what they were like, in the dark, lad, I suppose?"

"O, yes, I saw them down town and follered them."

"Splendid! Describe them—describe them, my boy!"

"One's the old deaf and dumb Spaniard that's ben around here once or twice, and t'other's a mean looking ragged—"

"That's enough, lad, we know the men! Happened on them in the woods back of the widow's one day, and they slunk away. Off with you, boys, and tell the sheriff—get your breakfast to-morrow morning!"

The Welchman's sons departed at once. As they were leaving the room Huck sprang up and exclaimed:

"Oh, please don't tell *any*body it was me that blowed on them! Oh, please!"

"All right if you say it, Huck, but you ought to have the credit of what you did."

"Oh, no, no! Please don't tell!"

When the young men were gone, the old Welchman said—

"They won't tell—and I won't. But why don't you want it known?"

Huck would not explain, further than to say that he already knew too much about one of those men and would not have the man know that he knew anything against him for the whole world—he would be killed for knowing it, sure.

The old man promised secrecy once more, and said:

"How did you come to follow these fellows, lad? Were they looking suspicious?"

Huck was silent while he framed a duly cautious reply. Then he said:

"Well, you see, I'm a kind of a hard lot,—least everybody says so, and I don't see nothing agin it—and sometimes I can't sleep much, on accounts of thinking about it and sort of trying to strike out a new way of doing. That was the way of it last night. I couldn't sleep, and so I come along up street 'bout midnight, a-turning it all over, and when I got to that old shackly brick store by the Temperance Tavern, I backed up agin the wall to have another think. Well, just then along comes these two chaps slipping along close by me, with something under their arm and I reckoned they'd stole it. One was a-smoking, and t'other one wanted a light; so they stopped right before me and the cigars lit up their faces and I see that the big one was the deaf and dumb Spaniard, by his white whiskers and the patch on his eye, and t'other one was a rusty, ragged looking devil."

" Could you see the rags by the light of the cigars ? "

This staggered Huck for a moment. Then he said :

" Well, I don't know—but somehow it seems as if I did."

" Then they went on, and you—"

" Follered 'em—yes. That was it. I wanted to see what was up—they sneaked along so. I dogged 'em to the widder's stile, and stood in the dark and heard the ragged one beg for the widder, and the Spaniard swear he'd spile her looks just as I told you and your two—"

" What ! The *deaf and dumb* man said all that ! "

Huck had made another terrible mistake ! He was trying his best to keep the old man from getting the faintest hint of who the Spaniard might be, and yet his tongue seemed determined to get him into trouble in spite of all he could do. He made several efforts to creep out of his scrape, but the old man's eye was upon him and he made blunder after blunder. Presently the Welchman said :

CORNERED.

" My boy, don't be afraid of me. I wouldn't hurt a hair of your head for all the world. No—I'd protect you—I'd protect you. This Spaniard is not deaf and dumb; you've let that slip without intending it; you can't cover that up now. You know something about that Spaniard that you want to keep dark. Now trust me—tell me what it is, and trust me—I won't betray you."

Huck looked into the old man's honest eyes a moment, then bent over and whispered in his ear—

"'Tain't a Spaniard—it's Injun Joe!"

The Welchman almost jumped out of his chair. In a moment he said:

"It's all plain enough, now. When you talked about notching ears and slitting noses I judged that that was your own embellishment, because white men don't take that sort of revenge. But an Injun! That's a different matter altogether."

During breakfast the talk went on, and in the course of it the old man said that the last thing which he and his sons had done, before going to bed, was to get a lantern and examine the stile and its vicinity for marks of blood. They found none, but captured a bulky bundle of—

"Of WHAT?"

If the words had been lightning they could not have leaped with a more stunning suddenness from Huck's blanched lips. His eyes were staring wide, now, and his breath suspended—waiting for the answer. The Welchman started—stared in return—three seconds—five seconds—ten—then replied—

"Of burglar's tools. Why what's the *matter* with you?"

Huck sank back, panting gently, but deeply, unutterably grateful. The Welchman eyed him gravely, curiously—and presently said—

"Yes, burglar's tools. That appears to relieve you a good deal. But what did give you that turn? What were *you* expecting we'd found?"

Huck was in a close place—the inquiring eye was upon him—he would have given anything for material for a plausible answer—nothing suggested itself—the inquiring eye was boring deeper and deeper—a senseless reply offered—there was no time to weigh it, so at a venture he uttered it—feebly:

"Sunday-school books, maybe."

Poor Huck was too distressed to smile, but the old man laughed loud and joyously, shook up the details of his anatomy from head to foot, and ended by saying that such a laugh was money in a man's pocket, because it cut down the doctor's bills like everything. Then he added:

"Poor old chap, you're white and jaded—you ain't well a bit—no wonder you're a little flighty and off your balance. But you'll come out of it. Rest and sleep will fetch you out all right, I hope."

Huck was irritated to think he had been such a goose and betrayed such a suspicious excitement, for he had dropped the idea that the parcel brought from the tavern was the treasure, as soon as he had heard the talk at the widow's stile. He had only *thought* it was not the treasure, however—he had not known that it wasn't —and so the suggestion of a captured bundle was too much for his self-possession. But on the whole he felt glad the little episode had happened, for now he knew beyond all question that that bundle was not *the* bundle, and so his mind was at rest and exceedingly comfortable. In fact everything seemed to be drifting just in the right direction, now; the treasure must be still in No. 2, the men would be captured and jailed that day, and he and Tom could seize the gold that night without any trouble or any fear of interruption.

Just as breakfast was completed there was a knock at the door. Huck jumped for a hiding place, for he had no mind to be connected even remotely with the late event. The Welchman admitted several ladies and gentlemen, among them the widow Douglas, and noticed that groups of citzens were climbing up the hill—to stare at the stile. So the news had spread.

The Welchman had to tell the story of the night to the visitors. The widow's gratitude for her preservation was outspoken.

" Don't say a word about it madam. There's another that you're more beholden to than you are to me and my boys, maybe, but he don't allow me to tell his name. We wouldn't have been there but for him."

Of course this excited a curiosity so vast that it almost belittled the main matter—but the Welchman allowed it to eat into the vitals of his visitors, and through them be transmitted to the whole town, for he refused to part with his secret. When all else had been learned, the widow said :

"I went to sleep reading in bed and slept straight through all that noise. Why didn't you come and wake me ? "

"We judged it warn't worth while. Those fellows warn't likely to come again— they hadn't any tools left to work with, and what was the use of waking you up and scaring you to death ? My three negro men stood guard at your house all the rest of the night. They've just come back."

More visitors came, and the story had to be told and re-told for a couple of hours more.

There was no Sabbath-school during day-school vacation, but everybody was early at church. The stirring event was well canvassed. News came that not a sign of the two villains had been yet discovered. ·When the sermon was finished, Judge Thatcher's wife dropped alongside of Mrs. Harper as she moved down the aisle with the crowd and said:

"Is my Becky going to sleep all day? I just expected she would be tired to death."

"Your Becky?"

"Yes," with a startled look,—"didn't she stay with you last night?"

"Why, no."

Mrs. Thatcher turned pale, and sank into a pew, just as Aunt Polly, talking briskly with a friend, passed by. Aunt Polly said:

"Good morning, Mrs. Thatcher. Good morning Mrs. Harper. I've got a boy that's turned up missing. I reckon my Tom staid at your house last night—one of you. And now he's afraid to come to church. I've got to settle with him."

Mrs. Thatcher shook her head feebly and turned paler than ever.

"He didn't stay with us," said Mrs. Harper, beginning to look uneasy. A marked anxiety came into Aunt Polly's face.

"Joe Harper, have you seen my Tom this morning?"

"No'm."

ALARMING DISCOVERIES.

"When did you see him last?"

Joe tried to remember, but was not sure he could say. The people had stopped moving out of church. Whispers passed along, and a boding uneasiness took possession of every countenance. Children were anxiously questioned, and young teachers. They all said they had not noticed whether Tom and Becky were on board the ferry-boat on the homeward trip; it was dark; no one thought of inquiring if any one was missing. One young man finally blurted out his fear that they were still in the cave! Mrs. Thatcher swooned away. Aunt Polly fell to crying and wringing her hands.

The alarm swept from lip to lip, from group to group, from street to street, and within five minutes the bells were wildly clanging and the whole town was up! The Cardiff Hill episode sank into instant insignificance, the burglars were forgotten, horses were saddled, skiffs were manned, the ferry-boat ordered out, and

TOM AND BECKY STIR UP THE TOWN.

before the horror was half an hour old, two hundred men were pouring down high-road and river toward the cave.

All the long afternoon the village seemed empty and dead. Many women visited Aunt Polly and Mrs. Thatcher and tried to comfort them. They cried with them, too, and that was still better than words. All the tedious night the town waited for news; but when the morning dawned at last, all the word that came was, "Send more candles—and send food." Mrs. Thatcher was almost crazed; and Aunt Polly also. Judge Thatcher sent messages of hope and encouragement from the cave, but they conveyed no real cheer.

The old Welchman came home toward daylight, spattered with candle grease, smeared with clay, and almost worn out. He found Huck still in the bed that had been provided for him, and delirious with fever. The physicians were all at the cave, so the Widow Douglas came and took charge of the patient. She said she would do her best by him, because, whether he was good, bad, or indifferent, he was the Lord's, and nothing that was the Lord's was a thing to be neglected. The Welchman said Huck had good spots in him, and the widow said—

"You can depend on it. That's the Lord's mark. He don't leave it off. He never does. Puts it somewhere on every creature that comes from his hands."

Early in the forenoon parties of jaded men began to straggle into the village, but

TOM'S MARK.

the strongest of the citizens continued searching. All the news that could be gained was that remotenesses of the cavern were being ransacked that had never been visited before; that every corner and crevice was going to be thoroughly searched; that wherever one wandered through the maze of passages, lights were to be seen flitting hither and thither in the distance, and shoutings and pistol shots sent their hollow reverberations to the ear down the sombre aisles. In one place, far from the section usually traversed by tourists, the names "BECKY & TOM" had been found traced upon the rocky wall with candle smoke, and near at hand a grease-soiled bit of ribbon.

Mrs. Thatcher recognized the ribbon and cried over it. She said it was the last relic she should ever have of her child; and that no other memorial of her could ever be so precious, because this one parted latest from the living body before the awful death came. Some said that now and then, in the cave, a far-away speck of light would glimmer, and then a glorious shout would burst forth and a score of men go trooping down the echoing aisle—and then a sickening disappointment always followed; the children were not there; it was only a searcher's light.

Three dreadful days and nights dragged their tedious hours along, and the village sank into a hopeless stupor. No one had heart for anything. The acci-

dental discovery, just made, that the proprietor of the Temperance Tavern kept liquor on his premises, scarcely fluttered the public pulse, tremendous as the fact was. In a lucid interval, Huck feebly led up to the subject of taverns, and finally asked—dimly dreading the worst—if anything had been discovered at the Temperance Tavern since he had been ill?

"Yes," said the widow.

Huck started up in bed, wild-eyed:

"What! What was it?"

"Liquor!—and the place has been shut up. Lie down, child—what a turn you did give me!"

"Only tell me just one thing—only just one—please! Was it Tom Sawyer that found it?"

HUCK QUESTIONS THE WIDOW.

The widow burst into tears. "Hush, hush, child, hush! I've told you before, you must *not* talk. You are very, very sick!"

Then nothing but liquor had been found; there would have been a great powwow if it had been the gold. So the treasure was gone forever—gone forever! But what could she be crying about? Curious that she should cry.

These thoughts worked their dim way through Huck's mind, and under the weariness they gave him he fell asleep. The widow said to herself:

"There—he's asleep, poor wreck. Tom Sawyer find it! Pity but somebody could find Tom Sawyer! Ah, there ain't many left, now, that's got hope enough, or strength enough, either, to go on searching."

CHAPTER XXXI.

NOW to return to Tom and Becky's share in the pic-nic. They tripped along the murky aisles with the rest of the company, visiting the familiar wonders of the cave—wonders dubbed with rather over-descriptive names, such as "The Drawing-Room," "The Cathedral," "Aladdin's Palace," and so on. Presently the hide-and-seek frolicking began, and Tom and Becky engaged in it with zeal until the exertion began to grow a trifle wearisome; then they wandered down a sinuous avenue holding their candles aloft and reading the tangled web-work of names, dates, post-office addresses and mottoes with which the rocky walls had been frescoed (in candle smoke.) Still drifting along and talking, they scarcely noticed that they were now in a part of the cave whose walls were not frescoed.

They smoked their own names under an overhanging shelf and moved on. Presently they came to a place where a little stream of water, trickling over a ledge and carrying a limestone sediment with it, had, in the slow-dragging ages, formed a laced and ruffled Niagara in gleaming and imperishable stone. Tom squeezed his small body behind it in order to illuminate it for Becky's gratification. He found that it cur-

tained a sort of steep natural stairway which was enclosed between narrow walls, and at once the ambition to be a discoverer seized him. Becky respond-ed to his call, and they made a smoke-mark for future guidance, and started upon their quest. They wound this way and that, far down into the secret depths of the cave, made another mark, and branched off in search of novelties to tell the upper world about. In one place they found a spacious cavern, from whose ceiling depended a multi-tude of shining stalactites of the length and circumference of a man's leg; they walked all about it, wondering and ad-miring, and presently left it by one of the numerous passages that opened into it. This shortly brought them to a bewitching spring, whose basin was encrusted with a frost work of glitter-ing crystals; it was in the midst of a

WONDERS OF THE CAVE.

cavern whose walls were supported by many fantastic pillars which had been formed by the joining of great stalactites and stalagmites together, the result of the ceaseless water-drip of centuries. Under the roof vast knots of bats had packed themselves together, thousands in a bunch; the lights disturbed

the creatures and they came flocking down by hundreds, squeaking and dart-
ing furiously at the candles.   Tom knew their ways and the danger of this sort
of conduct.   He siezed Becky's hand and hurried her into the first corridor
that offered; and none too soon, for a bat struck Becky's light out with its

ATTACKED BY NATIVES.

wing while she was passing out of the cavern.   The bats chased the children
a good distance; but the fugitives plunged into every new passage that offered,
and at last got rid of the perilous things.   Tom found a subterranean lake,
shortly, which stretched its dim length away until its shape was lost in the
shadows.   He wanted to explore its borders, but concluded that it would be

best to sit down and rest a while, first. Now, for the first time, the deep stillness
of the place laid a clammy hand upon the spirits of the children. Becky said—

"Why, I didn't notice, but it seems ever so long since I heard any of the
others."

"Come to think, Becky, we are away down below them—and I don't know
how far away north, or south, or east, or whichever it is. We couldn't hear
them here."

Becky grew apprehensive.

"I wonder how long we've been down here, Tom. We better start back."

"Yes, I reckon we better. P'raps we better."

"Can you find the way, Tom? It's all a mixed-up crookedness to me."

"I reckon I could find it—but then the bats. If they put both our candles
out it will be an awful fix. Let's try some other way, so as not to go through
there."

"Well. But I hope we won't get lost. It would be so awful!" and the
girl shuddered at the thought of the dreadful possibilities.

They started through a corridor, and traversed it in silence a long way,
glancing at each new opening, to see if there was anything familiar about the
look of it; but they were all strange. Every time Tom made an examination,
Becky would watch his face for an encouraging sign, and he would say
cheerily—

"Oh, it's all right. This ain't the one, but we'll come to it right away!"

But he felt less and less hopeful with each failure, and presently began to
turn off into diverging avenues at sheer random, in desperate hope of finding
the one that was wanted. He still said it was "all right," but there was such
a leaden dread at his heart, that the words had lost their ring and sounded just
as if he had said, "All is lost!" Becky clung to his side in an anguish of fear,
and tried hard to keep back the tears, but they would come. At last she said:

"O, Tom, never mind the bats, let's go back that way! We seem to get
worse and worse off all the time."

Tom stopped.

"Listen!" said he.

Profound silence; silence so deep that even their breathings were conspicuous. in the hush. Tom shouted. The call went echoing down the empty aisles and died out in the distance in a faint sound that resembled a ripple of mocking laughter.

"Oh, don't do it again, Tom, it is too. horrid," said Becky.

"It is horrid, but I better, Becky; they *might* hear us, you know " and he shouted again.

The " might " was even a chillier horror than the ghostly laughter, it so confessed a perishing hope. The children stood still and listened; but there was no result. Tom turned upon the back track at once, and hurried his steps. It was but a little while before a certain indecision in his manner revealed

DESPAIR.

another fearful fact to Becky—he could not find his way back!

"O, Tom, you didn't make any marks! "

"Becky I was such a fool! Such a fool! I never thought we might want to come back! No—I can't find the way. It's all mixed up."

"Tom, Tom, we're lost! we're lost! We never can get out of this awful place! O, why *did* we ever leave the others! "

She sank to the ground and burst into such a frenzy of crying that Tom was appalled with the idea that she might die, or lose her reason. He sat down by her and put his arms around her; she buried her face in his bosom, she clung to him, she poured out her terrors, her unavailing regrets, and the far echoes turned them all to jeering laughter. Tom begged her to pluck up hope again, and she said she could not. He fell to blaming and abusing himself for getting her into this miserable situation; this had a better effect.

She said she would try to hope again, she would get up and follow wherever he might lead if only he would not talk like that any more. For he was no more to blame than she, she said.

So they moved on, again—aimlessly—simply at random—all they could do was to move, keep moving. For a little while, hope made a show of reviving—not with any reason to back it, but only because it is its nature to revive when the spring has not been taken out of it by age and familiarity with failure.

By and by Tom took Becky's candle and blew it out. This economy meant so much! Words were not needed. Becky understood, and her hope died again. She knew that Tom had a whole candle and three or four pieces in his pockets—yet he must economise.

By and by, fatigue began to assert its claims; the children tried to pay no attention, for it was dreadful to think of sitting down when time was grown to be so precious; moving, in some direction, in any direction, was at least progress and might bear fruit; but to sit down was to invite death and shorten its pursuit.

At last Becky's frail limbs refused to carry her farther. She sat down. Tom rested with her, and they talked of home, and the friends there, and the comfortable beds and above all, the light! Becky cried, and Tom tried to think of some way of comforting her, but all his encouragements were grown threadbare with use, and sounded like sarcasms. Fatigue bore so heavily upon Becky that she drowsed off to sleep. Tom was grateful. He sat looking into her drawn face and saw it grow smooth and natural under the influence of pleasant dreams; and by and by a smile dawned and rested there. The peaceful face reflected somewhat of peace and healing into his own spirit, and his thoughts wandered away to by-gone times and dreamy memories. While he was deep in his musings, Becky woke up with a breezy little laugh—but it was stricken dead upon her lips, and a groan followed it.

"Oh, how *could* I sleep! I wish I never, never had waked! No! No, I don't, Tom! Don't look so! I won't say it again."

"I'm glad you've slept, Becky; you'll feel rested, now, and we'll find the way out."

16

"We can try, Tom; but I've seen such a beautiful country in my dream. I reckon we are going there."

"Maybe not, maybe not. Cheer up, Becky, and let's go on trying."

They rose up and wandered along, hand in hand and hopeless. They tried to estimate how long they had been in the cave, but all they knew was that it seemed days and weeks, and yet it was plain that this could not be, for their candles were not gone yet. A long time after this—they could not tell how long—Tom said they must go softly and listen for dripping water—they must find a spring. They found one presently, and Tom said it was time to rest again. Both were cruelly tired, yet Becky said she thought she could go on a little farther. She was surprised to hear Tom dissent. She could not understand it. They sat down, and Tom fastened his candle to the wall in front of

THE WEDDING CAKE.

them with some clay. Thought was soon busy; nothing was said for some time. Then Becky broke the silence:

"Tom, I am so hungry!"

Tom took something out of his pocket.

"Do you remember this?" said he.

Becky almost smiled.

"It's our wedding cake, Tom."

"Yes—I wish it was as big as a barrel, for it's all we've got."

"I saved it from the pic-nic for us to dream on, Tom, the way grown-up people do with wedding cake—but it'll be our—"

She dropped the sentence where it was. Tom divided the cake and Becky ate with good appetite, while Tom nibbled at his moiety. There was abundance of cold water to finish the feast with. By and by Becky suggested that they move on again. Tom was silent a moment. Then he said:

" Becky, can you bear it if I tell you something ? "

Becky's face paled, but she thought she could.

" Well then, Becky, we must stay here, where there's water to drink. That little piece is our last candle ! "

Becky gave loose to tears and wailings. Tom did what he could to comfort her but with little effect. At length Becky said :

" Tom ! "

" Well, Becky ? "

" They'll miss us and hunt for us ! "

" Yes, they will ! Certainly they will ! "

" Maybe they're hunting for us now, Tom."

" Why I reckon maybe they are. I hope they are."

" When would they miss us, Tom ? "

" When they get back to the boat, I reckon."

" Tom, it might be dark, then—would they notice we hadn't come ? "

" I don't know. But anyway, your mother would miss you as soon as they got home."

A frightened look in Becky's face brought Tom to his senses and he saw that he had made a blunder. Becky was not to have gone home that night ! The children became silent and thoughtful. In a moment a new burst of grief from Becky showed Tom that the thing in his mind had struck hers also—that the Sabbath morning might be half spent before Mrs. Thatcher discovered that Becky was not at Mrs. Harper's.

The children fastened their eyes upon their bit of candle and watched it melt slowly and pitilessly away; saw the half inch of wick stand alone at last ; saw the feeble flame rise and fall, climb the thin column of smoke, linger at its top a moment, and then—the horror of utter darkness reigned !

How long afterward it was that Becky came to a slow consciousness that she was crying in Tom's arms, neither could tell. All that they knew was, that after what seemed a mighty stretch of time, both awoke out of a dead stupor of sleep and resumed their miseries once more. Tom said it might be Sunday, now—maybe Monday. He tried to get Becky to talk, but her sorrows were too oppressive, all her hopes were gone. Tom said that they must have been missed long ago, and no doubt the search was going on. He would shout and maybe some one would come. He tried it; but in the darkness the distant echoes sounded so hideously that he tried it no more.

The hours wasted away, and hunger came to torment the captives again. A portion of Tom's half of the cake was left; they divided and ate it. But they seemed hungrier than before. The poor morsel of food only whetted desire.

By and by Tom said:

"*Sh!* Did you hear that?"

Both held their breath and listened. There was a sound like the faintest, far-off shout. Instantly Tom answered it, and leading Becky by the hand, started groping down the corridor in its direction. Presently he listened again; again the sound was heard, and apparently a little nearer.

"It's them!" said Tom; "they're coming! Come along Becky—we're all right now!"

The joy of the prisoners was almost overwhelming. Their speed was slow, however, because pitfalls were somewhat common, and had to be guarded against. They shortly came to one and had to stop. It might be three feet deep, it might be a hundred—there was no passing it at any rate. Tom got down on his breast and reached as far down as he could. No bottom. They must stay there and wait until the searchers came. They listened; evidently the distant shoutings were growing more distant! a moment or two more and they had gone altogether. The heart-sinking misery of it! Tom whooped until he was hoarse, but it was of no use. He talked hopefully to Becky; but an age of anxious waiting passed and no sounds came again.

The children groped their way back to the spring. The weary time dragged on; they slept again, and awoke famished and woe-stricken. Tom believed it must be Tuesday by this time.

Now an idea struck him. There were some side passages near at hand. It would be better to explore some of these than bear the weight of the heavy time in idleness. He took a kite-line from his pocket, tied it to a projection, and he and Becky started, Tom in the lead, unwinding the line as he groped

along.   At the end of twenty steps the corridor ended in a "jumping-off place."
Tom got down on his knees and felt below, and then as far around the corner
as he could reach with his hands conveniently; he made an effort to stretch
yet a little further to the right, and at that moment, not twenty yards away, a
human hand, holding a candle, appeared from behind a rock!   Tom lifted up
a glorious shout, and instantly that hand was followed by the body it belonged

A NEW TERROR.

to—Injun Joe's!   Tom was paralyzed; he could not move.   He was vastly
gratified the next moment, to see the "Spaniard" take to his heels and get
himself out of sight.   Tom wondered that Joe had not recognized his voice
and come over and killed him for testifying in court.   But the echoes must
have disguised the voice.   Without doubt, that was it, he reasoned.   Tom's

fright weakened every muscle in his body.   He said to himself that if he had strength enough to get back to the spring he would stay there, and nothing should tempt him to run the risk of meeting Injun Joe again.   He was careful to keep from Becky what it was he had seen.   He told her he had only shouted " for luck."

But hunger and wretchedness rise superior to fears in the long run.   Another tedious wait at the spring and another long sleep brought changes.   The children awoke tortured with a raging hunger.   Tom believed that it must be Wednesday or Thursday or even Friday or Saturday, now, and that the search had been given over.   He proposed to explore another passage.   He felt willing to risk Injun Joe and all other terrors.   But Becky was very weak. She had sunk into a dreary apathy and would not be roused.   She said she would wait, now, where she was, and die—it would not be long.   She told Tom to go with the kite-line and explore if he chose; but she implored him to come back every little while and speak to her; and she made him promise that when the awful time came, he would stay by her and hold her hand until all was over.

Tom kissed her, with a choking sensation in his throat, and made a show of being confident of finding the searchers or an escape from the cave; then he took the kite-line in his hand and went groping down one of the passages on his hands and knees, distressed with hunger and sick with bodings of coming **doom.**

CHAPTER XXXII.

DAYLIGHT.

TUESDAY afternoon came, and waned to the twilight. The village of St. Petersburg still mourned. The lost children had not been found. Public prayers had been offered up for them, and many and many a private prayer that had the petitioner's whole heart in it; but still no good news came from the cave. The majority of the searchers had given up the quest and gone back to their daily avocations, saying that it was plain the children could never be found. Mrs. Thatcher was very ill, and a great part of the time delirious. People said it was heartbreaking to hear her call her child, and raise her head and listen a whole minute at a time, then lay it wearily down again with a moan. Aunt Polly had drooped into a settled melancholy, and her gray hair had grown almost white. The village went to its rest on Tuesday night, sad and forlorn.

247

Away in the middle of the night a wild peal burst from the village bells, and in a moment the streets were swarming with frantic half-clad people, who shouted, "Turn out! turn out! they're found! they're found!" Tin pans and horns were added to the din, the population massed itself and moved toward the river, met the children coming in an open carriage drawn by shouting citizens, thronged

THE "TURN OUT" TO RECEIVE TOM AND BECKY.

around it, joined its homeward march, and swept magnificently up the main street roaring huzzah after huzzah!

The village was illuminated; nobody went to bed again; it was the greatest night the little town had ever seen. During the first half hour a procession of villagers filed through Judge Thatcher's house, siezed the saved ones and kissed them, squeezed Mrs. Thatcher's hand, tried to speak but couldn't—and drifted out raining tears all over the place.

Aunt Polly's happiness was complete, and Mrs. Thatcher's nearly so. It would be complete, however, as soon as the messenger dispatched with the great news to the cave should get the word to her husband. Tom lay upon a sofa with an eager auditory about him and told the history of the wonderful adventure, putting in many striking additions to adorn it withal; and closed with a description of how he left Becky and went on an exploring expedition; how he followed two avenues as far as his kite-line would reach; how he followed a third to the fullest stretch of the kite-line, and was about to turn back when he glimpsed a far-off speck that looked like daylight; dropped the line and groped toward it, pushed his head and

THE ESCAPE FROM THE CAVE.

shoulders through a small hole and saw the broad Mississippi rolling by! And if it had only happened to be night he would not have seen that speck of daylight and would not have explored that passage any more! He told how he went back for Becky and broke the good news and she told him not to fret her with such stuff, for she was tired, and knew she was going to die, and wanted to. He described

how he labored with her and convinced her; and how she almost died for joy
when she had groped to where she actually saw the blue speck of daylight; how
he pushed his way out at the hole and then helped her out; how they sat there
and cried for gladness; how some men came along in a skiff and Tom hailed them
and told them their situation and their famished condition; how the men didn't
believe the wild tale at first, "because," said they, "you are five miles down the
river below the valley the cave is in"—then took them aboard, rowed to a house,
gave them supper, made them rest till two or three hours after dark and then
brought them home.

Before day-dawn, Judge Thatcher and the handful of searchers with him were
tracked out, in the cave, by the twine clews they had strung behind them, and
informed of the great news.

Three days and nights of toil and hunger in the cave were not to be shaken off
at once, as Tom and Becky soon discovered. They were bedridden all of Wednesday and Thursday, and seemed to grow more and more tired and worn, all the
time. Tom got about, a little, on Thursday, was down town Friday, and nearly as
whole as ever Saturday; but Becky did not leave her room until Sunday, and then
she looked as if she had passed through a wasting illness.

Tom learned of Huck's sickness and went to see him on Friday, but could not
be admitted to the bedroom; neither could he on Saturday or Sunday. He was
admitted daily after that, but was warned to keep still about his adventure and
introduce no exciting topic. The widow Douglas staid by to see that he obeyed.
At home Tom learned of the Cardiff Hill event; also that the " ragged man's "
body had eventually been found in the river near the ferry landing; he had been
drowned while trying to escape, perhaps.

About a fortnight after Tom's rescue from the cave, he started off to visit Huck,
who had grown plenty strong enough, now, to hear exciting talk, and Tom had
some that would interest him, he thought. Judge Thatcher's house was on Tom's
way, and he stopped to see Becky. The Judge and some friends set Tom to
talking, and some one asked him ironically if he wouldn't like to go to the cave
again. Tom said he thought he wouldn't mind it. The Judge said:

"Well, there are others just like you, Tom, I've not the least doubt. But we have taken care of that. Nobody will get lost in that cave any more."

"Why?"

"Because I had its big door sheathed with boiler iron two weeks ago, and triple-locked—and I've got the keys."

Tom turned as white as a sheet.

"What's the matter, boy! Here, run, somebody! Fetch a glass of water!"

The water was brought and thrown into Tom's face.

"Ah, now you're all right. What was the matter with you, Tom?"

"Oh, Judge, Injun Joe's in the cave!"

CHAPTER XXXIII.

WITHIN a few minutes the news had spread, and a dozen skiff-loads of men were on their way to McDougal's cave, and the ferry-boat, well filled with passengers, soon followed. Tom Sawyer was in the skiff that bore Judge Thatcher.

When the cave door was unlocked, a sorrowful sight presented itself in the dim twilight of the place. Injun Joe lay stretched upon the ground, dead, with his face close to the crack of the door, as if his longing eyes had been fixed, to the latest moment, upon the light and the cheer of the free world outside. Tom was touched, for he knew by his own experience how this wretch had suffered. His pity was moved, but nevertheless he felt an abounding sense of relief and security, now, which revealed to him in a degree which he had not fully appreciated before how vast a weight of dread had been lying upon him since the day he lifted his voice against this bloody-minded outcast.

Injun Joe's bowie knife lay close by, its blade broken in two. The great foundation-beam of the door had been chipped and hacked through, with tedious labor; useless labor, too, it was, for the native rock formed a sill outside it, and upon that stubborn material the knife had wrought no effect; the only damage done was to the knife itself. But if there had been no stony obstruction there the labor would

CAUGHT AT LAST.

have been useless still, for if the beam had been wholly cut away Injun Joe could not have squeezed his body under the door, and he knew it. So he had only hacked that place in order to be doing something—in order to pass the weary time—in order to employ his tortured faculties. Ordinarily one could find half a dozen bits of candle stuck around in the crevices of this vestibule, left there by tourists; but there were none now. The prisoner had searched them out and eaten them. He had also contrived to catch a few bats, and these, also, he had eaten, leaving only their claws. The poor unfortunate had starved to death. In one place near at hand, a stalagmite had been slowly growing up from the ground for ages, builded by the water-drip from a stalactite overhead. The captive had broken

DROP AFTER DROP.

off the stalagmite, and upon the stump had placed a stone, wherein he had scooped a shallow hollow to catch the precious drop that fell once in every three minutes with the dreary regularity of a clock-tick—a dessert spoonful once in four and twenty hours. That drop was falling when the Pyramids were new; when Troy fell; when the foundations of Rome were laid; when Christ was crucified; when the Conqueror created the British empire; when Columbus sailed; when the massacre at Lexington was "news." It is falling now; it will still be falling when all these things shall have sunk down the afternoon of history, and the twilight of tradition, and been swallowed up in the thick night of oblivion. Has everything a purpose and a mission? Did this drop fall patiently during five thousand years to be ready for this flitting human insect's need? and has it another important object to accomplish ten thousand years to come? No matter. It is many and many a year since the hapless half-breed scooped out the stone to catch the priceless drops, but to this day the tourist stares longest at that pathetic stone and that slow dropping water when he comes to see the wonders of McDougal's cave. Injun Joe's cup stands first in the list of the cavern's marvels; even "Aladdin's Palace" cannot rival it.

Injun Joe was buried near the mouth of the cave; and people flocked there in boats and wagons from the towns and from all the farms and hamlets for seven miles around; they brought their children, and all sorts of provisions, and confessed that they had had almost as satisfactory a time at the funeral as they could have had at the hanging.

This funeral stopped the further growth of one thing—the petition to the Governor for Injun Joe's pardon. The petition had been largely signed; many tearful and eloquent meetings had been held, and a committee of sappy women been

HAVING A GOOD TIME.

appointed to go in deep mourning and wail around the governor, and implore him to be a merciful ass and trample his duty under foot. Injun Joe was believed to have killed five citizens of the village, but what of that? If he had been Satan himself there would have been plenty of weaklings ready to scribble their names to a pardon-petition, and drip a tear on it from their permanently impaired and leaky water-works.

The morning after the funeral Tom took Huck to a private place to have an important talk. Huck had learned all about Tom's adventure from the Welchman and the widow Douglas, by this time, but Tom said he reckoned there was one thing they had not told him; that thing was what he wanted to talk about now. Huck's face saddened. He said:

"I know what it is. You got into No. 2 and never found anything but whisky. Nobody told me it was you; but I just knowed it must 'a' ben you, soon as I heard 'bout that whisky business; and I knowed you hadn't got the money becuz you'd 'a' got at me some way or other and told me even if you was mum to everybody else. Tom, something's always told me we'd never get holt of that swag."

"Why Huck, *I* never told on that tavern-keeper. *You* know his tavern was all right the Saturday I went to the pic-nic. Don't you remember you was to watch there that night?"

"Oh, yes! Why it seems 'bout a year ago. It was that very night that I follered Injun Joe to the widder's."

" *You* followed him?"

"Yes—but you keep mum. I reckon Injun Joe's left friends behind him, and I don't want 'em souring on me and doing me mean tricks. If it hadn't ben for me he'd be down in Texas now, all right."

Then Huck told his entire adventure in confidence to Tom, who had only heard of the Welchmen's part of it before.

"Well," said Huck, presently, coming back to the main question, "whoever nipped the whisky in No. 2, nipped the money too, I reckon—anyways it's a goner for us, Tom."

"Huck, that money wasn't ever in No. 2!"

"What!" Huck searched his comrade's face keenly. "Tom, have you got on the track of that money again?"

"Huck, it's in the cave!"

Huck's eyes blazed.

"Say it again, Tom!"

"The money's in the cave!"

"Tom,—honest injun, now—is it fun, or earnest?"

"Earnest, Huck—just as earnest as ever I was in my life. Will you go in there with me and help get it out?"

"I bet I will! I will if it's where we can blaze our way to it and not get lost."

"Huck, we can do that without the least little bit of trouble in the world."

"Good as wheat! What makes you think the money's — "

"Huck, you just wait till we get in there. If we don't find it I'll agree to give you my drum and everything I've got in the world. I will, by jings."

"All right—it's a whiz. When do you say?"

"Right now, if you say it. Are you strong enough?"

"Is it far in the cave? I ben on my pins a little, three or four days, now, but I can't walk more'n a mile, Tom—least I don't think I could."

A BUSINESS TRIP.

17

"It's about five mile into there the way anybody but me would go, Huck, but there's a mighty short cut that they don't anybody but me know about. Huck, I'll take you right to it in a skiff. I'll float the skiff down there, and I'll pull it back again all by myself. You needn't ever turn your hand over."

"Less start right off, Tom."

"All right. We want some bread and meat, and our pipes, and a little bag or two, and two or three kite-strings, and some of these new fangled things they call lucifer matches. I tell you many's the time I wished I had some when I was in there before."

A trifle after noon the boys borrowed a small skiff from a citizen who was absent, and got under way at once. When they were several miles below "Cave Hollow," Tom said:

"Now you see this bluff here looks all alike all the way down from the cave hollow—no houses, no wood-yards, bushes all alike. But do you see that white place up yonder where there's been a land-slide? Well that's one of my marks. We'll get ashore, now."

They landed.

"Now Huck, where we're a-standing you could touch that hole I got out of with a fishing-pole. See if you can find it."

Huck searched all the place about, and found nothing. Tom proudly marched into a thick clump of sumach bushes and said—

"Here you are!   Look at it, Huck; it's the snuggest hole in this country.   You just keep mum about it.   All along I've been wanting to be a robber, but I knew I'd got to have a thing like this, and where to run across it was the bother.   We've got it now, and we'll keep it quiet, only we'll let Joe Harper and Ben Rogers in— because of course there's got to be a Gang, or else there wouldn't be any style about it.   Tom Sawyer's Gang—it sounds splendid, don't it, Huck?"

"Well, it just does, Tom.   And who'll we rob?"

"Oh, most anybody.   Waylay people—that's mostly the way."

"And kill them?"

"No—not always.   Hive them in the cave till they raise a ransom."

"What's a ransom?"

"Money.   You make them raise all they can, off'n their friends; and after you've kept them a year, if it ain't raised then you kill them.   That's the general way.   Only you don't kill the women.   You shut up the women, but you don't kill them.   They're always beautiful and rich, and awfully scared.   You take their watches and things, but you always take your hat off and talk polite.   They ain't anybody as polite as robbers—you'll see that in any book.   Well the women get to loving you, and after they've been in the cave a week or two weeks they stop crying and after that you couldn't get them to leave.   If you drove them out they'd turn right around and come back.   It's so in all the books."

"Why it's real bully, Tom.   I b'lieve it's better'n to be a pirate."

"Yes, it's better in some ways, because it's close to home and circuses and all that."

By this time everything was ready and the boys entered the hole, Tom in the lead.   They toiled their way to the farther end of the tunnel, then made their spliced kite-strings fast and moved on.   A few steps brought them to the spring and Tom felt a shudder quiver all through him.   He showed Huck the fragment of candle-wick perched on a lump of clay against the wall, and described how he and Becky had watched the flame struggle and expire.

The boys began to quiet down to whispers, now, for the stillness and gloom of the place oppressed their spirits.   They went on, and presently entered and followed

Tom's other corridor until they reached the "jumping-off place." The candles revealed the fact that it was not really a precipice, but only a steep clay hill twenty or thirty feet high. Tom whispered—

"Now I'll show you something, Huck."

He held his candle aloft and said—

"Look as far around the corner as you can. Do you see that? There—on the big rock over yonder—done with candle smoke."

"Tom, its a *cross!*"

"*Now* where's your Number Two? '*Under the cross,*' hey? Right yonder's where I saw Injun Joe poke up his candle, Huck!"

Huck stared at the mystic sign a while, and then said with a shaky voice—

"Tom, less git out of here!"

"What! and leave the treasure?",

"Yes—leave it. Injun Joe's ghost is round about there, certain."

"No it ain't, Huck, no it ain't. It would ha'nt the place where he died—away out at the mouth of the cave—five mile from here."

"No, Tom, it wouldn't. It would hang round the money. I know the ways of ghosts, and so do you."

Tom began to fear that Huck was right. Misgivings gathered in his mind. But presently an idea occurred to him—

"Looky here, Huck, what fools we're making of ourselves! Injun Joe's ghost ain't a going to come around where there's a cross!"

The point was well taken. It had its effect.

"Tom I didn't think of that. But that's so. It's luck for us, that cross is. I reckon we'll climb down there and have a hunt for that box."

Tom went first, cutting rude steps in the clay hill as he descended. Huck followed. Four avenues opened out of the small cavern which the great rock stood in. The boys examined three of them with no result. They found a small recess in the one nearest the base of the rock, with a pallet of blankets spread down in it; also an old suspender, some bacon rhind, and the well gnawed bones of two or three fowls. But there was no money box. The lads searched and re-searched this place, but in vain. Tom said:

"He said *under* the cross. Well, this comes nearest to being under the cross. It can't be under the rock itself, because that sets solid on the ground."

They searched everywhere once more, and then sat down discouraged. Huck could suggest nothing. By and by Tom said:

"Looky here, Huck, there's foot-prints and some candle grease on the clay about one side of this rock, but not on the other sides. Now what's that for? I bet you the money *is* under the rock. I'm going to dig in the clay."

"That ain't no bad notion, Tom!" said Huck with animation.

Tom's "real Barlow" was out at once, and he had not dug four inches before he struck wood.

"Hey, Huck!—you hear that?"

Huck began to dig and scratch now. Some boards were soon uncovered and removed. They had concealed a natural chasm which led under the rock. Tom got into this and held his candle as far under the rock as he could, but said he could not see to the end of the rift. He proposed to explore. He stooped and passed under; the narrow way descended gradually. He followed its winding course, first to the right, then to the left, Huck at his heels. Tom turned a short curve, by and by, and exclaimed—

"My goodness, Huck, looky here!"

It was the treasure box, sure enough, occupying a snug little cavern, along with an empty powder keg, a couple of guns in leather cases, two or three pairs of old moccasins, a leather belt, and some other rubbish well soaked with the water-drip.

"Got it at last!" said Huck, plowing among the tarnished coins with his hand. "My, but we're rich, Tom!"

"Huck, I always reckoned we'd get it. It's just too good to believe, but we *have* got it, sure! Say—let's not fool around here. Let's snake it out. Lemme see if I can lift the box."

It weighed about fifty pounds. Tom could lift it, after an awkward fashion, but could not carry it conveniently.

"I thought so," he said; *they* carried it like it was heavy, that day at the ha'nted house. I noticed that. I reckon I was right to think of fetching the little bags along."

The money was soon in the bags and the boys took it up to the cross-rock.

" Now less fetch the guns and things," said Huck.

"No, Huck—leave them there. They're just the tricks to have when we go to robbing. We'll keep them there all the time, and we'll hold our orgies there, too. It's an awful snug place for orgies."

" What's orgies? "

"*I* dono. But robbers always have orgies, and of course we've got to have

" GOT IT AT LAST ! "

them, too. Come along, Huck, we've been in here a long time. It's getting late, I reckon. I'm hungry, too. We'll eat and smoke when we get to the skiff."

They presently emerged into the clump of sumach bushes, looked warily out, found the coast clear, and were soon lunching and smoking in the skiff. As the sun dipped toward the horizon they pushed out and got under way. Tom skimmed up the shore through the long twilight, chatting cheerily with Huck, and landed shortly after dark.

"Now Huck," said Tom, "we'll hide the money in the loft of the widow's wood-shed, and I'll come up in the morning and we'll count it and divide, and then we'll hunt up a place out in the woods for it where it will be safe. Just you lay quiet here and watch the stuff till I run and hook Benny Taylor's little wagon; I won't be gone a minute."

He disappeared, and presently returned with the wagon, put the two small sacks into it, threw some old rags on top of them, and started off, dragging his cargo behind him. When the boys reached the Welchman's house, they stopped to rest. Just as they were about to move on, the Welchman stepped out and said:

"Hallo, who's that?"

"Huck and Tom Sawyer."

"Good! Come along with me, boys, you are keeping everybody waiting. Here—hurry up, trot ahead—I'll haul the wagon for you. Why, it's not as light as it might be. Got bricks in it?—or old metal?"

"Old metal," said Tom.

"I judged so; the boys in this town will take more trouble and fool away more time, hunting up six bit's worth of old iron to sell to the foundry than they would to make twice the money at regular work. But that's human nature —hurry along, hurry along!"

The boys wanted to know what the hurry was about.

"Never mind; you'll see, when we get to the Widow Douglas's."

Huck said with some apprehension—for he was long used to being falsely accused—

"Mr. Jones, *we* haven't been doing nothing."

The Welchman laughed.

"Well, I don't know, Huck, my boy. I don't know about that. Ain't **you** and the widow good friends?"

"Yes. Well, she's ben good friends to me, any ways."

"All right, then. What do you want to be afraid for?"

This question was not entirely answered in Huck's slow mind before he found himself pushed, along with Tom, into Mrs. Douglas's drawing-room. Mr. Jones left the wagon near the door and followed.

The place was grandly lighted, and everybody that was of any consequence in the village was there. The Thatchers were there, the Harpers, the Rogerses, Aunt Polly, Sid, Mary, the minister, the editor, and a great many more, and all dressed in their best. The widow received the boys as heartily as any one could well receive two such looking beings. They were covered with clay and candle grease. Aunt Polly blushed crimson with humiliation, and frowned and shook her head at Tom. Nobody suffered half as much as the two boys did, however. Mr. Jones said :

" Tom wasn't at home, yet, so I gave him up ; but I stumbled on him and Huck right at my door, and so I just brought them along in a hurry."

" And you did just right," said the widow :—" Come with me, boys."

She took them to a bed chamber and said :

" Now wash and dress yourselves. Here are two new suits of clothes— shirts, socks, everything complete. They're Huck's—no, no thanks, Huck— Mr. Jones bought one and I the other. But they'll fit both of you. Get into them. We'll wait—come down when you are slicked up enough."

Then she left.

CHAPTER XXXIV.

HUCK said: "Tom, we can slope, if we can find a rope. The window ain't high from the ground."

"Shucks, what do you want to slope for?"

"Well I ain't used to that kind of a crowd. I can't stand it. I ain't going down there, Tom."

"O, bother! It ain't anything. I don't mind it a bit. I'll take care of you."

Sid appeared.

"Tom," said he, "Auntie has been waiting for you all the afternoon. Mary got your Sunday clothes ready, and everybody's been fretting about you. Say—ain't this grease and clay, on your clothes?"

"Now Mr. Siddy, you jist 'tend to your own business. What's all this blow-out about, anyway?"

WIDOW DOUGLAS

264

"It's one of the widow's parties that she's always having. This time its for the Welchman and his sons, on account of that scrape they helped her out of the other night. And say—I can tell you something, if you want to know."

" Well, what ? "

" Why old Mr. Jones is going to try to spring something on the people here to-night, but I overheard him tell auntie to-day about it, as a secret, but I reckon it's not much of a secret *now*. Everybody knows—the widow, too, for all she tries to let on she don't. Mr. Jones was bound Huck should be here—couldn't get along with his grand secret without Huck, you know ! "

" Secret about what, Sid ? "

" About Huck tracking the robbers to the widow's. I reckon Mr. Jones was going to make a grand time over his surprise, but I bet you it will drop pretty flat."

Sid chuckled in a very contented and satisfied way.

" Sid, was it you that told ? "

" O, never mind who it was. *Somebody* told—that's enough."

" Sid, there's only one person in this town mean enough to do that, and that's you. If you had been in Huck's place you'd 'a' sneaked down the hill and never told anybody on the robbers. You can't do any but mean things, and you can't bear to see anybody praised for doing good ones. There—no thanks, as the widow says "—and Tom cuffed Sid's ears and helped him to the door with several kicks. " Now go and tell auntie if you dare—and to-morrow you'll catch it ! "

Some minutes later the widow's guests were at the supper table, and a dozen children were propped up at little side tables in the same room, after the fashion of that country and that day. At the proper time Mr. Jones made his little speech, in which he thanked the widow for the honor she was doing himself and his sons, but said that there was another person whose modesty—

And so forth and so on. He sprung his secret about Huck's share in the adventure in the finest dramatic manner he was master of, but the surprise it occasioned was largely counterfeit and not as clamorous and effusive as it might have been under happier circumstances. However, the widow made a pretty fair show of astonishment, and heaped so many compliments and so much gratitude upon Huck that he almost forgot the nearly intolerable discomfort of his new clothes in the entirely intolerable discomfort of being set up as a target for everybody's gaze and everybody's laudations.

The widow said she meant to give Huck a home under her roof and have him educated; and that when she could spare the money she would start him in business in a modest way. Tom's chance was come. He said:

"Huck don't need it. Huck's rich!"

Nothing but a heavy strain upon the good manners of the company kept

TOM BACKS HIS STATEMENT.

back the due and proper complimentary laugh at this pleasant joke. But the silence was a little awkward. Tom broke it—

"Huck's got money. Maybe you don't believe it, but he's got lots of it. Oh, you needn't smile—I reckon I can show you. You just wait a minute."

Tom ran out of doors. The company looked at each other with a perplexed interest—and inquiringly at Huck, who was tongue-tied.

"Sid, what ails Tom?" said Aunt Polly. "He—well, there ain't ever any making of that boy out. I never— "

Tom entered, struggling with the weight of his sacks, and Aunt Polly did not finish her sentence. Tom poured the mass of yellow coin upon the table and said—

"There—what did I tell you? Half of it's Huck's and half of it's mine!"

The spectacle took the general breath away. All gazed, nobody spoke for a moment. Then there was a unanimous call for an explanation. Tom said he could furnish it, and he did. The tale was long, but brim full of interest. There was scarcely an interruption from anyone to break the charm of its flow. When he had finished, Mr. Jones said—

"I thought I had fixed up a little surprise for this occasion, but it don't amount to anything now. This one makes it sing mighty small, I'm willing to allow."

The money was counted. The sum amounted to a little over twelve thousand dollars. It was more than any one present had ever seen at one time before, though several persons were there who were worth considerably more than that in property.

CHAPTER XXXV.

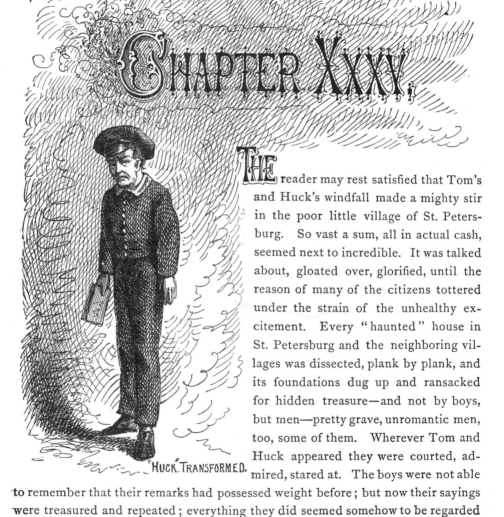

"HUCK" TRANSFORMED.

THE reader may rest satisfied that Tom's and Huck's windfall made a mighty stir in the poor little village of St. Petersburg. So vast a sum, all in actual cash, seemed next to incredible. It was talked about, gloated over, glorified, until the reason of many of the citizens tottered under the strain of the unhealthy excitement. Every "haunted" house in St. Petersburg and the neighboring villages was dissected, plank by plank, and its foundations dug up and ransacked for hidden treasure—and not by boys, but men—pretty grave, unromantic men, too, some of them. Wherever Tom and Huck appeared they were courted, admired, stared at. The boys were not able to remember that their remarks had possessed weight before ; but now their sayings were treasured and repeated ; everything they did seemed somehow to be regarded

268

as remarkable; they had evidently lost the power of doing and saying common-place things; moreover, their past history was raked up and discovered to bear marks of conspicuous originality. The village paper published biographical sketches of the boys.

The widow Douglas put Huck's money out at six per cent., and Judge Thatcher did the same with Tom's at Aunt Polly's request. Each lad had an income, now, that was simply prodigious—a dollar for every week-day in the year and half of the Sundays. It was just what the minister got—no, it was what he was promised—he generally couldn't collect it. A dollar and a quarter a week would board, lodge and school a boy in those old simple days—and clothe him and wash him, too, for that matter.

Judge Thatcher had conceived a great opinion of Tom. He said that no commonplace boy would ever have got his daughter out of the cave. When Becky told her father, in strict confidence, how Tom had taken her whipping at school, the Judge was visibly moved; and when she pleaded grace for the mighty lie which Tom had told in order to shift that whipping from her shoulders to his own, the Judge said with a fine outburst that it was a noble, a generous, a magnanimous lie—a lie that was worthy to hold up its head and march down through history breast to breast with George Washington's lauded Truth about the hatchet! Becky thought her father had never looked so tall and so superb as when he walked the floor and stamped his foot and said that. She went straight off and told Tom about it.

Judge Thatcher hoped to see Tom a great lawyer or a great soldier some day. He said he meant to look to it that Tom should be admitted to the National military academy and afterwards trained in the best law school in the country, in order that he might be ready for either career or both.

Huck Finn's wealth and the fact that he was now under the widow Douglas's protection, introduced him into society—no, dragged him into it, hurled him into it—and his sufferings were almost more than he could bear. The widow's servants kept him clean and neat, combed and brushed, and they bedded him nightly in unsympathetic sheets that had not one little spot or stain which he could press to his heart and know for a friend. He had to eat with knife and fork; he had to use napkin, cup and plate; he had to learn his book, he had to go to church; he had to talk so properly that speech was become insipid in his mouth; whithersoever he turned, the bars and shackles of civilization shut him in and bound him hand and foot.

He bravely bore his miseries three weeks, and then one day turned up missing. For forty-eight hours the widow hunted for him everywhere in great distress. The public were profoundly concerned; they searched high and low, they dragged the river for his body. Early the third morning Tom Sawyer wisely went poking among some old empty hogsheads down behind the abandoned slaughter-house, and in one of them he found the refugee. Huck had slept there; he had just breakfasted upon some stolen odds and ends of food, and was lying off, now, in comfort with his pipe. He was unkempt, uncombed, and clad in the same old ruin of rags that had made him picturesque in the days when he was free and happy. Tom routed him out, told him the trouble he had been causing, and urged him to go home. Huck's face lost its tranquil content, and took a melancholy cast. He said:

"Don't talk about it, Tom. I've tried it, and it don't work; it don't work, Tom. It ain't for me; I ain't used to it. The widder's good to me, and friendly; but I can't stand them ways. She makes me git up just at the same time every morning; she makes me wash, they comb me all to thunder; she won't let me sleep in the wood-shed; I got to wear them blamed clothes that just smothers me, Tom; they don't seem to any air git through 'em, somehow; and they're so rotten nice that I can't set down, nor lay down, nor roll around anywher's; I hain't slid on a cellar-door for—well, it 'pears to be years; I got to go to church and sweat and sweat—I hate them ornery sermons! I can't ketch a fly in there, I can't chaw, I got to wear shoes all Sunday. The widder eats by a bell; she goes to bed by a bell; she gits up by a bell—everything's so awful reg'lar a body can't stand it."

"Well, everybody does that way, Huck."

"Tom, it don't make no difference. I ain't everybody, and I can't *stand* it. It's awful to be tied up so. And grub comes too easy—I don't take no interest in vittles, that way. I got to ask, to go a-fishing; I got to ask, to go in a-swimming— dern'd if I hain't got to ask to do everything. Well, I'd got to talk so nice it wasn't no comfort—I'd got to go up in the attic and rip out a while, every day, to git a taste in my mouth, or I'd a died, Tom. The widder wouldn't let me smoke; she wouldn't let me yell, she wouldn't let me gape, nor stretch, nor scratch, before folks—" [Then with a spasm of special irritation and injury],—"And dad fetch it, she prayed all the time! I never *see* such a woman! I *had* to shove, Tom—I just had to. And besides, that school's going to open, and I'd a had to go to it—

COMFORTABLE ONCE MORE.

well, I wouldn't stand *that*, Tom. Lookyhere, Tom, being rich ain't what it's cracked up to be. It's just worry and worry, and sweat and sweat, and a-wishing you was dead all the time. Now these clothes suits me, and this bar'l suits me, and I ain't ever going to shake 'em any more. Tom, I wouldn't ever got into all this trouble if it hadn't 'a' been for that money; now you just take my sheer of it along with your'n, and gimme a ten-center sometimes—not many times, becuz I don't give a dern for a thing 'thout it's tollable hard to git—and you go and beg off for me with the widder."

"Oh, Huck, you know I can't do that. 'Taint fair; and besides if you'll try this thing just a while longer you'll come to like it."

"Like it! Yes—the way I'd like a hot stove if I was to set on it long enough. No, Tom, I won't be rich, and I won't live in them cussed smothery houses. I like the woods, and the river, and hogsheads, and I'll stick to 'em, too. Blame it all! just as we'd got guns, and a cave, and all just fixed to rob, here this dern foolishness has got to come up and spile it all!"

Tom saw his opportunity—

"Lookyhere, Huck, being rich ain't going to keep me back from turning robber."

"No! Oh, good-licks, are you in real dead-wood earnest, Tom?"

"Just as dead earnest as I'm a sitting here. But Huck, we can't let you into the gang if you ain't respectable, you know."

Huck's joy was quenched.

"Can't let me in, Tom? Didn't you let me go for a pirate?"

"Yes, but that's different. A robber is more high-toned than what a pirate is—as a general thing. In most countries they're awful high up in the nobility—dukes and such."

"Now Tom, hain't you always ben friendly to me? You wouldn't shet me out, would you, Tom? You wouldn't do that, now, *would* you, Tom?"

"Huck, I wouldn't want to, and I *don't* want to—but what would people say? Why they'd say, 'Mph! Tom Sawyer's Gang! pretty low characters in it!' They'd mean you, Huck. You wouldn't like that, and I wouldn't."

Huck was silent for some time, engaged in a mental struggle. Finally he said:

"Well, I'll go back to the widder for a month and tackle it and see if I can come to stand it, if you'll let me b'long to the gang, Tom."

"All right, Huck, it's a whiz! Come along, old chap, and I'll ask the widow to let up on you a little, Huck."

"Will you Tom—now will you? That's good. If she'll let up on some of the roughest things, I'll smoke private and cuss private, and crowd through or bust. When you going to start the gang and turn robbers?"

"Oh, right off. We'll get the boys together and have the initiation to-night, maybe."

" Have the which ? "

" Have the initiation."

" What's that ? "

" It's to swear to stand by one another, and never tell the gang's secrets, even

HIGH UP IN SOCIETY.

if you're chopped all to flinders, and kill anybody and all his family that hurts one of the gang."

" That's gay—that's mighty gay, Tom, I tell you."

"Well I bet it is. And all that swearing's got to be done at midnight, in the lonesomest, awfulest place you can find—a ha'nted house is the best, but they're all ripped up now."

18

"Well, midnight's good, anyway, Tom."

"Yes, so it is.   And you've got to swear on a coffin, and sign it with blood."

"Now that's something *like!*   Why it's a million times bullier than pirating. I'll stick to the widder till I rot, Tom; and if I git to be a reg'lar ripper of a robber, and everybody talking 'bout it, I reckon she'll be proud she snaked me in out of the wet."

CONCLUSION.

————

So endeth this chronicle. It being strictly a history of a *boy*, it must stop here; the story could not go much further without becoming the history of a *man*. When one writes a novel about grown people, he knows exactly where to stop— that is, with a marriage; but when he writes of juveniles, he must stop where he best can.

Most of the characters that perform in this book still live, and are prosperous and happy. Some day it may seem worth while to take up the story of the younger ones again and see what sort of men and women they turned out to be; therefore it will be wisest not to reveal any of that part of their lives at present.

THE END.

Catalogue of Books Published by the

AMERICAN PUBLISHING COMPANY,

HARTFORD, CONN.

BRANCH OFFICES, CHICAGO, ILL. & CINCINNATI, OHIO.

REVISED DECEMBER 1st, 1876.

ADVENTURES OF TOM SAWYER. MARK TWAIN's last work. 150 Engravings. New, Bright, and Refreshing. A Splendid Gift Book.

THE TRUE-BLUE LAWS OF CONNECTICUT. Edited by the HON. J. HAMMOND TRUMBULL, LL. D., with Historical Introduction. An entirely new rendering of a very old story. This book should be in the library of every lawyer and man of intellect, and read by everybody. It is as amusing as it is instructive.

GABRIEL CONROY. BRET HARTE's great Work. Now first published in book form. Critics have pronounced it the most fascinating work of the day. A beautiful Octavo volume of 533 pages, including cuts. 33 Full Page Illustrations.

Price in Cloth.	Cloth, Gilt Edge.	Library.	Half Morocco.	Full Morocco.
$3.00	$3.50	$3.50	$4.50	$7.00

THE BIG BONANZA: An authentic account of the discovery, development and wonderful exhibit of the great Comstock Silver Lode; Sketches of the most Prominent Men interested in the mines; Incidents and Adventures; Humorous Stories; Amusing Experiences; Anecdotes, &c., &c. A rollicking book, by the famous writer DAN DE-QUILLE, with an Introduction by Mark Twain. A book for the times. An elegant Octavo of about 600 pages, 66 full page and many text Engravings.

Price in Silver-Colored English Cloth.	Cloth, Gilt Edges.	Library.	Half Morocco.
$3.50	$4.00	$4.00	$5.00

MY WINTER ON THE NILE AMONG THE MUMMIES AND MOSLEMS: By CHAS. DUDLEY WARNER. Author of "My Summer in a Garden," "Back-Log Studies," &c., &c. A delightful book of Egyptian travel. Octavo, 477 pages.

Price in Cloth.	Cloth, Gilt Edges.	Library Style.	Half Morocco.	Full Turkey Morocco.
$2.50	$3.00	$3.00	$4.50	$7.00

BIBLE LANDS ILLUSTRATED. By Rev. H. C. FISH, D. D. A Pictorial Handbook of Bible Lands and Christian Antiquities. Interesting to both old and young. Over 900 Pages. 600 Engravings and maps.

Price in Cloth.	Cloth, Gilt Edges.	Leather (library style).	Half Morocco.	Full Morocco.
$3.50	$4.00	$4.00	$5.00	$8.00

D. L. MOODY AND HIS WORK. By the REV. W. H. DANIELS. The Author visited Great Britain and took part in the revival meetings there, and this book is a complete Biography of Moody and Sankey, and a full account of their labors in *Great Britain and America*, including those in Brooklyn, Philadelphia and New York. It is the only Original lives of these men out, and is Authentic. 519 Pages. 17 Full-page Engravings.

Price in Cloth.	Cloth, Gilt Edge.	Leather (library style).	Half Morocco.
$2.00	$2.50	$2.50	$3.50

WI-NE-MA (THE WOMAN-CHIEF) AND HER PEOPLE. By the HON. A. B. MEACHAM, Chairman of the Modoc Peace Commissioners, &c. This is the record of the heroic Indian woman, who at the risk of her own life saved the author from butchery at the time of the assassination of Gen Canby and part of his associates by the Modocs. 12mo. 168 Pages. 16 Engravings. Price in Cloth $1.00.

FAC-SIMILE OF GEN'L WASHINGTON'S ACCOUNT WITH THE UNITED STATES, FROM 1775 TO 1783. A Centennial Curiosity worth having. By permission of Congress the original account book of Gen'l Washington was taken from the archives at Washington, lithographed and printed, and this volume is a perfect fac-simile in every respect of the original. Price $2.50.

THE HISTORY OF DEMOCRACY, OR POLITICAL PROGRESS Historically Illustrated from the Earliest to the Latest Periods. By HON. NAHUM CAPEN. A work of the greatest value, and should be in every library. Large Royal Octavo, 677 Pages. Steel Illustrations.

Price in Cloth.	Library.	Half Morocco.	Full Tarkey Morocco.
$5.00	$6.00	$7.00	$9.00

UNWRITTEN HISTORY OR LIFE AMONG THE MODOCS. By JOAQUIN MILLER. A most fascinating Indian story, showing the real life of the Indian and the injustice he meets with. Octavo, 446 Pages. 24 Full page Engravings.
Price in Cloth, $3.00.   Library, $3.50.   Half Morocco, $4.50.

A BOOK ON TOBACCO: Its History, Varieties, Culture, Manufacture, Commerce, and Various modes of use in different parts of the World, &c. By E. R. BILLINGS. A complete novelty. 486 Pages. Nearly 200 Engravings.

Price in Cloth.	Gilt Edges.	Library Style.	Half Calf or Morocco.
$3.00	$3.50	$3.50	$4.50

MY CAPTIVITY AMONG THE SIOUX. By Mrs. FANNY KELLY. The extraordinary story of a woman captured by the Indians; her life among them; and her wonderful escape. Finely Illustrated on Wood and Steel. 300 Pages. 12mo.
Price in Fine English Cloth, $1.50.

THE UNCIVILIZED RACES: OR NATURAL HISTORY OF MAN. By the REV. J. G. WOOD, M. A., F. R.S. &c. An exact reprint of the English Edition, with large additions by an American traveller; an invaluable addition to a library; in one or two volumes, 1681 pages. 715 Engravings.

	Price in Cloth.	Leather (library style).	Half Morocco.	Full Morocco.
In one Vol.	$6.00	$7.00	$8.00	$10.00
In two Vols.	$3.75 each vol.	$4.50 each vol.	$5.00 each vol.	$6.00 each vol.

AGRICULTURE. By ALEXANDER HYDE. Being Twelve Lectures before the Lowell Institute, Boston. Mass. A rare book for the farmer. 12mo. 370 Pages. Price $1.50.

PEOPLE FROM THE OTHER WORLD. By COL. H. S. OLCOTT. The wonderful doings of the "Eddy Brothers," and other noted spiritualists, with tests applied by the author. 12mo. 492 Pages. 50 Full page Engravings.
Price in Cloth, $2.50.   Cloth, Gilt Edges, $3.00.   Half Turkey, $4.00.

BEYOND THE MISSISSIPPI. By A. D. RICHARDSON. Having an immense sale. A work too well known to need a description. 630 Pages, 216 Engravings.

Price in Cloth.	Cloth, Gilt Edges.	Leather (library style).	Half Morocco.	Full Morocco.
$3.50	$4.00	$4.00	$5.00	$8.00

PERSONAL HISTORY OF U. S. GRANT. By A. D. RICHARDSON. The only authentic and full life of this famous man. 560 Pages, 25 Engravings.

Price in Cloth.	Cloth, Gilt Edges,	Leather (library style).	Half Morocco.
$3.00	$3.50	$3.50	$5.00

FIELD, DUNGEON AND ESCAPE. By A. D. RICHARDSON. The noted record of the capture, imprisonment and escape of the lamented author during the civil war. 512 pages, 10 steel and wood Engravings.

Price in Cloth.	Cloth, Gilt Edges.	Leather (library style).	Half Morocco.
$3.00	$3.50	$3.50	$5.00

THE GREAT REBELLION; A HISTORY OF THE CIVIL WAR IN THE UNITED STATES. By HON. J. T. HEADLEY. The most complete and cheapest history out. 1206 Pages and 70 steel Engravings.

	Price in Cloth.	Em. Morocco.	Leather (library style).	Half Morocco.
In one Vol.		$5.00	$5.00	
In two Vols.	$3.50 each vol.	$4.00 each vol.	$4.00 each vol.	$5.00 each vol.

ILLUSTRATED HISTORY OF THE BIBLE. By J. E. STEBBINS. Containing Biographical sketches of most of the noted characters in the Bible. A valuable and instructive book. 608 Pages, 18 Full Page steel Engravings, 1 Map.

Price in Cloth.	Cloth, Gilt Edges.	Leather (library style).	Full Morocco.
$3.50	$4.00	$4.00	$6.00

HISTORY OF THE INDIAN RACES OF THE WESTERN CONTINENT. By CHAS. DEWOLFF BROWNELL. Brought down to end of the Modoc war. 760 Pages. 40 full-page Engravings, plain and colored.
Price in English Cloth, $3.50.   Leather (library style), $4.00.

EVERYBODY'S FRIEND: OR JOSH BILLING'S PROVERBIAL PHILOSOPHY OF WIT AND HUMOR. Profusely Illustrated by Thos. Nast, &c. 129 Engravings.
Price in Cloth, $3.50.   Cloth, Gilt Edges, $4.00.   Library, $4.00.   Half Morocco, $5.00.

THE NEWGATE OF CONNECTICUT. By R. H. PHELPS. A History of the celebrated Simsbury mines, the historical prison in which Tories were confined during the
Revolutionary war a hundred years ago, and used as a State's Prison for years afterwards.
The only book of its kind, and intensely interesting. Illustrated with views of the old
and present Newgate, and also of the Wethersfield State's Prison. 12mo. 117 Pages.
6 Engravings. Price in Cloth, 75 cts.

The foregoing Books are all new and just from the Press.

*SCRIPTURE READING LESSONS, AN AID TO FAMILY WORSHIP. By REV. J. T.
CHAMPLAIN, D. D. Destined to fill a place long void. To every family where Family
Worship is observed, it will prove invaluable. It covers the whole Bible and is free from
anything sectarian. It will be sold at an extremely low price in order to place it in the
reach of all.

*INDIA: ITS PRINCES AND ITS PEOPLE. By MRS. JULIA A. STONE. A Magnificent Book,
Splendidly Illustrated. It is a sensible, shrewd, American woman's description of India
and its People, after a residence there of years, during which she journeyed over all
parts of the country, up and down the Ganges, etc. A work of most thrilling interest.

* These two last named books are not yet published, but are now
nearly ready for the press, and will be issued as soon as practicable.

☞ Agents canvassing for any of the Books mentioned above or on
the preceding page are allowed to take orders for any of the following.
For many of them a constant demand exists, and the agent will realize
a large income from their sale without trouble.

SKETCHES NEW AND OLD. By MARK TWAIN. Among them the story of the
Jumping Frog. A beautiful parlor table-book. 320 Pages, 122 Illustrations.

Price in Cloth.	Cloth, Gilt Edges.	Leather (library style).	Half Morocco.	Full Morocco.
$3.00	$3.50	$3.50	$4.50	$6.00

INNOCENTS ABROAD: OR THE NEW PILGRIM'S PROGRESS. By MARK TWAIN. Everybody has heard of this book. Fully Illustrated. 652 Pages, 234 Engravings.

Price in Cloth.	Cloth, Gilt Edges.	Leather (library style).	Half Morocco.	Full Morocco.
$3.50	$4.00	$4.00	$5.00	$8.00

ROUGHING IT. By MARK TWAIN. A companion volume to Innocents Abroad. Full
of Twain's characteristic humor. 600 Pages, 300 Illustrations.

Price in Cloth.	Cloth, Gilt Edges.	Leather (library style).	Half Morocco.	Full Morocco.
$3.50	$4.00	$4.00	$5.00	$8.00

THE GILDED AGE. By MARK TWAIN and CHARLES DUDLEY WARNER. A tale of To-
Day. Wit, Humor, and Romance combined. 576 Pages, 212 Illustrations.

Price in Cloth.	Cloth, Gilt Edges.	Leather (library style).	Half Morocco.	Full Morocco.
$3.50	$4.00	$4.00	$5.00	$8.00

MY OPINIONS AND BETSEY BOBBET'S. By JOSIAH ALLEN'S WIFE. A home book,
full of humor, sarcasm, and instruction. One of the most amusing books ever written.
432 Pages. 12mo. 50 Illustrations.

Price in Cloth, $2.50.	Cloth, Gilt Edges, $3.00.	Half Morocco, $4.00.

THE GREAT SOUTH. By EDWARD KING. Illustrated from sketches by J. WELLS
CHAMPNEY. A record of journeyings in all the South in 1872 and 73. This book has won
a world wide reputation both for beauty and for faithful portrayal of the South as it is.
Magnificently illustrated. Large Octavo, 810 Pages. Maps and Engravings over 600.

Price in Cloth.	Plain Leather.	Half Morocco.	Full Morocco.
$6.00	$7.00	$8.00	$12.00

THE WORLD OF WIT AND HUMOR. An unique book. A collection of famous
humorous sketches and poems, from the pens of the most celebrated writers. Such
poems as "Nothing to Wear," "The Heathen Chinee," and "The Wonderful One-
Horse Shay," are here collected and illustrated, and scores of equally noted prose
sketches. A beautiful volume just adapted to the parlor table. Large Octavo, 500 Pages.
450 Engravings.

Price in Cloth.	Cloth, Gilt Edges.	Library.	Half Morocco.	Full Morocco.
$3.50	$4.00	$4.50	$6.00	$10.00

SQUIBS, OR EVERY DAY LIFE ILLUSTRATED By Palmer Cox. One of the funniest books
ever written. A record of sights seen by the author in his walks about town and sketched by him on the spot. A book to read and laugh over. 12mo. 500 Pages. 200 Engravings.

Price in Cloth, $2.00.	Cloth, Gilt Edges, $2.50.	Half Morocco, $4.00.

SIGHTS AND SENSATIONS IN EUROPE. By JUNIUS HENRI BROWNE. Travel and Sight-seeing in Europe, Ireland, Spain, Germany, Holland, &c; with an account of persons and places connected with the Franco-Prussian war. A book of rare and exciting interest. Octavo, 591 Pages. 70 Illustrations.

Price in Cloth.	Cloth, Gilt Edges.	Leather (library style).	Half Morocco.
$3.00	$3.50	$3.50	$4.50

OVERLAND THROUGH ASIA. By THOMAS W. KNOX. Pictures of Siberian, Chinese and Tartar life. A splendid work, full of interest. Octavo. 608 Pages. 193 Engravings.

Price in Cloth.	Cloth, Gilt Edges.	Leather (library style).	Half Morocco.	Full Morocco.
$3.50	$4.00	$4.00	$5.00	$8.00

THE GREAT METROPOLIS. A Mirror of New York. A complete showing up of the great Metropolis inside and out. By JUNIUS HENRI BROWNE. Octavo, 700 Pages. 26 Engravings.

Price in Cloth, $3.00.   Library, $3.50.   Half Morocco, $4.50.

HOLIDAY BOOKS. Most fascinating for Boys and Girls. Almost every page illustrated. STORIES ABOUT BIRDS. Price $2.50.   STORIES ABOUT ANIMALS. Price $2.50. PEBBLES AND PEARLS,   "   1.25.

THE HOLY BIBLE, with Apocrypha and Concordance (the authorized edition); to which are added Canne's Marginal References; Index and Table of Texts, and an account of the Lives and Martyrdoms of the Apostles and Evangelists. Illustrated with numerous beautifully executed Steel Plates. The cheapest Bible made.   Price $6.00 to $13.00

THE HOLY BIBLE, containing the Old and New Testaments. Translated *Literally* from the Original Tongues. By JULIA E. SMITH. Price $3.00.

TO THE PUBLIC.

It has been claimed that books sold by Agents are higher in price than those of equal value sold at book-stores. This belief often prevents persons from buying of an Agent. So far as our books are concerned, there is no foundation for such a claim. Please consider the following statements.

FIRST. Most of our books are fully illustrated, not only with full page but with text engravings. These illustrations must be printed on something better than ordinary book paper, and to be well executed it requires the whole book to be on fine, heavy paper suitable for the cuts, costing very high. Again, the printing of the text with cuts costs more than twice the price of plain printing. Hence, few books are printed with text engravings. For proof, we ask you to count up all you can remember of them, aside from ours. You will find they are very few. Publishers avoid them universally.

SECOND. We claim that we sell you books with from two hundred to three hundred engravings, finely printed on extra fine paper, and most firmly bound, as low as you can buy any book equal in *weight*, *size*, and *popularity*, which contain but few if any cuts, at any book-store; while you will be asked there for books illustrated as are our $3.50 ones (if they have any such) at least $5 or $6. We do not ask you to take our word for this, but to test it by enquiry and comparison. We certainly sell books lower than book-stores.

We allow our Agents exactly the discount on our price, that publishers allow the regular trade, and *no more ;* and as through our Agents we sell ten times more of our books than do the trade publishers, we can afford a better book for a given sum. We ask investigation on this subject that all may know whether we speak truly or not. We assert that no books of equal cost of the "BEYOND THE MISSISSIPPI," "THE INNOCENTS ABROAD," "OVERLAND THROUGH ASIA," "ROUGHING IT," and others of our books have ever been sold in this country at the price we sell them at.

THIRD. We employ only those Agents who enter into agreements with us, pledging themselves not to put any books into stores ; and it is only through unreliable Agents that they are seen there. The great popularity of our works, and their ready sale make it an object for the trade to get them. Having, by some means, obtained them, dealers sometimes sell our books at a reduced price even without profit to themselves. This is done to injure Agents, and the Subscription-Business, and is the sole and only ground for the current belief that the trade sell books lower than the subscription houses.

Our Agents are instructed by us to introduce our books, but never to press them upon those who do not desire them. We publish none but valuable and popular work, and we bespeak for our Agents a kind reception.

The *Atlantic Monthly* says of us and one of our books :

" If this book can make its way among the Subscription-Book public, it will do a vast service to literature in educating the popular taste to the appreciation of good reading, and the time will yet come when the Book-Agent will be welcomed at all our doors instead of warned from them by every prohibitory device."

Also says the *New York Journal of Commerce* :

" This is precisely the sort of book which every one ought to be glad to have thrust in his face and urged on his attention. The purchaser will be grateful to the agent who has induced him to buy it."

Such commendations from such authority speak volumes for our books.

AFTERWORD
Albert E. Stone

CULTURAL CONTEXTS

No American author has participated more fully in his or her country's life, during a crucial era of change, than Samuel L. Clemens. Merely to summarize the signal features of the life of the man known as Mark Twain authenticates this claim. Consider this incomplete review of personal and cultural events and aspects: childhood in a Mississippi River border town of the slaveholding South; piloting and journeyman printing along the great Midwestern river; brief Civil War service in the Confederate militia; westward adventuring along the Oregon Trail to the Nevada silver mines and California gold mines; newspaper reporting and humorous lecturing on the Pacific Slope and Hawaii; an eastward voyage via the Isthmus to New York City and a wider, more successful career as reporter, freelance writer, and lyceum lecturer; national and European travel by rail and steamboat, culminating in an around-the-world tour; marriage into the Eastern monied class and residence in Hartford's Nook Farm neighborhood of genteel writers and liberal clergymen; authorship of a succession of popular travel books and novels marketed by subscription; his own publishing company as one of several speculations, ending in the 1890s in bankruptcy.

In the course of this archetypal Gilded Age history Mark Twain also shared the political, social, and intellectual concerns of his contemporaries. Some of these were liberal Republican politics during and after Reconstruction;

Darwinism, determininism, and the Social Gospel; new psychological models of the mind; comprehensive disillusionment later, and bitter criticism of imperialism and racism in the wake of the Spanish-American War and Jim Crow. As reflections of his age, his books sometimes became plays on the New York stage; even more of them were translated into foreign languages, winning him worldwide acclaim. At the zenith of his remarkable (and sometimes tragic and tormented) career, the white-haired, white-suited Mark Twain modestly acknowledged what had already been said of him — this flamboyant American had become the most widely known literary figure on the planet.

At the center of this fabulous private and public life stand Mark Twain's twin monuments of fiction, *The Adventures of Tom Sawyer* and *Adventures of Huckleberry Finn.* In these two novels, one published in 1876, the other in 1885, live a pair of immortal boys. Tom Sawyer and Huck Finn are among America's undisputed contributions to the world's cast of unforgettable characters. As Bernard DeVoto put it, "these two boys have become the possessions of everyone. . . . they have become legends."[1] Indeed, Tom and Huck may be the youngest members of the pantheon, just as the United States was the youngest, rawest culture from which fictional legends emerged late in the last century. Out of a Hannibal, Missouri, boyhood and its fund of adult memories Mark Twain's fertile imagination distilled two fictional classics whose protagonists reappear in half a dozen lesser works published or left in manuscript at the author's death in 1910.

Though Tom and Huck (and, increasingly and controversially, Jim) are now hailed as cultural icons, they should be framed in their several historical contexts: not just Twain's worlds of the 1870s and 1880s or our 1990s perspectives, but also the 1830s and 1840s worlds of the white boys, the slave, and their village. Such recreations, moreover, should be anchored firmly in responses by the now millions of readers all over the world who have delighted in these books and revered their author. "I am eleven years old, and I live on a farm near Rockville, Maryland," wrote one of these admirers to the aging Mark Twain. "Once this winter we had a boy to work for us named John. We lent him 'Huck Finn' to read, and one night he let his clothes out of the window and left. The last we heard from him he was out in Ohio, and father says if we had lent him 'Tom Sawyer' to read he would not have stopped on this side of the ocean."[2]

Bernard DeVoto and a Maryland farm boy share an admiration cutting across age, time, and sophistication. Mark Twain would have smiled at their agreement. During his career he worked mightily to bridge such social and literary gaps. With part of his talent he courted the approbation of genteel middle-class readers who delighted in *The Prince and the Pauper* and *Joan of Arc*, two other stories about boys and girls. Yet another side of his self produced often hilarious satires of the cultural values of well-heeled consumers of culture. In these works he wrote unabashedly for what he often called the Belly and Members. Straddling these different and sometimes opposed audiences, Mark Twain explored and exploited a rapidly changing feature of the social landscape in the later nineteenth century — the simultaneous presence of literate, semiliterate, and illiterate groups in cities and countryside. All three classes, in fact, were found at Nook Farm, where genteel adults, children of all ages, and servants (blacks from the South, immigrants from Ireland) coexisted, even within the Clemens household. Moreover, as recent critics have pointed out, Tom, Huck, and Jim personify these groups and dramatize their differing notions of style, humor, morality — indeed, of reality itself. Hence it's not surprising that Twain published in the *Atlantic*, in the *St. Nicholas* magazine whose young readers included "Teedie" Roosevelt, and also in books (liberally illustrated like this facsimile) sold from door to door by subscription agents. When *Adventures of Huckleberry Finn* was banned from the children's sections of the Concord and Brooklyn libraries, genteel sensibilities were pleased while semiliterates laughed, as did their lip-smacking book salesmen.

Conflict and change indeed characterize at many points the whole cultural era 1865–1910. Mark Twain was perhaps most representative in being powerfully conflicted and constantly changing in his outlook and allegiances. Despite affection for the Belly and Members, he became comfortable in his success, symbolized by the gaudy Hartford mansion staffed by half a dozen servants. As a democrat and liberal Republican he supported reforms of government and business, whose cozy cooperation produced industrialization, trusts, railroad land grants, strikes, huge fortunes and grinding poverty, and eleven years of depression between 1873 and 1897. Yet one of his admired friends and his financial adviser was Henry H. Rogers, who Twain blithely admitted was one of the most rapacious of robber barons. As an ex-Southerner who grew up taking slavery for granted, this transplanted Northerner became a sympathetic patron of blacks and one of the first widely popular white writers to take black characters seriously. He poured hundreds of thousands into the fatally flawed Paige typesetter, then in *A Connecticut Yankee in King Arthur's Court* scathingly satirized American mechanical ingenuity and stock market know-how. If, as DeLancey Ferguson believes, "humor, like lyric poetry, is a form of self-dramatization,"[3] then this humorist's expression, by turns hilarious and mordant, dramatizes tensions deeply felt within and across the cultural horizon.

Doubtless the deepest and most fertile tension in Mark Twain's consciousness was his lifelong dedication to his boyhood experiences and outlook as these came into conflict with adult values and compromises. His ambivalence about and celebration of boyhood opened the richest vein in his art, impelling him to juxtapose the innocent, passive eye of childhood against mature wisdom, hypocrisy, and evil. Though Tom and Huck, the Prince and the Pauper, Joan of Arc and Philip Traum are permanent hallmarks of a powerful personal preoccupation, these figures became culturally significant as others — fellow writers, readers of all ages, parents and teachers, clergymen and librarians — felt likewise. Hence Twain and his contemporaries shared an intense nostalgia for childhood, the small town, and an antebellum America apparently light-years away from the often bleak and brutal conditions of their own day.

The Adventures of Tom Sawyer in particular epitomizes this cultural convergence. For *Tom Sawyer* was but one of a series of postwar novels celebrating boyhood by presenting the Bad Boy as a distinctively new American hero of fiction. Thomas Bailey Aldrich's *The Story of a Bad Boy* (1869) was probably the first in a notable succession; its popularity with both young and old soon spawned, besides Twain's book, Charles Dudley Warner's *Being a Boy* (1878), B. P. Shillaber's *Ike Partington and His Friends* (1879), Edgar W.

Howe's *The Story of a Country Town* (1882), Edward Eggleston's *The Hoosier Schoolboy* (1883), George W. Peck's *Peck's Bad Boy* (1883), William Dean Howells' *A Boy's Town* (1890) and *The Flight of Pony Baker* (1902), and Stephen Crane's *Whilomville Stories* (1900). These works are linked by a common thread. Each in different ways challenges or satirizes the Sunday School and secular stories of childhood published before the Civil War in places like the *Youth's Companion* and in the Peter Parley and Rollo books of Samuel Goodrich and Jacob Abbott. This genteel, pious literature championed the Good Boy, the Model Boy. As the presences of Sid Sawyer and Willie Mufferson in *Tom Sawyer* typify, later writers on childhood were resolutely anti-prig. Taking a more "natural," "realistic," or "vernacular" view of boyhood, these authors drew upon autobiography, satire, farce, social history, and even the psychological novel as modes of representing American childhood, and comic realism as basic technique. This breakthrough has had wide repercussions in twentieth-century American fiction, as the numerous young-person narratives by Sherwood Anderson, Ernest Hemingway, William Faulkner, Eudora Welty, Carson McCullers, J. D. Salinger, Truman Capote, James Baldwin, and Harper Lee, among many others, variously testify.

Because its author tried to make *Tom Sawyer* part of this juvenile culture — "my book is intended mainly for the entertainment of boys and girls," runs the final preface — there is a close link between this Bad Boy and his literary cousins. Comparing Tom with his fellow anti-prigs displays striking parallels and differences. First of all, Tom is no stereotype of the Bad Boy, the Natural Boy, the Human Boy. He is himself, an individual with distinctive traits, speech, social personality. Further, the ties connecting him to St. Petersburgh* are more complex and deep-rooted than is true of the other village boys. In spite of a veneer of farcical humor, Tom's adventures, unlike those of his fellows, become the serious process by which this boy matures. As a result, *Tom Sawyer* is more than a nostalgic re-creation of Mississippi

---

* I have retained the spelling "St. Petersburgh" with the "h" because it is that of the first American edition reproduced here, although it appears as "St. Petersburg" without the "h" in subsequent editions.

River life before the war, though it is that, too. Twain pays boyhood a greater compliment by making his Tom the vehicle of a full-dress study of personal identity in social terms at once genial and searching. But this unusual personal and cultural achievement was not pulled off easily or early, as we shall see by examining how, in the 1870s, amid all this social ferment, *The Adventures of Tom Sawyer* was made.

CREATION

"I have finished the book," Clemens wrote his novelist friend and editor William Dean Howells, "& didn't take the chap beyond boyhood. . . . If I went on, now, & took him into manhood, he would just be like all the one-horse men in literature & the reader would conceive a hearty contempt for him. It is *not* a boy's book, at all. It will only be read by adults."[4] This historic letter, written on July 5, 1875, announces neither the beginning nor the end of the creation of *The Adventures of Tom Sawyer*. Rather, it arrests attention at a crucial moment when the author reflects relief, pride, and confusion over his mostly completed manuscript. After all, *Tom Sawyer* was Mark Twain's fourth book but the first novel written solely by himself. "Solely," in this case, was not entirely accurate, for both before and after the summer of 1875 — right up to publication in December 1876, in fact — the author had help from many hands. Howells and Livy Clemens were chief prepublication critics. But the manuscript also reflected numerous memories, performances, writings, and social occasions where Twain's imagination of boyhood had been stimulated. For instance, the apprentice printer of 1855–56 wrote a comic letter in which bugs around the printshop light are described in language anticipating the novel's Sunday school "show-off" scene. A decade later, Twain found himself in Grace Cathedral, San Francisco, distracted by a fly and a long-winded prayer, much as Tom Sawyer would be in the St. Petersburgh church. Later still, during an 1872 evening at a London club, he amused his hosts with an account of whitewashing a fence in Hannibal. Other such details kept offering themselves to the reminiscing writer.

Apart from the "Boy's Manuscript" of 1870 (an abortive experiment in first-person narrative), probably the most famous and influential of early stimuli is the letter Twain wrote Will Bowen on February 6, 1870. Bowen, a close boyhood chum and one model for Tom Sawyer, had sent Twain a letter about his recent marriage to Livy; thanking him, Twain replied, "The fountains of my great deep are broken up & I have rained reminiscences for four & twenty hours. The old life has swept before me like a panorama; the old days have trooped by in their old glory again. . . ." Then followed a litany of names, spots, and scenes of Hannibal of yore. Sam's catching measles from his friend; "playing Robin Hood in our shirt-tails"; the slaughterhouse, Holliday's (Cardiff) Hill; the schoolhouse, Sunday school, the town pump; accidentally burning up "that poor fellow in the calaboose"; Laura Hawkins, "my sweetheart"; swimming in the stillhouse branch and drownings or near-drownings in the great river — all are boyhood memories from the 1830s and 1840s on their way to becoming memorable moments in Hannibal's future reincarnation.[5] At no point in this writer's rich career, it may now be argued, were experience, memory, emotion, imagination, *and* revision to come into more fruitful balance than in the evolving composition of *Tom Sawyer*.

Actual writing probably began in 1873, in Hartford. During that year, Twain was able to write about a hundred and twenty pages of manuscript, though he found many diversions, especially collaborating with his neighbor Charles Dudley Warner on *The Gilded Age*. Further writing had to wait until February 1874. Then, and later that summer at Quarry Farm, in Elmira, New York, he forged ahead, netting nearly four hundred more handwritten pages. In September 1874, another stoppage occurred. Among the usual social and lecturing distractions, Twain now became immersed in writing "Old Times on the Mississippi" for the *Atlantic*. Apparently this nostalgic act did not immediately refill the well of memory for *Tom Sawyer*. Though he now had some five hundred manuscript pages, that wasn't enough for a subscription book. Struggling under mounting financial pressures, the busy author returned in the spring to make a final push which finished the task — or so he thought when he wrote Howells.

This spasmodic composition of a favorite work, one DeVoto was to hail as the single work "most harmonious with his interest, his experience, and his talents,"[6] was soon repeated in the seven-year struggle to write *Huckleberry Finn*. Both books seemed to drift into existence. In *Tom Sawyer*'s case, Twain candidly invited first Howells, then his wife, children, and visiting mother to help improve his creation. "I wish you would promise to read the MS of Tom Sawyer some time & see if you don't really decide that I am right in closing with him as a boy — & point out the most glaring defects. . . . I don't know any other person whose judgment I could venture to take fully & entirely," he told Howells — and meant it.[7]

The author's anxiety here over his book's scope and audience reflected second thoughts about a prior notation on the corner of page 1 of the manuscript. This complete holograph manuscript, now in the Riggs Library, Georgetown University, is an invaluable guide. Moreover, present-day readers and critics everywhere can use it in Paul Baender's facsimile edition of the author's holograph manuscript of "The Adventures of Tom Sawyer" (1982). The note reads:

1, Boyhood & youth; 2 y and early manh; 3 the Battle of Life in many lands; 4 (age 37 to [40?],) return & meet grown babies & toothless old drivelers who were the grandees of his boyhood. The Adored Unknown a [illegible] faded old maid & full of rasping, puritanical, vinegar piety.

As Hamlin Hill remarks, "this marginal note represents . . . a very early if not the earliest plan for the plot of the new novel."[8] Yet as Howells' and others' responses came in, Twain began cheerfully to change his mind. "I finished reading Tom Sawyer a week ago, sitting up till one A.M. to get to the end, simply because it was impossible to leave off," Howells wrote on November 21, 1875. "It is altogether the best boy's story I ever read. It will be an immense success. But I think you ought to treat it explicitly as a boy's book. Grownups will enjoy it just as much if you do. . . . I have made some corrections and suggestions in faltering pencil." Then Howells added, "The adventures are enchanting. I wish I had been on that island. . . . I don't seem to think I like the last chapter. I believe I would cut that."[9] As it turned out, Howells suggested only thirty-one or so changes. His and Livy's roles as Victorian police-men have in this case been much exaggerated.

Mark Twain, apparently, had already begun to rethink *Tom Sawyer*. In an astonishing proposal dated July 13, 1875, he urged Howells to collaborate with him on a stage version, adding, "I have my eye on two young girls who could play "Tom" and "Huck.""[10] Later still, he revealed what liberties he ac-cepted from another participant in the creative process. "[True W.] Williams has made about 200 rattling pictures for it — some of them very dainty. . . . He takes a book of mine, & without suggestion from anybody builds no end of pictures from his reading of it."[11] Putting Williams to work so freely on a manuscript still being read and corrected by others was Twain's, not his publisher Elisha Bliss's, idea. Further rethinking and rewriting were encour-aged by numerous delays that stretched publication on through 1876. The American Publishing Company, hurting still from the 1873 depression, was slow in getting subscription agents in the field. Arranging for prior publica-tion in England with Chatto and Windus and a German edition with Tauchnitz, competition from Canadian pirates, and Howells' enthusiastic but embarassingly premature review in the *Atlantic* in May were additional headaches. Little wonder, then, that the author had time to delete and insert, substitute and rearrange. As Paul Baender points out, the *Tom Sawyer* manu-script reveals how Twain worked: an "extraordinary number of clear pages showed the speed Mark Twain could maintain, while changes showed careful deliberation in language and style."[12]

Still another element in this protracted birth was the fact that during the summer of 1876 the exasperated author began composing *Adventures of Huckleberry Finn*. Even though the greatest of American sequels was not to be finished for some years, Twain had ample opportunity to hone *Tom Sawyer* more carefully to emphasize connections and contrasts. His pair of fictional orphans were aligned in their separate stories to dramatize literary and social issues. Victor Doyno has deftly discussed some of these in *Writing "Huck Finn": Mark Twain's Creative Process*: romantic versus pragmatic temperaments; admiration for European nobility versus a native nonliterary egalitarianism; hypocritical Christianity versus superstitious beliefs; literacy versus semiliteracy as active agents and viewpoints in plots often sharing the author's penchant for farce, melodrama, and violence. One arresting bit of evidence suggesting that Twain was of two minds about his nearly finished book is a remark to Howells in the July, 1875, birth announcement: "I perhaps made a mistake not writing it in the first person."[13]

Though the incomparably vernacular voice of *Huckleberry Finn* may be more memorable, both novels brilliantly satirize the society within which their protagonists are embedded. Moreover, *Tom Sawyer*'s popularity with four generations of readers (old and young) may in this comparison go unexplained. Though second to *Huckleberry Finn* in sales during Twain's lifetime, *Tom Sawyer* in the twentieth century has sold the best of all his novels. With critics, too, Twain's first boy book is increasingly recognized as a well-made work of art. With respect to literary coherence and psychological penetration, among other attributes, this book is much more than its maker's somewhat offhand characterization — "simply a hymn, put into prose form to give it a wordly air."[14]

CHARACTER, COMMUNITY, AND THE CRITICS

Indeed, despite a history of interruptions and shifting notions about adults or children as audience, as well as reliance upon others' opinions to resolve the author's occasional confusions over content and style, Twain's first novel as completed and revised seems to show a conscious structure encompassing its diverse origins and intentions. Beginning as a standard Bad Boy in the initial seven chapters, Tom, though not the narrator, displays a marked individuality and way of taking his world and its challenges and opportunities. As his dreams reveal, Tom is graphic and literary in thought. From the outset, he is attuned to the adult world and has imaginative flair in dealing with elders and peers. He dreams of stalking into the church at the zenith of his piratical fame to impress the whole village. He leads his little gang to Jackson's Island, watches the steamboat's frantic passengers search for their bodies, grandly attends his own funeral, and pours the treasure on the table at the story's climax. As Judith Fetterly aptly observes, Tom is most clearly Mark Twain in his penchant to show off, to entertain, to orchestrate his and the community's relief from boredom and gratify their common love of the grandiloquent gesture.[15]

Furthermore, though Twain perhaps regretted not using a first-person narrator, he endowed his bookish boy hero with unmistakable freshness of speech. Among the many parallel episodes in the Bad Boy novels, cemetery scenes are melodramatic moments. Aldrich's Tom Bailey is an unconvincing participant in one such scene, because of the clumsy adult language put in his mouth. When Tom and Huck, however, huddle in the St. Petersburgh cemetery, before Dr. Robinson's murder, they whisper in more believable accents.

> "Hucky, do you believe the dead people like it for us to be here?"
> Huckleberry whispered:
> "I wisht I knowed. It's awful solemn-like, *ain't* it?"...
> "Say, Hucky — do you reckon Hoss Williams hears us talking?"
> "O' course he does. Least his sperrit does."
> Tom, after a pause:
> "I wish I'd said *Mister* Williams. But I never meant any harm. Everybody calls him Hoss."(87)

Twain's mixture of humor and horror here is convincing. Nor can it be simply attributed, as some would say, to a debt to Dickens' *A Tale of Two Cities* and young Jerry Cruncher. Any literary echo has been kept in the background. What's there instead is overall fidelity to individual voices and differences between a semiliterate Huck and a more socially attuned Tom. "Hoss" and "Mister" are nice ways of pointing up contrasts between genteel and vernacular, children's games and adult realities, and maybe even reserve versus candor. As such, they underline the protagonist's consciousness as he muses his way into mysteries.

As for so-called realistic language, Twain tamed the various "obscenities" in his original story so successfully that the overall tone of Tom Sawyer is scarcely rougher than are the novels of Aldrich or Howe — not to mention the timid Howells. DeVoto points out in *Mark Twain at Work* just how mild these obscenities actually were, how quick Twain was to outdo Howells and Livy in curbing his own crudities. The Missouri writer's reach for the living shape of language often halted as soon as he suspected how coarse "combed me all to hell" or a dog leaving church "with his tail shut down like a hasp" would sound to genteel juvenile ears. Other modifications were, however, more significant. His pruning of the scene in the schoolhouse between Tom and Becky (chapter 20) makes one profound change in the fabric and theme of *Tom Sawyer*. When Tom surprises his sweetheart peeking in Mr. Dobbins' anatomy book with its "handsomely engraved and colored frontispiece — a human figure, stark naked" (162), Becky tears the page. In fear and shame she berates Tom and flings out of the room. "What a curious kind of a fool a girl is," Tom thinks. "Never been licked in school! Shucks. What's a licking!" (163). The episode thus turns toward corporal punishment and away from young people's sexual curiosity. Originally, Twain had Tom thinking differently: "But that picture — is — well, now it ain't so curious she feels bad about that. . . . Suppose she was Mary and Alf Temple had caught her looking at such a picture and went around telling. She'd feel — well, I'd lick him." Howells' comment at this point was "I should be afraid of this picture incident."[16] Though the first version had escaped the Elmira eye of Livy Clemens, Twain killed his realistic impulse, with its play on the word "curious." Thus died the sole explicit reference to sexuality in *Tom Sawyer* — indeed, in all of Mark Twain's boyhood stories.

Of course, the author of *Tom Sawyer* and *Huckleberry Finn* (if not of *Pudd'nhead Wilson*) was a prude. As writer, he was hypersensitive to his readers' and his own timidities. Consequently, as a motive for human conduct in growing boys and girls, adolescents, or adults, sexuality is almost entirely absent from his fiction. Even in unpublished writings he exhibited unusual reticence. "There was the utmost liberty among young people — ," he wrote, recalling Hannibal in the sketch "Villagers of 1840–3," "but no young girl was ever insulted, or seduced, or even scandalously gossiped about. Such things were not even dreamed of in that society, much less spoken of and referred to as possibilities."[17]

Twain, in common with his contemporaries (even Stephen Crane), shied away from the fact of sexuality in curious young minds, not only because of convention but also out of deep-seated ambivalence in respect to time and change. Sexuality inevitably implied adolescence, growth toward adulthood. With part of his mind he turned his back on such implications, taking pains never to specify Tom's age. From the first, Tom and Huck were conceived as children of indefinite years. Presexual innocence absolved Twain from confronting certain aspects of maturity, especially physical love and marriage, which neither his abilities nor his predilections equipped him to develop satisfactorily. Boyhood, about which no one of his generation wrote better, was a safer, more congenial area of personal and social experience. There he could focus on timeless moments in late childhood or early adolescence in which a boy, poised between infancy and manhood, could face forward to certain grown-up problems — serious ones, too, like money and death, though not, in this book, slavery — and yet backward to a state before puberty. *Tom Sawyer*'s conclusion puts as explicitly as Twain was able this precarious position. "So endeth this chronicle. It being strictly a history of a *boy*, it must stop here; the story could not go much further without becoming the history of a *man*. When one writes a novel about grown people, he knows exactly where to stop — that is, with a marriage; but when he writes of juveniles, he must stop where he best can"(275).

Tom Sawyer is punctuated with moments embodying this quality of arrested time. Several take place on Cardiff Hill, that "Delectable Land, dreamy, reposeful, and inviting"(26). Others show Tom squirming at his school desk. The two sites are symbolic. One is natural and static, the other social and on the move. As unwilling schoolboy, Tom "ached to be free, or else to have something of interest to do to pass the dreary time" (72-73). Here Tom shows his double-mindedness, to face both ways, whether to escape back into time by doing something actively exciting, or to escape to the timeless woods and river. Thus the plot is constructed so that Tom's escape adventures are keyed to the temporal life of the larger community. In a way quite unlike Aldrich, Warner, Howe, or Howells, Twain has his boy predict or repeat in the boy world occurrences in the grown-up world. On the night after Tom and Joe Harper pretend to kill each other in the Robin Hood game, Tom witnesses the actual murder of Dr. Robinson. Similarly, Tom and Becky on a picnic narrowly escape from the same cave where Injun Joe meets a grim death. Readers can readily recall other parallels or anticipations.

The link between the two worlds is invariably Tom Sawyer. Joe Harper plays Robin Hood, and Huck watches the graveyard murder, but only Tom does both. Participating in this way means that Tom gradually experiences the cruelties, cupidities, greed, and responsibilities of adulthood. This maturation is the dramatic and satiric undercurrent during the early part of the book but becomes the major motif as his extended summer wears to a climax. In the process, St. Petersburgh assumes a larger role than do the locales of the other village Bad Boy stories. The town in *Tom Sawyer* emerges as more than the setting of a golden idyll; it sits for its portrait (one of the first in our literature) as a representative American community. People of all classes and castes inhabit Twain's town — lawyers and drunkards, white boys and girls, mulattoes and a young slave named Jim, schoolmasters and old maids and Indian half-breeds. Something suggesting the total social reality of a typical antebellum river town is sketched, as the author had already practiced doing for Obedstown and Cattleville in *The Gilded Age* and was to do for Hadleyburg, Dawson's Landing, and Eseldorf. In a real sense, the Revolt from the Village, a favorite if trite theme of twentieth-century novelists like Sinclair Lewis, begins with *Tom Sawyer* and *Huckleberry Finn*.

The inclusiveness of Twain's social catalogue may go unnoted simply because each event or institution emerges as part of a boy's daily life. The sweep of these experiences undercuts "the idyll of Hannibal" as it uncovers a community's hypocrisy, violence, desperation, and greed. DeVoto speaks for those who wish to ignore the whole picture when he writes, "This village, though violence underlies its tranquility as it underlies most dreams of beauty, is withdrawn from the pettiness, the greed, the cruelty, the spiritual squalor, the human worthlessness that Huck Finn was to travel through ten years later."[18] On the other hand, it is equally one-sided to see St. Petersburgh through the minatory eyes of Van Wyck Brooks. In *The Ordeal of Mark Twain* Brooks tends to treat even Tom's "rosy" town like the others "with their shabby, unpainted shacks, dropping with decay, the litter of rusty cans, the mud, the weeds, the dust!"[19] Though the cultural debate between

Brooks and DeVoto preoccupied critics during the twenties and thirties, their opposing pictures of frontier squalor or frontier vigor still find support among present-day admirers of *Tom Sawyer*.

Closely allied to the idyllic/satiric salvos between Brooks and DeVoto are later debates over the book's literary coherence and artistry. For it was all too simple for readers sold on "the idyll of Hannibal" to be convinced, as DeLancey Ferguson put it in 1943, that the flood of memories overcoming the nostalgic Mark Twain meant that "he had only to set them down. . . . nothing mattered but effectiveness of episode in his mind at the time." To Ferguson (and others, like Alexander Cowie), *Tom Sawyer* "in short grew as grows the grass; it was not art at all, but it was life."[20] Indeed, to Ferguson, the sole conventional plot character in the novel is Injun Joe. Cowie confirmed this view in 1948 by asserting that this story exists "in small units, which when added up (not arranged) equal the sum of boyhood experience."[21] (Despite this serious simplification, Ferguson's *Mark Twain: Man and Legend* remains, with Justin Kaplan's *Mr. Clemens and Mark Twain*, one of the best modern biographies.)

A contrary case, one that predominates today, was first advanced by Walter Blair as early as 1939. In the pioneering essay "On the Structure of *Tom Sawyer*"[22] Blair argued that Twain consciously organized and carefully revised his novel. Employing four distinct but interlaced plot lines — the love story of Tom and Becky, the Jackson's Island escape and return, the story of Muff Potter, and the Injun Joe story — he developed the initiation and maturation of a boy mischievous, active, *and* gradually becoming morally aware and responsible. This psychosocial trajectory, if Twain's early marginal notation on the manuscript's first page is credited, was to lead eventually to Tom Sawyer's "Battle of Life" and disillusioning return to St. Petersburgh. By the narrative's close, Tom is genially browbeating Huck into embracing a respectable life with the Widow Douglas. This demonstrates that the outcome of Tom's long summer of adventures is acceptance of a grown-up's compromising connection to society. Nothing Tom does in *Adventures of Huckleberry Finn* will alter this growing commitment. The contrast here with Jim is chilling, for the shadowy figure of the boy slave in *Tom Sawyer* becomes later the runaway whose spiritual and moral maturity, some readers feel, constitutes the moral center of Twain's sequel.

Many if not most critics of Mark Twain's fiction now agree with and have extended Blair's argument. From James M. Cox to Henry Nash Smith and Hamlin Hill, from Paul Baender, Charles A. Norton, myself, and John Gerber, the conviction has steadily spread that *Tom Sawyer* is indeed a carefully re-vised work of literary art. The definitive Iowa-California edition of *The Adventures of Tom Sawyer* (1982) and Baender's facsimile edition of the man-uscript lend textual weight to this interpretation.

If Mark Twain did become disenchanted with Tom Sawyer — after all, one image of Sam Clemens himself — then the boy's easy acceptance of village re-spectability remains in striking contrast with another side of boyhood exemplified by Huck Finn. Passive acquiescence to a beautifully corrupted community vitiates for many modern readers the flair, independence, and moral sensitivity Tom shows at key points earlier in the narrative. In a deep sense, Tom Sawyer has gone over to the real enemy — time. For his initiation, by turns admirable and incomplete, goes a long way toward bringing him out of the eternal moment of boyhood, symbolized by Cardiff Hill, and launching him on the stream of social time or history. The aging writer may have confirmed this disguised but disillusioning outcome for his character when he derisively termed Theodore Roosevelt the political Tom Sawyer of the Spanish-American War era. [23]

On all counts, Twain's initial exploration in fiction of his own childhood turned up no permanent Paradise by the river. "Those good old simple days" that he and his fellow Americans yearned for held a full measure of personal and social evil. This historical insight was perhaps not suitable (or even in-teresting) to good little girls and boys. But it was a perception and prophecy Mark Twain could not fully hide from himself. If *Tom Sawyer* began as a prose hymn to the personal and national past, it ended as also a deceptively detached study of a soiled society, one both static and changing. Like the Natural Boy himself, life and art proved a mixture of good and evil, of play and horror. This powerfully simple insight into a cultural moment and monument accounts for much of the book's century-long appeal and present significance.

NOTES

1. Bernard DeVoto, *Mark Twain's America* (Boston: Little Brown, 1932), 299–300.

2. *Mark Twain's Autobiography*, ed. Charles Neider (New York: Harper, 1959), 340–41.

3. DeLancey Ferguson, *Mark Twain: Man and Legend* (Indianapolis and New York: Bobbs-Merrill, 1943), 107.

4. *Mark Twain–Howells Letters: The Correspondence of Samuel L. Clemens and William D. Howells, 1872–1910*, ed Henry Nash Smith and William M. Gibson, with the assistance of Frederick Anderson, 2 vols. (Cambridge: Belknap Press, Harvard University Press, 1960), 1: 91–92.

5. *Mark Twain's Letters to Will Bowen*, ed. Theodore Hornberger (Austin: University of Texas Press, 1941), 18–19.

6. DeVoto, *Mark Twain's America*, 303.

7. *Mark Twain–Howells Letters*, 1:92.

8. Hamlin Hill, "The Composition and Structure of *Tom Sawyer*," *American Literature* 32 (January 1961), 386.

9. *Mark Twain–Howells Letters*, 1:110–11.

10. *Mark Twain–Howells Letters*, 1:95.

11. *Mark Twain–Howells Letters*, 1:121.

12. *"The Adventures of Tom Sawyer" by Mark Twain: A Facsimile of the Author's Holograph Manuscript*, ed. Paul Baender (Frederick, Md.: University Publications of America; Washington, D.C.: Georgetown University Library, 1982), xxxvi.

13. *Mark Twain–Howells Letters*, 1:91–92.

14. Quoted in Albert Bigelow Paine, *Mark Twain: A Biography*, 4 vols. in 2 (New York: Harper, 1935), 2:477.

15. Judith Fetterly, "Mark Twain and the Anxiety of Entertainment," *Georgia Review* 33 (Summer 1979), 382–91.

16. Bernard DeVoto, *Mark Twain at Work* (Cambridge: Harvard University Press, 1942), 13–14.

17. Quoted in Dixon Wecter, *Sam Clemens of Hannibal* (Boston: Houghton Mifflin, 1952), 173.

18. DeVoto, *Mark Twain at Work*, 23.

19. Van Wyck Brooks, *The Ordeal of Mark Twain* (New York: E.P. Dutton, 1920), 40.

20. Ferguson, *Mark Twain: Man and Legend*, 175–76.

21. Alexander Cowie, *The Rise of the American Novel* (New York: American Book Company, 1948), 609.

22. Walter Blair, "On the Structure of *Tom Sawyer*," *Modern Philology* 37 (August 1939), 75–88.

23. Justin Kaplan, *Mr. Clemens and Mark Twain* (New York: Simon and Schuster, 1966), 363.

FOR FURTHER READING

Albert E. Stone

For useful biographical insights into *The Adventures of Tom Sawyer* see, in addition to the major biographies by Paine, Ferguson, Wecter, and Kaplan, the manuscript "Villagers of 1840–3" printed in *Huck Finn and Tom Sawyer Among the Indians* (Berkeley: University of California Press, 1989). For more detailed discussion of Twain's composition of this and allied works, consult Charles A. Norton, *Writing Tom Sawyer: The Adventures of a Classic* (Jefferson, N.C.: McFarland and Company, 1983) and Victor A. Doyno, *Writing "Huck Finn": Mark Twain's Creative Process* (Philadelphia: University of Pennsylvania Press, 1992). Major critical and cultural discussions of *The Adventures of Tom Sawyer* abound; some of the most useful in augmenting or correcting earlier works by Brooks and DeVoto include the introductions and notes to the Iowa-California and facsimile manuscript editions by John C. Gerber and Paul Baender; Albert E. Stone, *The Innocent Eye: Childhood in Mark Twain's Imagination* (New Haven: Yale University Press, 1961); Henry Nash Smith, *Mark Twain: The Development of a Writer* (Cambridge: Belknap Press of Harvard University Press, 1962); and James M. Cox, *Mark Twain: The Fate of Humor* (Princeton: Princeton University Press, 1966).

ILLUSTRATORS AND ILLUSTRATIONS
IN MARK TWAIN'S FIRST AMERICAN EDITIONS

Beverly R. David & Ray Sapirstein

From the "gorgeous gold frog" stamped into the cover of *The Celebrated Jumping Frog of Calaveras County* in 1867 to the comet-riding captain on the frontispiece of *Extract from Captain Stormfield's Visit to Heaven* in 1909, illustrators and illustrations were an integral part of Mark Twain's first editions.

Twain marketed most of his major works by subscription, and illustration functioned as an important sales tool. Subscription books were packed with pictures of every type and size and were bound in brassy gold-stamped covers. The books were sold by agents who flipped through a prospectus filled with lively illustrations, selected text, and binding samples. Illustrations quickly conveyed a sense of the story, condensing the proverbial "thousand words" and outlining the scope and tone of the work, making an impression on the potential purchaser even before the full text had been printed. Book canvassers were rewarded with up to 50 percent of the selling price, which started at $3.50 and ranged as high as $7.00 for more ornate bindings. The books themselves were seldom produced until a substantial number of customers had placed orders. To justify the relatively high price and to reassure buyers that they were getting their money's worth, books published by subscription had to offer sensational volume and apparent substance. As Frank Bliss of the American Publishing Company observed, these consumers "would not pay for blank paper and wide margins. They wanted everything filled up with type or pictures." While authors of trade books generally tolerated lighter sales, gratified by attracting a "better class of readers," as Hamlin Hill put it, authors of subscription books sacrificed literary respectability for popular appeal and considerable profit.[1]

The humorist George Ade remembered Twain's books vividly, offering us a child's-eye view of the nineteenth-century subscription book market.

Just when front-room literature seemed at its lowest ebb, so far as the American boy was concerned, along came Mark Twain. His books looked at a distance, just like the other distended, diluted, and altogether tasteless volumes that had been used for several decades to balance the ends of the center table . . . so thick and heavy and emblazoned with gold that [they] could keep company with the bulky and high-priced Bible. . . . The publisher knew his public, so he gave a pound of book for every fifty cents, and crowded in plenty of wood-cuts and stamped the outside with golden bouquets and put in a steel engraving of the author, with a tissue paper veil over it, and "sicked" his multitude of broken-down clergymen, maiden ladies, grass widows, and college students on the great American public.

Can you see the boy, Sunday morning prisoner, approach the book with a dull sense of foreboding, expecting a dose of Tupper's *Proverbial Philosophy*? Can you see him a few minutes later when he finds himself linked arm-in-arm with Mulberry Sellers or Buck Fanshaw or the convulsing idiot who wanted to know if Christopher Columbus was sure-enough dead? No wonder he curled up on the hair-cloth sofa and hugged the thing to his bosom and lost all interest in Sunday school. *Innocents Abroad* was the most enthralling book ever printed until *Roughing It* appeared. Then along came *The Gilded Age, Life on the Mississippi*, and *Tom Sawyer.* . . . While waiting for a new one we read the old ones all over again.[2]

Publishers, editors, and Twain himself spent a good deal of time on design — choosing the most talented artists, directing their interpretations of text, selecting from the final prints, and at times removing material they deemed unfit for illustration.[3]

With the exception of *Following the Equator* (1897), books released in the twilight of Twain's career were not sold by subscription. Twain's later books, published for the trade market by Harper and Brothers, seldom contained more than a frontispiece and a dozen or so tasteful illustrations, rather than the hundreds of illustrations per volume that subscription publishing demanded. Illustration, however, remained a major component of Twain's later work in two important cases: *Extracts from Adam's Diary*, illustrated by Fred

Strothmann in 1904, and *Eve's Diary*, illustrated by Lester Ralph in 1906.

The stories behind the illustrators and illustrations of Mark Twain's first editions abound in back-room intrigue. The besotted or negligent lapses of some of the artists and the procrastinations of the engravers are legendary. The consequent production delays, mistimed releases, and copyright infringements all implied a lack of competent supervision that frequently infuriated Twain and ultimately encouraged him to launch his own publishing company.

In many cases, Twain took illustrations into account as he wrote and edited his text, using them as counterpoint and accompaniment to his words, often allowing them to inform his general narrative strategy and to influence the amount of detail he felt necessary to include in his written descriptions. In the most artful and carefully considered illustrated works, an analysis of the relationships between author and illustrator and between text and pictures illuminates key dimensions of Twain's writings and the responses they have elicited from readers. Examinations of even the most straightforward examples of decorative imagery yield insights into the publishing history of Twain's books and his attitudes toward the production process.

The original illustrations in Twain's works have often been replaced in the twentieth century by subsequent visual interpretations. But while Norman Rockwell's well-known nostalgic renderings of *Tom Sawyer* and *Huckleberry Finn* may tell us much about 1930s sensibilities, we would do well to reacquaint ourselves with the first American editions and the artwork they contained if we want to understand the books Twain wrote and the world they affected.

Illustrated books, like the illustrated weekly magazines that first appeared in the 1860s, were a significant source of visual images entering nineteenth-century homes. Because of their widespread popularity and the relative paucity of other sources of visual information, Twain's books helped to define America's perceptions of remote people, exotic scenes, and historic events. In addition to being an essential element of Mark Twain's body of work, illustrations are a documentary source in their own right, a window into Twain's world and our own.

NOTES

1. For background on subscription book publishing, see Hamlin Hill, *Mark Twain and Elisha Bliss* (Columbia: University of Missouri Press, 1964), chapter 1. See also R. Kent Rasmussen, "Subscription-book publishing" entry, *Mark Twain A to Z: The Essential Reference to His Life and Writings* (New York: Facts on File, 1995), p. 448.

2. George Ade, "Mark Twain and the Old-Time Subscription Book," *Review of Reviews* 61 (June 10, 1910): 703–4; reprinted in Frederick Anderson, ed., *Mark Twain: The Critical Heritage* (London: Routledge and Kegan Paul, 1971), pp. 337–39.

3. Beverly R. David, *Mark Twain and His Illustrators, Volume 1 (1869–1875)* (Troy, N.Y.: Whitston Publishing Company, 1986), discusses in detail Twain's involvement in the production of his early books.

Beverly R. David & Ray Sapirstein

Both Mark Twain and his publisher, Elisha Bliss, agreed that True Williams (1839–1897) should be the sole illustrator of *The Adventures of Tom Sawyer*.[1] Williams was a practical choice, since he worked on every book Twain had published with the American Publishing Company up to that point: *Innocents Abroad, Roughing It, The Gilded Age*, and *Sketches, New and Old*. Williams finished the designs for *Sketches*, published in September 1875, less than two months before he began work on *Tom Sawyer*. When the American edition of *Tom Sawyer* finally came off press in December 1876, it included approximately 160 of Williams' illustrations in its 275 pages. Twain also contributed, playfully adding two deliberately crude pieces of his own artwork: his longhand version of Tom's oath (95), not strictly an illustration, and Tom's "dismal caricature of a house," captioned "Tom as an Artist" (70).[2]

In *Sketches, New and Old*, Williams had followed a pattern of providing an appropriate illustration for the opening of each sketch, a half- or three-quarter-page vignette that featured the title in large, ornate letters engraved by the artist rather than set in type. Williams carried the same design scheme over into *Tom Sawyer* with minor modifications. His hand-rendered chapter headings included roman numerals, and the first word of each chapter was engraved by hand and integrated within the illustration. While decorative, the device was also functional: the large chapter-title illustrations added roughly twenty pages to a volume that was extremely short for a subscription book, a factor Twain and his publisher had to consider. Similarly, the cover of *Tom Sawyer* virtually duplicated the cover of *Sketches*, both a time-saver and a money-saver in that the cloth, type style, and stamp dies from *Sketches* could be reused.

Other graphic elements of *Sketches* were carried over into *Tom Sawyer*. The youngster from Twain's "Bad Little Boy" story (*Sketches*, 51) is unmistakably the Tom Sawyer who appears in the headpiece to chapter 4 (42). The ill-fated lad from the "Good Little Boy" story (*Sketches*, 60) has the forlorn features and starchy suit of Huck Finn as he appears in "Huck Transformed," the headpiece to chapter 35 (268). The grandmother with switch in hand in "History Repeats Itself" (*Sketches*, 271) is almost identical to Aunt Polly as she appears throughout Tom Sawyer and in her character portrait, the headpiece to chapter 19 (158).

However, the main characters are portrayed inconsistently. Throughout the story, Huck is identified by his outfit rather than by individualized traits; Williams followed Twain's text and dressed him "in the cast-off clothes of full-grown men," his hat "a vast ruin with a wide crescent lopped out of the brim" (64). And Tom's only consistent distinguishing feature is his checked pants. As he appears in the frontispiece, he hardly resembles the character Williams rendered throughout the book. Although the image is excellent in its detail and technical proficiency, it carries no sense of individuality or character, portraying a docile Model Boy with dainty curls and features, vacantly absorbed in reverie in an idyllic retreat. Twain's Tom, no doubt, would have tormented this boy mercilessly. The frontispiece seems the graphic equivalent of the affected verse Twain quotes in the Sunday school pageant, full of nostalgic pieties and predictable sentiment. Finally, Williams never seems to have settled upon a fixed age for his leading characters, possibly because of Twain's own lack of specificity. The Tom who scales the backyard fence to escape Aunt Polly's wrath in the opening chapter (18) seems several years younger than the near-adolescent who appears on the facing page.

Critics have faulted Williams for sporadic inattention to the text of *Tom Sawyer*. His depiction of the now iconic whitewashing episode is frequently cited as an example of this failure. In 1941, Warren Chappell wrote:

> [Williams] used a rail fence instead of a board fence which is described. For pictorial reasons, he might have cut down on the "thirty yards of board fence, nine feet high," but his measly rail fence is not suited to shielding Tom's actions from Aunt Polly in the ensuing scene.[3]

An illustrator could be expected to make such a mistake, but errors only rarely managed to elude Twain's close scrutiny. Twain was in contact with Williams while he was producing the drawings, but the author may not have had a clear vision of the fence either. He had described it originally as a four-foot fence in manuscript.[4] Similarly, Williams depicted Injun Joe without an eyepatch, overlooking Twain's description, but Twain vacillated as well, mentioning the character's "eyes" in two instances.[5] Given personal crises and his problems with publishing delays, the timing of the English edition, and Canadian piracy, Twain may simply have had too much on his hands to spend time tutoring his usually competent illustrator. Perhaps he felt that Williams, who was turning out reasonably satisfactory work, was best left to his own devices. The last thing Twain needed was a resentful True Williams sulking over a bottle of rum.

Both Twain and Bliss were well aware that Williams had a drinking problem. Bliss referred to him as "poor drunken Williams" while *Tom Sawyer* was in preparation, and in a letter to William Dean Howells, Twain wrote of him, "Poor devil, what a genius he has, & how he does murder it with rum."[6] Whether the cause lay in alcohol, indifference, personal problems, or elsewhere, Williams' work for *Tom Sawyer* was haphazard and occasionally uninspired. Twain had often railed bitterly at artists who failed to read his work carefully before illustrating it, a necessity he and Bliss repeatedly brought to Williams' attention. Overall, Williams did follow the details of the text, but in many cases he gave no more and no less than what Twain described; the result was a fair number of accurate but flat renderings of the characters and events in the novel.

The last drawing in *Tom Sawyer*, captioned "Contentment" in the list of illustrations, depicts Aunt Polly seated, smiling as she knits (274) — a direct reference to, though not an exact reproduction of, an illustration depicting Mrs. Partington, a character created by the popular humorist B. P. Shillaber. The original image appeared first on the masthead of Shillaber's weekly magazine of the early 1850s, the *Carpet Bag*, which also carried some of Twain's earliest literary ventures. Later the image served as the frontispiece for Shillaber's *Life and Sayings of Mrs. Partington* (1854). Mark Twain acknowledged that he used elements of Mrs. Partington in his conception of Aunt Polly, who closely resembles Shillaber's character in Williams' renderings. Since Twain and Shillaber were friends, it is almost inconceivable that Twain allowed Williams to rework a picture of Mrs. Partington and present it as an original. Though the actual intent of author and illustrator remains a mystery, the image was possibly a private joke between them, or perhaps between Twain and his mother, who were said to have joked about their own parallels with Mrs. Partington and her nephew Ike.[7]

Williams' taste for mischief, manifested in Twain's earlier works by his enthusiastic participation in comic hyperbole and slapstick, had to be curtailed somewhat for *Tom Sawyer*. Twain, courting respectability with this, his first noncollaborative novel, sought a more decorous presentation and left out much of the wry social satire with which he had made his reputation as a writer. Williams channeled his energy into subtly playful and spooky funereal chapter headings, incorporating dead branches, ravens, bats, gravestones, and ominous Gothic lettering. Other chapter headings showed artistic ingenuity and independence, such as the one formed by the billowing smoke from Tom's pipe (134), an image suggesting indulgent amusement with the boys' clandestine descent into waywardness. Williams' involvement with the text and playful sense of the macabre are particularly apparent in "Injun Joe's Two Victims" (103). He signed the image on a headboard that bears the inscription "Sacred to the Memory of T. W. Williams."

The artist's true mastery is evident in the skill with which he handled the scenes set at night. If by day his figures are stiff and clichéd, his nocturnal images evoke the evil that lurks in the darkness just beyond a lantern's circle of light. It matters little that the full moon seems to appear night after night, that his renderings aren't technically accurate or fastidiously faithful to the text. He didn't necessarily seek to convey the reality of a house at night but what the boys' imaginations wrought from the mundane. Using oblique lighting effects and dim outlines inventively, Williams created a drama and suspense that perfectly complemented Twain's portrayal of the boys' powerful imaginations. In his best moments, Williams demonstrated he could keep pace with Twain, conveying the spirit of the book wholeheartedly and substantially. Details of the night forest seem glimpses from a boy's-eye view. In his chapter headings, Williams presented the significant oracles that caught the boys' attention, the vivid phantasms of childhood's imaginative landscape: the owl perched on a blasted branch (85), the doom foretold by a stray dog howling at the full moon at midnight (93), a lonesome stern-wheeler gloomily churning the river (128), the haunted house half revealed by the broken light of the moon (198). The images ably capture the ghostly thrill of silent travel through a mysterious night world few sleepers see.

Williams' vertically oriented compositions show creative deliberation, often dramatizing the story with childlike vividness: the solemn child-swallowing vastness of the cave (220), Cardiff Hill looming like the Rockies (257), a streak of lightning crackling down the page (141). Appropriately, the imaginative terrain of Tom and Huck's adventures is more vibrant and alive than the adult reality that Williams treats superficially. With the exception of Aunt Polly, the adults come across as dull, drab props, as do the young heroes when in their restrictive place in the adult world. Although Twain did not write *Tom Sawyer* in the first person, Williams' best illustrations capture Twain's attraction to a child's point of view, thus demonstrating his inclination toward the revolutionary narrative strategy he would subsequently employ in *Huckleberry Finn*.

Twain thought highly of Williams' work on *Tom Sawyer*, writing to William Dean Howells,

> Williams has made about 200 rattling pictures for it — some of them very dainty. . . . He takes a book of mine, & without suggestion from anybody builds no end of pictures just from his reading of it.[8]

But the man himself has remained a shadowy figure, remembered largely through anecdotes about his alcoholism, which to a great extent has colored critical assessments of his work. After the publication of *A Tramp Abroad* in 1880, his last book for Twain, he disappeared from the historical record; with no formal academic training or credentials, he does not appear in any of the standard biographical reference works on artists. Now, however, thanks to the pioneering research of Barbara Schmidt, we are able to fill in some of the details of his life and career.[9]

Truman W. Williams was born in western New York in 1839, and spent his childhood in Watertown, New York. After serving in the Union Army during the Civil War, as an advance scout for Sherman's march to the sea, he settled in Hartford, Connecticut. Self-taught as an artist, he began working as an apprentice and then as an illustrator for the American Publishing Company. Throughout the 1870s, Williams illustrated many noteworthy travel and local-color books, including works by Stephen Powers, Joaquin Miller, E. R. Miller, Matthew Hale Smith, A. D. Richardson, and Thomas H. Knox, many of which served as models for Twain and were influential in determining the shape and scope of a successful subscription book. Williams also worked on several books by the humorist Marietta Holley ("Josiah Allen's Wife"), a personal friend who hailed from his hometown; he created the image of Holley's popular character Samantha, who appeared in serial novels over several decades. In 1876, the same year *Tom Sawyer* was published, he illustrated works by Bret Harte (*Gabriel Conway*) and Dan De Quille (*The Big Bonanza*), two writers intimately connected with Twain's Western years. In 1879, for the short-lived publishing company started by Frank E. Bliss, Elisha's son, Williams illustrated *The Life of the Honorable William F. Cody, Known as Buffalo Bill*; like the illustrator, Cody had been a scout under General Sherman, although he served in the West.

Following the death of Elisha Bliss in 1880 and the subsequent shake-up at the American Publishing Company, Williams began drawing for A. D. Worthington, another Hartford publisher, although he continued to work for American as late as 1884. Ironically, given the most frequently mentioned detail of his biography, he worked on *Platform Echoes* (1884), a reader by the temperance orator John D. Gough. In or around 1885, Williams married and moved to Chicago; shortly thereafter, his wife and infant son died in childbirth. Through the 1880s until 1891, he worked for the Belford-Clarke Publishing Company, which had pirated many of Twain's books for the Canadian market. At Belford-Clarke, Williams illustrated titles from George W. Peck's Bad Boy series, among others. In 1890 Belford published Williams' only book, *Frank Fairweather's Fortunes*, a runaway boy's story of circus life and adventures on the high seas and in Central America; that same year Williams released an illustrated volume of verse by his favorite authors, *Under the Open Sky*.

After Belford-Clarke was destroyed by a disatrous fire in 1891, Williams worked primarily for Rand McNally and Company, also in Chicago. Beginning in the 1870s, he had illustrated a number of books by the soldier and explorer Willard Glazier, like Holley, a personal friend; the 1892 edition of Glazier's *Headwaters of the Mississippi*, published by Rand McNally, demonstrates that Williams made the transition from pen-and-ink line drawings to watercolor-like wash drawings after the invention of photomechanical reproduction, a radical change that swiftly made dinosaurs of many illustrators and engravers. At the time of his death in 1897, Williams was working on John L. Stoddard's volumes of geographical lectures.

Williams' participation in all of Twain's subscription books through *A Tramp Abroad* ranks him as Twain's most significant and regular collaborator. In addition to forging the first images of Tom Sawyer, Huckleberry Finn, and an assortment of Twain's other popular characters, Williams was in no small measure involved in the creation of Twain's own public image, as he drew many of the caricatures of the author that appear throughout Twain's early work. His scribbly etchings greatly contributed to the puckishly satirical tone of the early subscription books, also a major component in the development of Twain's popular persona. Despite his relative obscurity and typically lowly status as a decorator of books, Williams' work addressed several crucial aspects of American history and culture — the West, the Civil War, impressions of foreign lands, and in *Tom Sawyer*, the idyllic innocence of boyhood and the rural past — and helped to create an American iconography that is still part of the national consciousness.

NOTES

1. Nathan M. Wood, "True Williams, Pen Drew Literary Giant of Old," *Watertown [N.Y.] Daily Times*, August 30, 1938, p. 11. Until recently, very little biographical information on Williams has been available. Unearthed by Barbara Schmidt, instructional media coordinator at Tarleton State University in Stephenville, Texas, and a regular contributor to the Mark Twain Forum on the Internet, this article provides significant biographical information about Williams, including his dates and publishing history. We are indebted to Barbara Schmidt for generously sharing this reference and her pioneering research on Williams' later career, which she is working on for a forthcoming article.

2. Explanatory Notes, *The Adventures of Tom Sawyer*, ed. John C. Gerber, Paul Baender, and Terry Firkins, The Works of Mark Twain (Berkeley: University of California Press, 1980), p. 523, n. 79.5.

3. Warren Chappell, "Tom Sawyer and the Illustrators," *The Dolphin: A Periodical for All People Who Find Pleasure in Fine Books*, no. 4, pt. 3 (New York: Limited Editions Club, Spring 1941), p. 251.

4. Explanatory Notes, p. 471, n. 46.12.

5. Ibid., p. 491, n. 189.8.

6. Elisha Bliss to Mark Twain, July 18, 1876, in *Mark Twain's Letters to His Publishers, 1867–1894*, Hamlin Hill, ed., (Berkeley: University of California Press, 1967), p. 100, n. 1; *Mark Twain–Howells Letters*, Henry Nash Smith and William M. Gibson, eds. (Cambridge: Harvard University Press, 1960), p. 121.

7. See J. R. LeMaster and David Haines, Jr., "Polly, Aunt" entry, *The Mark Twain Encyclopedia*, J. R. LeMaster and James D. Wilson, eds. (New York: Garland Publishing Company, 1993), p. 589.

8. *Mark Twain–Howells Letters*, p. 121.

9. See n. 1 above. All biographical details in the summary that follows are from Wood's article and correspondence with Barbara Schmidt.

A NOTE ON THE TEXT

Robert H. Hirst

This text of *The Adventures of Tom Sawyer* is a photographic facsimile of a copy of the first American edition dated 1876 on the title page. Although books printed from the first edition plates were manufactured until at least 1903, the earliest copies of the first edition came from the bindery on December 8, 1876. The *Hartford Courant* reviewed the book on December 27, and two copies were deposited with the Copyright Office on January 2, 1877. The copy reproduced here is an example of Jacob Blanck's "first printing": it is the earliest impression, on wove paper, made before minor errors crept into the preliminary pages (*BAL* 3369). It was very likely among the 9,378 copies printed and bound by the end of December 1876. The original volume is in the collection of the Mark Twain House in Hartford, Connecticut (810/C625adt/1876/c. 1).

THE MARK TWAIN HOUSE

The Mark Twain House is a museum and research center dedicated to the study of Mark Twain, his works, and his times. The museum is located in the nineteen-room mansion in Hartford, Connecticut, built for and lived in by Samuel L. Clemens, his wife, and their three children, from 1874 to 1891. The Picturesque Gothic-style residence, with interior design by the firm of Louis Comfort Tiffany and Associated Artists, is one of the premier examples of domestic Victorian architecture in America. Clemens wrote *Adventures of Huckleberry Finn, The Adventures of Tom Sawyer, A Connecticut Yankee in King Arthur's Court, The Prince and the Pauper,* and *Life on the Mississippi* while living in Hartford.

The Mark Twain House is open year-round. In addition to tours of the house, the educational programs of the Mark Twain House include symposia, lectures, and teacher training seminars that focus on the contemporary relevance of Twain's legacy. Past programs have featured discussions of literary censorship with playwright Arthur Miller and writer William Styron; of the power of language with journalist Clarence Page, comedian Dick Gregory, and writer Gloria Naylor; and of the challenges of teaching *Adventures of Huckleberry Finn* amidst charges of racism.

CONTRIBUTORS

Beverly R. David is professor emerita of humanities and theater at Western Michigan University in Kalamazoo. She is currently working on volume 2 of *Mark Twain and His Illustrators*, and on a Mark Twain mystery entitled *Murder at the Matterhorn*. She has written a number of sections on illustration for the *Mark Twain Encyclopedia* and her *Mark Twain and His Illustrators, Volume 1 (1869–1875)* was published in 1989. Dr. David resides in Allegan, Michigan, in the summer and Green Valley, Arizona, in the winter.

E. L. Doctorow is the author of *Welcome to Hard Times* (1960), *Big as Life* (1966), *The Book of Daniel* (1971), *Ragtime* (1975; National Book Critics Circle Award, 1976), *Loon Lake* (1980), *Lives of the Poets* (1984), *World's Fair* (1985; National Book Award, 1986), *Billy Bathgate* (1989; National Book Critics Circle Award, PEN/Faulkner Award, William Dean Howells Medal of the American Academy and Institute of Arts and Letters, 1990), *The Waterworks* (1994), and a volume of essays, *Jack London, Hemingway, and the Constitution* (1993). He lives in New York City and is Glucksman Professor of English and American Letters at New York University.

Shelley Fisher Fishkin, professor of American Studies and English at the University of Texas at Austin, is the author of the award-winning books *Was Huck Black? Mark Twain and African-American Voices* (1993) and *From Fact to Fiction: Journalism and Imaginative Writing in America* (1985). Her most recent book is *Lighting Out for the Territory: Reflections on Mark Twain and American Culture* (1996). She holds a Ph.D. in American Studies from Yale University, has lectured on Mark Twain in Belgium, England, France, Israel, Italy, Mexico, the Netherlands, and Turkey, as well as throughout the United States, and is president-elect of the Mark Twain Circle of America.

Robert H. Hirst is the General Editor of the Mark Twain Project at The Bancroft Library, University of California in Berkeley. Apart from that, he has no other known eccentricities.

Ray Sapirstein is a doctoral student in the American Civilization Program at the University of Texas at Austin. He curated the 1993 exhibition *Another Side of Huckleberry Finn: Mark Twain and Images of African Americans* at the Harry Ransom Humanities Research Center at the University of Texas at Austin. He is currently completing a dissertation on the photographic illustrations in several volumes of Paul Laurence Dunbar's poetry.

Albert E. Stone, professor emeritus of American Studies and English at the University of Iowa, is the author of *The Innocent Eye: Childhood in Mark Twain's Imagination* (1961), *Autobiographical Occasions and Original Acts* (1982), *The Return of Nat Turner: History, Literature, and Cultural Politics in Sixties America* (1992), and *Literary Aftershocks: American Writers, Readers, and the Bomb* (1994). He is also the series editor of fourteen volumes of Singular Lives: The Iowa Series in North American Autobiography, issued by the University of Iowa Press. He lives in Arrowsic, Maine.

ACKNOWLEDGMENTS

There are a number of people without whom The Oxford Mark Twain would not have happened. I am indebted to Laura Brown, senior vice president and trade publisher, Oxford University Press, for suggesting that I edit an "Oxford Mark Twain," and for being so enthusiastic when I proposed that it take the present form. Her guidance and vision have informed the entire undertaking.

Crucial as well, from the earliest to the final stages, was the help of John Boyer, executive director of the Mark Twain House, who recognized the importance of the project and gave it his wholehearted support.

My father, Milton Fisher, believed in this project from the start and helped nurture it every step of the way, as did my stepmother, Carol Plaine Fisher. Their encouragement and support made it all possible. The memory of my mother, Renée B. Fisher, sustained me throughout.

I am enormously grateful to all the contributors to The Oxford Mark Twain for the effort they put into their essays, and for having been such fine, collegial collaborators. Each came through, just as I'd hoped, with fresh insights and lively prose. It was a privilege and a pleasure to work with them, and I value the friendships that we forged in the process.

In addition to writing his fine afterword, Louis J. Budd provided invaluable advice and support, even going so far as to read each of the essays for accuracy. All of us involved in this project are greatly in his debt. Both his knowledge of Mark Twain's work and his generosity as a colleague are legendary and unsurpassed.

Elizabeth Maguire's commitment to The Oxford Mark Twain during her time as senior editor at Oxford was exemplary. When the project proved to be more ambitious and complicated than any of us had expected, Liz helped make it not only manageable, but fun. Assistant editor Elda Rotor's wonderful help in coordinating all aspects of The Oxford Mark Twain, along with literature editor T. Susan Chang's enthusiastic involvement with the project in its final stages, helped bring it all to fruition.

I am extremely grateful to Joy Johannessen for her astute and sensitive copyediting, and for having been such a pleasure to work with. And I appreciate the conscientiousness and good humor with which Kathy Kuhtz Campbell heroically supervised all aspects of the set's production. Oxford president Edward Barry, vice president and editorial director Helen McInnis, marketing director Amy Roberts, publicity director Susan Rotermund, art director David Tran, trade editorial, design and production manager Adam Bohannon, trade advertising and promotion manager Woody Gilmartin, director of manufacturing Benjamin Lee, and the entire staff at Oxford were as supportive a team as any editor could desire.

The staff of the Mark Twain House provided superb assistance as well. I would like to thank Marianne Curling, curator, Debra Petke, education director, Beverly Zell, curator of photography, Britt Gustafson, assistant director of education, Beth Ann McPherson, assistant curator, and Pam Collins, administrative assistant, for all their generous help, and for allowing us to reproduce books and photographs from the Mark Twain House collection. One could not ask for more congenial or helpful partners in publishing.

G. Thomas Tanselle, vice president of the John Simon Guggenheim Memorial Foundation, and an expert on the history of the book, offered essential advice about how to create as responsible a facsimile edition as possible. I appreciate his very knowledgeable counsel.

I am deeply indebted to Robert H. Hirst, general editor of the Mark Twain Project at The Bancroft Library in Berkeley, for bringing his outstanding knowledge of Twain editions to bear on the selection of the books photographed for the facsimiles, for giving generous assistance all along the way, and for providing his meticulous notes on the text. The set is the richer for his advice. I would also like to express my gratitude to the Mark Twain Project, not only for making texts and photographs from their collection available to us, but also for nurturing Mark Twain studies with a steady infusion of matchless, important publications.

I would like to thank Jeffrey Kaimowitz, curator of the Watkinson Library at Trinity College, Hartford (where the Mark Twain House collection is kept), along with his colleagues Peter Knapp and Alesandra M. Schmidt, for having been instrumental in Robert Hirst's search for first editions that could be safely reproduced. Victor Fischer, Harriet Elinor Smith, and especially Kenneth M. Sanderson, associate editors with the Mark Twain Project, reviewed the note on the text in each volume with cheerful vigilance. Thanks are also due to Mark Twain Project associate editor Michael Frank and administrative assistant Brenda J. Bailey for their help at various stages.

I am grateful to Helen K. Copley for granting permission to publish photographs in the Mark Twain Collection of the James S. Copley Library in La Jolla, California, and to Carol Beales and Ron Vanderhye of the Copley Library for making my research trip to their institution so productive and enjoyable.

Several contributors — David Bradley, Louis J. Budd, Beverly R. David, Robert Hirst, Fred Kaplan, James S. Leonard, Toni Morrison, Lillian S. Robinson, Jeffrey Rubin-Dorsky, Ray Sapirstein, and David L. Smith — were particularly helpful in the early stages of the project, brainstorming about the cast of writers and scholars who could make it work. Others who participated in that process were John Boyer, James Cox, Robert Crunden, Joel Dinerstein, William Goetzmann, Calvin and Maria Johnson, Jim Magnuson, Arnold Rampersad, Siva Vaidhyanathan, Steve and Louise Weinberg, and Richard Yarborough.

Kevin Bochynski, famous among Twain scholars as an "angel" who is gifted at finding methods of making their research run more smoothly, was helpful in more ways than I can count. He did an outstanding job in his official capacity as production consultant to The Oxford Mark Twain, supervising the photography of the facsimiles. I am also grateful to him for having put me in touch via e-mail with Kent Rasmussen, author of the magisterial *Mark Twain A to Z*, who was tremendously helpful as the project proceeded, sharing insights on obscure illustrators and other points, and generously being "on call" for all sorts of unforeseen contingencies.

I am indebted to Siva Vaidhyanathan of the American Studies Program of the University of Texas at Austin for having been such a superb research assistant. It would be hard to imagine The Oxford Mark Twain without the benefit of his insights and energy. A fine scholar and writer in his own right, he was crucial to making this project happen.

Georgia Barnhill, the Andrew W. Mellon Curator of Graphic Arts at the American Antiquarian Society in Worcester, Massachusetts, Tom Staley, director of the Harry Ransom Huma ities Research Center at the University of Texas at Austin, and Joan Grant, director of collection services at the Elmer Holmes Bobst Library of New York University, granted us access to their collections and assisted us in the reproduction of several volumes of The Oxford Mark Twain. I would also like to thank Kenneth Craven, Sally Leach, and Richard Oram of the Harry Ransom Humanities Research Center for their help in making HRC materials available, and Jay and John Crowley, of Jay's Publishers Services in Rockland, Massachusetts, for their efforts to photograph the books carefully and attentively.

I would like to express my gratitude for the grant I was awarded by the University Research Institute of the University of Texas at Austin to defray some of the costs of researching The Oxford Mark Twain. I am also grateful to American Studies director Robert Abzug and the University of Texas for the computer that facilitated my work on this project (and to UT systems analyst Steve Alemán, who tried his best to repair the damage when it crashed). Thanks also to American Studies administrative assistant Janice Bradley and graduate coordinator Melanie Livingston for their always generous and thoughtful help.

The Oxford Mark Twain would not have happened without the unstinting, wholehearted support of my husband, Jim Fishkin, who went way beyond the proverbial call of duty more times than I'm sure he cares to remember as he shared me unselfishly with that other man in my life, Mark Twain. I am also grateful to my family—to my sons Joey and Bobby, who cheered me on all along the way, as did Fannie Fishkin, David Fishkin, Gennie Gordon, Mildred Hope Witkin, and Leonard, Gillis, and Moss

Plaine — and to honorary family member Margaret Osborne, who did the same.

My greatest debt is to the man who set all this in motion. Only a figure as rich and complicated as Mark Twain could have sustained such energy and interest on the part of so many people for so long. Never boring, never dull, Mark Twain repays our attention again and again and again. It is a privilege to be able to honor his memory with The Oxford Mark Twain.

Shelley Fisher Fishkin
Austin, Texas
April 1996